FOR SALLY
WITH LOVE

ACKNOWLEDGMENTS

Many people in Macau and Hong Kong were kind enough to assist me while I wrote this book. Of those friends especially who offered hospitality and valuable help I would like to thank Jonathan Elwes, Jan Bochenski, Mike Keates, Elizabeth and John Brealy, Guy Cubitt, and Patti Dougherty.

PROLOGUE

DARK CLOUDS raced against the moon flooding the sea with patches of cold gold light, silhouetting the rakish superstructure of a converted gunboat riding into Hong Kong on the tail of a typhoon.

On the open bridge, deafened by wind, face stung by salt spray, stood the solitary figure of Nicholai the Russian; the colorful legends of the China coast had also bestowed on him, for his courage and skill as a smuggler, the raffish name, Snake Boat Man of Macau.

At his side a wiry Cantonese, Keng Po, guided the craft in its roller-coaster passage down the steep-sided waves. They were closing on the Hong Kong shore. Nicholai had picked up the lights of Aberdeen, the largest fishing harbor in the colony. He gave his orders in Cantonese, the language of the boat. Keng Po wrestled the helm around to the new course.

At the back of the bridge stood Udo the Bear, a giant of a European, naked to the waist, and hugely muscled. Before he met Nicholai he had earned his living as a street fighter in Macau, when then he would have crippled a man for the price of a meal; now he was Nicholai's first lieutenant.

In the engine room Lin Tsang clung to an overhead rail and anxiously surveyed the three thundering engines that had earned the *East Wind* its reputation as the fastest craft in the South China Sea.

"Enough," Lin Tsang said as he heard the propellers race once more clear of the sea. "*Enough*. The madman's killing you." Set into the bulkhead was a statue of the goddess A-ma, protectress of seamen. Lin Tsang, the most superstitious of the crew, commended his soul to her, then clambered up the ladder onto the deck.

Spray hit him like a solid wall, swept over the deck before he could close the engine room hatch. Around him dark wind keened and towering thirty-foot waves, foam whipping from their crests, swept past.

Lin Tsang found it even more terrifying on deck than in the claustrophobic confines of his engine room. He felt his stomach swoop as the *East Wind* corkscrewed down a storm wave that reared against the shelving coastline. The gunboat's steeply flared bows, designed to sit high on the plane, were submerged as it crashed into the trough at the bottom. The deck was swamped by a mass of broken water. Lin Tsang would have lost his grip and been swept away if Udo hadn't leaned down, seized him and effortlessly lifted him to safety over the bridge weather rail.

"He's crazy," Lin Tsang shouted to Udo against the tearing wind, knowing that Nicholai could not hear him. "He's getting crazier each time we make a run. The *East Wind* wasn't built to operate on a night like this. We should have waited for calmer weather and used our speed. You tell him—"

"I can tell him nothing these days," Udo snapped. "Anyway, we've relied on calm seas and our speed too often. He knows what he's doing."

Actually, Nicholai was drinking to numb his mind before each run, and everyone on the boat knew it. They stayed with him for the honor of being his crew; for the charisma of the man, even though it seemed his famous luck was beginning to desert him.

"Steer oh-two-oh." Nicholai caught Keng Po's anxious glance as the *East Wind* entered the channel. "Aberdeen," he confirmed. He was going to enter the second biggest harbor in the colony, but the risk was acceptable... the British would not expect a landing on a night like this. "The *bomban* in charge of the guard launch has been bribed. He'll see

12

nothing until it's too late. All the other police vessels will be safely tied up in the typhoon harbor."

Keng Po pointed ahead. "The harbor must have caught the edge of the typhoon." The swash of the sea had broken through in one place, forcing a narrow gap in the piled concrete blocks that formed the breakwater. Storm waves hurled themselves through it and shattered in the shallow water on the other side.

The *East Wind* slipped past the harbor mouth and entered Aberdeen— a floating city of fishing junks and sampans tethered together, pitching and tossing in rank after battered rank, rain-swept and battened down after thirty-six hours of force-ten winds. Here and there a vessel, unable to ride out the typhoon, had sunk, leaving only the tip of its mast visible.

IN ONE of the larger junks at the end of the rank closest to the breakwater, on deck under cover of a tarpaulin, a European with a harsh pockmarked face picked up the ex-gunboat in his binoculars. "He's come," Inspector Malloy said. "Dear God, you were right." Malloy's aching weariness fell away, shed like the skin of a reptile.

Deck Sergeant Lao Ch'en, lying alongside him, carefully eased his cramped limbs. Ancient Lao Ch'en was reaching the end of his career, many years of which had been spent hunting the Snake Boat Man, and now at last he'd outfoxed him, the hefty reward money almost within his grasp. "I knew he'd come as the typhoon blew itself out, and I knew he'd choose the best junk harbor in Hong Kong. The closer we get to catching him, the more he wants to taunt us. It's for his face—the man tries to hide that his nerve is going."

Tethered to the side of their junk, out of sight of the main channel, were two police launches. "Now," Malloy said. "I'm going to spring my trap now."

"Wait." Lao Ch'en grabbed Malloy's arm. "Wait until his boat is stopped and the sampans surround him, then we'll have him for certain."

THE EAST WIND glided toward the heart of the harbor, where the smaller sampans were moored. She carried no lights. Her lean, low outline was obscured by the forest of junk masts. The forehatch opened. Fat Sui Leong and an American army deserter, Tom Hakker, quietly lifted themselves onto the deck and prepared to offload the gold. A third man, Lo Fang, who had remained below, passed up an oilskin bag.

13

"No."

"Take it," he whispered harshly to Fat Sui Leong, who had felt the light round ball and knew instantly what it contained. "Dr. Sun has ordered that this reach the 14K."

Nicholai had been sweeping the harbor through his binoculars. "Make the signal," he ordered. A light flashed once from the ex-gunboat and a small flotilla of waiting sampans began struggling toward it across the choppy waters.

The *East Wind* carried one and a half tons of gold from Macau. Once it reached the sampans it would disappear from police informers' eyes as surely as if it had been scattered out at sea... these coolies were part of the all-powerful 14K Triad, and one *tael* of missing gold, one word out of place, would cost the coolie his life.

Nicholai swung his glasses to check his crew's progress on the foredeck. He spotted the oilproof sack being surreptitiously pushed through the foredeck hatch.

A sampan had jostled ahead of the others to draw alongside the *East Wind*. Lo Fang followed the sack through the hatch to ensure that it reached the right sampan.

"Bring that here," Nicholai told him.

Lo Fang reluctantly made his way to the bridge. Nicholai leaned down, took the bag from him and opened it. Inside lay a sticky black ball of opium, five catties worth, destined for the new heroin factories that were springing up in Kowloon. Nicholai's hatred of the drug was well known. It was a measure of his waning influence that anyone would have dared smuggle it aboard. But Lo Fang's place on the *East Wind* had been secured by Dr. Sun himself, which gave him courage.

"How many bags?" Nicholai asked quietly.

Lo Fang tried to boast. "Ten. Dr. Sun ordered a trial shipment—"

"Throw them overboard, and see that they sink."

Lo Fang glared up at him. "Do you dare rob Dr. Sun?"

"I carry no opium nor human cargo aboard my boat," Nicholai said. "That is my rule."

"Let it pass," Udo said behind Nicholai. "Pretend you haven't seen it."

"Are you and the rest of my crew in this too?"

"You know better than that. None of us are, except Lo Fang, and he always was Dr. Sun's informer."

"If you defy Dr. Sun," the helmsman warned, "if you make his man lose face, it will mean your certain death, and perhaps ours too..."

Lo Fang, overhearing this exchange, smugly prepared to go back to

14

work. But Nicholai, feeling reckless, damned the consequences. "The opium goes into the sea," he ordered the men on the foredeck. "And *you*"—he turned to Lo Fang—"go over the side after it."

"Dr. Sun will have his revenge—"

"You'll see us all in hell yet, Nicholai," Udo growled. But to ensure that his captain's orders were obeyed, the huge man swung himself lightly down from the bridge.

From the corner of his eye Lo Fang spotted Udo moving toward him, and rather than risk having his back broken he promptly threw himself into the greasy, heaving water.

Udo then turned from the portside rail and caught a glimpse of the black-and-gray launch that had crept up on them, and before he had time to shout a warning Nicholai saw it too and wrenched the engine telegraph handles down to full ahead.

The "crash-start" warning bell rang in the engine room. Lin Tsang, who had kept all three engines ticking over against such an emergency, rammed their throttles wide. The *East Wind* nearly stood on her stern as her triple propellers bit the water. The wash set up by the accelerating ex-gunboat overturned the sampans that had clustered around her, sending the little gold smuggler's bars, the precious evidence Malloy needed, to the mud-and-garbage-silted bottom of Aberdeen harbor.

Afraid of killing the coolies in the water, the police launch could not intercept the *East Wind*. "Go around them," Malloy ordered. "Don't stop to pick up survivors. If he's killed anyone I'll have him for murder."

"THEY'VE BLOCKED the southern exit," Udo reported as the *East Wind* reached the main channel. Through his binoculars he had picked up the silhouettes of two big seagoing police launches gliding forward, bow-to-bow, to close the breakwater entrance.

Nicholai turned north, weaving through the junk-strewn harbor toward the western entrance. Too late. Two police launches were positioned again, bow-to-bow, to block the exit.

"YOU CAN wriggle all you want, you bastard," Malloy said with great pleasure as his launch followed the *East Wind*, "but this time I really believe I've got you.". . . Malloy was not here to earn another commendation on his service record. He held a very personal grudge against Nicholai . . . "Just keep on his tail," he called to the deck sergeant manning the helm. "He's got no way out."

15

KENG PO, on the bridge of the *East Wind*, was echoing Malloy's comments. "It's no good, Hau-ye," he shouted to Nicholai above the slipstream. "There are only two exits from Aberdeen and they've closed both to us."

Nicholai had brought the *East Wind* careering back down the harbor, and now he spotted the narrow gap that the seas had forced through the southern breakwater. He tried to gauge the width of the gap; there was just enough room, perhaps two or three feet to spare on either side of his boat. Keng Po quickly understood what was in Nicholai's mind. "No, you'll kill us all—"

"Would you rather rot in a stinking Hong Kong jail?" Nicholai demanded, and steered the *East Wind* at the gap. "Tell Tsang," he said to Udo, "that I want all the power he's got." The engines trumpeted, the sound whipping away in the wind as the boat leapt forward.

His crew could see a wave curling high over the top of the breakwater; a thousand tons of raw energy gained from its long fetch across the South China Sea. Nicholai drove the *East Wind* at the maelstrom that came exploding through the gap.

The *East Wind*'s bows dove into the sea. The boat's impetus carried it forward, the bows lifting steeply, the light hull careering up the face of the wave like an express lift. The crest of the wave broke over the boat, boiled under its keel, creating enough water to clear the blocks, and then they were through and past the breakwater, the boat on its side surfing out of control down the back of the wave. They would have capsized in the deep trough below if Nicholai had not gunned the port engine, using all of its fourteen hundred horsepower to bring the bows around just in time to meet the next sea.

"HE'S SLIPPED through," Malloy shouted, half crazy with frustration and rage. "Go *after* him..."

The deck sergeant and Malloy would have risked their lives to settle the score with the Snake Boat Man, but no one else on their boat would...

"Even if we clear the gap we can't catch him now," the bosun told Malloy. "He has double our speed. We'll chase his wake all the way back to Macau."

He was, of course, right.

16

THE *EAST WIND* berthed in the Inner Harbor of Macau just before dawn. Chang Ch'en, the Syndicate's enforcer, waited with his bodyguards on the dock to escort Nicholai, the Snake Boat Man, to Dr. Sun's palace. Nicholai swung himself down from the bridge and made ready to jump ashore. Udo caught his arm. "I'm your friend," the big man argued, "I'm coming with you."

Nicholai shook his head. He was tall, dark-complected, descended, so he was told, from a noble Russian line. "No point in risking your life too," he said. "Stay with the crew."

Nicholai walked beside Chang to the waiting car. Shaken by his near capture, his nerves were in a worse state than he had dared let Udo and Keng Po know.

His step was light, Chang thought, not sensing how Nicholai felt, for a man whose career was over... Chang turned to the crew, allowing his jacket to fall open and reveal the gun in its shoulder holster. His message was clear; he carried out Dr. Sun's executions. . . .

FOR THE past one hundred years Macau had been Hong Kong's weak sister, dying slowly as her harbor filled with silt. Hong Kong, situated only forty-five miles due west across the Pearl River estuary, had robbed her of her trade with China. But then, it was said that Macau had never lived by honest toil.

The six-and-a-half-square-mile entrepôt was one of the most exciting cities in the East. Certainly it was the most lawless—a haven for smugglers, spies and blockade runners. Built on seven small hills, commanded over by the fire-gutted facade of a Christian cathedral, it was the oldest European settlement on China's soil—a city of ancient roofs and cobbled streets, smelling of sandalwood incense from the joss sticks that burned in the open doorways of the shops, mingled with the stench of mudflats at low tide.

Macau's Portuguese colonial rulers had lost much of their influence. The Communists showed no interest in assuming direct control, being content to manipulate behind the scenes. And so under Dr. Sun's leadership, a criminal organization known as the Macau Syndicate had grown in power until it rivaled the notorious 14K Triad, its sister criminal organization based in Hong Kong. Between the Syndicate and the Triad they now possessed fortunes greater than the exchequers of many countries. Macau still paid halfhearted homage to its Portuguese governor and chief of police, but it was understood throughout the South China Sea that Dr. Sun ruled here.

Dr. Sun had built his palace of rose marble from the profits of the illegal gold trade, and it dominated the city. A great banquet was now drawing to a close within the Crystal Room, the room he loved best in all his exquisitely furnished palace. Along either wall, in glass cabinets that rose from floor to ceiling, sparkled the finest collection of crystal in the Orient. The chandeliers that hung above the long polished table were reputed to be composed of diamonds.

Some thirty of Dr. Sun's closest companions were seated around the table, having enjoyed a sumptuous meal. They had learned from Dr. Sun that their Syndicate was now ready to depart from its illegal gold trade and switch to drugs and gambling.

Business over with, Dr. Sun relaxed. He was prematurely old from the ravages wrought on his body when he begged his way from Shanghai to Hong Kong during the great famine of '37. His lips formed a bloodless scar across his hollow-cheeked, sunken-eyed face, over which almost-transparent skin was stretched like faded parchment. The last two fingers of his left hand were missing. His upper eyelids were straight, all the curve being in the lower half; most disconcerting were his eyelids that closed upward, hooding his black-eyed glare.

In his high-backed chair at the head of the table, he threw back his head and laughed. It was the forced laughter of a man on the edge. The others around the table, drunk though they were, laughed with him overlong and loud to ensure those blazing black eyes didn't single them out. Every man there—pimp, racketeer, extortionist, thief—was terrified of Dr. Sun, and would go to any lengths to keep him in his current good humor.

Yu Shik Lieu, the ubiquitous comprador, the most powerful man in Dr. Sun's household, had no place at the banqueting table. His job was to keep alert, to watch for enemies among those present. He stood now by the door, overseeing the servants who scurried back and forth. As the laughter died away and conversation resumed further down the table, Dr. Sun signaled to the comprador, who caught the signal, the index finger of the left hand pointing against his master's thigh, and issued a soft-voiced order to a servant. The servant hurried away to see Lao Ta, chief of the Manchu bodyguards, whose men patrolled the palace grounds, and returned with a cloth-covered silver tray.

The comprador lifted the edge of the cloth and inspected the .38 caliber revolver that lay beneath. "Deliver it to the great lord Sun," he instructed. At that moment he caught the merest flicker of a movement; someone was spying on the banquet through a secret grill in one of the crystal cabinets. No one knew of its existence except Dr. Sun and his comprador.

The comprador left his post by the door and, motioning to Lao Ta to follow him, hurried into the next room, where a cubbyhole cunningly worked into the wall gave access to the spygrill. Lao Ta drew his gun, a heavy-caliber automatic, and took aim. The comprador threw back the curtain—and a pretty little girl, aged nine or ten, with huge dark almond eyes, spun from the grill.

Lao Ta's weapon was leveled at her head. The comprador swept the girl up in his arms. "Fool," he whispered to Dr. Sun's daughter, Crystal Lily, "you little fool... even you could have died for spying on your father."

From within the Crystal Room came the loud report of a pistol shot, then a scream of pain, the sounds setting the crystal ringing all around the room. It was a sound Dr. Sun enjoyed. The girl broke free of the comprador's arms, ducked past Lao Ta and ran from the room as though all the devils in Macau were chasing her.

Thomas Wu, tall, lean, elegantly dressed, sat three places down on the left of Dr. Sun. He was Dr. Sun's personal secretary, once almost his adopted son until the birth of Crystal Lily made all hope of that impossible. He remained sober, too fastidious a man to indulge in the drunkenness and gluttony of the others. He listened instead for unguarded snippets of conversation from the powerful men around him, later to report them to his master. He had seen Dr. Sun lift the napkin and take the gun from the platter when he thought no one was watching.

Thomas Wu knew what was going to happen. He dared not move, but the color left his face and he imagined his legs going numb. Dr. Sun was about to round off his banquet by playing "Who is the lucky man?" Others had spotted the gun being lowered under the table. Without a word being spoken, without any discernible change of expression, a current of fear circuited that table. The gun went off. The guest next to Thomas Wu clutched his leg where the bullet had lodged below his knee, and screamed. Dr. Sun lifted his still smoking revolver and smiled. The other men around the table smiled with him as the servants hurried forward, lifted the unfortunate man from his chair and carried him away.

The comprador waited for Dr. Sun to regain his composure, silently thanking his ancestors that the news he had to break had come now. Shooting at one of his companions' legs under the table at the end of a banquet always put Dr. Sun in a good temper... he believed it made his hospitality memorable. "Great lord," the comprador whispered in Dr. Sun's ear, "Chang has brought the Snake Boat Man to the palace. He wants to see you."

Dr. Sun was in an expansive mood. "Bring the Snake Boat Man here, see that he has an honored place at my table."

"...Great lord, the gold run was not successful"—the comprador steeled himself before delivering the next piece of news—"worse, the Snake Boat Man discovered the opium and he threw your man Lo Fang overboard..."

"*Where is he?*"

"In the antechamber, lord."

Dr. Sun pushed back his chair and strode from the room. Thomas Wu followed after him.

Dr. Sun had managed to control some of his anger by the time he confronted the Snake Boat Man, knowing that Nicholai, of all his men, was not afraid of offending him. He dismissed Chang, then to Nicholai: "How much gold did you lose?"

"A quarter of a ton, maybe less."

"You did not take proper precautions, you've grown careless."

"I took all the precautions I could. Someone from here tipped the British off. Inspector Malloy of the Hong Kong police was waiting for me—"

"Excuses. You let Malloy and that deck sergeant of his, Lao Ch'en, outsmart you. But never mind the gold now, what about my man, Lo Fang?"

"He disobeyed my orders. You know I carry no drugs on the *East Wind*."

"Nicholai"—Dr. Sun spoke with unaccustomed patience; any other man would have been dead by now, but Dr. Sun possessed an almost superstitious regard for Nicholai—"the trade you and I built is ending. The world will soon operate a free market in gold. Heroin is the new gold of Macau. It is easy to conceal, light to carry, and the profits are far larger than you or I can imagine. I know that your wife, the beautiful Li Wen, was an addict, and I am aware of the struggle you both went through to wean her from it. But bad memories of her death cannot stop you now—"

"I will not run drugs and I will not run refugees. You have skin boats to do that. I've come to tell you that I retire. I'm finished with you—"

"No one leaves my service. No one *ever* leaves me. Their service ends

20

when they die. You were just a starving *fang quoi* when I rescued you from certain death in the Inner Harbor and made you number one among my captains—"

"I've repaid my debt to you many times over."

"You can never repay me for your life. It belongs to me."

"Take it, then." Nicholai turned and walked out of the room, expecting at any moment to feel a bullet in the back. He made it through the door, but he still had to get out of the palace, and its walls were guarded by Dr. Sun's Manchu bodyguards.

Hiding at the top of the grand staircase, little Crystal Lily watched him leave, her eyes nearly as big as she was.

"Let Chang kill him," Thomas Wu urged. "You must protect your face. He has humiliated you, all Macau will soon know—"

"Great lord," the comprador interceded against Thomas Wu, who glared at him, "remember he has a boat crew waiting for him in the Inner Harbor. Remember also that if you kill him Udo will come to revenge his captain; and not even Chang, your enforcer, or Lao Ta will relish defending you from the Bear seeking a blood debt. Besides, the Snake Boat Man is your creation. You saved the *gwilo* from a stinking death in the Inner Harbor. His legend among our people has become your legend, his glory is your glory. If you destroy him now you will destroy part of yourself. Let him go."

Dr. Sun nodded, turned on Thomas Wu. "Get out of my sight, you dog's turd, and do *not* tell me how to deal with the only man I have ever loved."

Nicholai had reached the hall before the entrance doors when he heard the patter of light feet chasing after him. He turned as the girl rushed into his arms. "Take me with you," Crystal Lily said, "please take me with you, don't leave me here." He stooped down to her and her face pressed against his chest. As a despised girl-child she was neglected by her father, in constant and real danger from enemies inside his palace. Nicholai was a god to her, the only man she could trust and look to for protection. She saw none of his weaknesses, only his strength, and she loved him with a near-adult passion.

Like Crystal, Nicholai had no one. His own childhood he blanked from his mind where he could. The Hong Kong police were growing more expert at protecting their coastline, and tonight his nerve had, he realized, finally failed him. He was running away, and he knew it. He wanted to be strong, at least for the girl, but he couldn't save her. "I can't take you with me," he said, all the hurt he felt for them both in his eyes, unable to explain to her the power of her father. "Neither you nor I would leave this palace alive."

She was a tough child; she had to be, he thought, to have survived so long. She very rarely cried, but he felt her crying now, sobbing against his chest.

To hell with it... he picked up Crystal Lily and carrying her in his arms, retraced his steps to the antechamber.

Dr. Sun paid no attention to his daughter's tears; he was stunned by Nicholai's return... the madman apparently had no concern for his own safety.

"You get your child out of this snake pit," Nicholai told him. "Send her away now to an English or American school. If you won't pay for her, I will."

"Don't you instruct me on her welfare," Dr. Sun said. No one had spoken to him like that in twenty years.

"Then I'll take her with me."

"You'll never get past the palace gates."

The comprador whispered, "I beg of you, hold back your anger. Send her far away to the Golden Mountain"—he used the Macanese euphemism for America—"she can learn and grow strong there... here she remains just another target for your enemies."

Dr. Sun weighed the alternatives. He held up his hand to signify a peace between himself and Nicholai. "The child goes to America, and you may retire from my service. But you must leave Macau and never return in my lifetime."

Nicholai accepted his sentence of exile without a sign.

"Some day," Dr. Sun went on, "my daughter will rule the Syndicate in my place, and she may call on you for the debt you now owe me. Do not refuse her. She asks in my name."

Nicholai set the child down. "I love you," she said, terrified of losing him. "Write to me in... in America?"

He brushed the tears from her face. His gray eyes were smiling like the sun dancing on a summer sea. "I won't forget you," he promised...

MACAU
1981

CHAPTER 1

UNEASILY ASLEEP in a four-poster double bed was a beautiful girl in her early twenties. She awoke as her amah stirred beyond her bedroom door, her hand reaching automatically for the .9mm caliber pistol under her pillow. The hollow light of dawn filtered through the huge bulletproof picture window on the west wall of her bedroom; beyond was her private courtyard garden surrounded by a high brick wall with an electrified fence on top. Guard dogs and the same Manchu bodyguards, now elderly men, who had once served her dead father patrolled the walls.

Crystal Lily got up, wrapped herself in a thin silk gown, walked through the study attached to her bedroom and out onto the marble balcony. Her face, deep in concentration, held an ivory-carved stillness as she watched the tropical dawn break, the sky changing from pastel to crimson as the sun came raging up out of the South China Sea.

She had returned from the University of Hawaii to her birthplace just one month before to inherit control of the Macau Syndicate on the death of her father, the notorious Dr. Sun.

Below her spread the tiny Portuguese-ruled island. In the fifteen years she had been away its skyline had altered almost beyond recognition. The seedy yet colorful four-hundred-year-old buildings were abruptly being swept aside; Macau, having reached an accommodation with China, had been given a reprieve. Gaudy hotels and casinos rose along the Praia Grande to cater to the new boom in tourism and gambling. Only the junk-crowded Inner Harbor still pulsated with the life force and rhythms of the old Macau.

For a moment the rising sun caught the junk masts and the narrow cobbled streets leading off the Inner Harbor in a noose of light, and once again Crystal Lily sensed the deep secrets, the heart of the city that had been her father's domain. For her the six-square-mile enclave, including the islands of Taipa and Colôane, that had been founded by traders, adventurers and soldiers of fortune still held the memories of her childhood with its aura of illicit excitement and danger. Indeed it represented the greater part of her soul that had remained unwesternized, that had made her long to come home...

A faint scratching sounded against her bedroom door, as though her caller were hesitant to intrude. *"Gong dai sen chai,"* she called out in half-remembered Cantonese.

The comprador, Yu Shik Lieu, now a much older man, stooping, entered her private rooms. He had served her father nearly his entire life, and he hated bringing her his news. "Failure," he said as gently as he could. "The junk carrying the gold to the 14K Triad was intercepted before it could reach Hong Kong."

"And my crew?" A soft wind off the sea was pressing her thin gown against her body, stirring the lustrous black hair that fell to her waist.

"All dead except one," the comprador answered, reluctant to meet her cool gaze. "A vessel belonging to your fleet found him hiding among the wreckage in the Soko Islands."

"Can he identify his attackers?"

"He claims he saw nothing. Fear, I believe, has erased his memory. By this evening his body will be found floating out to sea."

"Let him live."

"My lady, he was part of a crew that failed you. To let him live would be to lose face, your father would never have permitted—"

"And what will happen if I fail to pay my father's debt to the Triad?"

"They will, I am afraid, join with your enemies in the Syndicate to destroy you. As you know, your father was banker of the 14K Triad, and a large portion of the gold bullion held in the vaults below this palace represents the profits from the Triad's share of the drug business. Profits were laundered through the Syndicate-owned casinos, converted into gold and held safely out of reach of the Hong Kong authorities in Macau."

"Won't they allow me to convert the debt into a paper currency of their choice? Why do I have to pay them in gold?"

"Because the Triad is outlawed in Hong Kong, and the least complicated method for them to make or receive large transfers in the colony is in gold. The Triad's debt falls due on the last day of August. The gold must reach them before then or your life..." He could not finish the thought. He did not have to.

Crystal Lily's amah, one of the staff of sixteen servants who moved quietly through the great rooms of the palace, placed a tray of fragrantly steaming tea in the study.

"Come with me," Crystal Lily ordered the comprador.

The old comprador shuffled after her into the study. He had held the most important position in Dr. Sun's household as adviser, intermediary, confidant. Respected for his shrewdness and trusted by Dr. Sun, he was feared by his subordinates; the comprador alone knew the cells of power, all the innermost secrets of Dr. Sun. He was also the one man who could bring Crystal Lily down, except up to now no comprador of a powerful Macanese house had ever betrayed his master. By every tradition he would stay loyal, and in return the comprador's family had become rich and powerful. He had only a few months to live before his emphysema-scarred lungs would cease to function, but Crystal Lily knew that his wisdom and guidance would be worth a battalion of gunmen in her coming fight for survival.

"There is obviously a well-placed traitor in my household," Crystal Lily said. "No one else knew where the junk would make its landfall."

The comprador shrugged. He more than anyone understood the extent of the power vacuum left by Dr. Sun's death.

"My lady, each man in this household served your father. Each man's loyalty was tested many times. But loyalties, I realize, can change. I will investigate. Now you must prepare yourself. You have less than forty minutes before the inner council of the Syndicate meets."

"Has Chen Kitung come back from Canton?"

The comprador nodded. "He will attend the meeting."

"So today we will know China's answer." Crystal Lily shook her head

27

wearily. "Except I know it already. The governor of Canton will vote against me."

"If he does, then one man in the inner council will already have been chosen to succeed you. I advise you to find him . . . before he tries to kill you . . ."

Macau had really changed very little, she thought.

Yu Shik Lieu waited in the study while Crystal Lily showered and changed into a western-style two-piece suit. She wore a minimum of makeup and piled her hair into a bun at the nape of her neck. Before leaving she paused in front of her father's shrine that was set into an alcove in one corner of her study. Red candles and incense sticks burned around an ancestor jar containing his bones. Facing the sea with the mainland of China behind the Fung Shui was a perfect resting place for it, and yet, instead of resting, his spirit seemed to pervade the palace; she often thought she could actually *feel* his brooding presence.

"Father," she now prayed before the ornate gold-and-red-backed shrine, "the other members of the Syndicate resent me. Especially as a woman. There is a serious challenge to my leadership. I know as long as I stay within these palace walls they can't harm me, but I also know that I am being encircled before a coup. You had few friends, and I have inherited all your enemies; wherever I turn for help I am blocked. My servants don't like serving a woman and are already beginning to desert me. I can only trust the advice of your old comprador. If they have chosen a new leader how will I know him? Please . . . help me . . . I am your daughter, your blood is my blood . . ."

She left the study and joined the comprador, who escorted her down the stairs.

"Remember," he said, "you are rich and vulnerable, these men are greedy. Let them grow bold."

She understood immediately the shrewdness of the old man's advice . . . if they fought like wolves over her she perhaps could divide them, eliminate them one by one. Remember, she told herself, you are your father's daughter. She took a deep breath and nodded to Yu Shik Lieu to open the door.

Four men waited inside the Crystal Room. They alone comprised the inner council of the Syndicate. At an impatient signal from the comprador they rose grudgingly to pay his lady respect. In her father's day they would not have dared sit before she entered the room.

Rocky Lee, a ladies' man, made no secret of his approval of Crystal Lily. The severe suit she had chosen to wear could not disguise the figure beneath. Her face was sultry, almost feline, and her ivory skin smooth. Few men failed to notice her lips, full and sensuous, not to mention her almond-shaped eyes framed by long, dark lashes.

What a waste of such a delicious morsel, Rocky Lee thought. Instead of attempting to rule the Syndicate this one would be better employed in one of the brothels off the Street of Happiness...

Crystal Lily took her place in her father's chair at the head of the table. Her comprador sat to the right and slightly behind her. His would be the only notes made of the meeting and they would never leave the palace.

Her eyes fell on a scuffed wooden begging bowl, hand-carved into the shape of a dragon boat. Her father had used this begging bowl to keep from starving on his journey from the waterfront slums of Shanghai to Macau. After he had made his fortune he had placed it there in the center of his priceless collection of crystal to remind him of the life of suffering he had come from. If his enemies had ever hoped for mercy they had only to look at that begging bowl... *Help me*...

On her left sat Chang Ch'en, the Syndicate enforcer responsible for discipline among its members and the labor unions. A squat, brutal-faced man with rounded shoulders and a balding skull, he was dressed in a silk tunic of pearl gray. Feeling his gaze on her, Crystal Lily glanced up, noted that his small, deep-set eyes flickered just a fraction of an inch below hers before he turned away. Chang never looked anyone directly in the eye.

"My lady," he murmured while the comprador read through the agenda for the meeting, his lips pressed into an anticipatory smile, "I hear one of our junks was lost last night. I will, of course, investigate."

Crystal Lily was quite certain he would do no such thing. She remembered it bruited about the palace during her childhood that her mother's death had been no accident, that Chang had murdered her on Dr. Sun's orders. Crystal Lily put no faith in Chang's loyalty to her now, especially if he thought she might try to avenge her mother. And in a power struggle with the inner council, surely this would be the man assigned to kill her. Her eyes fell on his huge hands resting on the table. A sadist, he had survived numerous assassination attempts, always saved by some animal sixth sense.

Crystal Lily felt a shiver of loathing and fear start up her spine, and turned to the governor of Kwangtung Province's unofficial representative in Macau. He had just returned from a private briefing in Canton. Kitung was a fat, smiling man whose appearance was like that of a benign Buddha—from the scrupulously shaven, shining dome of his head to the folds of his well-nourished flesh.

When the new leadership swept to power in China during the Revolution of 1949, Dr. Sun had sought out Chen Kitung to act as his liaison with the Communists. Those were difficult times for the enclave, but Chen Kitung's job was to see that vast amounts of graft reached Canton. Later, when Chairman Mao unleashed the Cultural Revolution, Chen Kitung and the governor of Kwangtung Province successfully walked the delicate tightrope between the rival factions while many others failed.

Crystal Lily knew that Chen Kitung had no desire to assume control of the Syndicate—he had reached an age at which he preferred a peaceful life—but he had survived so far because he had always been able to pick the winning side...

Kitung's expression as he reported on his visit to China betrayed nothing; he was too good a diplomat for that. Crystal Lily, watching him closely, knew there would be no slip of words, no signs to warn her if and when the balance of power had shifted radically out of her favor. Yet her life depended on finding this out. And now her years of comparative safety in Hawaii were ripped away, replaced by the terrors of a childhood spent in Macau—a time when her own instincts for survival had been honed and fine-tuned. She concentrated, her senses now sharpened to signals that were well hidden but nonetheless there. The guarded veil behind Chen Kitung's eyes when he looked at her, the subtle hint of betrayal in his unaccustomedly sweating face...yes, all her old instincts were at work, and she was all but certain that the governor of Canton had turned against her...had agreed to support a male successor to Dr. Sun's female heir...

She knew that this was the final move against her already shaky power base, the one that the other members of the Syndicate had been waiting for. They would feel licensed now not only to dispose of Crystal Lily and her leadership, but also to take over and profit by her enormous fortune—five tons of gold bullion that Dr. Sun had stashed in the vaults below this palace against such an eventuality. And out of that bullion, two tons was owed by Crystal to the 14K Triad in Hong Kong.

Crystal Lily fought to control her panic. The die was cast, what hope was there of dividing these men...what chance did she have against them?...Whatever, she warned herself abruptly, she had no time for such girlish self-indulgence. What would her father have done? He would have destroyed them all. Very well, quickly, which of these men has been chosen to replace you? She forced herself to concentrate. Not Chen Kitung, not Chang the enforcer... no one would trust him. Who then...?

The comprador sat watching his protégée. The effort of concentration had penetrated the beautiful stillness of her face—she had sensed something. He guessed that she could read men's faces as her father had done, that instinctively she would discover, sense these men's treacheries, find their weaknesses. The old comprador almost felt relieved. With this young cub in her father's place, all was not yet lost...

Rocky Lee sat midway down the table on Crystal Lily's right. In his early forties, he was a good-looking Chinese if in a flashy sort of way. Unlike the others, who were very conservative when it came to displaying any signs of wealth, Rocky Lee covered himself in gold and diamond rings and chains. He regularly appeared in the society columns of the Macau and Hong Kong newspapers, always linked with the latest movie starlet about. The others disapproved of his flamboyance but could find no fault with his management of their drug operation or with the gambling that now provided a major portion of the Syndicate's income.

Lee had built a power base among his drug traffickers, and he was ambitious—of that Crystal Lily had no doubt. But she also dismissed him as an immediate threat. He was not a leader, and far too much of a hedonist to win support from this self-consciously conservative group of men.

Still... *someone* had instigated the move to depose her. Which left only Thomas Wu. She had noticed that he sat apart from the others at the far end of the table, poised as though already impatient to assume leadership. He was in his fifties, lean-faced with a flattened nose and narrow, reptilian eyes...

Thomas Wu was born on the island of Coloane, the bastard son of an African sergeant serving with a Portuguese colonial army battalion once stationed there and of an outcast Chinese mother. His mixed blood made him quick to resent any imagined humiliation, and with a store of bitterness always just beneath the surface, he was by far, Crystal Lily felt, the most dangerous of them all. As a child Wu had watched his mother starve to death in a back alley of Colôane village, and was said to have made a vow by her corpse that neither he nor his descendants would ever know such racking poverty again. He joined the wandering armies of child street beggars who invaded Macau during the famines that swept China, somehow managing to attract the attention of Dr. Sun, who took the clever boy into his family as a possible heir. The birth of Crystal Lily

31

soon ruined any hopes young Wu had. The boy was put to work first as a clerk in one of the Syndicate-owned banks, and later in the position of Dr. Sun's personal secretary. He rather quickly demonstrated the business acumen needed to take the Syndicate into the twenty-first century, but Crystal Lily had always discounted any challenge from him for the simple reason that the Chinese, inherent racists, would distrust any leader not wholly Chinese. Even so, he was the cleverest man there. Could he now have somehow persuaded the others to support him? she wondered.

Crystal Lily appeared deceptively vulnerable to the men gathered around the table. They expected to find a naiveté inherent in her sheltered American education, but when she lifted her face all their attention fastened on her deep black eyes. This young woman *had* power, a visible force that made them remember her father. All except Wu were abruptly uneasy. He raised his eyes to her—his oldest rival, the girl-child of Dr. Sun who had robbed him of his inheritance, and they were eyes that dared openly if briefly to show his sense of triumph...

So she had discovered her enemy, who left her in no doubt that he felt confident enough to strike at her, and very soon... She adjourned the meeting and quickly left the room; her comprador and bodyguards would escort the members of the Syndicate from her palace.

THE COMPRADOR found her later in her study. She was seething, blotches of red marring her high, perfect cheekbones. Unable to sit, she moved about the room like a cat.

"So, the governor is against me?" she exploded.

"It was to be expected," the comprador said quietly. "Do you have any idea whom they have chosen to replace you?"

"Thomas Wu, of course... that scum who was almost my brother by adoption. I saw the treachery and the arrogance in his eyes. We must act now before he does. He knows the Triad has called in my father's debt to them."

"Wait, my lady, wait. You are safe inside this palace. Thomas Wu is a clever enemy. He is squeezing you, hoping to force you into some act that will leave you vulnerable and open to him."

"I have a deadline to meet," she reminded him. "If I don't deliver the gold by the last day of August the Triad will join with Wu to destroy me. I can't fight both of them and now the governor of Kwangtung, too. Damn, he must think he has me squeezed between his fingers like an ant," she raged, knocking a chair across the room.

But as suddenly as it began the tantrum was over; her icy self-control returned. They had underestimated her; she *had* the courage to fight back, and they would discover she was indeed her father's daughter—as ruthless and cunning as he. No. More so. After all, she was also a woman...

"I need an ally. I've known for some time that I would. How many messages have we sent to the Snake Boat Man?"

"Two."

"And he still hasn't answered?"

"No."

"Then I must go to Hong Kong to see him. He won't refuse me face-to-face." She hoped. "Make the arrangements."

"My lady, you must not leave this palace, it would be terribly dangerous for you—"

"I'm already gambling with my life. I must have help, and the only man I can turn to is the Snake Boat Man."

To Nicholai, whom she had never forgotten.

CHAPTER 2

"**SLOW DOWN,**" the captain of Crystal Lily's boat ordered. They were fifty minutes out of Macau, headed for Hong Kong. "Watch for the beacon on the land." With barely a tremble the high flared bows of the launch touched the water, the deep throb of its diesel engines slowed.

Crystal Lily stood beside the captain on the bridge of her ChrisCraft as it entered Victoria Harbor. In the evening it was one of the most spectacular scenes in the world, with the island of Hong Kong lying to the south, Kowloon on the mainland of China to the north and the harbor dividing the land like a small inland sea surrounded by skyscrapers.

On first sight it seemed to her they were sailing into a pool of darkness surrounded by a skyline of blazing lights alive with noisy activity. A Cathay Pacific Tristar on final approach for Kai Tak Airport soared overhead. Double-decker Star Ferries churned back and forth across the harbor at full speed, impatiently blowing horns at the junks and bumboats in their paths.

But it was the lights reflecting from the skyscrapers on the oily waters that especially held Crystal Lily. The magic, the excitement of Hong Kong never failed to move her, regardless of how many times she had seen it... Her eyes drank in sight of the buildings, the boats, the flashing beacons on the buoys, the brightly lit American warships lying at anchor on the Wanchai waterfront and the flashing neon signs of the bars on the waterfront, always beckoning to the men on those warships.

"Four hundred yards..." the leadsman called from the bow as the ChrisCraft approached the landing stage. "Two hundred yards." The captain needed his full attention to guide the ChrisCraft around the ferries and walla-walla water taxis plunging around him. "Fifty yards... ten yards..." The leadsman took hold with his casting pole for coming alongside.

And then, the final order came from the captain: "Tie up the boat. Stop engines."

The boat secured, Crystal Lily was escorted ashore by four well-muscled bodyguards. The captain took note of her departure with regret. Although she had no way of knowing it, tonight was the first and last time he would have occasion to serve the late Dr. Sun's beautiful daughter... what a waste, he thought, then shrugged away his conscience. Thomas Wu would pay well for the information he had to offer, and in these troubled times it only made sense for a man with a family to place his loyalty with the strongest side...

INSIDE THE terminal Crystal Lily ignored the long immigration lines and made her way to a private office, walked unannounced through the half-open door. A European senior immigration officer glanced up from his work, recognized her and stiffened nervously as she placed five passports on his desk.

"I would like entry visas," she said. It was less a request than a command.

"As you know, your father was never given entry to Hong Kong—"

"Then you must convince your superiors to treat me differently."

"I'll see what I can do." The official returned a few minutes later and handed her back the passports. "I can only give you twenty-four hours' clearance without going to a higher authority—"

"That will do." She turned to leave and her bodyguards surrounded her, using their shoulders to clear a path through the terminal.

Once on the street she again took in the heady excitement of Hong Kong, the frenetic energy that characterized the richly diverse, teeming city.

Within moments two rented Mercedeses rolled up to the curb; Crystal Lily got into the lead car. The comprador was waiting for her, his frail body resting uncomfortably against the back seat.

"Did you have any problems getting a visa?"

"No, it was well arranged."

The comprador checked on her bodyguards—counting the two with him, there were five who had remained behind. "You have left the palace well guarded?"

"Yes."

"Thomas Wu will have learned about our journey by now, but not even he can move against the palace without support from the others. Still, we must not give him time to gain support. We must be back within six hours, no later than that."

Crystal nodded as she opened her window, letting in the noises of the street and the pungent aromas from the sidewalk restaurants. The cars slowly nosed through the crowd of people and traffic along the waterfront. Ahead was a magnificent fifty-story skyscraper that housed the main offices of All Asia Trading, the most prestigious of the five *hongs*, or trading houses, of Hong Kong. After passing the building the cars swung right, climbing toward the Peak, a single steep mountaintop that dominated the island. Tires squealed as the cars rounded the narrow hairpin corners, the deep boom of their exhausts resounding off the stone-banked walls. Up through Magazine Gap they drove, passing through some of the most expensive real estate in the world, into clearer, cooler air, leaving the city fumes behind. Dense green vegetation grew over the banks, and blocks of flats, seemingly mined into the vertical mountainside, fell away in Lilliputian tiers below.

"Does he still live alone?" Crystal Lily asked the comprador, hoping her voice wouldn't betray what she secretly hoped.

"Yes, except for a servant."

"Could he need money?"

"I think not, he amassed great wealth while working for your father..."

The comprador studied her. Everyone knew about the Snake Boat Man's reputation, and he worried that Crystal Lily was putting too much hope on it... or could the affection he suspected she still held for Nicholai have swayed her? "He has been retired for fifteen years," the comprador

36

reminded her, "and I have heard he is drinking heavily. Why don't you choose a younger man?"

She shook her head. "I trust no one else."

The cars neared the summit of the Peak, turned into Lugard Road and pulled up in front of a pair of imposing metal gates. The driver climbed out and identified himself in front of a video screen set into one wall. A whir of electric circuits, and the gates swung open. The cars rolled down a steeply winding tunnel into a large basement. The doors clamped shut, forming a second barrier from the road. Bodyguards were reaching for their weapons even as the banks of overhead flourescent lights flooded on, and a gray-haired, sad-faced Kuomintang soldier, badly wounded in the service of the Snake Boat Man, limped across the concrete catwalk that spanned the basement above the cars. "Tell your men to remain—" But before he could finish the sentence the bodyguards had already fanned out. One of them, running up the steps to the catwalk, pushed the old man against the railings and frisked him.

"The Snake Boat Man's servant," the comprador said to Crystal Lily, recognizing the former soldier. "You are Ah Chuen," he called up. "I remember you now. My lady, the daughter of Dr. Sun, has come to speak with the Snake Boat Man."

The bodyguards, after searching the basement, were now slipping through the doors at either end of the catwalk into the main property. The comprador and Crystal Lily followed them into a small, well-tended garden. Ah Chuen hurried after them.

"You will wait here," he said, gruffly. Unable to control the bodyguards, he felt himself to have lost face. "My master performs his *t'ai-chi ch'uan* exercises now, after which he meditates."

"And after that," a deep, resonant voice said from the top of the steps leading to the house, "I drink a little whiskey and then I go to bed. And I do the same thing night after goddamn night. Welcome."

Nicholai hurried down the steps and took Crystal Lily in his arms almost as if to toss her into the air and then hug her as he had done so often when she was a child. And she felt the shock tingle through her body at the remembered strength of his arms, delighted to feel him near her again. All of the love that she felt in him now and needed so badly, she knew she could return many times over... She pressed her face into his chest, savoring the comfort he seemed to offer. She would gladly have stayed where she was... but then she felt his grip slacken—the closeness of the young woman reminded Nicholai that the girl he knew was gone, her place taken by a woman of poise and power. He let his hands fall to his sides, not so much out of embarrassment as out of respect for a beautiful lady who, after fifteen years, was now a stranger to him.

"It's been a long time," he said, his eyes seeming to drink in the sight of her.

Lily looked up at him anxiously. The Snake Boat Man, in his late forties, was still very trim, his intelligent seafarer's eyes set wide apart in a sensitive, chiseled face. She'd been afraid that he'd allowed himself to deteriorate, that the rumors of his drinking were true, but on seeing him her fears were swept aside... to Crystal Lily he was still godlike, a man who could instill confidence, a man who could succeed where others failed. She was keenly aware of the attraction he held for her, but she was not afraid of its power... I love you, she thought, I always will. His gray eyes still danced for her like the sunlight on a summer's sea, his voice so familiar and warm with memories...

Nicholai turned to Yu Shik Lieu, more stooped and wizened perhaps, Nicholai thought, but with the same quickness of mind that allowed him to think nine ways at once. There was little love lost between the two men now; the comprador's loyalty was clearly with Crystal Lily and he trusted no one, not even the Snake Boat Man.

"Do you want to search me, too?" Nicholai said mockingly, though his tone wasn't harsh. He was wearing a loose embroidered silk robe that left him feeling cool and fresh in the heat of the night.

"That will not be necessary," the comprador said, "but for your safety, make no sudden gestures that could be misunderstood."

Yu Shik Lieu shot a look of warning at the bodyguards who had taken up covering positions in the wings of the house and in the garden.

As the men spoke Crystal Lily had been quietly surveying the house, which was tucked away into a ledge of the mountain, offering complete privacy. It was a modern, multileveled building horizontally cantilevered, together with its ornamental gardens, on concrete and steel beams. The construction alone seemed a remarkable feat of engineering, she thought, and must have cost him a fortune.

"You didn't answer when I sent for you," Crystal Lily said, flashing Nicholai an accusing look.

He shrugged. "I don't work for your father anymore."

"I understand that. He's dead. And I've inherited the Syndicate."

"So I've heard. And I want no more to do with it."

"Was he really that evil, Nicholai?" she asked, using the name she had always known him by.

"I believe so." His tone was neither cruel nor apologetic.

38

She walked over to a wrought-iron railed parapet, below which was a sheer drop. The view looking down over the ships in the harbor and across to the lights of Kowloon on the other side was magnificent. It was one of those rare, still, clear nights in July with a white moon rising over the sea. She sensed his deep disapproval, knowing that he'd wanted her to stay in Hawaii. Still, he couldn't blame her for trying to reforge old family bonds.

"Do you remember," she said, "when I was a little girl, the stories you told me when you visited the palace? And once, when there was a moon as beautiful as this, you took me to my bedside window and told me the story of the love affair between the cowherd and the weaver girl, and how the disapproving gods turned the lovers into stars and flung them to opposite ends of the heavens? And how the lovers still met only once a year, on the seventh night of the seventh moon, by stepping across the skies on a bridge made by the outstretched wings of magpies?" She shook her head, remembering how those times offered a temporary escape from the loneliness and fears of her childhood.

"What do you want from me?" Nicholai asked quietly.

She turned to him, her face beautiful in the moonlight. "I want you to help me. When my father died I became the rightful heir to the leadership of the Syndicate. As you can imagine, the others are trying to get rid of me."

"How can I help you? I'm no gunman—"

"That's not what I mean," she said impatiently. "These men are being assisted by my father's business partners in Hong Kong. Billion Dollar Choy is about to make a bid for Asian Trading, the Princely Trading House. As you know, that's the last great bastion of British control over the Hong Kong marketplace. Billion Dollar Choy has close links with the 14K Triad and has appealed to them for help. The head of the Triad has agreed to finance part of the share raid against Asian Trading, and then to coordinate labor unrest in Asian Trading companies. They're timing it to make its share value plunge. In return they want a piece of the Princely House. The Triad will use that as a legitimate front to spread their power throughout Australia, the East and America."

The comprador, who had been hovering just within earshot, added anxiously, "And now the Triad, in order to finance their part in the Asian Trading share raid, have called on my lady to repay their loan to her father in the currency it was issued in—gold bullion, nearly two tons of it."

"And so to finance their raid I have to deliver the gold from my vaults in Macau to Hong Kong," Crystal Lily said. "Naturally they've given me a deadline. If I don't meet it the Triad will certainly join with those in the Macau Syndicate to destroy me."

"There is no gold trade anymore," Nicholai said. "It ended in the sixties—"

"I realize that. There are few good captains left. I've already made three attempts to send junks carrying small quantities of gold to Hong Kong. Each time they've been intercepted, as any run I try to make will be..." Surely he could sense how she wanted him to help her, but he kept silent, damn him.

"I've decided to gamble everything on moving all the gold in one shipment. I'm asking you to come out of retirement, make one last run, like you did for my father in what I believe some call the good old days." She smiled. "Land the gold for me in Hong Kong, Nicholai."

He shook his head. "I'm too old," he said, "too long retired. Find someone else—"

"You're the *only* one I can turn to," she said, embarrassed to find she was pleading with him. "If I can cancel the threat from the Triad there's still a chance that I can beat the Syndicate. You were my father's best sea captain. You were one of the few people who weren't afraid of him, who had his respect, and I trust you. There are other captains around, but you're still the best there is." Did he believe her?

He seemed unmoved.

"You owed a debt to my father," she said, her voice hardening. "I'm calling on it now."

"Why not leave Macau while you still can?" Nicholai advised. "Go back to America, find yourself a young man and settle down, have a family—even if you did manage to get the gold to Hong Kong, do you think your struggle would be over?"

The strain had begun to creep into Lily's face. Her eyes flashed. "What are you saying? Because I'm a woman, I should meekly turn over my inheritance just because someone else wants it?" There was a coldness in her voice that startled Nicholai... it was too familiar... "I won't do it. And as for marriage, Madame Mao Tse-tung once said, 'Sex is engaging in the first rounds, but what sustains interest in the long run is power.'"

Nicholai studied her face, realized that this stunning young woman, in spite of all her years in America, was no different and apparently no less determined than her father. And with that realization he knew that nothing he could say would divert her.

He turned his head away from her as he leaned against the balustrade. Staring down at the harbor, he felt his mind flood with memories of the many mistakes and miscalculations that had lead to his last unsuccessful run. He would have agreed to her request without hesitation, but he worried that *he* had changed. When he left Macau he was like a man going down in flames, his nerve gone...but he could hardly tell her that now.

"The days when a boat could slip unnoticed from Macau to Hong Kong have gone," Nicholai said, "especially if word got out, as it would, of its cargo. Once that much gold is on the sea bound for the Triad everyone will be after it. Making a gold run today is very different from twenty years ago. Hong Kong has built itself an impressive line of defenses. Boats are more sophisticated, faster. It would be suicidal even to try a gold run now."

But Crystal could sense him wavering. He'd always been a proud man, a romantic hell-bent to survive in an age of realists. She aimed for the chink in his armor.

"Why have you been living alone up here for the last fifteen years? People already talk about you as though you were dead, and in the next fifteen years, while you stare down at that harbor, they'll forget you...I never have."

Nicholai kept silent for a long moment, his hands gripping the railings. A surreptitious glance and Crystal Lily was shocked to see the anguish in his face. She had no idea, of course, that for all those years Nicholai had been full of guilt for having abandoned her, his crew and his boat on that night he escaped from Macau. Dr. Sun hadn't needed to send him into exile...he was going anyway. And it had taken fifteen years for him to dry himself out, slowly pull the pieces of his life back together, try to learn a new way to live. The only way he could do it was to leave his past behind, isolate himself. In spite of his wealth and prestige he had forced himself to stay alone in this eyrie on the Peak until he was sure that his inner battle was won. But the years that passed had been a bloodless, empty, lonely sort of existence for him. And what Crystal Lily offered him now was an unexpected spark of hope...It was the best and only chance he had...

Pride would never have allowed Nicholai to come down from his mountain eyrie for himself. He had needed Crystal Lily to pull him back. Yet at the same time he resented her for finding his weakness so easily...it made him too vulnerable to her, and in a way that especially bothered him...

"All right," Nicholai said, turning abruptly to her. "I'll see if such a run is still possible. When is your deadline?"

"August thirty-first."

He calculated swiftly. It was now the beginning of July. That left slightly less than seven weeks.

Again she could anticipate his thoughts before he could speak them. "The Triad will not extend the deadline," she said, "but I'll have a fast, modern boat waiting in Macau."

There was little more to be said. Nicholai escorted her back to her car and operated the switches that opened the gates. "I'll be in contact with you," he promised.

Moments later his servant found him watching the car's taillights disappear. "You agreed," Ah Chuen challenged him.

"I said I would think about."

"I knew it was bad joss to allow her to come. You could never say no to that girl, from the time she was little higher than your knee. Now you have agreed to risk everything on a run that will almost certainly result in your death."

The Snake Boat Man shrugged. "She needs me," he said quietly. "She has given me the chance to come back from the living dead and make one last run... I at least owe it to her father... more, I owe it to myself."

CHAPTER 3

"**WHO IS** he?" the ChrisCraft captain demanded of the stranger at the comprador's side. The captain had made a deal with Thomas Wu to deliver Crystal Lily to an ambush at sea, but not even the comprador, he figured, could have guessed that.

"Your replacement," the comprador answered. He had no information; he was acting on instinct. "The journey's over for you. You will remain in Hong Kong until I send for you."

The captain swung around to Crystal Lily, who had climbed to the bridge to watch the boat's departure from Hong Kong. He would have appealed to her, but her face showed that she supported her comprador. He shrugged at the inevitable and stepped off the boat.

"Take us back to Macau by a different route," the comprador instructed his new captain. The throbbing engines settled down to a steady beat;

spray rose from the ChrisCraft's bow wave as it turned from Hong Kong and gathered way.

"Are all these precautions of yours really necessary?" Crystal Lily asked impatiently once they were out of earshot of the crew.

"You are accustomed to American ways. This is China, the only route linking Macau and Hong Kong is by sea, and the Syndicate may be waiting."

She spent the rest of the journey in silence. On one level her meeting with Nicholai had been successful but on the personal side it seemed to have been a disaster. Throughout her childhood and the years spent in the narrow confines of a convent, then later at the University of Hawaii she had always kept her love alive for Nicholai. Other men she met somehow seemed callow and weak compared to him. For years she had longed for this reunion. When it finally came she realized she hadn't fully understood the anguish she seemed to have caused him. She had been too young to understand the downward spiral he was on before he left Macau. Now she felt after their reunion that her ambition to control the Macau Syndicate had offended him. It seemed to her an unjust reaction. After all, she'd been groomed her whole life for this inheritance. Nicholai knew that, but now that she was fighting for what was hers, he seemed to resent her... well, so be it, she thought, but her disappointment was keen, and in spite of her willingness to forgive, it was difficult to forget...

Now having reached Macau's territorial waters the ChrisCraft followed the channel—cut like a narrow ribbon between dangerous mud shoals and sandbanks that had closed the Inner Harbor to all but the shallowest draught vessels. Hydrofoils and jetfoils bringing gamblers in from Hong Kong used it frequently, but they moored against the jetties on the south-eastern edge of Macau, which could be used only in clement weather.

The boat now passed under the new bridge linking Taipa Island with Macau, and on into Ou Moon, gateway to the Sea Mirror Bay. A necklace of lights from the Praia Grande glinted softly on the sea, while old-fashioned junks trailed their fishing nets across the bay. In only an hour's journey Crystal Lily felt that she had stepped back in time and place. If Hong Kong was a vibrant, modern city not unlike New York, then Macau still captured the romance of the East, possessing a dark magic uniquely its own.

Armor-plated limousines waiting on the quayside for Crystal Lily's boat quickly swept her and her entourage along the banyan-tree-lined streets toward the palace.

Only when they were safely inside the car did the comprador begin to relax. The two cars roared through the night streets in convoy—the comprador and Crystal Lily in the lead vehicle, the bodyguards behind.

So far so good, he thought with relief as they neared the palace. From the corner of his eye he noticed a battered Roads Department truck pull out behind them. It was late for such a vehicle to be about, and no member of the municipality would have authorized road work near the palace without first checking with the comprador. But Yu Shik Lieu was tired, less attuned to the warning signals than usual.

A steel grill that guarded the palace entrance began to rise as they approached, and the heavy car surged forward. Suddenly the switches were reversed and the grill dropped. The head car screeched to a halt, its hood rammed against the grill's bottom rim. The limousine behind them, unable to stop, slammed into their rear.

The Roads Department truck following the convoy, its massive fenders reinforced with steel, plowed into the rear limousine, shunting it across the road like a toy. Gunmen with nylon stocking masks jumped from the back of the truck and surrounded it. A jack was rammed under its rear axle and its wheels were lifted off the ground, pinning Crystal Lily's bodyguards inside.

The truck reversed, then accelerated, its rear wheels smoking on the cobbled street.

"Get *down*, my lady," the comprador ordered, trying to pull her beneath the seat as the truck's jagged fenders tore into the armor plating; the impact nearly rocked the heavy vehicle over onto its side. With a shriek of tortured metal the truck freed itself, shuddered into reverse, and backed away for another charge.

"Use the radio," the comprador called to the driver. "Hurry, find out what's happened to our men in the palace." The truck again charged the car, ripping into the right-hand side. Crystal and her comprador were thrown to the floor, but the specially armored limousine proved tough. The front of the truck was wrecked, its buckled fenders jammed against its front wheels. It tried to disengage, then stalled.

Remarkably, the shell of the limousine remained intact. Chang, the enforcer, monitoring the action from one of the dark side streets around the palace, let loose a gang of coolies. "Remember," he told the half-starved men, "you will be paid only if you spill her blood." The coolies began to attack the limousine, smashing their long bars against the door hinges and windows, trying to make an opening large enough for the gunmen behind them to step in and shoot the occupants of the car.

The comprador raised himself, his arms forming a protective circle around Crystal. Steel-pointed crowbars stabbed at the glass only inches from her face, but she stared back without flinching at the men wielding them. If we live through tonight, the comprador promised himself, I'll see that word of this child's courage spreads throughout Macau.

It was less than two minutes into the ambush when guards inside the palace responded. Staccato bursts of submachine-gun fire ripped down from the palace walls, leaving two of the coolies dead, others wounded. As more guards appeared the gunmen finally broke and ran.

Crystal Lily's Manchus in the second limousine quickly freed themselves, humiliated by their loss of face and ready to pursue.

"Escort my lady to the palace," the comprador ordered, calling them back. "Get rid of those vehicles and the bodies, then send Lao Ta to me." The comprador's voice barely controlled his rage, knowing the attack had been only moments from succeeding.

A SHORT while later the comprador made his way to Crystal Lily's rooms. He found her standing on the balcony, looking out over the walls of the palace. "My lady," he called to her anxiously, "come away from there. Until we find the traitor in your household it's best you show yourself as little as possible.

Crystal did not move. "They've turned my home into a prison. To stand out here in the sun or the moonlight is the only freedom I have left. I won't be denied that... Why didn't they attack us at sea?"

"They had no time to arrange it."

"Did you identify the dead men?" she asked, turning to him suddenly. "Were they Chang's soldiers?"

The comprador shrugged. "Perhaps, but I believe this is the work of Thomas Wu and that for once he acted too quickly or he might have succeeded. Depend upon it, he will strike again and soon. We have to find a way to delay him for seven weeks."

Lily had been thinking the same thing. She was silent for a moment as she considered a scheme she'd had in mind since she first learned the Syndicate was trying to depose her. "Comprador, would you say Thomas Wu is a greedy man?"

"Too clever to be overly greedy."

"And the others? Are they greedy men?"

"Yes," the comprador agreed without hesitation. "They are greedy men."

"What if they thought that by waiting a few weeks they could take everything I own at once and at almost no risk to themselves? Would they then force Thomas Wu to wait?"

"I believe they would."

"Well then, Wu and the others will expect some sort of retaliation for tonight's attack. We won't do anything. My enemies in the Syndicate must believe they've won. Let them think I am preparing to leave the palace taking as much of the gold as possible."

"This is a very dangerous course," the comprador protested. "Once you appear to accept defeat more and more of your servants will desert you. There will be no turning back if this fails."

"I need *time*. I have to appear vulnerable in order to rob them of a sense of urgency," she said tensely. "The Syndicate must be aware of my preparations to leave. Let them think they can choose the moment when I transfer the bullion to the boat as their best time to destroy me." As she spoke she remembered the sharp, pointed crowbars driving straight at her face and shivered at the thought of how close they had come to succeeding... even she had found it hard to believe that the glass was able to withstand such a savage beating. But her fear was quickly forgotten as she remembered the source behind the attack, and a bitter rage swept through her.

"If I can only anticipate where and when they'll strike, that will give me the advantage I need."

The shock of the attack, too long suppressed, was swamping her now. She felt ill, her skin had become clammy and she reached out to the balustrade for support. "You can go now, comprador," she said. "I need to rest..."

The old amah, squatting patiently with her back against the passage wall, looked up as the comprador closed the door behind him. "My lady?" she asked him, "does she need me?"

"No. Let her rest."

"I hear she was brave..."

"Truly," he muttered as he shuffled away. "That girl has the blood of her father in her veins and *dew neh loh moh* on her enemies who forget that."

THE COMPRADOR was resting on a low silk-covered couch in his quarters when Lao Ta came to make his report. Lao Ta's name meant Old Big or Number One. He was a stocky, bull-necked, balding man with small, ratlike eyes and a dirty drooping moustache. As leader of Crystal Lily's bodyguards, the Manchus inherited from her father, he was the second most powerful man in the palace after the comprador. Until now she had considered them the most trustworthy servants she had left, and they still inspired fear in her enemies.

The comprador sipped his jasmine-scented tea while Lao Ta waited uneasily for him to speak. "What happened?" The comprador's voice was unnaturally quiet.

Lao Ta shrugged his rounded shoulders in a surly fashion, trying to hide his considerable loss of face. "Lord," he said, "someone interfered with the grill's mechanism... both that and the doors behind it were jammed fast."

The comprador nodded, understanding immediately what had happened. Any vehicle entering the palace, once having passed under the grill, was then blocked by a door. In the chamber between the door and the grill the vehicle and its occupants were thoroughly searched before being allowed onto the grounds. The bodyguards inside, trapped behind the door, were unable to reach the street to support them.

"At first we worked on the switches," Lao Ta said, "then we heard the fighting in the street. We tried to reach the wall, but the door to that was locked from the inside and we had to waste time breaking it down."

"Have you any idea who the traitor could be?"

"No," Lao Ta said, his eyes fierce. "But lord, I *promise* you he is not among my men."

"The security of this palace is your responsibility, not so?"

Loa Ta braced himself. "Yes, lord—"

"—Then find me this traitor, and quickly, or my lady will have both our heads."

The comprador knew that the morale of the servants would drop sharply after tonight. He leaned back, signaling that the questioning was over.

Lao Ta was stunned. He'd expected to be dismissed from his position at the very least. "Is that all, lord?"

"No," Yu Shik Lieu said, searching the other man's face behind half-closed eyes. "At this time I take opium. Never have I needed it more. My chest is so tight I can hardly breathe. Will you join me? It is a long time since we've smoked together as friends."

Lao Ta's heart had been beating at a trip-hammer rate. He had fought alongside Chang in the early gang wars, and his position in Dr. Sun's household had been secured by the enforcer. Would Yu Shik Lieu remember that after all these years? Of course he would... Yu Shik Lieu forgot nothing. This wizened, infirm old man was as dangerous as a small but deadly snake that hides in the dust and strikes without warning. "Lord," Lao Ta said carefully, trying to hide his suspicion, "I cannot. You offer too great an honor to one who is disgraced."

They both knew that if Lao Ta remained and shared opium with the comprador his face would be restored with his men. There could be no greater expression of trust. But why? Lao Ta asked himself anxiously. Yu Shik Lieu had never been generous with those who made mistakes...

"Who better than you and I can understand the trouble that lies ahead," the comprador said pointedly. "Come, let us join together and if not we, then perhaps our clans may survive."

Lao Ta wondered if his ears were deceiving him. Could this be the beginning of a proposition of some kind? Yu Shik Lieu would be far too subtle to make any approach directly. Think, Lao Ta urged his confused brain. With this wily old man you have to understand what is meant, not what is said... what does he want from me?

The comprador rang a silver bell and a handsome middle-aged woman came into the room. "Number three wife, fill another pipe for my friend." The woman returned and presented a second pipe to Lao Ta. The stem was fashioned out of beautifully carved ivory that had yellowed with age; the jade tip felt cool against his lips.

"The pipes are a matched pair made for my father in the days when China was for civilized people," the comprador said as he signaled to his third wife. She knelt beside him, took a pinch of thick, sticky black resin and deftly rolled it into a ball. She smeared the ball over a tiny pinhole pierced in the spherical bowl of the pipe, held it over a candle flame and quickly handed it to the comprador as the opium smoldered alight.

Next she prepared a pipe for Lao Ta, who lay on a couch beside her husband. He knew at once that the opium was of the finest quality in the Orient, imported especially for the comprador from the Mau Hill tribes who grew the fragile poppies on the Burmese-Thailand border. He sucked the rich, sweet-tasting smoke into his lungs, exhaling through his nose. It had none of the acrid aftertaste of nicotine. Almost immediately he felt as though his mind had been freed, and a deep sense of relaxation crept over him. "Lord," he said, finding his courage more easily now, "forgive me this question, but there is a rumor that greatly troubles me. Indeed, it troubles every servant here."

"What is it?"

"Is it true that your doctors say you only have a short time left?"

The comprador smiled ruefully to himself. There were no secrets

49

anywhere in Macau, except the ones he kept to himself. "For your ears only, then, and because you will have to start taking on more of the workload, yes, it is true."

Which must be why I am here, Lao Ta thought. "How long, lord?"

"Four to six months, perhaps more. Long enough to see us through the present troubles. Anyway, well before then my lady will have left Macau."

So, Lao Ta thought, taking the bait in his eagerness, the Syndicate *had* won, she'd made her decision to leave... "Will you be going with her?"

"No. I am too old to leave here. She will choose a new comprador, someone more suited to present times."

"And the rest of us?"

"You have your mistress. You don't need me to teach you how to serve her well."

Lao Ta caught the sharp note in the comprador's voice. Even so, alerted as he was now to every innuendo, he had to wonder if this cunning old man was telling him the truth, or testing him... he watched the comprador breathe in the smoke of the freshly made pipe and hoped that the old man would fade into opium-induced dreams before he did.

"It takes me a little longer each time before I dream," the comprador said, "and when I do my dreams must dwell on that which is beautiful and refreshing, not the pain in this old body. Would you mind if my wife played a little music?"

"No, lord. Of course not." Lao Ta was finding it impossible not to be flattered by this show of hospitality.

"You will appreciate it, I assure you. It is the music of the old China, of a life we understood. My third wife's family were scholars for generations pasts, and she was taught to play the *chin*."

Before taking up a rare wooden instrument—its strings made of well-twisted silk instead of catgut—she lit incense sticks... their spicy, thin smoke rising in a spiral of fragrance, bringing remembrance of thyme hillsides and the fresh-scented fields of northern China.

"She was taught always to burn a little incense before the goddess of music to invoke her presence before playing," the comprador said quietly. The woman moved between them so that they could both hear the ethereal music, still and cool as though floating on the incense in the room. It seemed the strings she plucked were scarcely vibrating as their magical sounds drew the men nearer with joy to the great empty peace within.

"Ah, third wife," the old man said dreamily, "you are a treasure beyond price. Your cool hands soothe me, the beauty in your face brings me eternal joy, your music touches my heart." He paused, his voice becoming anxious. "Lao Ta, should anything happen to me within the next few weeks, I charge you to protect third wife and all my clan."

"My lord," Lao Ta struggled to answer as he hovered near unconsciousness, "I will be her servant as I am yours."

"Listen again to her music and you will learn why I treasure her . . . even more than opium she can set this tired soul free. Tell me, my friend," Yu Shik Lieu murmured, "are we together?"

Lao Ta heard the question, but his dreamlike state beckoned him and he was unable to reply or to think clearly about the sincerity of the old comprador.

CHAPTER 4

A STEADY flow of polite conversation eddied around the gleaming dinner table at Government House in Hong Kong. White-gloved servants cleared the last course away before the formally dressed men in dinner jackets and women in low-cut evening gowns, the swell of their breasts and their carefully tended faces lit in the glow cast by silver candelabras.

Clair Denning, wife of the taipan of Asian Trading, felt a hand touch her thigh, her dinner partner's fingers lightly but confidently caressing her skin in a gesture that was at once so intimate and so demanding that it inflamed her entire body.

She stopped speaking to her neighbor in mid-sentence and turned back to the naval officer seated on the other side of her.

"Ma'am," he said in a low voice, his eyes seeming to burn through her, "I guess I just had to find out if you were wearing anything underneath that dress."

Clair's hand went down and lightly brushed his hand upward. Well, now he knew, and she could feel his excitement rising as she knew it would...Clair was a beautiful woman with natural blond hair cascading over her suntanned shoulders. Her eyes were hazel, flecked with green, and she met his gaze, taunting him. "Steady, captain," she whispered, but her voice betrayed the huskiness of awakened sensuality.

"Commander, ma'am," he corrected her.

"Does it matter?"

"Not right now, it doesn't."

"I meant to ask you earlier which is your ship?"

"The guided missile destroyer. We're anchored off the Wanchai waterfront."

"Oh, I've seen it. You've made her beautiful tonight, all those lights."

"That's my ship, ma'am," he said. "And I'd like to show her to you sometime."

He was dark and youthful-looking in his navy dress uniform, from a southern Italian heritage, she guessed, and he hadn't taken his eyes off her from the moment she walked in the door wearing a stunning silk sheath dress slit up one side to her thigh.

Clair had been well satisfied with the effect of her entrance. Every man in Government House, whether he braved his wife's angry glare and looked up or not, knew when she arrived. Loathing the boredom of the governor's dinner parties, she had flirted throughout the evening with the naval officer. At first it was nothing more than the usual civilized exchanges, but they soon became more obviously flirtatious until she felt his hand touch her thigh and knew that they were passing the point of no return.

Joss Denning sat across from his wife and some way down the table. He had noticed something. Clair caught the troubled look in his eye and smiled innocently at him. This ought to take the bastard's mind off business for a while, she thought maliciously.

The talk swept past them toward the head of the table. "Your Excellency, the latest figures put four out of every five people in the colony as refugees," Bevan, the taipan of Wentworth's, said to the governor, "and now I'm told that we're expecting a new influx. Surely this can't go on...What does the administration plan to do about it?"

"We've already taken severe measures against them," the governor said. "What more would you have me do? I can't very well order the police to shoot them on the beaches."

"What intrigues me is why the refugees scramble so hard to get past the colony's defenses in the first place," a hunched, graying writer with the London *Daily Telegraph* said. "Surely they must realize that this is the only human habitation in the world that knows when it's going to die—in nineteen ninety-seven, of course. When the lease on the ceded New Territories expires and nine-tenths of the colony has to be handed back to China." He glanced at the faces around him with shrewd, heavy-lidded eyes. "What's going to happen to all of you then, gentlemen?"

"Same old subject crops up every time the taipans get together with the governor," Clair said in a bored tone. "The bastards are shit-scared of losing all their money."

"So would I be if I had the kind of money that's invested here," the officer replied. He was aware that the seductive woman beside him belonged to a very august company. Her husband and the other taipans, the great managers of the five major trading companies gathered at the table, were the merchant princes of Hong Kong and each enjoyed the social privilege as well as enormous wealth and power that the position brought. Descended from freebooting, opium-trading ancestors, they ruled over the most successful, fiercely independent and competitive free market system in the world. The companies represented at the table paid a minimum of tax and had succeeded in turning a barren, waterless island, whose population had risen from a few thousand to nearly five million within the last fifty years, into one of the most prosperous corners of the earth.

Lady Caley, sensing the direction the conversation was taking, signaled to the women that it was time for them to retire. This was the part of the evening that Clair hated most.

"Name the day and I'll show you my ship," the commander pressed her, concerned that he might lose contact with her later in the drawing room.

"I'll do better than that," Clair said softly as she got up. "Slip away from here and I'll show you Government House."

As the men moved their glasses down to the governor's end of the table the commander edged away. Five minutes later he found Clair waiting in the shadow of a wide terrace. A heavy fragrance drifted in from the garden. "Those flowers are wonderful," she said, inhaling the fragrance as he took her hand.

"What is it?"

"Moon flower. Come and see." She led him into the hot, tropical darkness of the garden. "There," she said breathlessly, resting her back against a tree, "now can you smell the jasmine as well?" Over her shoulders the lighted windows of Government House cast shadows in the garden, reminding her of the other dull-faced taipans' wives now gathered dutifully around the governor's lady. But the danger in being where she was took over her senses. She raised her face to his and he kissed her, his weight pressing her against the cool, smooth bark of the tree. His hand went in through the slit of her dress and slid across her thighs. "No," she said, twisting away from him, "we can't now...the governor is expecting trouble in Hong Kong and there are Gurkha guards patrolling the garden." But he was beyond caring about the danger...she'd held him anticipating long enough. Now he wanted satisfaction.

He pinned her against the tree like a butterfly, his hands pulling her dress around her waist. His knees parted her thighs, his back arched. "Oh," she whispered thickly, her arms around his neck, riding up on him. "Oh damn you, you feel so good." He thrust into her, slowly at first, then gaining strength until her body moved in rhythm with his. She reached her climax before him and buried her face in his neck to drown her sobs.

Suddenly there was the sound of soldiers marching on the graveled path, but Clair didn't have the strength to stop him. "Come quickly," she whispered. "For God's sake, come quickly." He had been on the brink and his body suddenly spasmed as though he'd been struck in the solar plexis. "Be quiet," she said, covering his mouth with her hand. Then he, too, caught the clink of weapons, the sound of footsteps.

They stood quietly, pressed against the tree, as a Gurkha patrol marched past not ten feet from them.

"That, ma'am, as one of your greatest generals once put it, was a damn close run thing."

"You performed quite well for an American," Clair said, recovering her cool poise.

"And you are a delicious English bitch. When can I see you again?"

"When you've learned that I'm not English. I'm Hong Kong born."

"That makes a difference?"

"It certainly does. Can you think of anyone else who would have introduced you to Government House in this way?"

In the dining room the conversation among the taipans and other guests continued; the French consul general seemed momentarily perplexed. "What banks can continue to finance you against such a deadline?"

"We still have sixteen years to go before the lease expires," Hugh Maplin of the Kowloon Peninsula Bank said. "Something will be negotiated by 'ninety-seven. Our biggest headache is the exploding birthrate in the squatter camps and sampan harbors. We simply don't have the land or the services to keep pace with it. I warn you, if we don't find an answer to that problem soon we won't have to worry about handing the colony back to China when the lease expires. It will have exploded at the seams by then."

"The United States Navy would surely miss the use of your harbor," the American admiral in command of the destroyer squadron said anxiously. He had noticed that the young commander was missing and hoped to hell he wasn't up to something that would get them in trouble with the British. "As I understand it, Your Excellency," he said to the governor, "they'd be mighty glad for you to extend the lease. After all, isn't a major portion of China's foreign currency earned through this colony?"

"There will be no extension of the lease in its present form," Joshua Denning said. He was not a big man, but he was strong and steadfast, and he had worked hard in the last five years to save Asian Trading from the brink of financial disaster. "That is, unless we can find a way that leaves the Chinese leadership with absolutely no alternative... after nearly a century and a half of fighting off foreign domination they're not apt to permit anyone other than Chinese to own their land."

"We should have asked Denning in the first place," Waglen of Hughes and Greylin said, unable to hide his bitter dislike for the taipan of Hong Kong's Princely House. "The rest of us old China hands know we can do nothing but wait and hope that those policy makers in Peking reach a favorable decision—but he's got a theory."

"Let's hope it's anchored on a stronger foundation than his own company," Bevan said dryly. He turned to Denning. "I see your shares have taken another knock on the Hang Seng Index today."

"You'll get burned if you try to sell me short," Denning warned the men. "It's just a temporary drop."

Joshua Denning at the age of thirty-eight was, with the exception of its founder, the youngest taipan in the history of Asian Trading. Unlike his predecessors, he hadn't been born to the position; instead he had married well and worked his way up to rule over the Princely House. Despite its many special privileges and responsibilities, it had required a painful learning process and, to the dismay of the other taipans, he'd met the challenge. Along with the resentment he regularly felt from the men, the tightly knit group of matrons who ruled European society in Hong Kong also took pains to remind him of his humble beginnings. So Joshua Denning became a loner, driving himself to succeed, despite the odds, and when the other taipans had tried to claw off attractive bits and pieces from his struggling company they had found themselves savagely rebuffed.

"What do you think China's going to do?" the British writer asked, interested by what Denning had to say.

The governor was aware that the British government and Peking were in the midst of very delicate negotiations and he didn't want the subject bandied about his dinner table before strangers. "Shall we join the ladies," he said, signaling to Denning to drop it. "Oh, and Joss—" the governor took Denning's arm as the others filed out of the room "—a word with you."

Sir Howard Caley was tall, lean with an aristocrat's well-bred features and twinkling blue eyes that disguised a truly Machiavellian mind when it came to defending the colony, which he knew to be the last jewel in the faded British Empire.

Trevelyan, the colony's secretary for security, had remained behind as well. A short, rotund, reputedly devious Cornishman with years of experience in keeping law and order in Hong Kong, he was ruthless in protecting a domain that was used by many rival nations as their chief listening post on China. His problems were further magnified by Nationalist Chinese agents who plotted street battles and assassinations against Communist agents, and the Triads who stored bombs and weapons for both factions in cock lofts, squatter camps and resettlement areas.

Over the years Trevelyan had developed an uncanny instinct for sniffing out trouble, earning him the respect of even the Chinese underworld. In appearance he was the opposite of the governor, but together they created a formidable team.

"Sorry to spring this on you," Trevelyan said, "but I've got something I want you to see, off the record, of course, and it couldn't wait. Will you follow me?" They left the dining room through the service door, making their way to the governor's spacious, book-lined study.

A fourth man waited for them there. He was stockily built, with hard eyes and a pockmarked face. "This is Superintendent Malloy. He's with Special Branch," Trevelyan said. By normal standards Malloy should have reached a higher rank at his age, but his bungled attempts to catch the one smuggler colorfully known as the Snake Boat Man fifteen years earlier had blocked his promotion—a bitter fact that Malloy had never forgotten.

"We know each other." Malloy nodded, then lifted a series of twelve-by-twelve-inch black-and-white photographs from a folder on the governor's desk. "Have a look at these," he said to Denning. The photographs were of four-hundred-ounce gold bars. "Notice the Royal Cypher imprint. We've identified these bars as having once belonged to us. They were looted from British banks during the Japanese occupation. A short while ago the marine police picked up rumors that a junk smuggling gold was intercepted between Macau and Hong Kong and sunk with all hands. There was no further evidence to back these rumors so we were inclined to discount them as a figment of some informer's imagination. Then these bars turned up during a police raid on a Triad-operated heroin factory in Aberdeen—"

"I've been asking myself," Trevelyan interrupted, "why, after all these years, should gold looted from the colony start finding its way back to Hong Kong? Well, the information Malloy's just received is that it was en route to the 14K Triad, and he tells me this shipment represents only the tip of the iceberg."

Malloy took the photographs from Denning and returned them to the folder. "Most crimes committed in the colony are related to drugs," he said, "and as you know, the drugs are supplied by the Triads. A little over three years ago the police narcotics division managed to secure sufficient evidence against the 14K to break it up, for a while. The Triad's members scattered into street gangs. They've caused us plenty of headaches, but nothing serious enough to be regarded as a real threat to the colony. Now a new san-chu has been appointed. We know who he is but can't prove anything yet, and he's too prominent a local figure to be treated with anything but kid gloves. Our informers tell us that he's been reorganizing the 14K. Any large transfer of funds to them could greatly enhance their power at a time when, with China watching our every move, we need to keep civil control in Hong Kong. This is a serious situation, gentlemen... you'll recall that the Independent Commission Against Corruption now estimates that no less than twenty percent of the police force already belongs to the Triad."

"We can't afford to lose any more ground to them," the governor put in. "If what Malloy says is true, if there is another large shipment of bullion due to the 14K Triad, then we've got to stop it from reaching them."

"How?" Denning asked. "It's not illegal to hold gold here anymore."

"It damn well is if it's going to one of the Triads," the governor said emphatically.

"All the leads we have keep pointing back to Macau," Trevelyan said. "First the marine police picked up a rumor of a junk from there being intercepted. We've recently learned that Dr. Sun's daughter has paid a visit to her father's old sea captain, the so-called Snake Boat Man . . . an amusing name, certainly."

"Who in the hell's the Snake Boat Man?" Denning asked irritably. It was late and he was anxious to reclaim his wife and go home.

"If you'll think back some fifteen years," the governor said, "you'll remember stories of a very successful smuggler who operated between Macau and Hong Kong. We never could catch him before he retired. Maybe he's thinking of making another run—"

"—Why are you involving me in this?" Denning asked. "Surely it's a matter for Mr. Malloy . . . I've got more than enough on my plate. As you heard tonight, someone's selling Asian Trading's shares short on the market."

"Ah, yes, about your company," Trevelyan said. "You're aware no doubt of the rumor that tomorrow your shares are going to be dumped on the Singapore and London exchanges as well. Have you any idea what's going on?"

"At the moment the situation is still unclear," Denning said cautiously. Did these men know something he didn't?

The governor knew of the work Denning had put into Asian Trading. Over the last five years he had proved his tenacity by keeping the crippled Princely House afloat—there was no doubt about his part in that. But he wondered if the young taipan had the stamina left to stay the course. It was common knowledge that Denning's marriage was in trouble, and on top of that—or because of it—he clearly was driving himself too hard. There was a great weariness in the taipan's eyes that no amount of rest could relieve, and the governor recognized the danger signals of a man about to crack. He wondered if Trevelyan had picked it up . . . They were going to need the Princely Trading House, with all its influence and multitude of interests throughout the Far East, to unlock sources of information presently unavailable to the Hong Kong administration.

"Don't mean to pry into your business, of course," the governor said, "but of the five major British-run companies in Hong Kong, yours would appear to be the most vulnerable to a share raid. Can you hold the line? You're aware, of course, that while Her Majesty's government is negotiating with China for the future of Hong Kong we can't afford any change in the status quo."

"Your Excellency, we've been getting stronger every year," Denning lied. The Hong Kong marketplace was like a shark's pool—if there was one thing Denning had learned, it was that it never paid to show any sign of weakness. "The Princely House will fight off an attack if it comes."

"Doré Brothers have already been swallowed by Billion Dollar Choy," the governor said.

"That was the lesson for the rest of us. We've strengthened our defenses since then."

"Last year when Sir Ten Ying-Ch'ao got control over McDonald Swithens the struggle was between legitimate business concerns," Trevelyan added. "This year that might not be the case, especially if some of the wealthy Chinese have grown impatient with the British *hong*'s virtual ownership of Hong Kong."

"What are you getting at?" Denning asked, impatient for something more than the vague hints they were dropping.

"I've been picking up bits and pieces of information," Trevelyan said. "Nothing fits yet, but I have a hunch that your problem and ours may be connected."

So that was it... based on some security official's "hunch" they were securing his cooperation with as elegant a piece of blackmail as one could wish. They were mad to think he'd go along with their scheme...

"What do you want from me?"

"The Princely House had traditional contacts with the Macau Syndicate, especially with their gold operation," Trevelyan said, probing for information about the connection.

"That was long before I became taipan." Asian Trading had indeed acted as shippers for gold purchased on the London bullion market and delivered it to the Syndicate in Macau. "We acted within the laws of that time. Macau never had any restrictions on the purchase of gold—"

"It's amazing how many millions of ounces they were able to absorb without putting any of it back on the market," Trevelyan observed dryly. "In any case, it looks as though the gold is coming back now, and into the Triad's hands."

"Our sources in Macau have never been strong," the governor said, "and we're finding the Portuguese particularly unhelpful in answering our queries concerning the Syndicate. We know the Princely House still has excellent contacts in Macau and we would like to use them...Can you get your people close enough to the Syndicate to find out what's going on?"

Denning weighed the alternatives. It would mean putting Asian Trading contacts at risk in Macau. On the other hand he needed to know what was brewing as much as the governor and Trevelyan...

"All right. I'll have my contacts dig about and see what they can come up with, but if there is a share raid mounted against my company, can I look to you for support?"

"As long as your enemies remain within the law there's damn little I can do to help you," the governor replied. "You taipans have always seen to it that I have less real power than the Jockey Club. But I promise you this—unofficially I shall help you in every way I can. Well, now," the governor said, confident that he'd secured the taipan's cooperation, "I'm neglecting my guests and your wife must be wondering what I've done with you."

"General Li..." Malloy prompted the secretary for security.

"Ah yes, the general. You may have heard of him," Trevelyan said to Denning. "He ran Madame Mao's security force during the rule of the Gang of Four. It was thought that he had managed to survive her, but he fell from grace a few months ago and now he's believed to be heading for Hong Kong, where he'll undoubtedly stir up trouble. Naturally that would be embarrassing for us...the border with China is being closely guarded, but he may come through Macau. Would you have your contacts watch for him there?"

Denning said he would, then made his way back along the passage to the reception rooms with the governor and Trevelyan.

"I have a heavy day tomorrow," he said. "If you and Lady Caley will excuse me I'd like to slip away."

The governor nodded, knowing the pressure Denning was under. "Of course...ah, there's your lovely wife..."

Clair was in the hall on the arm of the naval officer, her hair and makeup obviously disheveled.

"Your Excellency, I've been showing off Government House to the American navy," she said gaily. The men could guess what she'd been doing, but she didn't care. She looked at her husband, catching the look of pain that flashed through his eyes. Let him suffer, she thought...he deserves it.

The Dennings drove home in silence. Clair knew that her behavior would bring no recriminations from him, no shouted arguments in front of the servants. It was as if he had learned to accept her nature, had resolved to stay married to her in spite of it—and she hated him for that. She resented his dedication, his self-discipline and the puritan Scottish Presbyterian standards he tried to live up to. His great passion outside Asian Trading were horses and the sea, and once she had been jealous of all three—of anything, for that matter, that kept him from her. She had loved him so passionately that to be with him was to feel a melting at the very core of her existence... But his smile, once leisurely and disarming, had grown hard, and the cool, detached wit that she had so enjoyed in him was gone. Now they rarely slept together, but she had found ways to take care of that...

Clair stretched herself luxuriously, studying her husband's profile in the dim light of the car. Slim and deceptively frail looking, he lacked the great physical presence of a born taipan, but perhaps that was growing in him... His eyes were a pure blue, like sapphires, and his hair was still thick and auburn-colored. She thought with half-remembered hunger of his smooth body, his long, sensitive fingers and the beautiful set of his head. God, how she had loved him then, when she had been the toast of Hong Kong standing out from the other girls like a single candle flame in a darkened room, and he the gorgeous moth she had chosen, against her family's wishes, from within the ranks of the Princely House. Well, Clair reassured herself, all that may be gone, but I still hold the flame and there are others to attract...

The car climbed a steep tarred driveway, finally pulling up before their mansion. Clair got out, but her husband remained. "Aren't you coming?" she asked abruptly.

He shook his head. "I have to go to the office."

Damn him, she thought furiously. No matter how she tried to hurt him, he still managed to make her feel rejected. She had seen him with the governor and the secretary for security and knew that something important must be breaking. "Whatever it is, you don't have to spend the night at the office. Can't you deal with it in the morning?"

"Clair," he said, barely able to contain his anger—it hardly seemed worth it anymore—"don't you understand what I've been trying to do? I've got very few shares in the Princely House compared to those you and your family own, and yet all these years I've been doing my damnedest to save your inheritance. But you still don't understand that even now, because you've never had to work for a damn thing in your life."

She cast about for a way to hurt him. "Joss, darling, no one in Hong Kong forgets for a moment that you were never born taipan of the Princely House—you just worked your way up from office boy." She knew it was a lie. He'd been the cleverest accountant they'd had. "Still," she threatened, "there are a growing number who would like to see the family back in control, not some clerk who married the boss's daughter. Don't forget that."

Denning tapped the chauffeur on the shoulder, signaling him to drive on. Turning back to the house, Clair knew she'd won the exchange, as she usually did, but it gave her no pleasure... only an unexpected sick feeling at the thought of actually losing him.

THE CHAUFFEUR let Denning off at a side entrance to the Asian Trading building in the central district of Hong Kong, and he quickly unlocked the door to his private elevator that would carry him up to the fiftieth floor.

The corridors were silent, the thick carpets deadening his footsteps. Prints of the famous company-owned clipper ships that once traded tea and opium, silk and silver, lined the walls. The boardroom and the directors' offices occupied the fiftieth floor; his suite was one floor above, with a balcony looking directly over the harbor from which he could watch his trading ships enter and leave port. Denning glanced in at the communications room. Brass clocks lined one wall, each showing the time in Tokyo, Sydney, Singapore, Riyadh, Paris, London, New York, and before each clock was a desk with a single black telephone connected to an outside line. In a few hours, when the stock exchanges opened around the world, the telephones would begin ringing, bearing the bad news. He collected the closing financial reports on the telexes and carried them up the spiral stairway to his suite.

From the wall behind his desk the portrait of Tiernan, the founding taipan—half pirate, half genius—stared down at him. Tiernan, a giant of a man, had seen the potential in this barren island, fought for it in the opium wars, survived shipwreck, famine and plague to make Asian Trading the foremost company in Hong Kong. From the very beginning his company was respected by the Chinese before all other *hongs*, referred to always as the Princely House.

Denning's appointment had come at a critical time. In the fourteen years of the previous taipan's rule, the company had slipped steadily from its dominant position in the marketplace. With relentless work, insight and courage Denning had managed to stop the slide, and for the last couple of years the Princely House had been fighting back. But in doing so he had made enemies, enemies he could easily have lived without— many of his senior directors distrusted him, resenting the young Chinese blood he was rapidly promoting, as well as other changes that disregarded the unspoken code of behavior they were accustomed to.

He opened the sliding doors and walked onto the balcony, thinking again of what his wife had said. He felt weary and alone but, damnit, not broken. Not yet. My father worked all his life for this company, he reminded himself, and so have I. I'm proud of it, proud to be a taipan. Even housed in this modern skyscraper the essence of the old company still remains. I've never forgotten the history of this company, nor the fact that millions of peoples' savings are invested with me; thousands of employees depend on me for their survival. That matters to me. I'm part of them. Clair will never understand that. If the Princely House fails, then I fail too, with everything I have.

In a moment he would have to return to his desk and work through the maze of interlocking companies that made up the framework of Asian Trading. He would have to find the weakness there that his enemies must have discovered, and somehow block them. The lights of a police launch on the water far below caught his eye, and he remembered Trevelyan's warning. "Who in hell is Dr. Sun's daughter and this Snake Boat Man," he found himself wondering aloud, "and what do they have to do with the survival of this Princely House?"

His answer would come in a fashion, and sooner, than he could possibly imagine.

CHAPTER 5

NICHOLAI STOOD on the upper deck of the *Tai Shan*, a modern white ferry that regularly plied the route from Hong Kong to Macau.

It steamed out of the Lantau Channel, crossed the invisible line known as the Square Boundary that divides Hong Kong's territorial waters from China. To the south, scattered like jade pieces, lay the Niu-T'ou Islands, the largest of which had been used as a Communist gunboat base to watch over the entrance to the Pearl River estuary.

The ferry captain, a white-haired, wrinkled-faced Welshman who'd known Nicholai from his gold-smuggling days, joined him. "In case you're wondering, the gunboats still operate from there." The captain had served in the South China Sea for thirty-seven years, eighteen of them on the ferries to Macau. "Anybody know that you're coming back?"

"No."

The sun burned down through masses of drifting clouds gathering for rain, and the limpid sea seemed to wilt under the heat. Soon the ferry reached the shallow waters outside Macau. The landfall was as Nicholai remembered it—mud shoals that barred the Bay of Ou Moon drawn up in a fierce yellow line across the darker yellow of the sea. That and the distant hills of China gave him his first pang of returning home.

The ship passed to port the long spidery spans of the bridge to Taipa Island, built during Nicholai's long absence. That and the many other changes that had altered the centuries-old skyline of Macau filled him with regret. He'd heard about the gambling boom, and now he was seeing first-hand the evidence of it—towering above the once graceful Praia Grande was a gaudy, gold-tiled structure that, to Nicholai, was an affront to the island's natural landscape. One circular wing was topped by a massive stone replica of a roulette wheel, its entrance designed to form gaping tiger's jaws. The casino was reputedly one of the largest outside of Las Vegas. In the background the atmosphere of the old city reeled under the onslaught of more hotels and casinos that seemed to crowd the sea front.

The *Tai Shan*, engines dead slow, its propellers churning mud, drew alongside the jetty in the Outer Harbor. "Do you want me to smuggle you ashore?" offered the captain.

"It's not necessary. It's been such a long time, no one will remember me."

Macau was a free port and there were no customs officials to contend with. Nicholai was making his way to the street after a cursory immigration check when he felt a hand touch his arm. It was an immigration official who had spotted him through the window of a back office.

At his request Nicholai followed the man to his office. "Don't enter Macau," the official said.

"I have an invitation from the head of the Syndicate."

"There are men more powerful than she who would advise against it. Go back to Hong Kong now."

"Do you propose to cancel my visa?"

"No, I have no authority to do so."

"Then I will return to Hong Kong in my own time."

The official shrugged. "It's none of my business, I merely warn you for your own safety."

Nicholai neglected to show his gratitude... The Avenue da Amizade lay in the soft light of dusk under a canopy formed by the branches of the banyan trees. The sounds and smells of the city, at least, were as

Nicholai had remembered... in the evening air there lingered the perfumed scents of joss sticks and sandalwood smoke, and the old-fashioned street lights along the seawall danced on the water.

At the jetty Nicholai signaled for a pedicab. A coolie in shorts and a sweat-stained vest nodded at Nicholai's instructions, then stood on his pedals, his calf muscles bulging, his lips pressed against teeth worn down from chewing sugarcane.

Nicholai felt the old spell of Macau tug at him as the pedicab glided silently along the wide seafront. For the past fifteen years his life had been without direction. He needed to reestablish his identity in the city that had molded his character. He was no longer sure of his achievements, even less of himself. His thoughts were of the years spent away from Macau... it seemed they had trickled through his fingers like sand in an hourglass... what, he asked himself, did he have to show for them?

The coolie braked in front of the entrance to the small, securely walled Portuguese admiralty dockyard. Nicholai used Crystal Lily's name to pass the guards, then walked toward the stone quay where her ChrisCraft was moored. The luxury vessel's lines showed that she had been built for speed, but he noted that her superstructure, with its useless flying bridge, rose too high above the water, making her silhouette easy to spot against a night horizon, and she drew too deep a draught. She would never make it out of the bay, let alone to Hong Kong against determined opposition...

He climbed back into the pedicab. "Go on, go on," he ordered in Cantonese. The coolie continued to pedal slowly along the sea road to the old Inner Harbor, then watched in amazement as the *gwilo* got out and walked down to the water's edge.

With all its memories of misery and pain, this was Nicholai's beginning, here among the seagoing junks clustered five deep in the narrow channel between Macau and Communist China. Washing hung from a forest of bare masts, crews squatted on the decks for their evening meal. He wandered deeper into the Inner Harbor along the Barro d'28 Mario, where shipwrights, for lack of space, constructed junks on cradles over a canal littered with scrapped and sunken vessels. Nicholai stood in the dark among the shanty homes built on stilts over the water, recapturing the memories of his youth... he listened to the chatter, tasted the spicy aroma of evening meals cooked over open fires of fresh-cut wood shavings, clean and sharp amid the stench of garbage floating on the water.

It was here he had nearly starved to death as a child, and the fishermen, grumbling at their own poverty, took him in, fed him on scraps and let him work on their boats—a white coolie serving the poorest Chinese.

At the start he had often wondered who his father was. He could remember his mother, a beautiful White Russian refugee who, like many others, had fled from the Russian Revolution across the Siberian border to China. To support her child she danced, as it was euphemistically called, on the long bar in Shanghai. She used to tell her son that she was a countess, that they were descended from a long and noble line of Russian aristocracy, then died before he could submit her to any close questioning.

At the age of eight Nicholai found himself alone in the Nanking Province, fleeing before the Japanese invasion of China. He came to Macau, one among thousands of refugees. Without papers, without knowledge of his own surname or benefit of a clan, he barely survived on the waterfront. It was here that he learned the importance of having a name in China... The peasant Chinese survived through their extended family system; without it, a man—and especially a boy like Nicholai—was just so much human rubbish destined for an early grave.

In the first years he had earned his living by scraping human excrement into buckets, crawling in the fetid spaces between decks, begging the crewmen to save their waste from the sea. The Chinese vegetable growers ashore treasured human dung, calling it the noble fertilizer, and he sold it to them in exchange for enough to eat. The junk people had contemptuously given him the name *Nay buk dum si lowe*, meaning white dung carrier, but he at least survived where others died, and he gained in strength. Soon he was doing a grown man's job on the fishing junks and, acknowledging his stubborn grasp on life, the peasants changed his name with grudging respect to *Suen Lo Hsu*, the ship's rat. That was the second of his names. From there he graduated to seaman and then to navigator, but the grinding poverty they all faced was merciless. He made just enough to keep from starving, there seemed no way out of his wretched life... until Dr. Sun, learning of his skill at guiding a vessel over the treacherous bars and sandbanks, gave him a job on his fast smuggling boats.

It was the one debt Nicholai could never repay. To be freed of the Inner Harbor, where the difference between life and death lay in a bowl of rice, was his salvation. He put his considerable talents to work, eager to justify himself to Dr. Sun, and three years later, at the age of seventeen, was given command of his own vessel. The legend of the Snake Boat Man had begun. Still, the cruelty of his early life in the Inner Harbor had left an indelible mark on him, with scars that would never truly heal...

The dour Tanka fishing clans ignored Nicholai, a courtesy they extended to any stranger. Then a woman drying her child in a doorway recognized him. Word sped quickly through the shanties and across the water to the junks. Fishermen came out of their homes, forming a line on either side of the passage he would have to take to get back to the road. "Snake Boat Man—" It was a whispered greeting deep in their throats as he passed among them. They held up their children to touch him for luck... here was a man who had proved it possible to break free of the Inner Harbor. Here was a legend come back to life. An old woman plucked at his arm. *"Haw-ye, we thought you were dead."*

"No. I went away and now I've come back." He was moved that the peasants still living there remembered him—he, too had known what it was like to starve, to have to fight for a living space in their world. He had felt forgotten, and now it seemed he was still remembered. He was feeling better...

"Lord," the coolie spoke over his shoulder as he pedaled Nicholai back along the sea road, "have you returned to help the Lady Sun?"

"Does she have support?"

"A little. Much more if you join her."

"Take me to her palace, brother. And for your own safety drop me some way before the gates. Tell no one that you saw me."

"THE SNAKE Boat Man is here," the comprador said, showing him into Crystal Lily's study. He said the name with pride.

She gestured to the comprador to leave, poured a whiskey and soda and handed it to Nicholai, hoping that he hadn't changed his drink. He took the glass out onto her balcony and stood looking down over the roof-tops of Macau, over the Praia Grande to the bay.

Crystal Lily walked up softly and stood beside him. "I'm glad you've come." She followed his gaze, aware of—and grateful for—the special feeling that they still shared. "It was on a night like this, I remember, that you used to take Li Wen sailing in your pleasure junk on the Bay of Ou Moon. It was just the two of you, and even as a little girl I can remember feeling so jealous of her... You were the toast of Macau then, you could have had any woman you wanted. I remember how the servants gossiped in amazement that you were always faithful to her. I always respected you for that."

"When I married her," he said, "she became so much a part of me that there was only room for her." Nicholai turned to face Crystal. He had been wondering how to explain this to her, and was surprised that the warmth and tenderness he felt for her actually made it easier.

"In the last years of the gold trade each run I made grew harder, the Hong Kong police learned my ways, and they brought in faster boats and better detection equipment. Every morning when I brought the *East Wind* back to the Inner Harbor Li Wen would be standing on our balcony overlooking the channel, watching for me. Ah Chuen would tell me that sometimes during an especially difficult run she would sense it and stand on the balcony all night, looking out to sea. She believed in me, she always did. I, on the other hand, had lost all confidence in myself near the end. She was all that kept me going. When she died I felt as though everything I believed in, everything I had, was gone. I began to think I was just another refugee who had managed to claw his way out of the stinking sewers of the Inner Harbor and then had fallen right back.

"You have to understand that money or power for its own sake means little to me, to most men like me. What we own, what we value, is our pride, our courage. When I left you that last night I was nothing again. My pride and my courage were gone. You didn't realize it, you were much too young, but I was little more than a drunk whose nerve had finally cracked. I had to leave Macau before everyone realized just how hollow the reputation your father had so adroitly built about me had become." He paused, not sure of the effect his words were having on her. "I failed you once before. Are you sure you want to trust me again?"

"You *never* failed me. You came back to face my father. No other man would have done that. It was only because of you that I was sent to America. I wouldn't have survived otherwise. You were the only man my father ever loved, and I loved you more. Nicholai, you are the Snake Boat Man of Macau. I remember asking the servants how you got your name, and they told me how your boat was said to wriggle like a snake through the sandbanks and reefs and islands that separate Macau from Hong Kong. All along the coast, among the fishing clans in the harbors, even on the police boats, you were a legend. 'The Snake Boat Man,' they'd say, and spit for luck, 'no one can catch him.' Even the Hokolo and Tanka sea gypsies who spend their whole lives on their junks and respect no one still tell stories about your exploits. Each one is more daring than the next as they try to top one another until the truth has perhaps become confused with fiction. But who cares... Nicholai, you are a legend, you are alive, and I still believe in you..."

"You wanted to know what I've been doing these last fifteen years," Nicholai said. "Well, I've dried out. Now I drink for pleasure, not because

70

I need it. And I've been doing a good deal of thinking. Fifteen years' worth, to be exact."

"And now? Will you still make the run for me?"

"Yes."

He had not disappointed her, especially not by his honesty, and she felt another powerful surge of affection for him. The lines in his face spoke to her of all the troubles of his life, and in them she found the strength of his character. Instinctively she recognized that in spite of his years away, here was a man who could still command the world he lived in. But she also knew that he was a man to be won, not commanded. And she respected him for it.

"Have you inspected my boat?"

"Yes. It's not suited to the kind of run I have in mind. I'll choose my own boat, recruit my own crew, and I'll need to pay them well."

"Money isn't a problem," Crystal Lily said. "Come with me." They took the lift from her study down to the vaults hewn from the rock below the palace. She switched on the lights, and through the thick bars of a steel grill he saw small ramparts of stacked four-hundred-ounce gold bars.

"How much of this do you want me to carry?"

"All of it. It weights almost five tons." Crystal indicated the gleaming stack on her left. "Just under two tons is owed to the 14K Triad. The rest is mine."

Nicholai calculated that at current rates she was worth something over fifty million United States dollars. "Why did Dr. Sun accumulate so much in one place?"

"At the time of his death my father had no faith in anything else. He never understood that as long as it was trapped in the vaults by his enemies it was worthless to me, unless I could move it. Which is up to you."

The telephone rang on the wall beside her. She answered it. "The chief of police is here," she said. "Will you see him with me?"

"Of course. In the meantime, do everything you can to keep your boat safe in his harbor," he said as they returned in the elevator to her rooms.

"Why? You just said you have no use for it."

"Because we are going to use your boat as a decoy to keep Thomas Wu's attention away from mine."

DA COSTA, Macau's chief of police, was shown into the room moments later. "My lady," he said, "you wished to see me?"

Da Costa had removed his hat, revealing a stubby crew cut. He was an overweight man, bulging out of his immaculately pressed uniform, sweating profusely in Macau's humid heat. His eyes met Nicholai's in startled recognition. Theirs had been an uneasy relationship, but Da Costa respected the Snake Boat Man. He recovered quickly. "You have found an ally, I see."

Crystal Lily got to the point—her American training, Da Costa suspected. "As you know from the attack made on me two nights ago, certain members of the Syndicate resent my succession to power. I have to know what friends I can count on."

"Your father was my benefactor, my lady," Da Costa said. "With his most generous help I have been able to educate my children in good schools in Portugal. I have also been able to buy a small farm in Oporto for my retirement."

"Which I believe is to be soon?"

Da Costa sighed. It was all he looked forward to now. "Very soon, my lady. I leave Macau at the end of September."

"Can I count on your loyalty and the assistance of your police force until then?"

Da Costa squirmed. "My lady, you will never find me personally ungrateful to the House of Sun, but the Portuguese administration cannot take sides in a dispute over succession within the Syndicate. It would end in humiliation for us. We cannot predict the outcome, and we would have to coexist with whomever was the winner."

She caught Nicholai's eye but he remained silent. "So you will remain neutral?"

"For the good of Macau, my lady, yes."

"I assume you know that I have to make a delivery of gold to the 14K Triad?"

"All of Macau is aware of that, my lady."

"Can you at least allow my ChrisCraft to remain within the sanctuary of your admiralty harbor?"

"My lady," Da Costa said, obviously relieved, "that I can do for you. We are almost as anxious as you that this gold leave Macau. We have no wish to find the 14K here looking for it. Let them ravage the Hong Kong police."

"So when my boat leaves, you can assure me that it will receive no interference from your police launches?"

"My lady, since the government of Kwangtung Province has ordered that deck guns on our launches be removed we have no power to stop you. On the night you leave my launches will be discreetly withdrawn to a safe distance. I only wish I could be of more help. All I ask, for the sake of the gambling and tourist industry, which, after all, your Syndicate controls, is that you not indulge in the overt war of succession that nearly destroyed Macau when your father seized power."

"Put your request to those who are trying to undermine my succession," she said coldly. "I am the legal heir, you know." Legal, if only by an ancient and special law, she thought wryly.

The comprador showed Da Costa to the door.

"Nicholai, how long can you stay?" Crystal said, turning to him eagerly once they were alone. She felt softer, kinder . . . happier when he was with her.

"I need an hour of your time to decide on our plans. Then I have to go."

"Where?"

"To find an old friend."

Udo, she guessed, trying to hide her disappointment. "I want to go with you, but I'm trapped here. Remember to take care while you're in Macau. Word will get around quickly that you're helping me, and my enemies will be your enemies."

Her warning wasn't necessary, as Nicholai's thoughts rushed ahead, planning. He felt again the familiar surge of being on top, in control.

IT WAS late by the time Nicholai's taxi crossed the bridge to Taipa, then over the long sea causeway to Coloane Village. He was dropped off in the village square and made his way through a maze of narrow lanes to an unmarked doorway. Udo the Bear, as he was known, did not advertise his restaurant—he expected his customers to know where to find him.

Nicholai let himself into a medium-sized room with a tiled floor, pink walls and a bilious green ceiling. Fortunately for Udo his reputation as a cook made up for his sense of decor. He was serving at the far table, dressed in a sweat-stained T-shirt and baggy trousers. Well over six feet tall, he had the menacing battered face of a prizefighter. When Nicholai had known him he had kept himself very fit; now he had let himself go and was running to fat.

Nicholai passed unnoticed behind Udo and took a seat at an empty table against one wall. Above him was a shrine to Udo's personal god of the Three Warriors; at its tiny altar he'd lit candles and incense sticks.

Udo slopped some wine into glasses at a table of eight tourists, then raised the bottle to his lips, finishing it. "You like my food?" he growled, slapping one of the tourists on the back. The tourist nodded nervously... The restaurant was justly famous—the bread was home-baked, the prawns and fish stew all cooked in one great wok were magnificent... but the tourist had the distinct impression that he'd be thrown through the window if he did anything less than agree.

Udo turned moodily to his less than spotless kitchen for more wine, unaware that he was fast reaching the point where he no longer bothered to serve wine to his customers, drinking most of it himself. The local patrons, accustomed to trouble this late in the evening, had already drifted away.

Udo was halfway back across the room when he recognized Nicholai. He stared for a moment in disbelief, then moved quickly toward him. Although the big man was drunk, he maintained a certain grace, his weight balanced on the balls of his feet, and had no difficulty negotiating his way around the chairs and tables.

Nicholai watched him approach warily, knowing too well his old friend's explosive temper and the fact that when drunk, he tended to use his fists to express himself when the right words couldn't be found. "You ran out on me, on all of us!" Udo's face was a mixture of anger and the affection he still felt for Snake Boat Man. He reached out and touched Nicholai's cheek, as if to check if he were for real. He slapped him, an act of affection, but with the clout of a bear's paw that sent Nicholai's head snapping aside. "It's been a long time." Udo said, "and never a word..."

Nicholai shrugged off the blow. "There didn't seem any point..."

Udo looked down at his belly. "See? I've grown fat and old and the women laugh at me now. And when I've drunk too much and start talking about the old days, no one believes it was me. But those were our good times, Nicholai, when you and I were important men around here. Now everyone thinks we're dead."

From the front door came the sound of more patrons crowding into the tiny restaurant. "Get out of here," Udo shouted without turning his head. "We're closed."

"You too," he warned the table of tourists. "Get out. There's no charge." But their way was blocked as they got up to leave. Chang, the Syndicate's enforcer, backed by ten of his men, stood in the doorway.

"I'm sorry," Nicholai said, realizing the trouble he'd brought. "They must have followed me here."

Chang moved over to one of the tourists, seized the unsuspecting man by the hair, plunged his face into his plate, then lifted it covered with the remains of fish stew. The others at the table stared in terror. "This restaurant no good now," Chang announced in a raspy explosion of broken English. His men began herding the others against the wall. "You no come here more time." Chang made a cut off gesture with his hand. "This place finished, unstand?"

He reached up and swept the candles and joss sticks from the altar, setting the cheap print curtains on fire.

As Chang continued to persecute the tourists Udo let out a soft whistle until a boy's face appeared around the kitchen door. He made a quick chopping motion; a moment later the boy was darting past Chang's men with a huge meat cleaver.

"Keep out of this," Nicholai warned. "You said yourself you're getting too old and fat."

"Do I have a choice?" He'd sobered up considerably. Udo grabbed up the cleaver from the boy, kicked the table away and went after Chang. There wasn't enough room for the huge man to fight at his best, but by the time he reached Chang he was carrying five of Chang's men on his back. As Nicholai joined in to help his friend he was attacked by three of Chang's bodyguards. The men went down in a tangled heap of body blows and kicks until the last thing Nicholai remembered was the sound of flames and the tourists screaming.

He regained consciousness as he was being dragged over the stones to a dirt alley and lifted his head enough to see the flames that swept through the restaurant. Chang leaned over and satisfied himself that Nicholai was conscious. "Leave Macau now," he warned. "You will not get another chance." As quickly as he'd come, Chang and his band of thugs were gone.

"UDO?" NICHOLAI crawled over to his friend. Udo's face was swelling from his forehead to his chin. He spat out blood and a broken tooth, then levered himself up against the wall.

"The Syndicate?" Udo asked.

"They've gone."

"What did you come here for anyway?"

"I'm going to make one last run. A big one—more gold than we've ever carried. But first I think maybe I should help you start another restaurant—"

"—Are you crazy? Look, I don't know about you, but this has been no good for me. I've been bored, fighting with my customers, drinking the profits, I was hoping Sun's daughter would have the sense to go to you."

As they spoke the boy Nicholai had seen earlier was running back and forth with buckets of water, trying to douse the flames.

"Shouldn't we try to help him?" Nicholai asked in spite of his pain.

"No." Udo slumped back. "Let it burn. They've done me a favor." His mouth was dry. "Fool Boy," he shouted. "Leave the fire alone. Get in there and get me some wine."

"Who's Fool Boy?"

"Some woman I knew claimed he was my kid and dumped him on me. He's not all there in the head but he helps in the kitchen . . . thinks you're some kind of god—I told him a lot about you."

"What happened to the boat?"

"I've taken good care of her." Udo groaned, testing his limbs before he got up. "The *East Wind*'s up on blocks in a boat shed. Fool Boy and I watched over her."

"Do you know where any of the old crew are?"

"I heard Fat Sui Leong's dead. He died in a knife fight in the Wanch. And some woman poisoned Sammy Lee for his money. The others are scattered. I don't know," he bent painfully over Nicholai. "We'll have to look around the waterfront. When's the run?"

"The end of August."

"Can you stand? Here . . ." He offered to help as Nicholai struggled to his feet.

"We're going to need some place to hide up with the boat," Nicholai said. "There's a refugee camp near Ka Ho. Do you know it?"

"Yes, it's next to the leprosarium. No one goes there if they can help it. It's run by German Alice, remember her from the old days?" He put his arm out to support Nicholai and the two men shuffled stiffly down the alley with Fool Boy following in their wake. "There's a small bay right below the camp," Udo said. "She needs money for her people. If you can pay she'll hide us."

It had been years since Nicholai had taken such a beating. "This isn't a great start. Not only do we have to take on the Syndicate, we're going to have to smuggle the gold past Hong Kong's hovercraft, helicopters and navy gunboats. You're sure you are still interested?"

"We can do it," Udo said gruffly, "the question is, where are we going to find a crew damn fool enough to sail with us?"

76

CHAPTER 6

"DA COSTA, I've called you here," Thomas Wu said, looking up at the chief of police, "because I want you to order the removal of Madame Sun's ChrisCraft from its berth in the Portuguese harbor." Chang, the Syndicate enforcer, stood by Thomas Wu's side. Further back in the office sat the still, Buddhalike figure of Chen Kitung.

"The privilege of occupying a berth in our admiralty harbor was granted as a mark of respect to her father," Da Costa said nervously. "We cannot withdraw it without seeming to take sides—"

"Are you prepared to refuse the wishes of the Syndicate?"

"I do not refuse," Da Costa replied hastily. "The harbor is under Portuguese control and as you know is neutral territory. I merely seek to maintain the status quo."

"She intends to use this craft to run gold to Hong Kong," Chen Kitung said from behind them.

"We cannot stop her," Da Costa insisted, regretting his promise to Crystal Lily.

"All you have to do is order her ChrisCraft's removal from the protection of your harbor," Thomas Wu repeated. "We'll see to its destruction."

"Lord Wu"—Da Costa paid him the courtesy of a mandarin's title—"the gold belongs to the 14K Triad. Frankly, we would be glad to be rid of it."

"Understand, Da Costa," Thomas Wu's voice grew hard, "we have no intention of allowing her boat to leave Macau waters, loaded or unloaded."

"What happens beyond Macau waters in not my concern. But I would remind you to attack her boat in our harbor would be an act of humiliation that we Portuguese could not ignore." Da Costa felt he had retreated far enough. Wu's insolent manner had forced him into a show of defending his dignity. "I am well aware that we occupy only a formal presence here, and that your succession to leadership of the Syndicate is backed by the governor of Kwangtung Province. But if you or he decide to disregard our neutrality, if you deliberately set out to humiliate us after all these years of peaceful coexistence with China and the Syndicate, then we would be prepared to sacrifice the status quo and appeal directly over the governor's head to Peking."

Da Costa's threat had its desired effect. Chen Kitung caught Thomas Wu's eye and discreetly shook his head—he wanted no ripple of this matter to reach Peking.

"Very well," Thomas Wu said, furious and a little surprised at the stubborn streak that had suddenly appeared in the usually passive police chief. "Her boat is safe, but only as long as it is in your harbor."

After Da Costa had left, Chen Kitung, levering his bulk from the chair, said, "Be satisfied, you have insured that her boat is useless to her, and I have a message for you. The governor of Kwangtung Province asks a special favor. A valued colleague of his has fallen from grace in Peking... he wishes him to reach Hong Kong safely. Can you find two places among the refugees making the run tonight?"

"Does he wish to send them by fast boat?" Wu asked. The captains of the small high-speed refugee vessels, skin boats, charged nearly thirty thousand dollars a head.

"No. The British are on full alert for the fugitives. Let them take their chances in a sampan. At least that way if they're caught, with luck, they may not be recognized..."

*　*　*

H.M.S. SCIMITAR, a low gray Royal Navy attack craft, scythed through the night sea like a shark. Only a small lick of white water flaring from its sharply raked bows betrayed the passage of the ship, running without lights through the water as it patrolled the eastern sector approaches to Hong Kong.

The captain, a tall blond British lieutenant, was seated in the command chair on the open bridge. Ahead a beacon flashed twice every ten seconds. "Waglen light, sir," said the helmsman at the wheel. To the southeast toward Ninepins Islands the masthead lights of legitimate fishing junks bobbed like fireflies against the dark expanse of sea.

Apart from one narrow land border with Communist China, Hong Kong is surrounded on three sides by water. The British patrolled these waters with every force at their disposal in their nightly battle against the illegal immigrants who came looking for refuge in the colony. Yet despite the barbed wire barricades, the Gurkha soldiers in the New Territories adjoining China and the navy and police patrols, when the sea was calm enough, the refugees without fail would cross it by the hundreds.

No one could tell for sure, but it was estimated that fifty percent died in the attempt—great hammerhead sharks in Mirs Bay claimed the lives of many, while others who couldn't swim simply drowned. Those without money to buy a place in a sampan even tried to float across the bays from China on inflated pig's bladders or hessian sacks filled with pingpong balls, their children strapped to their backs. Or they fashioned inflatable rafts from plastic ponchos, carefully sewn together. While many did manage to slip through, often when the dawn came the police found and collected pieces of punctured plastic and the bodies that the currents washed up against the mud flats.

Tonight's patrol had a different purpose. At the back of the open bridge, gripping the rail, was the squat, stocky figure of Special Branch Superintendent Harry Malloy. Malloy was hardly a seaman, and as the humid salt wind buffeted his face he tried not to watch the swells that creamed along the vessel's sides.

A radar scanner just above where he stood turned with a low cranking hum. It was a device so sensitive that the operators working below deck could pick up a fishing float at one-and-a-half miles. "We have a contact, we have a contact," the operator's voice came through the bridge amplifier. "Come round to red four-hundred distance three miles. Definite contact."

79

The captain picked up the microphone. "What does it look like?"

"Too small to tell at this distance, sir, but it could be a sampan riding low in the water."

The captain switched the speaker system through to the rest of the vessel. "Captain to crew. All hands to quarters—we're closing in on a contact."

He turned, deferring to the Special Branch officer. "Do you want to brief them?"

Malloy slowly shook his head. He felt too sick to move. "You warn them..." he began, then changed his mind and reached for the microphone. "We know that an agent loyal to the old regime in Peking is going to try to make a crossing tonight. For those of you who remember the bloody riots in Hong Kong during the Cultural Revolution...well, this bastard helped organize them and he's coming here to stir up more trouble. It's important that we intercept him. Is that clear? The man is almost certainly armed, so take care when you approach anyone on the water." With that Malloy, feeling queasy, signed off and braced himself against the railing to wait.

A LEAKING, rotted seventeen-foot-long sampan sailed through the darkness toward Hong Kong. Its occupants, crammed together shoulder to shoulder, had been at sea for three days. Most of that time was spent waist-deep in water, bailing constantly to keep their craft afloat. Now they could see, blazing on the horizon against the night sky, the lights of Hong Kong.

The refugees had fought storms for the first thirty-six hours, and the women and children were so exhausted that they were held upright only by the press of the bodies in the boat. Most of them came from the same farming commune in the Kwangtung Province of China, having been led down the coast by a fisherman who owned a hand-held compass. Just before reaching Hong Kong waters the sampan had been intercepted by Thomas Wu's high-speed launch. Several of the male refugees were taken off onto the launch, their places in the sampan taken by two strangers.

The first warning the refugees had of danger was the deep throb of marine engines pounding up from behind, then the flared bows of the modern attack craft materialized through the light sea mist.

A young girl standing in the bow of the sampan, the swells breaking over her, looked bitterly at the lights of Hong Kong. She knew they'd been caught well within the Square Boundary that separated the colony's water from China. Within twenty-four hours the other peasants would be returned to China to receive a year's sentence in a detention camp before being sent back to their commune for more punishment. She and her father, however, would not be so lucky... She felt her father's hand on her shoulder and turned to him. "When the British take us prisoner, don't identify yourself with me," General Li Ch'en said. "No matter what happens, remember your training. Your survival is important for our country..."

In one final, desperate act before capture, peasants began tearing up and throwing overboard the names and addresses of their relatives in the colony, hoping to protect them. General Li Ch'en and his daughter added their papers to those already littering the wake.

The *Scimitar*'s searchlights seared through the dark, scanning the sampan. The peasants, petrified by the armed vessel that drew alongside, offered no resistance. A few of the men resignedly pulled down the torn sail and shipped aboard the steering oar. Without the sail to stabilize them, their cockleshell craft began to rock and plunge dangerously in the swells.

At first Malloy thought there were eight, perhaps ten refugees in the sampan, then he made out more and more heads covered in gray plastic hoods, hiding from the blinding glare of the searchlights. "Eleven men, six women and four children," he counted... twenty-one bodies packed into the leaky boat. He stood in the shadows and watched them being pulled up one by one through the railings and onto the deck. The captain joined him. "Navy's going to catch hundreds of illegals tonight. How in the hell are you going to spot the man you want among this lot?"

"Because I know the bastard's face as well as I know my own, and so does each of my men. As soon as we've got them all aboard I want your sailors to search that sampan."

A shaven-headed peasant, so thin that his bones hardly filled his baggy canvas clothes, was being pulled through the rail, trying to keep his face from the light... General Li Ch'en had fallen from favor with the new regime governing China, and for the last four months had been hunted by the men in his own security force. Hunger and exhaustion had so ravaged his face as to make him almost unrecognizable, but Malloy spotted him. He had been bloodied in the vicious street battles of the sixties when the Red Guards, organized by this man, had used everything from bombs to razors and acid against the police and had nearly taken Hong Kong.

81

"That's him," Malloy called out. A burly British sailor immediately pinned the general's arms while Malloy went forward, frisked him and quickly removed the gun he found strapped to his body. The general offered no resistence; his face showed only a calm acceptance of his fate. The sailor handcuffed him while Malloy stood back, weighing the gun in his hand. "Take him below," Malloy ordered, unable to hide his satisfaction at this night's work, "and see that he's guarded at all times."

The rest of the refugees assembled on the pitching deck allowed themselves to be searched and herded along with the dumb resignation of animals. But in one young and strikingly attractive woman, Malloy saw a look of such utter wretchedness that even he felt pity for her... saw in her lovely face all the days of rocking at sea, the fear, the weariness and the hopes of freedom wasted. But in her manner there was still a glimmer of courage, a defiance that demanded they recognize her dignity as a human being.

Malloy's eyes kept searching her out, in spite of his attempt to ignore her. There was a captivating air about her, an incandescent innocence that could move a man to try and destroy that innocence, or fight to protect it. Malloy knew instantly what he wanted of her, and a reckless idea crossed his mind, one totally against his training.

"Rendezvous with a police launch," Malloy told the lieutenant, "I'll take the general and the illegals off your hands and leave you to get back on patrol."

The lieutenant was glad to oblige. His craft was designed for high-speed chases, not for use as a prison ship. As the *Scimitar* flashed up her main jet engines a sixty-foot-long flame erupted from the huge exhaust ports in the stern. The engines rumbled and the vessel sprang across the sea, the spray from its planing bows rising higher on both sides than the bridge.

Malloy made his way to the stern where the refugees were seated on deck in the shelter of the engine-room superstructure. They had been so weakened over the days by the violent motion of their sampan that many of them could no longer sit erect or hold up their heads. The girl, whose face still fascinated him, supported an older woman, whose head rested in silent misery on her breast.

The *Scimitar* made its rendezvous with a police launch in a sheltered bay in the New Territories. Malloy waited until the rocky shore was only a couple of hundred yards away, then he summoned one of the peasants. He questioned the man briefly in broken Mandarin, then sent him to rejoin the others. Next he summoned the girl. "*Nāi oōi m̄ oōi Koñg Ying-*

82

mān, you can, cannot speak English?" he demanded in Cantonese dialect; his Mandarin was weak and he didn't want to risk any misunderstanding.

"*Ngōh oōi Koñg Ying-mān.* Can speak English," she said quietly.

"Where do you come from?"

"Shanghai."

That, and the fact that she spoke English accounted for the difference in her looks, Malloy thought. This was no peasant, probably a student trying to escape. "What's your name?"

"Mae Ling."

"Can you swim?"

She nodded, tried to read the stranger's face.

"Well enough to reach shore?"

The girl glanced over the rail, measuring the distance between the shore and the navy vessel and nodded again.

"My name," he said, pronouncing the words slowly, "is Harry Malloy and I live at apartment two-twenty, New World Mansions, Pok Fulam." He gave the local translation for Pok Fulam. "Repeat that." She did so.

"All right, if you make it, contact me there. But if you're caught, keep your mouth shut. Understand?"

"Lord, can you help the others?"

"No. Only you." The penalty for aiding an illegal was severe, and he cursed himself for a fool as he told her, "Go over the side when I call the guard away."

The lieutenant was maneuvering his vessel alongside the police launch. "Bring me that one now," Malloy ordered, motioning toward an old woman. As the guard brought her forward Malloy dismissed the girl, sending her back to join the others. The guard let her pass along the narrow catwalk. In a moment she was behind him, sheltered from the other sailors by the engine-room ventilators, and from the corner of his eye Malloy saw her slip over the side. His mind ticked off the seconds as he fired questions at the old woman.

A lookout on the bridge finally spotted the girl striking out for shore and sounded the alarm. The *Scimitar*'s searchlights blazed out, and Malloy ran up the steps to the bridge. He stared for a moment after the swimming figure, pretending to assess the odds on recapturing her, then seeming to reach a decision . . . "Leave her," he ordered briskly. "The police will pick her up in the morning. Transfer General Li Ch'en and the illegals to the police launch. I've got the big fish I came to catch." As Malloy spoke he noticed, with relief, that the girl hads been swallowed up in the darkness.

83

"That was a girl of unusual beauty for a peasant," the lieutenant said to Malloy, not quite daring to voice his suspicions but letting Malloy know that he'd noticed her too. "If she makes it she's going to find there are more sharks waiting for her in Hong Kong than there ever were in Mirs Bay."

Malloy shrugged and turned away.

"What are your plans for the general?" the lieutenant called after him.

"He'll be returned to China, where they'll execute the bastard," Malloy said, obviously pleased with himself.

THE POLICE launch reached Victoria Harbor just before dawn. The street lights were still burning and the ships remained lit, but the windows of the towering buildings gazing down on the harbor were dark and the tops of the buildings on the mid-levels of the peak were shrouded in mist.

Inspector Rem Choy, Malloy's assistant, was waiting for him on the dock. He had spent most of the night clinging to the bows of a bucking dinghy in Deep Bay and was soaked through.

"I've got him," Malloy said as he stepped off the boat. "Have headquarters contacted the Communists yet?"

"They're anxious to have the general back as soon as possible."

"Anything else?"

"Yes. The secretary for security wants your report on his desk before his nine o'clock briefing with the governor."

"Shit. I'm supposed to take Jenny to the airport." He weighed his priorities. He'd promised to have breakfast with her before she left...well, Jenny would have to wait.

Malloy was not attractive in any ordinary sense of the word, but he did appeal to a certain kind of woman, and those who had lived with him eventually discovered the same thing: he was essentially a violent, insensitive man, taking special pains to dominate them in such a way that they lost all confidence in themselves, becoming completely dependent on him. Often they were beautiful women, accustomed to being indulged by a wealthy father or husband—until they met him. To keep their sanity they somehow convinced themselves that Malloy's savagery was a deep, exciting expression of love. Malloy simply used them.

He picked up Jenny in the foyer of his apartment building in Pok Fulam. She was a lovely auburn-haired woman who had left her husband for him and was returning to England to visit her children. "I've just called a taxi," she said, not attempting to hide her anger.

84

"Cancel it." He shrugged an apology. "I've had a busy night."

They slowly made their way through the morning traffic to Kai Tak. Neither spoke.

"Whom do you plan to replace me with?" Jenny finally said. "After all, I'll be gone for a whole month."

"Does it matter? Besides, I expect you'll bribe Ah Ming for all the details."

Jenny shrugged. "I hardly need to. The last time I came back I found some tart wearing my clothes."

Malloy smiled at the memory of her going after him with a pair of scissors... She made taunting her a real pleasure. "They're your precious brats you're leaving me for, not mine."

He parked the car while Jenny checked in, and found her again in the departure lounge; her British Airways flight to London was on final call.

"See you in a month," he said. He pulled her to him, sliding his hands under her arms so that they were level with her breasts. She had lasted longer than the others, and he knew that he was going to miss her voluptuous, willing body in bed. But he had plans to ease his loneliness.

"Harry, you're such a bastard," she whispered in his ear before she kissed him. "You think you have us all worked out. Well, maybe just once you're wrong..." And then she was rushing off to join the last of the passengers filing through the doors.

He raised his hand in mock farewell. He bloody well didn't have her wrong, the snotty bitch...

He drove straight back to his apartment to shower and change. Ah Ming, the amah, was crying as she clattered about the kitchen.

"Shut up," Malloy ordered, annoyed by the sobs that disturbed his morning peace. "Your precious Missee she back one month. Count on it."

"Missee she gone. She not come back."

"What..." Malloy had just stepped into the shower. He snatched a robe and strode into the bedroom, dripping wet.

The amah pointed to an envelope on Jenny's dressing table; he promptly ripped it open.

"Good-bye, you bastard," Jenny had written in her bold, flowing hand. "God knows how you managed to keep me this long, but this time I won't be back. P.S. I didn't want to make a scene so I've told Ah Ming to send on my clothes. Good riddance. J."

Malloy turned on the amah. "Why in hell didn't you tell me she was leaving?"

"Missee say no tell. She say you no likee—"

"Damn straight, I no likee . . . you're fired, *chow hai*. Get out of here—no, wait. She wants her things, does she?" His hand swept across Jenny's dressing table, sending bottles of perfumes crashing to the floor. He ground the broken glass under his heel, then reached for her suitcases and pulled them down. "Pack the pieces for her." He opened her closet, seized an armful of dresses and began ripping them apart. "Let's see how Her Highness likes wearing these for another man." He sat on the bed as the weeping amah packed. "That bitch, I'll get to her . . . no one walks out on me . . ."

CHAPTER 7
HONG KONG

NICHOLAI AND Udo walked the few blocks northwest of Kai Tak to the ancient walled city of Kowloon. Their route took them through slums, but a taxi carrying Europeans would have attracted more attention than they wanted—or needed. They were dressed in loose, open-necked shirts, cotton trousers and comfortable coolie sandals. The temperature was well into the nineties and the humidity was so high that moisture seemed to drip from the air.

At this time of the year most westerners wilted when separated from their air conditioners, changing their sweat-stained shirts two and three times a day. But these men hardly noticed the heat, having spent their entire lives in the Orient, and, though European by descent, they had through the years adopted Cantonese manners and gestures, so much so that they were able to mingle with the noisy street throngs without the Chinese being aware of the strangers in their midst.

They were headed for the old city of Kowloon—a slum that lay buried behind a crumbling facade of shops. They left the sunlight behind and climbed down a rotting ladder to enter a subterranean world populated by thieves, thugs and drug smugglers.

The old city, a one-square-mile area that because of a treaty dispute dating from 1898 was still under the control of China, had simply been left to rot; police rarely went there and when they did they were armed and in groups of three or four.

Vendors selling everything from children to stolen jewelry lined the gloomy basement passages. Sweatshop owners used illegal immigrant labor to churn out jeans and plastic toys. They worked in cramped box-wood shacks constructed on stilts over fetid drains that rushed along half-closed tunnels. As they made their way along dimly lit alleyways the two men had to duck to avoid the tangle of live electric wires overhead where sweatshop owners tapped into the main electric power cables.

It was well known that heroin, bought freely here for two hundred and eighty American dollars an ounce could easily be sold for six hundred dollars just across the harbor on the island. The irony of it was that Communist China had no problem with drugs while Hong Kong, founded to further Britain's opium trade, spent tens of millions a year to try and control its use among its own population.

The trouble began in 1946 when the police closed down the opium dens. Resourceful addicts switched to heroin because it could be injected quickly and lacked opium's distinctive aroma.

Lin Tsang, the man Nicholai was looking for, was an opium addict. He was also the best engineer the *East Wind* ever had, and he was a good friend as well.

The walled-city watchmen, members of street gangs serving out their probationary period in menial tasks, slouched in the doorways, their eyes following the two men as they passed. It was unheard of for *gwilos* to enter a place where even the beggars mugged each other, yet these men appeared unconcerned. At first it was thought they were crazy, but when they realized that Nicholai took each turn through the maze of passages with confidence and that the big man following him walked lightly, watching his back, they figured these were two *gwilos* with powerful Triad connections and were best left alone.

Nicholai turned into an alleyway of unlicensed dentists, who for a considerably reduced fee practiced their profession the old-fashioned way, using the most primitive tools. From their hovels skulls and secondhand sets of dentures leered into the gloom. They pressed on through basements of dilapidated buildings that almost met in the middle, stopping all light from filtering down. The walls narrowed until both men found it difficult to squeeze their shoulders through; finally the alley opened into a small courtyard. A steep wooden ladder leaned against a shack that had been tacked on bamboo stilts to the side of a building.

Nicholai pushed open the door. He knew the word of his presence would spread quickly and wasn't surprised to find two guards waiting for him. The shack, a vetting area, was inconspicuous among the rest of the buildings. A door had been knocked through the brick partition wall, leading into a multistory apartment block, the front of which was in the legitimate part of Kowloon. Two of the apartments had been converted into an opium den for those traditionally minded Chinese who could still afford their vice. In the event of a police raid the customers could be smuggled through this shack to safety along the alleyways of the walled city.

A fat, cold-eyed Chinese, his hair plastered down with a lavender-smelling brilliantine, warily approached the two men. "*Mat-yĕ shi?* What is the matter? *Nḡi shik-in mē?* Do you wish to smoke?"

"*Ngōh m̄ shîk-in.* I don't smoke. *Ngōh yāu kōh p'ang-yāu, kui kin Lin Tsang.* I have a friend named Lin Tsang," Nicholai said. "*Seūng nḡoh seung kin kūi.* I want to see him."

"*M-hai kūi ch'ut-cho'h hui.* No, he has gone." The fat man glanced a warning at his guards—he didn't want a report made of this conversation and switched from the pitched tones of Cantonese. "You speak English?"

"Of course." Nicholai changed language abruptly. "Where is he? He still owns this place, doesn't he?"

"No. He died some time ago. I'm the new owner."

Lin Tsang had used his share of the money when the boat paid off to buy the apartment block. The opium den was created merely to indulge a vice that he knew he had under control.

"I don't believe you," Udo said harshly, blocking the doorway with his great bulk. His message was clear.

As the fat man quickly reviewed the few people left who could still be interested in Tsang he began to suspect Nicholai and Udo's identity. "Please make no trouble," he said nervously. "Apart from my guards I am protected by the 14K Triad. I assure you, you would never leave the city alive."

"What happened?" Nicholai said.

"He was unable to come to a satisfactory arrangement over the profits of his business with the 14K. I was more reasonable."

"Where can we find him?"

The fat man knew it would be foolish to lie to Nicholai . . . he spread his hands in a gesture of apology as he said, "His bones await their return to China in the Hotel of the Dead."

THE PREMIUM on land in Hong Kong is such that the freehold on a choice six-by-three gravesite is worth up to twelve thousand American dollars. Most Chinese cannot afford to pay such an amount, and the usual solution is to rent a grave for six years, after which, in special ceremony, the skeleton is unearthed, the bones are cleaned by relatives, then reverently stacked in precise ascending order from feet to skull in a pottery urn known as an ancestor jar. The Chinese believe that there exists an invisible bond between the living and the dead. The urn is then either taken home to the family shrine or placed in a smaller, less costly space where the Fung Shui is propitious. For the traditionalists there is a large building situated by itself at one end of Kowloon, known simply as the Hotel of the Dead.

NICHOLAI AND Udo moved through the corrugated iron door of a warehouse in which row on row of human remains were stacked—the rich in ornate polished coffins made of specially imported Liuchow wood, the poor in battered cardboard suitcases. Here they remained in the musty silence until the day when they could be returned across the border to China and buried at last in the villages of their ancestors.

"Lin Tsang," Nicholai wrote for an aged caretaker who limped away to check on it, then returned with a ladder and a younger assistant. "This way," he said as he continued back down the numbered rows. The suitcase was finally located on a shelf fifteen feet up. "Do you want to see it?"

"Yes."

The locks presented no problem. Nicholai and Udo brushed off the dust and gingerly opened the case. The bones had been packed according to the instructions laid down by Confucius. Nicholai lifted out the skull and turned it over. The bone at the back of the cranium had been crushed. Tucked away among the rest of the skeleton was a small canvas bag that held a jade ring fashioned into the shape of a dragon, Lin Tsang's totem of good fortune. Evidently his murderers had been too superstitious to take it. In a colony where ancestor worship made any unattended grave suspicious, Nicholai thought, what better place to hide the remains of Lin Tsang...

"I always thought he'd be too cunning to let himself end up this way," Udo said sadly. "No one loved the good life like Lin Tsang... Remember how he used to tell us to follow the four bests... eat at Kwangchow—the best food. Dress at Hangchow—the best silk. Marry at Soochow—the best girls. Die at Liuchow—the best wood for coffins. He was very superstitious about that—he wanted to be well buried."

Nicholai closed the suitcase and summoned the caretaker. "What instructions do you have concerning this man?"

The caretaker shrugged, indicated the label. Men buried in suitcases earned him little *cumshaw*; he didn't concern himself over them. "His relatives wish him sent back to China like the others, when the borders open again."

"He has no relatives except us," Nicholai said. The caretaker knew better than to obstruct these men. Nicholai took out an envelope, stuffed it with money and handed it to the caretaker. "We'll bury him here in Hong Kong. Call an important Fung Shui man and see that he finds a most propitious gravesite. Let this Fung Shui man know that this is my good friend whose spirit I wish to protect."

The Fung Shui man, a master in the science of reading fate in the winds, land and water, was supposed to provide a gravesite where the juxtaposition of terrain guaranteed the deceased good fortune and protection from evil spirits.

Nicholai was Chinese enough to believe in the spirit world. He also had the distinct feeling that wherever his old friend Lin Tsang was, he could use all the help he could get...

MAE LING spent the next twenty-four hours hiding in the mountainous, broken country of the New Territories. On the second evening, driven by hunger, she made her way to a small stone house village set in rocky fields.

An elder found her waiting by the communal well at the end of the village, and she promptly threw herself before him, begging for protection. The village was populated by the Hakkas, a close-knit, hardworking community of people. As Mae Ling was led along the single street, people came to their doorways to stare at her, their faces cold and unwelcoming. They recognized at once that she was a stranger from the mainland— the villagers in the New Territories had long ago stopped welcoming illegal immigrants. The population of Hong Kong had exploded in the last ten years—there was scarcely room even for their own clan members, and with each new illegal immigrant who managed to evade the police the survival of the others was increasingly threatened.

Mae Ling was brought before the matriarch of the clan, who regarded her with the same suspicion of the other villagers. Mae Ling was wearing a shapeless black coolie tunic and a battered broad-rimmed straw hat covered her head, but even so the matriarch noted her beauty and hissed angrily at the men crowding at the doorway of the tiny room.

"Do you speak Cantonese, child?" she asked in a dry, reedy voice.

Mae Ling nodded. "A little."

"Where are you from?"

"Shanghai."

"Ah, a city girl." The matriarch had been sure of it. More than that, this tall, straight-backed girl had the landlord class in her ancestry. Her eyes were very dark with that double light in them, the whites clear like fine china. Her forehead was smooth and broad, her nose and cheekbones were not flat like a peasant's but well shaped, and her lips were generous and soft over perfectly formed teeth. This was a fine and gentle girl, made for love.

"Do you have relations here?" It was an important question. If a girl was plain or had powerful relations within the colony who might inquire after her, then the matriarch simply handed her over to the police. On the other hand, if she were attractive and without the protection of close relatives, then the villagers supplemented their income by selling the girls to the Wo Hop To Triad, which specialized in prostitution.

"I have an uncle," Mae Ling said.

"Is that all?"

"Yes."

"What does he do?"

"He is in the police."

"Does he expect you?"

"Oh no," Mae Ling said. "He would lose his job."

True, the matriarch reflected. It was especially difficult for the police to help their relatives from the mainland. The penalties if they were caught were twice as severe. "Give me his address," she now said. "I will send a message to him telling him you are here and, if he wishes, he may send for you. Meanwhile you may stay here. It would be dangerous for you if you were seen in the fields. Do you have money for your food?"

"No, I lost everything on the boat."

"Well, no matter, your uncle will pay us. I am old and infirm and you may serve me until he comes."

"Thank you," Mae Ling said, deeply relieved. Her eyes flickered to the men in the doorway, and she was doubly grateful for the protection of the matriarch. "My uncle and I will do our best to reward you."

92

"I'm sure you will, my child," the matriarch said, her eyes cold and calculating. "A messenger will leave in the morning." This girl could bring them a nice sum of money, the matriarch thought. It would be a pity to lose her.

MALLOY WAS late. An attractive Chinese secretary ushered him into the secretary for security's office. Trevelyan was seated behind his large desk, facing the window. He finished his telephone conversation and curtly waved Malloy to a seat.

"I've read your report."

Malloy searched through his pockets for a cigarette, then remembered that Trevelyan was a fanatical anti–smoker. "The tip-off was good. Where did it come from?"

"The taipan of the Princely House picked it up from his sources in Macau." There was a note of accusation in Trevelyan's voice as he spoke.

Malloy ignored him. It wasn't his fault that Her Majesty's miserly government had neglected Macau all these years. "Denning's neck is as much at stake over this as ours," he said.

The two men had, through the years, nursed an intense dislike for each other. Malloy was one of the most efficient officers in the force, but his abrasive personality always managed to work its way under the secretary for security's skin. More, they were too much alike to trust each other.

"I believe that some time ago this Nicholai... this Snake Boat Man nearly ruined your career."

Malloy's defenses were immediately up. "That's correct and I—"

"You are, I take it, old adversaries?"

"Yes..." Malloy replied cautiously, wondering how much digging through old files Trevelyan had done...

In 1965 Malloy, newly recruited into Special Branch and eager to prove himself, had managed to arrest one of Nicholai's crew on Hong Kong territory. In an attempt to make the man inform on his colleagues, Malloy beat him half to death in a cell below Tai Tam police station. The scene of the beating had been staged so as to appear that Malloy had defended himself in an attack by the prisoner, and nothing came of it—until a short while later when Malloy was kidnapped on his way to work and held prisoner in the pitch-dark hold of a junk for a week. When he was released he was in much the same battered physical condition as the man he'd arrested.

93

It was impossible to suppress the abduction of a police officer, and in the course of the inquiry that followed, Hong Kong's newspapers carried stories noting that Malloy's injuries were similar to those of the crewman. Malloy was subsequently charged with the torture of a prisoner, but he was far to shrewd to let the charges stick. Still, the public warning he'd received from the Snake Boat Man was a humiliation suffered by the entire police force, and Malloy's career had nearly come to an abrupt end. Physically Malloy was tough—in fact, tougher than most. No one had beaten him so thoroughly before or since. But it wasn't the pain, it was the loss of face that still rankled him. That, and the fact that his prospects for promotion had stalled at the rank of superintendent...

"Do you know what became of the Snake Boat Man?" Trevelyan said.

"He's been retired...must be ten, fifteen years." My God, Malloy thought to himself, had it been that long?

"Where is he now?"

"Last time I checked he was living in a house on the Peak. Keeps to himself. He's got his Hong Kong belongership now. All his papers are in order. As long as he keeps out of trouble I can't touch him."

"If you knew him so well when he was a smuggler," Trevelyan said, "why didn't you throw him in jail instead of letting him retire into a luxury on the Peak neither you nor I can afford?"

It struck home, reminding Malloy of what he considered the biggest personal failure in his career. "There was a time when I would have given my pension to catch him," Malloy said with quiet intensity, "and I *still* would."

"Well, now you'll have your chance. He's coming out of retirement to work for the heir to the Macau Syndicate. She's persuaded him to make one last gold run. A big one. I want you to stop him."

At last, Malloy thought, I'll have the bastard. "How far can I go?"

Knowing well what Malloy was asking, Trevelyan framed his reply carefully. "He's a citizen of this colony. You'll, of course, want to stay within the law. Other than that..." He spread his hands expansively, giving Malloy the sign he wanted.

"Will you back me?"

"If you mean protect you should you go too far and get caught again, no. I don't have to take that risk." Trevelyan stood up, indicating the interview was over. "As I understand it, you have a long-standing personal score to settle with the Snake Boat Man. That is why I chose you. I suggest you not let him get the better of you this time."

CHAPTER 8

A **LARGE** vegetable truck came for Mae Ling early in the morning. "I have good news for you," the matriarch said. "Your uncle will help you. A space has already been prepared in the truck where you must hide. Do not come out under any circumstances unless you are told."

Mae Ling noted how the driver and his two assistants were appraising her. The driver stepped forward, snatching her hat from her head. "He wishes to make sure your description matches with that given by your uncle," the matriarch said, seeing Mae Ling's startled reaction.

The driver motioned Mae Ling to move out of earshot, but she could still hear his voice raised in argument with the matriarch. "No," he was shouting in Cantonese, "that's an impossible price to pay—"

"What price?" Mae Ling asked. "For what?"

"It doesn't concern you, your uncle will pay," an elder said, taking her arm and steering her toward the truck. "You have brought enough danger to our village, now get inside."

The villagers were standing in a semicircle around her, leaving her with no choice but to climb into the back. The door was slammed shut and padlocked. She found the hiding place hollowed out between the crates of vegetables and lay in the semidarkness while the truck lurched over the potholed road toward another village. . . .

A short time later the truck stopped. Another young girl, obviously frightened, was helped into the back, holding tight to her worldly possessions in a small cloth-bound bundle.

They drove on, then stopped again. This time two girls were herded into the back, one of them so badly beaten that she was barely conscious. There was little point in pretense now as one of the assistants stationed himself in the narrow space left between the crates and the back door of the truck.

The wood-slatted sides of the truck let in just enough light to make out shapes, and the noise from the truck muffled the girls' voices from the guard. Mae Ling helped tend to the injured girl. "Who are you?" she whispered.

"She not hear you," the girl who had been brought in with her said. She spoke with the thick accent of a peasant from the Gwangadung Province. "So-Yun my name. And you . . . ?"

"Mae Ling."

So-Yun turned. "That is who?" She motioned to the fourth girl crouching in the corner.

"I don't know," Mae Ling said. "She's too frightened to speak."

"Hey you," So-Yun called to her, "what name?"

"Ying Ch'ao," the girl blurted. "We now go which-place?" she asked, realizing something was very wrong.

"You not know, *heya?*" So-Yun asked.

"No," Mae Ling said quietly, bracing herself against the bumpy road. "Why is this girl hurt?"

"I talk with this one piece girl little bit only," So-Yun said. "She immigrant, like us, was brought by Triad and used as prostitute."

"How could they make her do that—?"

"Triad have system called stamping their property. Take one piece girl some place away, rape her until she no fight them. Do what they say." So-Yun's voice had lost some of its toughness as she spoke.

"They wouldn't dare," Mae Ling whispered, shaken. "I told them that my relative was a policeman."

"Triad see you no reach him until they plenty sure you no have way back from life they teach you," So-Yun said. "One piece girl tell me even after Triad sell you to brothel they send protectors, escort you all time, use you maybe fifteen customers a day. They think this one piece girl broken in but she escape, now take back and Triad use her, make warning to others."

"If you knew all this, why did you let them put you in the truck?" Mae Ling felt a sickening jolt of desperation go through her.

"I learn last night only by whispering through wall to one piece girl, then what I could do? I would run away they catch me, or police catch me, send me back China. No," So-Yun said determinedly, "let them take me safe journey Hong Kong, then I escape. You can help me?"

"What do you want to do?"

"Trouble," So-Yun admitted. "I think not they put guard in truck. We have kill him, eh?"

"How?" Mae Ling asked. "He's enormous."

"I have knife." So-Yun drew out a flat-handled stiletto that had been strapped to her inner thigh.

"... If we somehow manage that, what then?"

"We wait truck in Hong Kong open. I put knife in face of first man I see then, he scream, we run."

Mae Ling realized it was the best they could hope for. Once we're out of the truck we'll split up—it will make it harder for them to catch us...

"You can help us?" So-Yun turned to Ying Ch'ao, who had not moved from her crouched position in the corner.

"No," Ying Ch'ao said, nervously. "Oh no, I not kill guard, not with knife."

"This one piece man maybe rape you in few hours' time," So-Yun told her angrily. "That make it easier?"

"Leave her alone," Mae Ling said. "She'd be no help to us anyway."

"But you help me?" So-Yun asked.

"Yes... have you ever killed a man with a knife?"

"No, you have?"

"No... but I know something about it."

"Where you learn? Were you Red Guards?"

"Something like that. You had better give me the knife."

"He big man," So-Yun said. "Fat, ribcage protect his heart."

"I am going to try for his throat. It's more difficult, but with a small knife there's a better chance of killing him."

"You make sound we come back kill you," So-Yun told Ying Ch'ao. "Tell me you," she said with renewed respect for Mae Ling, "what want me do, eh?"

Mae Ling moved closer to the girl and whispered her plan. She knew it might not work, but it was all they had...

THE TRUCK turned onto a tarred surface, making the ride smoother. The guard was crouched in a narrow space by the door, his back resting against a barricade of vegetable crates that almost reached the roof. He heard the noise of someone crawling over the crates above his head and glanced up. So-Yun grinned at him roguishly. "Hey you," the guard ordered, "get back." She ignored him and climbed down to the floor.

"Listen," she said in the same dialect he used, "I have got to take a pee."

She was mocking him with her hips. "Too bad. You have to wait until we get to Hong Kong." He heard the noise of another body coming over the crates and landing lightly beside him.

"This my friend," So-Yun said as Mae Ling smiled demurely at him. "She has got to take a pee too. How long till we get to Hong Kong?"

"About—" The guard saw the flash of steel out of the corner of his eye but was too late to stop it. With all her might Mae Ling plunged the blade through the carotid artery and up toward his brain. A rush of sticky, warm blood spilled over her hands. The guard slid down, his heels drumming on the floor in a death spasm that lasted no more than a few seconds.

So-Yun checked for a pulse. "Dead," she pronounced.

"Thank all the gods." Mae Ling breathed a sign of relief. "I had nightmares about what he would have done to us if we'd only wounded him." She searched his body, found a knife and a bone-handled garroting wire. "All right," she called to Ying Ch'ao, "you can come out now." There was no answer.

"We her leave," So-Yun said disgustedly.

"What about the injured girl?"

"Can do nothing." So-Yun shrugged. "I know name her relatives. I tell them where to look for her if I get away."

They covered the body as best they could with vegetables, and Mae Ling used the inside of her tunic to wipe the blood from her hands and arms. The truck had climbed over Razor Hill and was entering the Eastern Pass to the city. They heard the scream of jets landing and taking off from Kai Tak Airport. "It can't be long now," Mae Ling said. "Where are you going? Have you got relatives?"

"I have boyfriend wait me. He swim across Deep Bay last year. Better I not tell you where in case they catch you." The truck was crawling along in heavy traffic. It pulled onto the side of the road and parked. The two girls first heard the engine switch off, then the cab doors slammed shut.

"They come now," So-Yun said. "Remember, you through run crowd, let all people see knife. No one person want stop you."

A fist banged on the door. "Is everything okay in there?"

So-Yun braced herself. "Okay..." She grunted, imitating the dead guard.

The padlock was unlocked, the door swung open. Mae Ling was temporarily blinded by the light. She made out a figure poised to swing himself over the tailgate and went for him with her knife raised. The driver let out a startled yell as the knife slashed a deep gash across his face, narrowly missing his eye.

So-Yun threw herself at the driver's assistant and they both sprawled on the ground. Mae Ling, landing on top of them, stabbed at his hand as he grappled with her for the knife. The driver was clutching his slashed face, screaming for help. They heard the sound of footsteps rushing toward them along the road. "Run," So-Yun shouted.

The girls charged up a flight of steps and found themselves in the resettlement area behind Kai Tak Airport—massive slums in the sky where the refugees who had been granted sanctuary and the boat people who had lived afloat in Sampan Harbors all their lives had been resettled in thirty-story apartment buildings. They ran through canyonlike spaces between buildings where wash hung from long bamboo poles from each apartment, and the children gazed down through wire meshing strung across the balconies to keep them from falling out. Behind them the girls heard the word being passed to the street gangs, the most junior members of the Triad who controlled petty crimes in the resettlement areas.

A street market ran the length of a road. "In here," So-Yun panted. She touched Mae Ling's arm just before they plunged in among the noonday shoppers. "Tsòi kìn, good-bye," she said, and disappeared.

It started to rain, the water dribbling off the tarpaulin roofs hung with naked light bulbs. Mae Ling elbowed her way through the shoppers who milled before fish-sellers or fingered squawking chickens in wicker cages. She pushed past butchers displaying their bloody meat beneath red light bulbs and stalls selling fresh fruit, vegetables and twenty different kinds of rice. For the moment it was the perfect place to hide; carefully she put the knife inside her jacket. Music blared, joss sticks burned and the smells of different foods cooking was everywhere. It was her introduction to the slums of Hong Kong, and she let herself be swept along by the crowds.

At the end of the market was a sign indicating the direction of the mass transit railway. Mae Ling had been told about that. She ran down the steps, joined a queue in front of one of the computer-operated turnstiles. It took her only a short time to realize how it worked. She pressed her body against the young man in front of her, who didn't mind... it wasn't until some time later that he realized his pocket had been picked. She quickly changed direction, bought herself a ticket and joined another queue.

MAE LING got off the train and found her way into a small shop in the Hanoi Road. The door was closed and barred. She kept knocking on it until a man appeared from the window above and called down to her that the shop was closed.

"Where is the owner?" Mae Ling demanded.

"He's gone."

"Where? I must see him."

"Who are you?"

Mae Ling gave her father's name. The effect was startling. The window slammed shut, and a few seconds later the door opened and she was dragged inside... After Chairman Mao Tse-tung's death the left wing, his wing, of the Communist Party went through a series of defeats culminating in the downfall of his widow and her supporters, and Hong Kong was to have been the base for carrying on the left wing's revolutionary struggle, of which Mae Ling's father was a part... "You are Ho Chen, my father's contact here?" Mae Ling asked.

The man nodded. "When he didn't come I realized that your father had been captured."

"He will *not* betray you."

Ho Chen was not convinced. "Once he's in the hands of the security apparatus he will have no alternative... I've instructed our people to leave at once. Even now I am packing—"

"—Where are you going?"

"To Singapore, on this afternoon's flight. We will meet there."

"Please, take me with you."

"Have you travel papers?"

"No, nothing."

"Then it's impossible. And as the daughter of General Li Ch'en the British and Communist agents will soon be scouring Hong Kong for you. Did your father give you anything for me?"

"No, he destroyed all his papers before he was captured. But I have

100

something of value..." Mae Ling tore a small hole in the lining of her jacket and unstitched a slim waterproof package. "Instructions from my mistress Chaing-Ching." She used Madame Mao Tse-tung's revolutionary name. "She is ill, without friends and sentenced to die. Among these papers is a message that is deeply personal to her; the chairman sent it in the last days of his life."

Ho Chen opened the package, unrolled a single sheet of fine rice paper. The brushstrokes were distinctive for Chairman Mao Tse-tung— in addition to being one of the world's great revolutionary leaders he had also been a noted calligrapher and poet... "You have been wronged," he wrote to his wife. "Today we are parting for different worlds. May each keep his peace. These few words may be my last message to you. Human life is limited, but revolution knows no bounds. In the struggle of the last ten years I have tried to reach the peak of revolution. I was not successful, but you must continue. If you fail your body will shatter, your bones will break..."

The chairman had accurately foretold his wife's fate, Ho Chen thought grimly. "Is this the original?" he asked, holding the paper reverently.

"It is. My mistress charged me to take it out of China to safety. Her relationship with the chairman was demeaned throughout her trial. She asks that when we bring China back to the path of the true revolution this message be published so our people will know she acted as she did on instructions from the chairman... Take it," Mae Ling said, knowing that her presence was endangering Ho Chen. "Keep it safe. Somehow I will join you in Singapore."

Mae Ling then left quickly. She took a train out to the Tse Wan housing area, where she found herself among more towering blocks of apartments, the only difference among them being the number painted in huge letters on each building's side. She searched for the address of her only remaining contact in Hong Kong—a distant cousin of her father. She hoped that as a policeman, a senior sergeant with more than thirty years' service behind him, he would protect her. If she could prove their relationship, then according to Chinese custom he was obliged to do so.

Mae Ling knocked on the door of an apartment seventeen stories above the ground. A woman in her late fifties answered it. "Mother," Mae Ling said respectfully, "I bring you greetings from your family." The woman slammed the door in her face. Again Mae Ling knocked until the woman grudgingly opened the door a crack.

"Go away," the woman said in a low voice, knowing by the shabby clothes and accent that the girl was an illegal immigrant.

"I want to see my father's cousin," Mae Ling insisted.

"He's not here."

"When will he be back?"

"Later. Go *away*. He help you, he lose pension then whole family starve. Go," the woman said angrily, pushing her to break her hold on the door.

Mae Ling was too weary to argue any more. She let the door close.

"Wait," the woman called from the inside. Mae Ling heard her grumbling inside the flat, then she opened the door wide enough to throw out a handful of coins and paper money. "This all we can give," she said. "Tell no piece person you came here."

MALLOY WAS working late in his cramped apartment in Pok Fulam when he heard a scratch at his door. He was immediately alert; he'd received no announcement of a visitor from the doorman. The scratch came again. He put down the dog-eared file on Nicholai, the Snake Boat Man, that he'd been reading, slipped a gun into the pocket of his robe and opened the door.

Mae Ling, exhausted, was leaning against the doorjamb. She had been walking around for hours before she found his address. Malloy recognized her immediately. She said nothing, only raised her face to look uneasily at him, trying to hide her fear of him. But she had run out of alternatives. He was truly her last resort.

Malloy glanced quickly down the corridor before he pulled her inside. "Anybody see you come?" His fingers painfully gripped her arm.

She shook her head, dizzy with hunger and fear. "No one. I slipped past the doorman..."

"Who else knows you're in Hong Kong?"

She told him about the Triad, leaving out the part about the murder. She was fairly certain that the Triad would dispose of the body quietly rather than risk police involvement.

"Your escape will have lost them a lot of face," Malloy warned, thinking swiftly. "Not to mention the money they stood to make on you. They'll still be looking for you. Anyone else?"

"I went to relatives but they wouldn't let me in." Mae Ling's voice was bitter.

"I'm not surprised. Do you know what the penalty for aiding an illegal is now?"

She shook her head.

"The head of the family picks up five years' imprisonment." He could

102

see that she was nearly dead on her feet. "Here, drink this," he said, but with no kindness in his voice. She felt the raw spirit burn its way down to her stomach, warming her. "I'll get you something to eat."

She sat at the kitchen table trying not to wolf down the food he'd set before her. "Why are you helping me?" she asked when she finished.

"I'd say that's my business," Malloy told her. "Now get out of those clothes and take a bath."

Malloy waited until he heard her lower her body into the water, then walked into the bathroom. She had no choice but to let him stare at her.

"Go on," he ordered.

Slowly she began to soap herself and as she did he leaned over the tub, letting his fingers leave a lingering trail of foam on her stomach and down into the silken black hair between her thighs.

She had driven all thoughts of Jenny from his mind—she was more than just beautiful, she was exquisite, captivating, with a body as perfectly proportioned as any he'd ever dreamed about... He'd known from the moment he saw her that he wanted her, that he'd give anything to possess her, and now that she'd come to him for refuge he could do it his way...

The dangers in harboring her only inflamed his lust, and he reached for her, not willing or able to wait until she finished her bath. "Please..." she tried to shrug his hands off her shoulders... "tomorrow, I'll let you do it tomorrow... tonight I'm too tired—" She gasped as he took hold of her hair and wrenched her out of the bath, half carrying, half dragging her, all wet and soapy, to the bedroom, where he threw her onto the bed. She was too frightened to protest, although instinctively she tried to draw herself into a ball and her hands went down in a feeble attempt to protect herself.

Malloy pulled his robe off. She couldn't avoid seeing his blood-gorged cock jutting between his legs. All she could think was to keep herself away from it. Her weariness now gave way to panic as she frantically writhed across the double bed.

Malloy caught her easily, forced her legs apart. His back arched as he drove himself into her. She opened her mouth to scream at the pain but he quickly covered it with his hand... on and on he thrust into her, making her feel as if she were splitting apart. She bit his fingers, raked his back, but the more she fought against him the more he seemed to enjoy it. The fire between her thighs had spread to her stomach. As he rode her exhausted body she felt it would never end, she could take no more, surely she would die...

His rhythm slowed, then he began to pound again, harder and harder.

She was so full of him, so possessed by him—it seemed her entire consciousness was centered between her thighs. The pain was consuming. She had always been able to cope with pain, but now she felt the heat of a fire that burned with a different flame.

And, in spite of herself, she began to meet his thrusts, arching her hips against his. Malloy was startled. "Damn me, you gorgeous bitch," he muttered, half intrigued, and half disappointed. "You're *enjoying* it, by God..."

He took her body, using it in every imaginable position, again and again until the room looked as if a hurricane had swept through it as, finally, they slept sprawled together on the mattress, the bedclothes scattered over the floor....

The alarm went off at seven A.M. Malloy, naked and chilled by the air-conditioning, stumbled from the bed into the kitchen to make himself some coffee. Mae Ling followed and stood draped in a sheet in the doorway. She said nothing, unsure where she stood with him.

"Can you cook breakfast *gwilo*-style?"

She shook her head. "I can learn... I can learn anything." She knew the effect that would have on him. It was necessary, she reminded herself. She had nowhere else to go...

Late for Trevelyan's morning security briefing, he dressed quickly and as he did he told her to stay. "And don't answer the phone. Don't touch anything in the drawers. Don't do *anything*. Understand?" He went to the closet and took out a thigh-slit *cheongsam* that only the most delicate Chinese figure could do justice to. "Tonight when I get home, be wearing this. I'll bring you paint for your nails and your face. I want you to look like a tart. Then I'm going to rip it off you, so see that you're wearing nothing underneath."

104

CHAPTER 9

STANLEY PRISON is a modern, top security, white-walled structure set on the edge of Tai Tam Bay. It was visiting hours there as Nicholai waited his turn to be shown to an interview window.

Tom Hakker, escorted by a prison warden, took his place on the other side of the window. His head was shaved as a protection against lice, and his pale pinched face had an unhealthy pallor from the long years spent in prison. He waited until the warden had moved away before he asked, "Why are you here?"

"I'm looking for a gunner," Nicholai said, "and you're the best I know."

"Damn right I am," Hakker said, "but I'm not getting much practice in here."

"How much longer have you got?"

Hakker shrugged. "Twelve years if I'm real lucky. Why? You planning to make another run?"

"Maybe."

"Could you get me out of here?"

Nicholai glanced over Hakker's shoulder to the high barred windows and alarms. "It looks like a tough place to break out of."

"You've got contacts—or if you don't any longer you can get them. Sounds like you might be needing me..." The pinched, hollow-eyed face took on a cunning expression. "Man, I was good, really good with a point five. If you get your ass in trouble you're going to need a man like me."

"What did you do?"

"You saying you don't know?"

"No."

"That bastard Ah Chuen," Hakker said. "When the cops picked me up I tried to get a message to you, figured you'd help one of your old crew. It looks like Ah Chuen didn't pass it on. That servant of yours was always trying to protect you. He sent a message back saying not to contact you again. And they had my ass in a sling—"

"What happened?" Nicholai interrupted. Hakker was an American, a latecomer who had joined his crew just before the boat paid off. Nicholai's sense of loyalty to him was limited.

"It was that girl I married. Remember her? Used to follow me around like a shadow?"

Nicholai remembered. She hadn't been much more than a child when Hakker bought her off one of the houses in the Street of Happiness in the bad old days of Macau.

"Well," Hakker said, "Fat Sui Leong didn't like the way I was treating her, or maybe he wanted her himself, I don't know. One night we got drunk and started a knife fight and somehow she got in the way and I killed her. I killed Fat Sui Leong too. Hell, if we'd been in Macau with old Da Costa as chief of police it wouldn't have been a problem. A man could buy his way out of trouble there. But we'd all moved to Hong Kong by then and the bastards here put me away for murder. If I hadn't been so drunk that night the judge swore he would have hung me. Anyway, I got life. Unless..." Hakker paused, his eyes narrowing. "You're ready to get me out of here, I know you can do it. All I need is a little help from the outside..."

To hell with you, Nicholai thought as he got up from his chair and signaled the warden that the interview was over. Fat Sui Leong had been a good friend of his.

"Hey, where you going?"

Nicholai leaned in close to the grill. "Hakker, you always were a vicious bastard. You stay where you are. I'll find another gunner."

"You bastard," Hakker screamed as he pounded against the window. "One day I'll get out of here, I'll settle with you too..." His voice trailed Nicholai as he made his way down the long prison corridor...

IT TOOK just under three hours to sail from Hong Kong to Cheung Chau Island. Nicholai made the trip hoping to find Keng Po, the last member of his old crew.

The lovingly restored teakwood junk, now rarely used, entered the harbor and maneuvered among the hundreds of fishing junks that packed the shoreline. A community of some five thousand Chinese gave birth, worked and died on board these junks, rarely setting foot on land.

Wen Yuan, a seasoned, craggy-faced boatman, brought the junk alongside the pier. Nicholai jumped, landing surefootedly on the slippery planks. After easing the junk's bows back toward the harbor where Wen Yuan would lie off and wait for him, he joined the press of people crowding along the narrow seafront street. All along the landward side rickety shops pressed lopsidedly against one another, crowded with a jumble of brightly painted Chinese signs. In the middle of the street was a fresh fruit and vegetable market. Among the stalls were tables protected from the sun by brightly colored awnings.

Udo was waiting at the far table. He had finished his *dim sum* and was sipping a bowl of green tea. "I got your message," Nicholai said as he drew up a chair. "Where is he?"

The big man stirred uncomfortably. "Remember what the old Keng Po was like?"

Nicholai nodded. The Keng Po he remembered had bright eyes, the look of a fox terrier and no scruples whatsoever. He was a born fixer with a superb talent for bribery. His greatest coup was when he had managed to spirit away two pedestal-mounted machine guns from a shipment the Macau Syndicate was slipping through the blockade to Communist China. It was during a particularly lawless time along the coast, and the machine guns had provided their boat with an almost unbeatable edge over its competitors.

"Well, you're not going to believe me," Udo said, "so you'd better see for yourself." He led the way through narrow streets to the Pak Tai Temple. A crowd dressed in white mourning clothes thronged the entrance as a procession of Buddhist monks filed past, clashing cymbals and ringing hand bells.

"Who died?" Nicholai asked, afraid it was Keng Po.

"The senior headman of this island. The monks have made the journey from their monastery over on Lantau Island especially for his funeral."

Udo nudged Nicholai. "Look." He nodded in the direction of one of the approaching monks. At first Nicholai did not recognize Keng Po . . . his head was shaved, his small figure swathed in a coarse saffron robe, and amber-colored prayer beads fell in a long curve from his neck.

"I don't believe it," Nicholai muttered. He could have imagined Keng Po as the incense master in a Triad, a business tycoon, or even in jail—but never as a Buddhist monk.

Keng Po was equally startled to see his old boss. Dropping out of the procession he thrust his begging bowl at Nicholai, who numbly stuffed some money into it and received a blessing.

Keng Po understood right away why Nicholai and Udo had sought him out. He motioned to them to follow him into the annex of the temple. From where the three men stood they could see the altar lit by tiers of candles wreathed in incense smoke.

"Another run?" Keng Po asked quietly.

Nicholai nodded.

"Who else is left?" Keng Po said, turning to Udo.

"Only you, me and Nicholai. But that's a pretty good base to start from. And only you know where the *East Wind*'s guns are hidden."

Keng Po paused for a moment, his eyes resting on the distant altar before he turned to the two men. The look on his face was their answer.

"They're buried beneath my monastery. When do you leave?" he asked Nicholai.

"As soon as I can get a crew together."

"It's been a long time, Nicholai." Keng Po bowed his head in a gesture of regret toward the Buddha figure dominating the altar. He had found a more pressing loyalty that he couldn't ignore. "Quickly," he said, "find me some clothes to change into before I lose my nerve . . ."

KENG PO jumped aboard Nicholai's junk. The others had found him a pair of slacks, a shirt and a baseball cap to cover his bald head. Even so, he felt a strange shyness among his old friends. It was going to take some time to emerge from the anonymity of a strict Buddhist order. "Where do we go now?" he asked as the junk left Cheung Chau and set a westerly course.

"We're going to make a trial run," Nicholai told him. "I want to see how much our old smuggling routes have changed. We'll start in the Soko Islands."

HALF A day later the junk wound its way through the chain of islands that marked the southwestern limit of Hong Kong's territorial waters. Thirty miles to the west across the estuary lay Macau. To the north and not much further up river was Canton, the principal city of China's Kwangtung Province. The great Pearl River estuary that flowed into the South China Sea at this point divided the three, which together comprised an area rich in history, the jealously guarded gateway to China.

The junk sailed through a cluster of small islands covered with green scrub and rock and largely uninhabited. The Snake Boat Man scanned the sloping shoreline, noting the coves with their white sand beaches and the rocks that jutted just above the sea. He was refreshing his memory of half-forgotten reference points...much of Nicholai's success as a smuggler lay in his detailed knowledge of Hong Kong's craggy coastline. He knew every rocky bar, cove and channel on each of the two hundred and forty islands within Hong Kong's territorial waters, and the same number again of islands in China's waters, any of which he could use to hide from the Hong Kong police.

"We've got company," Keng Po said as he approached Nicholai. He was pointing over Nicholai's shoulder to a sleek gray patrol boat flying the red flag of China and hurtling through the sea on a course parallel to theirs—until it abruptly changed course and veered south.

Nicholai focused his binoculars on it. "*Hoi kung*, seventy-three-foot class," he said, "armed with twin point-five machine guns and capable of forty knots." Suddenly another vessel rounded one of the islands, skimming like a flat stone over the surface, churning up curtains of white spray from its air cushions as it converged on the trespassing *hoi kung*'s wake. "British Royal Navy hovercraft, Rolls-Royce-powered, speed over fifty knots. It's shadowing the *hoi kung* along the international boundary... The British have established a coast watcher's station at Shek Tse Po equipped with radar and the latest night observation devices. They'll have sent in the hovercraft. When we come through here from Macau they'll be the first to pick us up."

"I thought you'd retired," Keng Po said. "Where did you get all this information?"

"Oh, I kept in touch." Nicholai allowed himself a smile. "Just in case." He called to Wen Yuan at the helm. "I've seen enough, take the junk down to the San-man and Tan Kan islands, then we'll sail into Hong Kong."

IT WAS late afternoon when the junk rounded the Stanley Peninsula on Hong Kong Island. A lighthouse flashed on top of a two-hundred-fifty-foot-high cliff that rose starkly above the sea. Beside it stood a sophisticated satellite and radar-tracking station. Keng Po looked up at the complex array of aerials and dishes. "That wasn't here when we last used this route," he said, obviously disturbed. "At fifty miles those men on the radar can count the hairs on your head."

"From you all they'll get is a reflection," Udo said, grinning. They passed Stanley, which was no longer a village but a mushrooming town. The junk sailed on into Tai Tam Harbor below Mount Collinson. In the 1960s it had been small, sleepy sampan harbor. Now it was jampacked with junks, pleasure craft and some of the most expensive real estate in the world sprawled around its shoreline. "Goddamn," Udo said as he took in the changed complexion of the land. "It's only been fifteen years but I hardly recognize it. If we made a run into Stanley now we'd likely drop the gold off at somebody's front door."

The north side of the island, dominated by Victoria Harbor and the city, was to be avoided. The junk sailed on around the south coast, past Cape D'Aguilar and along Shek O and Big Wave Bay. Expensive homes now lined the cliffs above the beaches where they once landed gold.

"It's no good," Udo finally said. "This whole coastline is out for us."

"You're wrong," Nicholai told him. "The more crowded it is both on sea and land the more difficult it is for the British to spot us. We have to find a landing site near a road or at least a track we can get a truck onto. Crystal Lily will need to move the gold before the Hong Kong police can cordon and search the area. My first choice is still the island, but there's something I want to show you both."

Nicholai sailed his junk into Joss House Bay and anchored it before dawn in the lee of Junk Island. From there he could watch the eastern entrance to Victoria Harbor. "The Royal Navy has a fast attack craft," he told them. "It's the same class of boat as the *East Wind*, except it's forty years advanced. She patrols at night to catch the skin boats and returns around this time to harbor." . . .

As the misty gray dawn was breaking the men on the junk heard the high-pitched whine of what sounded like an aircraft approaching over the water. "H.M.S. *Scimitar*," Nicholai said. The sound grew louder, the whine becoming a howl, then a thunderous roar. A sleek, futuristically

110

designed attack boat barreled out of the mist and flashed past the anchored junk.

"She's spent a good night's hunting," Udo said. He had spotted in the lee of her raked bridge a group of illegals cowering under the eye of armed British sailors. Two huge jet exhaust-ports in her stern glowed an angry red, and her wash hit the junk, tossing it about like a matchbox.

"I've seen her enter and leave harbor but never this close," Nicholai said as the attack craft disappeared from sight. There was an unusual note of respect in his voice. "I believe she can do more than forty knots and she's equipped with the most modern detection devices. If she gets on our tail she's going to be hard to shake off."

"*Hau-ye*," Keng Po said, staring after the *Scimitar*. "I'm beginning to think we're crazy to try this . . . everything has changed while we've been away. Hovercraft, radar, jet boats—we never had to deal with those."

But Nicholai refused to accept defeat in advance. "Whatever the British have got," he said firmly, "I believe I can beat them."

"What if the Communist Hoi Kungs decide to intercept us when we cross the international waters between Macau and Hong Kong?" Keng Po challenged.

"I can outfox them too." He hoped.

Nicholai steered his junk out of Joss House Bay through the Fat Toung Mun Channel, a broad reef closing down to a rocky neck two hundred yards wide with swells breaking on either side. It was used by shipping during the day, and he had to put his helm hard over to avoid a tug pulling a rusted sand barge.

"They come through all time," Wen Yuan shouted over the sound of the engine. "Shortcut to Hong Kong."

The junk sailed east to the Ninepins, a rocky spine of islands jutting sharply over the horizon. The silhouette of the weather-worn cliffs changed constantly as they approached. Ships regularly avoided the Ninepins because of their treacherous reefs lying just below the water. Nicholai knew it was possible to take a boat through if the navigator could remember how the reefs lay in relation to the cliffs. "We'll come here," Nicholai said, "if we have to shake them off."

After he had practiced navigating the junk through the islands he set course to the north, searching for alternative landing sites if the police made it impossible for him to reach Hong Kong Island.

The New Territories, owned on lease from China, were less crowded and possessed spectacularly rugged scenery. To reach Rocky Harbor Nicholai took his junk through Sau-si-Mun, a channel so named by the Chinese because it was shaped like a key and difficult to navigate. Nicholai knew that it was dangerous to use this route even in calm seas, that in a swell it could be terrifying. There were only feet to spare between the rocks and the boat, and the waves built up in the middle. Nicholai had to draw on all his skill to bring the unwieldy junk hard over at exactly the right moment, then back into the center of the channel before tacking around another of its jagged, wave-lashed promontories. A white marker beacon, placed there by the police who used the channel, had been painted on the rocks of the promontory. On a hilltop above it lay the ruins of a monastery, supposedly haunted by the ghosts of the men who had lost their lives to Sau-si-Mun.

The roar of the surf, the sting of the wind-driven spray on his skin... Nicholai felt that after so many years away it was damn good to be alive... Keng Po glanced at him, saw the clear look of determination on his face. He understood well that Nicholai was testing his own nerve and skill and feeling more confident in the process...

The junk sailed into the shelter of Rocky Harbor. Stretching before them was a great flooded valley with just the ridges of the mountaintops showing. An empty, silent place, the distant hilltops barren of trees were colored in green and browns. It was a sea and landscape of very special beauty, dusted with a misty light.

They sailed on as the junk explored mile after mile of Rocky Harbor. On the right lay a new stone causeway; above it the High Island reservoir, and then Urn Island blocked their passage north. Nicholai turned and looked behind him to take in the whole expanse of Rocky Harbor from the tip of Urn Island to the islands at its mouth, feeling he could use the Sau-si-Mun Channel as an alternative escape route to the sea.

Now he steered the junk to the right side of Urn Island, where the water was green and narrowed like a river mouth with steep shrub-covered banks. He was looking for a landing place within reach of the road linking the High Island reservoir with the trunk roads through the New Territories to the city. At Tsen Chu Wen he found what he wanted. An old vehicle track came right down to a pier at the water's edge, and except for a few derelict houses the village was deserted.

He would try to land the gold on Hong Kong Island. If he failed, then this would be his choice for the final run. "I've seen enough," Nicholai called to his crew. "Let's go home."

CRYSTAL LILY left her rooms, making her way down the main stairway of the palace. She knew she should have waited until Nicholai was ready to speak to her, but she was impatient to see him again and couldn't restrain herself from going to the comprador's office, where she knew the two men were meeting.

Both got up as she entered. Nicholai's gray eyes searched her face for signs of stress—given her age and lack of experience in such matters, he was worried about how well she was holding up in the isolation of the palace, living with the knowledge of the danger that surrounded her. She *was* looking strained, he thought, but she left him in no doubt that she had untapped reserves of courage.

"Nicholai," she said warmly, relieved that he'd arrived in Macau safely, "have you planned your route?"

He nodded wordlessly, and although he offered no greeting, the warmth in his eyes assured her.

Nicholai unfolded the chart he'd brought. "I'll round Coloane," he said, pointing to the map, "and run deep into the South China Sea to avoid Communist patrols." He penciled a line down the ninety-first and forty-third longitude, joining them along the fifty-third latitude line. "Hong Kong's territory"—he indicated the area of land and islands within the square—"I'll cross the border here in the shelter of the Soko Islands."

"The British have established a coast watcher's station on the tip of Lantau Island," the comprador said, pointing to a spot northwest of the Sokos.

"I know," Nicholai said. "I'll create a diversion to draw the hovercraft stationed there away from me... My first choice for a landing spot is here"—he pointed to Tai Tam Harbor on the south side of Hong Kong Island. "The second"—Nicholai traced his finger around the rocky coastline—"is here below the cliffs of Shek O. If both those options fail I'll hide out in Communist waters beyond the Ninepins Islands, and then I'll make a final run in from the southeast to here." He traced the route through Rocky Harbor to the deserted hamlet he'd discovered by Urn Island. He turned to the comprador. "You must have your men waiting to unload the gold at each of these places."

"Use the third landing place only if you are in extreme difficulty," the comprador advised. "Its distance from Hong Kong makes it improbable that we will be able to hide the gold from the British land forces there before dawn."

When the meeting broke up Crystal Lily took Nicholai by the arm and led him to the Crystal Room. It was, as it was once for her father, her favorite room in the palace.

"Did you ever attend council meetings of the Syndicate?"

113

"No *gwilo* could attend," Nicholai said, wondering why she should ask such a question. "Nor did I ever have any desire to get that close to the inner sanctum."

"But you knew my father better than anyone," she said, trying to draw him out, to talk of her father and the old days of Macau.

Nicholai walked around her, resting his hands on the back of her father's carved chair. "I remember his weakness for indoor pistol practice." He smiled, teasing her. "You hid over there"—he pointed in the direction of the spy grill—"that last night and watched him fire off a round under the table to see, as he put it, who was the lucky man."

"Luckily Lao Ta and Yu Shik Lieu found me, but I can remember running through the palace as though all the devils were after me." Crystal found she could laugh at the memories now and turned to Nicholai, feeling a renewed surge of affection for him. "The only stories I ever heard of my father were those secretly told by the servants about how he built this palace on the blood of starving peasants. What happened to my mother?" she said, her mood suddenly becoming serious.

"Ask the comprador."

"I can't. He may have been involved in her... her murder, and if he thought I owed a blood debt against him it would affect his loyalty to me..."

She had a shrewd mind, Nicholai thought, when it came to understanding men... the fate of her mother must have haunted her for years and Nicholai knew that she was asking for the truth from him now.

"Your mother was a great beauty, high-born from one of the principal families in Macau. Your father married her to gain the social prestige he so badly wanted. She was terrified of him, so much so that one day shortly after the palace was completed she left—you, and everything she had. She begged for protection from the Catholic bishop of Macau, but he was a cowardly man. He waited three days before deciding to take her in, afraid of making an enemy of your father. By then it was too late... your mother was found drowned in the bay. Some people say it was suicide, others say your father ordered her death. I honestly don't know the truth of it..."

"Then unless I can force the truth out of Chang, who after all was executioner for my father, I will never know—"

"Stay away from Chang."

Crystal bit her lip; her feelings were becoming increasingly confused. In her heart she wanted to hate her father, but now that she was in his position, she was beginning more and more to identify with the beggar

114

who built the House of Sun. "My mother left to save her own life, yet she left me here defenseless," she said at last. "By running away she made my father lose face at a time in his struggle for power when... when he would really have no option but to punish her. She must have been a selfish, spoiled woman—"

"You support your father?" Nicholai was surprised at her ability to rationalize her mother's death.

"I understand him better now that I have taken his place," she admitted, beginning to recognize the loneliness that came with his position. "But I'll never forgive Chang, who certainly must have carried out her murder."

In so many ways now she reminded Nicholai of her father... While he could, in a sense, admire her for her strength, her quickness of mind, it bothered him to think of her life running the same course as his. "Weren't you happy in Hawaii?" he asked.

"Yes... but I also felt out of place..."

"Couldn't you have settled down, built a career for yourself there, married?"

She nodded. "A doctor offered me a *proper* life with him there." It was true, but she said it mockingly. "And there was a charming Irishman who even threatened to follow me here when I told him I was leaving."

"My God, Crystal, you had more than enough chances. Why did you come back?"

"Because Macau is in my blood. And I am my father's daughter."

"There's still time to give this up," he told her, ready to give up his own drive to prove himself again for her sake. "We can get out of Macau right now. I'd rather use my boat to run you to the Philippines than have you risk your life in a struggle against the Syndicate—"

"No, I'll never allow the likes of Thomas Wu to beat me. I'm committed to this struggle, Nicholai. For my father's sake as well as my own..."

"Crystal, you don't owe that old bastard. And you'll too quickly get the taste for absolute power. Believe me, Crystal, once you have it it's hard to give it up. But it'll corrupt you just as it did your father..."

Crystal stiffened at his words; her dark eyes flashed a dangerous warning. "You seem to disapprove of me, but what about your own life? Have you been so perfect?"

"No," Nicholai said evenly, refusing to back down to her anger. "There's much I've done that still haunts me, which is why I got you away from Macau when you were still a child. But you've none of the excuses your father had. Or I have. You've never had to watch one beggar choke another to death in a fight over a bowl of rice. In the year I joined the exodus from Shanghai more than twenty-nine thousand bodies were found in its rivers and streets. In Blood Alley behind the Bund on one winter's night alone the police picked up six hundred frozen bodies." His eyes were alive with the anger and pain of his memories. "What can you know of the kind of life that spawned men like your father and me?"

When Nicholai spoke like this, so obviously caring for her, wanting, as he always had, only the best for her, she remembered how she had grown up idolizing him, how much she still loved him...

And Nicholai, at the same time, was struck with the realization that he no longer felt for her as a child who had long ago needed him for a parent. His feelings were those of a man who found himself wanting her as a woman. Wanting her badly. And she sensed this...

They stood facing each other, and without thinking he took her by the shoulders, pulling her against him—then stopped.

He knew that he could not afford to allow their relationship to develop any further, or it would surely destroy them both. It took enormous willpower for him to let his arms drop. "I served your father," he said quietly, "and now, when you need me..."

Oh yes, I do, she thought, in more ways that one... But she could not bring herself to say so. Not now. She could, though, take some comfort from the way he looked at her... You want me too, I see it, I feel it in you when you look at me. She wanted him to take her into his arms, but she refused to tell him so...

"You must make a choice," Nicholai said. "If you're determined to assume power here, the absolute power needed for a woman to rule in the East, then you cannot have a relationship as a woman with any man..."

She well understood that by "any man" he meant himself.

"He will become your weakness rather than your strength, your servants will be envious of his access to you, and through him they'll plot to attack you. You must always be alone—just as your father was. It's the price you pay for power..."

Nicholai could see Crystal was not willing to accept this. She only thought he was trying to influence her to leave Macau, betraying the love and trust she'd put in him for so many years...

"I expect the power and wealth I've inherited will bring its own compensations," she said, wanting to hurt him as much as his seeming rejection had hurt her. "I see no reason to change my mind now. *I will not.*"

"So be it. But play each man against the other, as your father did. I assure you, Lao Ta and your comprador will resent any lover of yours, but that's the risk you take. Remember that you must trust no one. I guarantee that your enemies will strike at you through the one you trust the most."

Night was falling; the stars were beginning to come out over the bay. It was now safe enough to travel. "I have to go, my junk is waiting to take me back to Hong Kong." He walked to the door, then turned to her.

"Nicholai," she said, her voice sounding vulnerable. "What about you? Can I trust in you still?"

"You know the answer," he said, and left.

CHAPTER 10

"WELL?" SUPERINTENDENT MALLOY glanced up as his assistant, Inspector Rem Choy, came into their third floor office in the Royal Hong Kong police building.

"The Snake Boat Man's definitely trying to contact his old crew," Rem Choy said, slipping into a chair.

"Has he had any success?"

"None that I know of, but even if he doesn't he shouldn't have too much trouble recruiting a new one."

Choy's obvious remark rankled Malloy; he needed facts and he wasn't going to allow a subordinate's inefficiency to deter him this time...

"Have you got anything we can use against him yet?"

"Nothing. Nor are we likely to until he actually makes his run. Oh, he's going to make another run, I'm dead certain of that. Our *mae chi*"—

he used the Chinese slang for informers—"all have the word."

"I suppose we can expect no help from Da Costa in Macau?"

Inspector Choy shrugged. "That's the Snake Boat Man's old stomping ground. What I still can't figure out is what the Triad intends to do with all that gold if he can land it here—"

"—Well, now you know what's foremost on the secretary for security's mind these days," Malloy said abruptly. The rest of the staff gave Malloy high marks as a professional, but few if any liked him—he was known as a bully, but damned good at his job. Rem Choy was one of the few who wasn't intimidated by Malloy—he knew how to handle him, and simply tolerated his gruff manner and insults.

"Oh, and there's one other thing that's just come in," Choy reported. "Remember the girl who escaped that night you took General Li Ch'en? Well, the I.I. patrols still haven't found her and Peking's raising hell. It turns out she was Li Ch'en's daughter and they know she was on that boat with him. According to their report she's quite some lady. She was attached to Madame Mao Tse-tung's staff during the last days of the Gang of Four. We now know that General Li Ch'en's plan was to secure a temporary base outside China from which to attack the present leadership in Peking. She was supposed to help him. They had documents from Madame Mao linking their cause with hers and the late chairman's. They hoped to use it to stir up trouble with the left-wing cadres here. Li Ch'en didn't have the documents with him so Peking figures she must have them—and she's loose somewhere in Hong Kong."

The news hit Malloy like a kick in the stomach. For the first time in many years he felt genuine fear. My God, he thought, twenty years in Special Branch and I've let that bitch set me up. He could imagine what the Communists would do to him if they found out she was operating from *his* apartment...

"It's all in here." Choy slid the report across Malloy's desk. He noticed the blood had suddenly drained from Malloy's face. "Anything wrong? What's the matter?"

"I'm fine," Malloy said quickly. "I want you to brief our men. Tell them to put the squeeze on the waterfront. Let the boat people know that anyone recruited by the Snake Boat Man can figure on spending the rest of his life in Stanley Jail. And just so they realize we're not fooling around, shake a few of their leaders down, hard. They'll understand that there's no place left in Hong Kong for so-called legends." He grabbed the report, started to go through it.

"Now get out of here," he told Rem Choy. "I've got work to do."

119

* * *

MAE LING heard the key grind in the front door lock of the apartment. As she went to unlatch it Malloy burst through the door. "Bitch," he said, kicking the door closed behind him. He slapped her hard across the face. "You bloody little bitch." At first she thought he was acting out another of his fantasies and remained where she'd fallen on the floor. But the look on his face told her this was much more than a sex game.

"Tell me again," Malloy said, stalking around her. She braced herself, certain that his boot would land in her ribs at any moment. "Where was it you came from?"

"Shanghai," she said, hoping she sounded convincing.

"And your father's dead?"

"Yes, yes." Panic took hold of her as she realized just what this man was capable of doing. Her dress had ridden up and she tried to use her body to distract him. He was not interested...

"And your mother and younger brother are living in poverty waiting for you to make enough money to send for them?"

"Yes, I've already told you that—"

"Liar, you're a liar." He hit her again across the mouth, then knelt down to grab her hair, lifting her face to his. "Now tell me the truth before I beat it out of you. Did you really think you could make such a fool out of me? Do you know who I am?"

Mae Ling *did* know—and she also knew she had no place else to go.

During the night Malloy thought that he'd fallen half in love with her, but now he was like a man waking up from a spell. Any kindness he'd shown her was gone, replaced by an overwhelming desire to get back at her for humiliating him.

He had checked carefully before going into the building to make sure he was not walking into a trap set up by her left-wing friends. "Don't move." He released her, throwing her back to the floor.

She watched as he searched the apartment, looking for documents that he thought might have been planted there, ripping out drawers, turning over the bed, throwing clothes from his dresser. He searched the bathroom, the kitchen, still found nothing. "All right, damn you, where are they?"

"What? What are you looking for?"

"The documents you and your father brought with you."

"There *are* no documents. My father threw them over the side of the sampan when we saw we would be captured." She read the violence in Malloy's eyes and flinched before he struck her again. "You *have* to

120

believe me, we knew we would be searched. Think..."—she used all her powers of persuasion to try to convince him—"if you had been in our place, what would you have done? We hoped that without the documents to identify us, we could still pass as refugees."

"All right, you bitch. Give me the addresses of your contacts here. The people who were going to help you—where are they?" He tightened his grip on her hair. "*Now.*"

"Nothing," Mae Ling gasped. "I had nothing... my father held all the papers and he destroyed them. It was safer that way. Why else did you think I came here? If I had contacts I would have gone to them—"

"—And that relation you went to for help?"

"His name is Lao Ch'en, a retired deck sergeant in the police. He's not involved. He knows no one, nothing led to him. He was to be used as a fallback only if everything else went wrong."

Malloy half believed her. He knew that her father was a professional like himself, and he'd keep everything from the girl—which is what Malloy himself would have done.

"You two didn't really believe you could raise enough support for Madame Mao Tse-tung? She's finished, forgotten. No one here is going to help that old bitch anyway."

"The workers in China are disillusioned with the government's modernization program," Mae Ling said defensively. "Many thousands of senior officials lost their positions when the new regime took power. They are ready to unite with us—"

"You're five years too late." He still didn't quite believe her story, but he was too concerned with saving his own skin to worry about any threat she might pose to the colony.

"What are you going to do with me?"

Malloy ignored her, left her huddled against the wall while he went to pour himself a drink, wondering how best to get rid of her.

He'd always intended to kick her out once he'd satisfied himself with her. But that was when he had thought of her as just another refugee who would sink into the Hong Kong underworld without so much as a ripple. If any questions had been asked it would have been his word against hers. That risk was acceptable. But this girl was different—she was no simple peasant, and if she so desired she could identify his apartment, his clothes and personal possessions well enough to satisfy people in his own department that she'd been there. And he knew too well that most of them would be only too anxious to believe her. He needed some way to get her out of Hong Kong and back to China, where the Peking government would deal with her. The immigration authorities would have to catch her, he reasoned. But it had to be done when she was clear of him and in such a way as to compromise her so that if she did try to incriminate him it would look like a frame. After all, her father had been in a position to know something about who he was...

His eyes went now to his briefcase, which he'd dropped by the door. It contained the file on the Snake Boat Man... and an idea began to form in his mind. He thought he saw a way he could use the one to trap the other, destroying them both. The more he thought about it the more the notion appealed to him...

"Maybe helping you wasn't such a bad idea after all." His tone wasn't quite so threatening now. "You may not know this, but your cousin was a senior police sergeant in the marine section in the days when they hunted the Snake Boat Man. He knew him well."

"The Snake Boat Man?" Mae Ling asked warily. She guessed that Malloy was concocting something that could hardly be good for her.

"He's an old man by your standards," Malloy said contemptuously. "Instead of living like a fat cat in a mansion on the Peak he ought to have rotted in jail these last twenty years. You're going to help me put him there."

"How? What must I do?" She didn't care how he answered—if this was a chance to save herself, well, she'd take it...

"What you're good at, you beautiful lying bitch. Spy on him for me. Make him fall for you. Then you'll report to me. Now get up and come over here." He waited for her impatiently, then opened his briefcase and took out a file. "In the next twelve hours I'm going to brief you fully on this man. He's no fool so pay attention, because tomorrow you're going back out on the streets. It's up to you to find a way to reach him—"

"I *cannot* go back on the streets. Please... the Triad will pick me up. They're looking for me, you said so yourself..."

She wondered whether to tell him about the murder but decided against it. It would only give him more to use against her.

"You've no choice."

"You know what they'll do to me." She raised her face to him, her lovely brown eyes looking directly at him. "Do you have no feelings for me at all?"

"Look at it this way," Malloy said. "If the police catch you, you'll be sent straight back to China, where as you know they'll execute you. On the other hand, if the Triad gets you, the worst that can happen to me is that instead of screwing you for free I'll have to pay for it. Either way I win and you lose. Do we understand each other?"

She nodded.

"Good, then you play it strictly my way, and if I get the Snake Boat Man, I'll see that you get a ticket out of here." He needed to give her some hope...

"To where?"

He shrugged. "Thailand, the Philippines, Singapore. Where do you want to go?"

"I have relations who would help me in Singapore," she said, allowing her need to hope get the better of her.

"I'll remember that," Malloy told her. And see that she never reached them...

NICHOLAI AND Keng Po sat side-by-side in a tiny sampan that was being paddled from the stern across the rain-squalled waters of Aberdeen Harbor by a straw-hatted old woman.

"The man's a lunatic," Keng Po warned. Rain dribbled through the stubble regrowing on his shaven head. "I'm sorry I found him for you."

"You told me he was good with engines," Nicholai said.

"By reputation he's a genius with any kind of machinery," Keng Po agreed, "but he's also unstable. I tell you he'll be trouble for us."

"Maybe we need to find someone who's a little crazy. We've searched the whole waterfront and no one with any sense will join us."

"Lord," the old woman interrupted. "Black devil work this place." She pointed to the dripping hulk of a seagoing junk that was laid up in the harbor for repairs.

"Take me alongside," Nicholai ordered, then turned to Keng Po. "Did you tell him who we were or what we wanted?"

"Are you crazy? I told him nothing. I never thought I'd have to see the bastard again." He followed Nicholai up the ladderway to the deck of the junk.

"I'm looking for a *gwilo* known as Sammy Fifth Street," Nicholai told the captain, who was taking shelter under a strip of canvas by the tiller. The captain spat, then hollered down into the fish-stinking hold. Some time later a tall, thin black man, an American, came on deck wiping his hands on a piece of oily cotton.

"You looking for me?" he seemed annoyed at the intrusion. He had a big egg-shaped head set on narrow shoulders and a gaunt, wide-eyed look. Dressed in a pair of oily jeans and T-shirt, he seemed oblivious to the downpour.

123

In spite of Keng Po's prior warning Nicholai was struck by the raw intensity on the man's face. Here, Nicholai thought, was an outcast: his hatred for the whole human race seemed to boil up inside him, ready to explode.

"I heard you were looking for someone to take you out to a Vietnamese refugee ship?"

"You a skin-boat operator, man?"

"No, but I'm interested in making a deal with you," Nicholai told him.

The man looked away, then let out a bitter laugh. "It sure doesn't take long for you skin-boat operators to hear. Well, I'll tell you this like I told it to the others... I don't give a damn if the going rate for bringing in a refugee is thirty thousand dollars a head. All I've got is fifteen thousand dollars. Nothing else. The rest went to pay to get my woman and child out of Vietnam. So you take it or leave it."

"I don't want your money," Nicholai said quietly.

"What do you want then, honky?" His nerves were raw and he was deliberately offensive, a man who imagined slights and readily looked for enemies. His face was marked by countless fights. Keng Po, watching quietly in the background, was willing to bet that few of Fifth Street's teeth were his own.

"I'm told you worked as an engineer on the United States Navy fast boats in Vietnam," Nicholai said, refusing to take the bait.

Fifth Street looked away—most of his scars were from that war—and gave his clipped, nervous laugh again. He was a highly intelligent man who had come to have so little faith in himself that he would turn his head away to hide how insecure and vulnerable he really felt.

"I'm good with engines," Fifth Street said, his voice filled with a kind of bitter pride. At least that skill he would still believe in. He glanced around the deck, half expecting Nicholai to challenge him. "I've kept this stinking heap moving through the water when its engines should have rusted clean through the bottom. Anyway, what are you offering?"

"Two hundred thousand dollars for a few weeks' work."

In spite of himself Fifth Street looked startled, if skeptical. "I've sweated eighteen hours a day for two months in this stinking harbor while I've waited for news of the refugee boat, and I've barely made enough to stay alive. Who do I have to kill to get that?"

"No one. Just make one run as the engineer on my boat. The cargo is gold."

Fifth Street now knew who this man was. "You've got to be crazy if you think anyone's going to work for you. The police have got this

124

waterfront sewn up, and the message is loud and clear. You're headed for only one place and so is anyone who joins up with you. Me? I've got my woman and child coming in on that refugee boat and we've been apart too long for me to go down now. No price is worth that."

Nicholai knew better than to argue with him. "Think about it," he said as he made his way to the ladder. "The weather reports predict bad storms in the next week, and I've seen some of those refugee boats. They don't ride out storms too well. If you should need my help don't leave it too long.". . .

"What did I tell you," Keng Po said, unable to hide his relief as they reached the sampan. "He's a madn͏ 1, we don't need him."

Nicholai thought differently. If he'd read Fifth Street right, and he thought he had, he could handle him. "Unless you or Udo feel confident about working on high-precision marine engines that haven't been used in fifteen years, we're going to wait for him to contact us."

"No," Keng Po protested. "You heard what he said—"

"He'll be in touch. He has to. Where do you think he's going to find a skin-boat operator to run his family into Hong Kong for fifteen thousand dollars?"

IN HONG KONG, where there are no areas left for playgrounds and parks, the street market becomes the hub of the community.

Old men of the Tsz Wan Shan housing area sat on concrete benches playing checkers while the women, with their youngest child strapped to their backs, shopped among the stalls for the family's evening meal. Each egg was carefully tested under a light. No vegetable vendor would even consider trying to package his produce—everything was laid open to painstaking inspection, then weighed and wrapped in bamboo leaf. After centuries of near-starvation food was of such importance to these Chinese that their common greeting was still, "Have you had rice yet?"

Mae Ling waited among the women in the market until the time of the evening meal, when she felt sure to catch her father's cousin at home. She climbed the stairway to the seventeenth floor, listened until she heard a man's voice inside, then knocked on the door.

An old man opened it. He was well into his sixties with a kind, healthy, weathered face. His eyes were a faded brown from years of exposure to the sun's glare off the sea.

"I am Mae Ling," she said, keeping her voice low. "I am of your clan. I claim your protection."

"I have heard," Lao Ch'en whispered, but his hands did not relax their grip on the door. "My wife spoke to me of you. I am sorry. You cannot stay here. It's too dangerous for us—"

"But I've no one else to turn to." The strain was clear in her face. "The Triad has tried to sell me into prostitution. I escaped from them but I can't hide any longer. If you cannot help me then I've decided to kill myself rather than let them take me." Mae Ling said this with such conviction that the old man was left with no doubt she would actually do it. He wavered between his loyalty to the law, which he had upheld all these years, and his obligation to a member of his clan. Although after the Communist revolution his side of the family had chosen to live in Hong Kong, his Chinese sense of family was so strong that a cousin was as close as a sister.

She was also a fresh and beautiful child. But what ultimately persuaded Lao Ch'en to help her was that he was reaching the end of his time, and if she killed herself, her spirit could well trouble his in the afterlife. "Come in," he said, opening the door, "we will have to think what to do with you, my daughter."

His entire apartment occupied less space than a modest-sized living room in any western country, thanks in part to the population explosion brought about by the influx of refugees. And in spite of the colony's building program the waiting list for an apartment in a block like this was normally twelve to fifteen years.

The Ling family housed seven adults in the open area, using to the maximum the thirty-five square feet allotted per person by the housing authority. Two members of the family, about to go on night shift at a nearby factory, rested on a two-tiered bunk by the door. Another two-tiered bunk was placed along the wall. Opposite that was a half-sized table that could just fit four people. Wooden shelves held the few cooking and eating utensils the family owned. A cot was squeezed into a corner for the baby.

Although relieved to be taken in, Mae Ling knew that to lose this home would be disastrous for the Ling family. "I will not stay long," she promised.

An old woman was squatting over a spirit stove on the tiny balcony that doubled as a kitchen. When she saw Mae Ling she turned away, muttering angrily. But Lao Ch'en, having now accepted her into his family, fussed over her, bringing her tea and sitting her down at the table with the others who were eating their evening meal.

Later that night when they could find a quiet space to sit together, he said, "I was glad when your father left Hong Kong. His politics were

126

different from mine and he caused a great deal of trouble here." Lao Ch'en was aware of the political changes that had been sweeping through the mainland and knew why she had escaped. "Does your father intend to join you?"

"No." Mae Ling told the half-truth quickly. "He will remain in China." Lao Ch'en could see that she didn't want to talk about their family in China and didn't pursue the matter.

"I've been retired from the police force for some time," he said. "It's not easy to live on a government pension. If you are caught here, as you will be if you stay, then they'll take my pension away and put me in jail." Having said it he realized the effect it would have, and he touched her arm gently. "I'm sorry, child, pay no attention . . . it's just an old man thinking aloud. I don't wish to add my burden to the one you already carry."

He leaned back against the wall, turning thoughtful. "You say the Triads are also looking for you? Well, in sheltering you I have put myself beyond the law. People will talk, they will find you through their *mae chai*. How will I protect you from them? We must think, what shall we do to hide you?"

"Father," Mae Ling said, subtly offering him the respect—due to his age and relation to her—that she would have given her own parent, "I heard in the streets some talk of the Snake Boat Man and I remembered my father telling me that you had some dealings with him."

Lao Ch'en nodded, unable to hide an old man's delight in the chance to reminisce. His association in the hunt for the Snake Boat Man had earned him a small place in the history of the coast. "Again and again we almost trapped him . . . By the end I'd learned his ways so well I could follow him in the dark, but the government gave us boats that could do only twelve knots while his could do thirty. No wonder we never caught him . . ."

She now put the question that Malloy had ordered her to ask. "Would he help me?"

"We were enemies," Lao Ch'en said, surprised at her notion. "This man was born in the East. He is as much Chinese as he is *gwilo*. If I ask him for help he would spit in my face. That is not the answer."

"You both have retired with honor," Mae Ling persisted. "And because he was once your enemy, he would gain great face now if he helped you."

She could see that her relation had no wish to place himself in his former enemy's debt. But she also knew that the Ling family was anxious

127

to be rid of her. She had shown Lao Ch'en a solution and left him to chew over the matter while she crept into a bunk vacated by one of the night shift workers.

Lao Ch'en's wife gave him little rest that night and continued to nag him the next morning. *She* was in no doubt as to what he should do.

He was forced to swallow his pride at last.

"Child," he said to Mae Ling, "perhaps your suggestion about the Snake Boat Man has merit. He could protect you. He is the one man outside the law whom the Triads would hesitate to touch, and perhaps he still knows ways to get you out of Hong Kong to safety. I will see what I can do."

She was about to ask if he knew where to find the Snake Boat Man, thought better of it and held back.

LAO CH'EN returned to the tenement the next evening clearly pleased with himself. "I hear the Snake Boat Man lives in a truly magnificent house on the Peak. I have telephoned his servant," he told Mae Ling proudly, "and he will see me."

Mae Ling smiled prettily. She was not proud of what she was doing, but she had to survive... even if the price was serving a sadist like Malloy...

CHAPTER 11

MAE LING and Lao Ch'en waited until dark before they started down the stairs of the tenement building. Not wanting to risk using public transportation, they took a taxi to the Snake Boat Man's home.

As they waited for the steel doors to open, Mae Ling caught from the corner of her eye the departing taxi's brake lights suddenly glow red as the taxi was halted by two men midway down Lugard Road. Malloy's men checking on her?

Ah Chuen, the Snake Boat Man's servant, let them into a high-ceilinged, split-level living room. Its enormous windows offered a breath-taking view from the harbor over to the New Territories and beyond to the massive, brooding landmass of China. "Wait here and touch nothing," Ah Chuen ordered, not bothering to hide his disdain for such poorly dressed peasants, then left them to find Nicholai.

Lao Ch'en couldn't help noticing that this one room was larger than his whole apartment . . . the obvious wealth of the Snake Boat Man only humiliated him more.

"All this must belong to a very rich man," Mae Ling whispered, glancing about. She'd quickly sensed the absence of a woman's hand in its furnishings.

"And a very powerful one," Lao Ch'en told her, trying to hide his nervousness.

NICHOLAI SAT with Keng Po and Udo on the terrace, lingering over supper. A fountain in the courtyard cooled the humid night air. When the wind stirred from the right direction they caught the impatient siren blasts of Star Ferries from far below as they churned back and forth across the harbor. It was one of the most beautiful, if restless, views in the world.

"How could you ever consider giving up all this?" Keng Po asked as Nicholai pushed a bottle of wine toward him.

For the past fifteen years each man had gone his own way, and the three of them, nearly strangers to one another, had used the night for renewing old ties.

"Because like you," Nicholai said, "I need more in my stomach than a diet of prayers and loneliness. Besides, Hong Kong has changed from the city I once loved, there are even more changes to come. It's time for me to move on, perhaps out of the East altogether." His gray eyes sparkled. "Besides, what better way for a smuggler to leave here than after one last successful run?"

"Why's our friend feeling so damn pleased with himself?" Udo muttered to Keng Po. Hong Kong made him feel uncomfortable—it was too big, too crowded and this house was too rich for his blood.

"The engineer contacted him today," Keng Po told him.

"Is he joining us?"

"He wants to talk," Nicholai said. "I'm meeting him tomorrow."

"Why not tonight?"

"There's no hurry."

"It's dangerous for us to wait here," Udo said impatiently.

"He's right," Keng Po said. "The British aren't fools. If we wait too long they'll find a way to stop us from leaving the colony."

It was then that Ah Chuen approached Nicholai's chair. "The policeman and his relative are here. I've put them in the living room as you instructed."

130

"This won't take long," Nicholai said as he got up.

Keng Po put out an arm to stop him. "You're a fool even to think of helping that man. If he'd had his way you would be in a cell right now, not living here—"

"That was a long time ago."

"He hates your guts—they all do in the police."

"At least he was an honest cop. One of the few who wasn't using his job to feather his own nest. I respected him for that. Besides, I'm anxious to see what the years have done to him."

"He must want a favor badly to come here. Be careful it's not a trap," Udo warned.

"All I have to do is listen," Nicholai said lightly as he left the room.

"And then," Keng Po called after him, "say *no*." . . .

Mae Ling felt Nicholai's presence even before she noticed that he was in the room. He was a powerful man who created a physical force all his own—and, she thought, one of the most attractive men she'd ever seen. Mae Ling felt considerably less anxious about the task she had been sent to do.

Lao Ch'en bowed jerkily from the waist in greeting. "My eyes cannot believe the splendor of your home," he stammered.

"Thank you. You are welcome guests. Has my servant brought you refreshments?"

"I have already trespassed upon your hospitality," Lao Ch'en demurred, motioning to Mae Ling. "My relative is an illegal immigrant . . ."

Mae Ling had been careful to stay in the background, but now she felt the Snake Boat Man's penetrating eyes turn to her. Many men had stared at her—she was accustomed to that—but he was different . . . she could detect neither lust nor even appreciation in his look. Instead it seemed he recognized her and was startled by this meeting . . .

"What can I do for you?" Nicholai said, turning to Lao Ch'en. The older man had rehearsed his speech many times over but now it vanished completely from his mind. "You and I were enemies once. I cannot pretend it was otherwise," he began, feeling some of the old resentment returning that this hunted criminal had always eluded him. Now here he was living in a veritable palace while Lao Ch'en sweltered in the slums of Tsz Wan Shan.

"I had a fast boat," Nicholai said with an edge to his voice, "but as I remember, your tenacity and your knowledge of this coast were nearly my undoing."

Damn fools, Mae Ling thought. Why dredge up the past? In another

131

moment they would be at each other's throats... she caught her cousin's eye, reminding him of the purpose of their visit.

"I have come to ask a favor." Lao Ch'en thought this final humiliation would be his undoing. "It is for my relation here. The Triad is looking for her. They transported her to the city from the New Territories. She escaped from them. It is common knowledge what they will do should they recapture her. She has turned to me for help, but I cannot save her except to have her sent back to China, where she tells me our family is disgraced. I have no powerful friends, no influence, and in helping her I have already put myself outside the law... You are the only man we know of, unconnected with the Triads, to whom we can turn for help. Will you find a way to get her out of the colony?"

"Do I have your word that she is from your family?"

"You have my word," the old man said, and Nicholai believed him.

"Did anyone see you come here?"

"No one. We were very careful, I assure you."

"Then I will help you. Leave the girl with me."

"I have money saved," Lao Ch'en offered, deeply relieved.

"—These days I hear the skin-boat captains charge upward of thirty thousand dollars a head for a journey only as far as Macau," Nicholai reminded him. It wasn't a matter of money. Lao Ch'en knew that.

"I will find whatever is required for my relative's safety," Lao Ch'en replied stubbornly. His family's savings over the last twenty years would hardly cover that amount of money, but his pride would not allow him to take anything more from his old enemy than he was prepared to repay.

"Be certain I will call on you for it later," Nicholai said, impatient with the policeman's stubborn pride.

"Until I have repaid you," Lao Ch'en said formally before he left. "*Ngaw Him Nei.*" Nicholai understood the Chinese oath that bound him, upon permanent loss of face, to repay the debt, no matter the cost. He realized now why Lao Ch'en, in his long career, had never accepted graft...

Nicholai waited for them to follow his servant out of the room, then threw open the louvred doors leading to his study. Above his desk was a portrait of Li Wen, his wife. He studied her face carefully. The two women were not the same, but there was something there... He thought he saw it in the expression in her eyes, in the delicate curve of her mouth, in her fragile beauty that was captured by the artist in such a way that it bore a striking resemblance to the girl he had just agreed to help.

132

A hollow sadness filled him. He had needed Li Wen's special under-standing to help heal the deep scars that remained from his struggle for survival in the Inner Harbor, and her love had given him a much-longed-for inner peace. When after six years of marriage she died of cancer, he had never looked for another woman to replace her. He had no desire to. Only lately, with the sudden realization that he was growing older, had he begun to feel a special loneliness and a need to fill it.

Nicholai became aware of someone standing in the doorway. He turned to see the girl silently waiting to be noticed. If she recognized herself in the portrait, she gave no indication.

"In helping me," she said quietly, "you have placed yourself in danger. How can I thank you?"

"There is no need. I was a refugee once. I know what it's like."

Unconsciously she had moved her head until her profile matched that of the portrait. "Come with me," Nicholai ordered. She didn't understand the tone in his voice—it was almost as though she had hurt him...

He led her out onto the terrace where Udo and Keng Po were waiting.

"Nicholai," Keng Po said sharply, "will you never learn to say no?" He turned to the girl, eyeing her suspiciously. "What is your name?"

"Mae Ling," she said as she looked about the room, sizing up the men. Nicholai was clearly the leader and Udo, judging from the size of the man, provided the force. Keng Po, she guessed, survived by his wits and was the shrewdest judge of human nature. She would have to be very careful with him.

"Where are you from?" he asked.

"Shanghai."

"And your father, what did he do?"

"He lectured at the university," she lied.

"Where did you learn to speak English?"

"I studied to join the foreign service." Which at least was almost true.

"She's exhausted," Nicholai said, saving her from further interrogation. "You can speak to her tomorrow if you want. Have you eaten?" he said, turning to her.

Mae Ling nodded, grateful for the reprieve... Malloy hadn't warned her about Keng Po.

"Then Ah Chuen will show you to your room. Tomorrow he'll see about getting you some forged papers." Mae Ling followed the old servant obediently. There was something about this Nicholai, she thought, that would make her task that much easier... It seemed almost too good to be true.

133

* * *

"SO YOU agreed to help her?" Keng Po said once Ah Chuen had shown her out of the room.

"Yes."

Keng Po sat quietly for a moment...he remembered that Li Wen had died at about this girl's age, and hoped his friend wasn't looking for something that was gone forever. "Don't search for your dead wife, old friend. She's not there." He knew how stubborn Nicholai could be, and the trouble it had gotten him into in the past. "Besides, at your age you should have learned to treat beautiful women with extreme caution."

"Too long in a monastery has made a philosopher out of him," Udo grumbled.

"But not a very good one, I'm afraid." Nicholai didn't wish to discuss his decision any further. What was done was done. "I could have imagined you as anything but a monk." Nicholai was on edge, still haunted by Mae Ling's face.

"When we all split up I was forced to take stock of my life," Keng Po said. "I thought it wise to prepare my soul against damnation in the afterlife. We Chinese have always been cynical about religion. We believe only because, for many of us, life is too intolerable not to—we all expect to be cheated in the end. Except maybe you, Nicholai."

The men were feeling mellow, and their talk flowed as freely as the wine they drank.

"You once believed there was some point to this life," Keng Po said, glancing at his old friend. "It made you dangerous, even to your friends. All believers are dangerous—they expect life to provide answers, they don't expect to be cheated. When you locked yourself away up here, did you find what you were looking for?"

"No. No more than you did."

"Me, I wasn't looking for anything," Udo said as he drained the last drops of wine from the bottle. "I cooked good food, drank wine, chased women and lost all my money gambling. Well, thank God we're together again," he said, clapping each of them on the shoulder. "I was no damn good on my own."

"I'VE GOT the taxi driver downstairs," Rem Choy reported to Malloy later that evening. "He's confirmed dropping the girl off at the Snake Boat Man's house."

So Mae Ling was in place. Clever girl, Malloy thought. She had moved fast. He was leaning back in his chair with his feet on his desk, the air conditioner humming behind him. He'd been waiting for hours for Choy's report, and had decided against going back to his apartment. Somehow it seemed empty without her there...

"Good. Now get search warrants," he ordered, "and tell our men to move into position. I want that house surrounded."

"It's like a fortress," Rem Choy warned.

"I *know* that." He gave his assistant a look that told him to withhold any more of his gratuitous remarks.

"What time do we go in?"

Malloy thought of Mae Ling with the Snake Boat Man and resisted the temptation to go in immediately. "Give them time to settle down," he said. He knew that most people are in their deepest sleep in the hours before dawn. He needed precious seconds that would provide to break through the doors.

"We'll go in at three-thirty."

MAE LING had been shown to a small room next to Ah Chuen's. Earlier that evening on her way through the house she had asked all innocently of the Snake Boat Man's servant, "What lies that way, *lao tsu?*"

"The guest wing."

"And there?" She pointed to the staircase.

"That way leads to my master's quarters. No one goes there," he told her sharply.

"Has he a *tsip?*" A *tsip* was a concubine.

"*No,*" Ah Chuen said irritably. This girl is sure to bring trouble, he thought as he limped on ahead of her.

She calculated her next move as she lay on her bed staring up through the dark at the ceiling. Three years as personal aide to Madame Mao Tse-tung in the bloodiest period of political infighting the Chinese Communist Party had ever experienced had taught her a great deal about survival. It was obvious she could not trust Malloy... her only concern now had to be to save her own skin. And in any way necessary...

Mae Ling steeled her mind and body for what lay ahead. She needed the Snake Boat Man as an ally, and had to find a way to make him one. He was powerful, of that she was certain—he could make all the difference to her survival. She remembered the way he'd looked at her earlier... there seemed to be signals, but she wasn't sure she could read them. Malloy was right about one thing—he wasn't a man easily fooled.

She waited until the house was silent, then crept up the stairs to

Nicholai's suite, not sure how she would be received. He woke up as she opened the door. "I was afraid of being alone," she said quietly. "I couldn't sleep."

Nicholai reached out to her, feeling for a brief moment that it was Li Wen, that she was with him again... Mae Ling dropped her clothes to the floor and crawled into the bed, her back warm against him. He touched her breasts, and she curled herself into a ball, her knees tucked against her chest. He could feel her shivering, and was brought back to reality... Fool, Nicholai thought, she's been in the hands of the Triad, she must be terrified of men... The girl was as much a prisoner as a guest in his house. Her safety depended on his goodwill... naturally she would do anything to earn it. Well, he wouldn't take her this way. He slid his hands from her breasts and put his arms lightly around her. "No," he said when she turned and dutifully offered him her body. "There'll be time enough when you're ready."

He held her tightly now, but in a way that wasn't threatening. In spite of herself Mae Ling was moved by this man's kindness. She felt herself relax, and suddenly the terror of the past few days caught up with her. Sensing her fear, he spoke quietly to soothe her. "You've come too far, tried too hard for freedom to let go now." He leaned over her and put on the light. The gray eyes that searched her face were so penetrating that it almost seemed he could read her mind.

He touched her face gently, and the kindness in his gesture brought stinging tears to her eyes. "I will see that you reach safety," he reassured her.

She knew she would never forget this face, weathered and strong... Surely he was a man who understood pain, but there was something more—he was a powerful man, born to command, with a will stronger than her own—and she knew she didn't have the strength to fight him. Nor would she have to... she took his hand and held tight to it. He had understood her fear, but instead of taking advantage of it, as Malloy and so many others had, he'd treated her with compassion. Overcome with his kindness and his strength, she got down on the floor and knelt in front of him, her head bowed.

"Lord," she whispered, her face wet with tears, "I thank you for taking me in, for your gentleness with me."

Nicholai got out of bed and pulled her to her feet. She laid her head against his chest. He put his cheek against her smooth black hair. "Take me now," she said, lifting her face to be kissed. "I'm ready, truly I'm ready..."

Nicholai carried her back to the bed. She felt soft against him, her skin and breath smelled sweetly of crushed flowers. He was a gentle, commanding lover, and she found herself gladly letting his lips and hands explore her body, bringing her to a pitch of genuine passion, and she gave back to him as full a measure of relief as she received...

LYING BESIDE him afterward as he slept, Mae Ling smiled, pleased with herself. This man was strong, but she was sure now that she could win him, perhaps even make him fall in love with her. And Malloy? She had been giving a good deal of thought to him, unable to forget the way he had used her, was still trying to use her. If she did as she was instructed, what then? Could she believe his promise? In sending her to this Nicholai, Malloy could easily be setting them *both* up for the police... This man breathing gently beside her would go to jail for aiding an illegal, and she would be sent back to face execution in China. Malloy would be rid of them both that way... Suddenly she was alert, her mind racing... Malloy would have men watching the house. Certainly he would know she was there. She had to alert Nicholai that they were both in danger. Still, he was her way out of the colony, she would need to be careful about what she told him...

She leaned over to awaken him. It wasn't difficult, since he slept lightly. "What is it?"

"Lord," she said, just the right note of concern edging her voice. "You asked my relative earlier if anyone had followed us here. We came by taxi, and as it turned away after dropping us, I believe I saw it stop at the bottom of the road. At the time I thought little of it, but I remember now two men leaning in through the window, questioning the driver. Could they have been watching your house...?"

Nicholai was instantly alert. "I don't know. What did they look like?" He felt her shrug beside him. "They were far away and it was dark. I couldn't see their faces."

Nicholai swung over onto his side of the bed and checked his watch. It was a little after three A.M.

"Was I right to wake you?" she asked nervously. "I didn't wish to alarm you, but I was concerned for your safety and—"

"You did well," he said. The night was nearly over and he instinctively felt a sense of danger in the silence of his house. "Get dressed and tell Ah Chuen to come to me."

He woke Keng Po, then Udo, explaining briefly. They met Ah Chuen

137

shuffling toward them on slippered feet from a vantage point on the roof. He had caught the glow of a poorly shielded cigarette. "Men by the gates," he told Nicholai.

"How can we get out of here without using the road?" Keng Po asked.

"There's another way down the mountain," Nicholai said. "Come with me."

They followed him silently through the garden to the edge of the terrace, which was cantilevered on reinforced concrete beams off the mountainside. Nicholai knelt, lifting a flagstone at the foot of the parapet. In a hollowed-out space beneath it was a rope ladder. He reached down, releasing the bolts that held the hatch shut at the bottom, and the ladder snaked down the sheer forty-five-foot drop to the mountainside below.

SITUATED ON a small ledge of rock almost level with the terrace and three hundred yards away was an observation post set up by two members of the Hong Kong police Special Branch. They took turns scanning the house through a pair of light intensifier glasses.

It was John Wong's turn to watch. He pressed the rubber eyepiece against one eye, switched it on and waited the split second for the shimmering light green field to appear on the scope. The outline of the house, magnified as if by ordinary binoculars, was etched like a black-and-gray negative against the background of green. He swept the scope along the terrace and up over the house to the road. He caught the glow of the same cigarette Ah Chuen had spotted, and at a quarter of a mile range the lighted tip burned a fuzzy blur across the sensitive scope. He knew that would be Mike Li by the gates. Stupid bastard... Wong lowered the scope. If Malloy caught Li with that cigarette he'd cut his balls off.

"See anything?" Wong's colleague, an older, heavier man, was stretched out on the ledge beside him.

"No. Just that stupid Mike Li's cigarette. It's quiet as a grave across there." He waited for the blur to fade, then brought the light intensifier down onto the terrace again. At the very bottom of the scope he caught the outline of the rope ladder and a girl's head disappearing from view.

Wong quickly reached for the walkie-talkie by his side. "Subjects leaving the house. They've dropped a ladder off the terrace." He swung the scope to the bottom of the ladder, where Udo was holding it steady for the girl.

Malloy waited, hunched in the car on Lugard Road. He heard Wong's report on the radio net and knew before he could reply that he was already

138

too late. "Go after them," he barked into the radio, vowing to have somebody's head.

Keng Po reached the bottom of the ladder as the police began to smash through the outer doors of the house. "Hurry," he shouted up to Nicholai.

Nicholai, the last to descend, knew that his servant Ah Chuen was too crippled to scramble down the ladder. He also knew even Malloy would not harm a weak, infirm old man. He would lose face. "Delay them as long as possible. I'll send you a message from Macau about what's to be done with my house." He wrapped a thick coil of rope around his shoulders and went down the ladder. The policemen on the ledge opposite the house had fixed him clearly in their scope. They shouted at him to stop as he plunged through the dense undergrowth until he found the water-worn path he was looking for. It snaked sharply down the mountainside. The others hurried after him, Udo bringing up the rear.

John Wong and his colleagues fell on the slippery earth, cursing in the dark as they ran through shoulder-high scrub, trying to cut Nicholai off.

By the time Nicholai stopped at the top of the bank Mae Ling and the others were scratched and muddied and gasping for breath. The bank was paved with stone, too steep to climb down without risking a twenty-foot fall to the wet, oily surface of the tarmac road below. Seasonal rain had caused mud slides to wash away much of the vegetation, and there was nothing within reach for Nicholai to secure his rope to.

Four hundred yards further up the mountainside John Wong had lost his radio in a crashing fall. In the glow of street lights below he could see now where the Snake Boat Man was headed. He raised his pistol and fired several shots into the air, signaling to Malloy the direction of the chase.

Nicholai knew that they had to act quickly. He wound one end of the rope around his shoulder and lowered the other over the side of the bank, digging his heels into the mud to anchor himself. "You first," he said to Udo, who was the heaviest. Keng Po and Mae Ling tried to help as Udo scaled down the side of the bank. Mae Ling went next, then Keng Po took over the rope. He weighed barely one hundred and twenty pounds and his heels were dragged toward the edge, his back arched painfully, as Nicholai went down. As soon as Nicholai's feet touched the tarmac Keng Po sent the rope sailing after him so that the police could not use it.

"Are you ready?" Keng Po called down anxiously. Nicholai and Udo moved into position under him to break his fall. Keng Po dove head first from the bank, flattening out his body before landing between Nicholai's and Udo's locked arms. Even though his fall was broken, the shock of his landing brought all three men down in a tangled heap and it took several moments for them to decide that no one was seriously hurt.

Udo wheezed happily, despite having taken Keng Po's knee in his stomach, momentarily knocking the wind out of him. "We're back in action again, the same team just like before..."

"Speak for yourself," Keng Po muttered as Mae Ling helped pull him to his feet. "We're fifteen years older and you nearly broke my back." He turned to Nicholai. "What now?"

"Over the road and straight down. The police aren't going to get down that bank in a hurry, and the going gets easier from now on. I keep a spare car in a garage just below here. Looks like I'm finally getting a chance to use it."

MALLOY STEPPED through the doorway into the Snake Boat Man's house. The lock had been burned away with an acetylene torch and Rem Choy, following him, grimaced at the stench of burned paint and scorched metal.

"Search this place thoroughly," Malloy told his men. "Strip everything down. You know who the owner is, gentlemen," he said, "he's in no position to complain."

"What about the girl's relative? The taxi driver can identify him. Shall we bring him in?" Rem Choy asked.

"He *was* one of us..." Malloy said thoughtfully. "We'll leave him for a while. He won't be going anywhere... Who's this?" he asked as Ah Chuen was brought up to him, pinioned between two policemen.

"The Snake Boat Man's servant, sir," one of the policemen replied.

"No doubt you're going to tell me there was no one in the house all night but yourself," Malloy said sarcastically.

"That's correct, master." Ah Chuen wasn't easily intimidated. Around him policemen had begun pulling down curtains, overturning drawers and ripping the fabric off the furniture. He saw through the study doors one of them reach up for the portrait of his late mistress. "Get away from there," Ah Chuen called out, trying to wrench himself free of his guards.

"Bring him along with me," Malloy ordered. He walked to the edge of the terrace and looked down at the escape ladder, still in place. "Not the act of an innocent man, would you say?" Ah Chuen kept silent.

Knowing he would get nothing more out of the servant that night, Malloy signaled Ah Chuen's guards to take him away.

"The Snake Boat Man's got half an hour's start on us," Rem Choy said as he took in the view from the terrace. "Where do you think he's headed?"

"Where would you go if you were an old smuggler?" He ignored Rem Choy for a moment, thinking of Mae Ling. Of course she had tipped off the Snake Boat Man. That bitch was going to suffer, he promised himself, he'd be sure of that. She wasn't out of the colony yet.

"The harbor, you fool," he said to Rem Choy as he turned back to the house. "He owns a junk doesn't he? Get hold of marine police headquarters. I want a general alarm put out. I want all junks leaving Hong Kong side harbors searched before dawn."

CHAPTER 12

NICHOLAI LED the others toward the breakwater of Aberdeen Harbor and down a flight of worn stone steps near the water's edge, where he signaled with a penlight. A short time later a sampan came alongside rowed by Wen Yuan, his boatman.

"Have the police been watching you?" Nicholai asked him.

The boatman smiled happily. "Yes, lord, but it wasn't hard to shake them off. I've been going to sea by day and bringing the junk back to a different mooring each night."

He rowed the sampan back to Nicholai's junk. It had undergone a complete transformation since the police surveillance started. Gone were its spotless decks and polished brass fittings that identified it as a rich man's pleasure craft. Instead, like countless other junks, nets hung from the mast and the deck was filthy, littered with all the paraphernalia of a hardworking fishing junk.

"Can we still slip out of here?"

"There's a police launch on guard at the harbor entrance, lord. But those pigs can't tell one junk from another at night." Wen Yuan was from the Hokolo tribe, Nicholai remembered, a nomadic people who held a fierce hatred for all forms of authority...

"I'm taking the sampan," Nicholai said as the others climbed on board. "Get the junk ready for sea. I'll be back in twenty minutes."

"Where are you going?" Keng Po asked, clearly upset at the news of a delay.

"I've got an engineer to collect."

"For God's sake, send for him later."

"No. I'm not leaving without him."

Nicholai rowed down the lines of moored junks and tied his sampan to the painter of the hulk where Sammy Fifth Street worked. He climbed quietly onto the deck, stepping over a sleeping watchman, and found Fifth Street curled up in a corner of the deck under a tarpaulin. He shook the man awake.

"Hey! What's going on, man?" Fifth Street reluctantly opened his eyes, recognizing Nicholai. "It's not even morning yet."

"Look," Nicholai said, crouching beside him, "I've no time to bargain with you. Are you with me or not?"

Fifth Street propped himself up on his elbows, trying to clear the sleep from his head. "You bring in my woman and child off a refugee boat that's coming in and either I'll find a way to pay you in one week or I'll work on your boat." He peered into the darkness, trying to see Nicholai's face. No one had ever trusted him before, and he wasn't accustomed to asking for favors—but now he was convinced this was his only hope for rescuing his family. "I'm the best damn engineer you're ever going to get—"

"You've got a deal. But I'll land them in Macau. Anything you want to get for them in the way of travel papers you can do just as well there. Hong Kong is off limits to me for a while. Get your things together— we're leaving now."

"Something I ought to warn you about," Nicholai said as he rowed Fifth Street back to his junk. "Refugee boats are trying to get into Hong Kong all the time. Are you sure your woman and daughter are on this one?"

"The description fits, all right. A Philippine's coaster spotted the boat two days ago near the Tan Kan Islands about thirty miles southeast of here. They said the crew is in bad shape. It's the only reason I didn't argue with you about Macau."

Nicholai noticed Fifth Street's concern as they came alongside his junk. "Don't worry," he told him, "this isn't the boat we'll be using to make the run."

The others were waiting impatiently as they came on deck. "Calls himself Fifth Street," Nicholai said, introducing him to the others. "He claims to be the best engineer we're going to find. Here..." Nicholai tossed Fifth Street the straw hat, black cotton smock and baggy trousers of a coolie. "Put these on. There's a police launch on guard at the harbor entrance, and in this light we'll need to pass as Chinese at fifty feet."

Fifth Street changed silently. He felt less than sure of himself with these three men, whose reputations were legendary on the waterfront.

"I've got a deal with your boss," he said gruffly to Udo and Keng Po. "We go out and get my family off that refugee boat and either I pay you for the ride or I work your boat on the run—in which case I'll do my job, don't worry. Other than that I've nothing to do with any of you. Clear?"

Keng Po ignored him, but Udo decided to put this tense stranger at ease. "Welcome aboard, friend. You know your way around boats, I'm told, so give me a hand getting this one ready for sea."

Fifth Street stared at him. "Screw you. I'm paying for this ride, one way or another. *You* can haul ropes, honky." He turned and walked to the bows.

Udo's face slowly filled with rage. "You tell me as soon as you're finished with that scrawny asshole," he said, turning to Nicholai, "because when you're through I'm going to drop him over the side."

"He's got chips on both shoulders. Leave him be."

With that Nicholai started the engines and the junk slipped quietly through the harbor for the open sea. Wen Yuan, Keng Po and Mae Ling busied themselves on deck preparing the nets. There were several other junks already on the move, making an early start for their daytime fishing grounds.

"Keep out of sight," Nicholai called to Udo. "You're too big to pass as Chinese."

Beyond the breakwater a low black-and-gray police launch rode, the silhouette of its machine gun protruding from its foredeck. On board the *bomban*, a twenty-four-year-old European police inspector with only a month's experience stood on the deck, frustrated at his mission. "It's bloody impossible," he complained to his deck sergeant. "There must be twenty junks at a time slipping back and forth from the fishing fleets. I can't search them all." He knew that the other police launches were spread just as thinly along the coastline. "Where's the bloody navy, why can't they help?"

"Navy patrols Square Boundary, sir," the deck sergeant replied. He spotted a junk attempting to slip past, swung his night glasses after it. "Stop that one, sir."

The junk ahead of Nicholai had altered course as soon as it spotted the police launch, trying to make its way out to sea. The police launch's searchlights flashed out the international "stop" signal, then closed in on it. The other fishing boats waiting to be searched milled about in confusion, their captains cursing the police for the delay. In that moment of confusion Nicholai managed to slip away. He caught a gleam in Wen Yuan's eyes and nodded back toward the junk now being searched. "A relative of yours?" he asked, only partly serious.

Wen Yuan laughed. "My nephew, lord."

"How much do I owe him for that?"

"I told him ten thousand dollars if we got through. He's the greatest robber in my clan, lord."

Nicholai knew that Wen Yuan would split the profits with his nephew, but the diversion had been cheap at the price.

Fifth Street, still at the bow, could hear the squeal of ropes running through blocks on deck as the mainsail was raised. The stars were fading. Dawn was not far off. The junk heeled in the following wind, and the great bat-winged sail whispered above his head.

THE ABERDEEN fishing fleet had been working all night in an extended crescent between Waglen Light and Tathong Point. In another half-hour they would be bringing in their nets, ready to crowd into the harbor and deposit fresh catches for the morning markets. Nicholai's plan was to mingle with them, and as soon as the opportunity presented itself move over the Square Boundary and out of Hong Kong waters.

He joined the fishing fleet and ran with them as they made their last sweep of the night out toward the Boundary. As they turned away, he ran on.

The sea wind cried in the rigging as the rising sun cast a red streak across the eastern horizon. Astern, the lights of the fishing fleet beckoned like clusters of fireflies on the dark water. Udo stood next to Nicholai at the helm while Keng Po and Wen Yuan climbed high into the rigging. They scanned port and starboard through binoculars, searching the dark purple-blue of the sea for a pursuing launch.

145

Fifth Street fidgeted, aware of the mounting tension on the boat. He made his way back to Nicholai at the helm. "When did you last have someone check your engines?"

Nicholai indicated the automatic controls by his side. "I only use them for emergencies."

Fifth Street opened the engine hatch. "I'll go down and take a look." He found a pair of nearly new diesels capable of producing more than enough power for the small junk. He crouched in the confined space, glad to be doing something with his hands, and busied himself checking them over.

Three miles ahead, dead on the Boundary and watching the fishing fleet on radar, was the H.M.S. *Scimitar*. The fast attack craft's jet turbines had been shut down; it was running dark and silently on its auxiliary diesel engines. In its wheelhouse a British seaman, spotting the junk on his radar screen, reported over the intercom to the captain, who was conning the vessel from the open bridge above. "Contact, green one-seven-oh. Looks like a junk that's broken away from the others, sir, and he's headed for the Boundary."

The young blond lieutenant turned to a lookout armed with a pair of powerful night glasses stationed beside him on the bridge. "Can you spot him?"

"No, sir. Must be running without lights."

"Stand by to fire up main engines," the lieutenant said. "We'll go in and pick him up. Let MARPOL know what we've got," he ordered the wireless operator.

In the control room at marine police headquarters Malloy took the message. He knew instinctively that it had to be the Snake Boat Man. With so much navy and police activity going on at that hour no other smuggler would risk trying to break out. "I don't care if you ram him," Malloy radioed to the lieutenant. "Don't let him get away. When you pick him up, you should find a girl with him." Malloy hoped the lieutenant wouldn't recognize her. "Hold her under close arrest and see that she speaks to no one. She's wanted for interrogation by Special Branch."

KENG PO was the first to spot the *Scimitar*. He picked up the high white plume of its wake and yelled a warning down to the deck. As he did so the *Scimitar*'s searchlight began to flash out the familiar "halt" signal.

Nicholai moved quickly, spinning the helm down hard, at the same time throwing open the engine throttles. The diesels below him burst into a full-throated roar as the junk surged forward. "Slacken off the sail," he yelled. "Udo, get forward. I'm going straight at him—you know what to do."

The *Scimitar*, its jet turbine engines howling, its siren screaming into the sea, had cut off the junk's path of escape.

"It's coming straight for us," the *Scimitar*'s bosun yelled.

"Hold your course," the captain ordered. He had the junk visual too, and could see its bows curving toward him. The bosun was well aware that his high-speed, technologically advanced craft was no match in a collision with the more heavily built junk. His nerve broke first. He spun his helm and the wake of the *Scimitar* churned as it heeled hard over.

Udo ran the length of the deck and hung, bare-chested and sweating, in the rigging as the bows of the junk shaved the starboard quarter of the *Scimitar*. He expertly judged the moment, then lunged at the crew member, who stood manning the submachine gun. The seaman felt Udo's massive arm circle his waist as it swept him, frozen in panic, into the sea.

A sharp-eyed sailor at the stern of the *Scimitar* saw the seaman swept overboard, yelled a warning to the bridge. The *Scimitar* was forced to cut its engines and circle back to pick up its crew member. Nicholai let out a sigh of relief.

DAWN WAS breaking as Nicholai raced his junk along the jagged shoreline of Koh Tan Island where the cliff face fell away to rocks pounded by the South China Sea swells. The Square Boundary passed through the southernmost tip of the island. Nicholai crossed it as the *Scimitar* caught up from behind.

"That craft must be doing close to forty knots," Fifth Street said, his head poking up through the engine hatch. He was obviously impressed by the *Scimitar*'s performance. "What have you guys got in Macau that's going to match that?"

"*Teng Eung*," Nicholai said. "The *East Wind*—wait 'til you see her... Haul up the Portuguese flag," he then told Keng Po.

The *Scimitar* drew up alongside, but by now both vessels were nearly half a mile into international waters.

"We're a Portuguese craft," Nicholai shouted across the water, "registered in Macau. You have no right to interfere with us."

"We'll be in touch with the Macau authorities about you," the lieutenant said abruptly.

"You do that." Nicholai felt he had nothing to fear from the threat.

"You damn near killed one of my men back there," the lieutenant said, unable to hide his fury at being outwitted. He spotted the girl on the deck of the junk—undoubtedly the one Malloy had been asking about. That was someone else whose reputation had taken a beating tonight, but that was no worry of his. "You should have stayed retired," he told Nicholai. "Cross this border again and we'll be sure to put you in jail where you belong—"

"You've had your chance," Nicholai said. "I'll be coming back, only next time I'll bring a faster boat—"

"I'll be waiting for you…" the lieutenant warned as he heeled the *Scimitar* away.

FIFTH STREET remained alone on the foredeck until later that morning when Mae Ling brought him food.

"Those are the Tan Kan Islands coming up ahead," she said. "The Snake Boat Man wishes you to know that your wife's vessel should be in sight in another hour."

Fifth Street thanked her, this time speaking without anger or sarcasm.

Mae Ling looked at him with open curiosity. "How did you come by the name 'Fifth Street'?"

"It was my navy name and I guess it stuck." He shrugged, unbending a little. "My father didn't hang around long enough to leave me his name. Neither did my old lady, for that matter. I was found near the corner of Fifth Avenue and Forty-second Street, in New York. The institution I was raised in gave me a name out of the telephone book, but I didn't take to it." Somewhat unexpectedly, he found himself willing to show a different side to Mae Ling—she didn't make him feel threatened…

He tasted the food, then handed the plate back to her. "I don't want their food."

Mae Ling had already guessed that the person Fifth Street hated the most was himself, but she also knew that if properly handled he could be a useful ally should she need him. "I'm a refugee too," she said. "I truly hope we find your wife and child safe."

He flashed her a brief smile of gratitude. "Thank you," he said quietly, and turned back to search the sea ahead for the boat. She didn't think he noticed when she left him, but he did.

FIFTH STREET had deserted his wife and child just before the fall of Vietnam, and he found himself in recent years torn with guilt. He'd been

148

an American sailor, finished with war, anxious to return to the only life he knew, back in Harlem. He saw no place in that life for an Asian woman and a kid tagging along. In spite of his talents with machinery, he couldn't settle down, managing to alienate fellow workers or management at every job. When he tried to start up a business of his own, he failed miserably... During the years that followed occasional smuggled letters from his wife did get to him, telling between the lines about the misery and starvation they were suffering. The arrival of the letters began to trigger his guilt to the point where he knew he had to find them... In Vietnam he had used her as a temporary wife, not especially caring whether she was with him or not. But once away from Asia and the war—and friendless—he realized how much she had meant to him, and he very much wanted to see his daughter again. He sent whatever money he could raise to help them bribe their way onto a boat leaving Vietnam—his overriding concern now was to bring them to safety and make up for the years he'd left them to make do on their own. He wasn't certain he could do that, but he knew he at least had to try...

THE TAN KAN chain of islands protect Hong Kong from the prevailing winds, and as the junk rounded from the east the greater power of the swells lifted its bows. An hour later Fifth Street let out an excited shout, recognizing the refugee boat from the description he'd been given. "There she is!" It was still well in international waters, limping slowly toward Hong Kong. A big seagoing junk, it was weatherbeaten and listing heavily. As the distance closed, Fifth Street could see the struggle the crew had just to keep the hulk afloat, wearily working at the clanking hand-operated pumps. Dirty brown bilge water gushed over the side in a long continuous stream. Fifth Street eagerly scanned the deck, trying to spot his wife, but he recognized no one.

Nicholai brought his junk to a halt and stood a short ways off.

"Hey... what are you waiting for?" Fifth Street yelled, hurrying over to him. "Bring us alongside."

"It's not smart to go close until we know how many refugees they have on board," Nicholai said. "If they're desperate enough they'll jump ship like a lot of drowning rats and swamp us. Have you spotted your wife and child yet?"

"No."

Nicholai, sensing trouble, said quietly, "I'll go with you. We'll take the sampan."...

Fifth Street and Nicholai hauled themselves up onto the slippery, sloping deck of the junk. The crew, half-starved and dressed in rags, moved about in a daze among groups of listless refugees. The deck, too, was in a shambles; anything that could possibly be of value had been ripped out, including the compass. Nicholai took stock of the scene with a practiced eye. "They've been boarded by pirates," he told Fifth Street grimly.

"What the hell do you mean ... pirates?"

"They lie in wait for refugee vessels off the coast of Vietnam like vultures."

"Oh my God, where's my wife and kid—?"

"Give me their names."

"Eva Khiem and Jenny."

"Wait. Let me ask them." But Fifth Street ignored him and plunged below deck in search of his family.

The skin-boat operators who usually met the refugee vessels at sea demanded a fortune for the last fast journey through the blockade into Hong Kong. Those who couldn't afford the price surrendered to the police and took their chances of survival in the lawless, overcrowded refugee camps.

The crew now gathered silently around Nicholai, their eyes dull. They had nothing left to lose, and perhaps this tall, strong-faced *gwilo* could bring them some form of salvation.

"Does anyone here speak Cantonese?" Nicholai asked. An old man shuffled forward. "Have you an Eva Khiem and her daughter Jenny on board?"

The old man stared down at his feet, slowly shook his head.

"What happened?"

The old man told him much the same story that had been repeated every year since the fall of Vietnam ... of an old leaking boat being run down by the more modern Thai fishing vessels ... of the refugees stripped and searched, the women and girls passed from man to man and raped over and over. Any male refugee who tried to protect them was viciously beaten. Then the pirates looted the boat, ending their siege by dumping the water supply over the side. For people already seriously weakened by privation, strength and hope quickly died...

Fifth Street reappeared on deck. "I can't find them, I *know* they were on this boat..." He grabbed the old man, and when the torn clothing came away in his hands he tightened his grip until his fingers pressed through the wasted flesh to the bone. "Goddamn you, where are they?"

"Let him go." Nicholai's sharp order brought Fifth Street back to his senses. "It's not his fault. They were boarded two days out of Vietnam.

150

The pirates dumped all the food and water they couldn't use over the side. He figures fifty percent of his crew have died since then. I'm sorry, but your wife and child...they were among them..."

The old man, understanding Fifth Street's angry grief, muttered something to Nicholai. "He says that he's very sorry," Nicholai translated, "but they couldn't keep the bodies. They were buried at sea."

"Is he telling me the truth?" Fifth Street said, loosening his grip.

"I'm afraid he is."

"I want to know how they died."

"You'd be a fool to ask."

Fifth Street's eyes filled with tears, but he stayed calm. All his life, from a childhood spent in institutions, to surviving in the streets of Harlem and later in the navy, he had known what it was to be kicked in the gut over and over again. He told himself he could cope with this. Face it...he'd half expected it not to work out...what the hell ever did...? He clenched his hands. As long as he could keep from thinking of the way they died, maybe he could keep his sanity. Still, it was his fault, he'd abandoned them, and he would somehow have to live with that...

Nicholai felt the deck moving sluggishly under his feet as he searched the horizon for any signs of help for the refugees, but it was clear of any vessels.

"This junk isn't going to stay afloat for more than a few hours," he told Udo and Keng Po after he had signaled them to come over the side. "I'm going to transfer these refugees to my junk."

"How many are there?"

"I counted thirty-two."

"What then?" Keng Po asked. He could see no point in saving thirty-two refugees when a quarter of a milliion more would make the same trip during the year. It would be better to leave them to their destiny...fate was not something to be tampered with... But Nicholai was no lover of fate.

"Land them on one of the Tan Kan Islands," Udo suggested. "At least they'll be safe there."

"That's Communist territory." Fifth Street shook his head. "They'll be sent right the hell back to Vietnam. After what they've been through, we can't do that to them..." His family had been part of this pathetic group, and now he felt a responsibility to those who'd survived. "I say we take them with us to Macau—"

"That's the craziest idea I've ever heard," Keng Po said. "Anyway, who gave you a vote—?"

"I've just joined you, I'm one of you. Damned right I have a say."

151

Nicholai turned to him. "Are you sure you want to do that?"

"Hell, what more have I got to lose? Only now the deal is that you take these people to Macau. I know you've got influence there. You can protect them..."

"He's right," Nicholai said quietly. "We'll take them to Macau."

"Hey, you!" Keng Po called to Fifth Street as he turned away. He'd had about enough of him and his ideas. "You'd better be *damned* good with engines..."

The refugees were finally packed into the junk, cramming every corner of the deck.

"Rig up some shelter from the sun and share the food and water we've got," Nicholai told Mae Ling and Wen Yuan. He waited for Udo to come back from opening the stopcocks of the refugee junk... he wanted to leave no evidence for the police or the Communists.

The hulk was already settling fast when Udo came over the side. Several of the refugees let out a low moan as their boat slipped beneath the waves. For many of them its demise broke the final link that bound them to their home and loved ones. Nicholai took over the helm and brought his junk onto course for Macau.

CHAPTER 13

SHORTLY BEFORE sunset that night the junk rounded the tip of Ka Ho, the northern promontory of Coloane Island. Before them lay a series of half-moon-shaped bays separated from one another by steep rocky spines. On the tip of one promontory stood a church sheltered by majestic pagoda trees. Mounted below its bell tower was a large cross on which was carved the figure of the crucified Christ. The church was surrounded on three sides by the sea, the Christ figure looking directly over the wreck of a refugee boat that had floundered onto the rocks in a storm and sunk. No one had survived.

"The Leper Church of our Lady of Sorrows," Udo told Mae Ling as the junk slipped into the bay below it. "On top of the promontory is a leper colony. Nearly eighty lepers live there with their families, who stay to look after them. On the right—" he motioned toward a three-story building surrounded by a high wire fence—"is a mental asylum. It's run by the Salesian Fathers too. In the next bay is a Vietnamese refugee camp. Macau, you know, is just a little part of Mainland China, and part of its territory is two islands connected by a bridge and a long causeway—there's Taipa and this one, Coloane. Coloane is the furthest from the city and still mostly underdeveloped. With the lepers and refugees... no one wants to come here"—he grinned, glad to be back—"except us."

The church bells tolled a warning as soon as the junk was spotted. As it entered the leper's bay a boy dived off one of the rocks, swam to the junk, hauled himself over the side and flung himself into Udo's arms. He had swum better than he walked. His left leg was lame and he dragged it behind him as he crossed the deck. Udo hugged the boy, lifting him high into the air. "My son," he said proudly to Mae Ling. The boy, in his early teens, was very thin, with a pathetic eagerness to please. But it wasn't until he greeted Mae Ling shyly, anxious to win her approval, that she noticed the dullness in his eyes. "I call him Fool Boy," Udo said fondly, cuffing his son's head. "He may be slow but he has courage, and somehow he gets there in the end."

A small crowd led by a large, raw-boned European woman had gathered at the water's edge by the time the junk's keel grounded on the shallow sand bottom of the bay. "I thought you intended to slip into Macau quietly," German Alice called out to the junk. "I hadn't expected you to bring me another boatload of refugees—"

"Can you find room for them?" Nicholai asked as he waded ashore to her.

She shrugged. "For the ones who reach here we always make room, somehow." She was as broad-shouldered as she was tall, in her sixties with gray hair cut like a steel helmet about her tanned square face. She had the air of a no-nonsense woman as she stood astride in open sandals, wet from the sea, wearing a faded linen skirt and mannishly cut shirt.

"This is Alice Van Heffelin, the doctor in charge of the camp," Nicholai said, introducing her to the others.

Alice had noticed Mae Ling at once and wondered where this beautiful girl fitted in... She also instinctively felt she would bring trouble... "Call me Alice," she said, her eyes friendly. "There's no time for formalities here."

"The British will have notified the Macau authorities that we've brought in refugees," Nicholai said as he watched them file wearily off the junk.

"There's no problem as long as their keep isn't going to cost the enclave."

154

"We'll pay."

"You've paid us more than enough already. Since you've brought us your boat we've been able to provide our refugees with better food and medical facilities. Fortunately Father Saludes isn't here to worry himself about breaking the law, and I would rob God himself to care for these people." Alice took Nicholai's arm and led him along the beach.

"Where is Father Saludes?"

"He has cancer. He was ordered to return to Portugal, though the poor man would rather have stayed on and died here. His replacement hasn't been appointed yet so I'm having to carry this on my own."

"What about the United Nations refugee commissioner?"

"He lives in an hotel in Macau and we never see him," Alice said, not hiding her disgust. "I hear he drinks a bottle of whiskey before ten in the morning and travels first class all over the world. But I can't get him to come twenty kilometers to the camp where our people need help. He prefers to talk, talk, talk about them in the comfort of the United Nations... But enough of my problems," she said, pausing. "You'll want to know what we've done with your boat. Look around you," she said proudly. "What do you see?"

Nicholai carefully studied the shoreline. "Nothing."

"Look higher up." Blending inconspicuously with the dense vegetation above the beach was a long bamboo shelter of the kind used to house refugees.

"The boat?"

"Yes."

He was impressed. "How did you get it out of the water and up there?"

"We used logs to make the slipway and winches to pull it up. My refugees and my lepers are men of many talents. They were more than willing helpers."

Fool Boy had limped hurriedly ahead of the party up the narrow strip of beach. The boat was his greatest source of pride, and he wanted to be the first to show it to them. They waited while he pulled open the large bamboo doors.

"How long will you be staying?" Alice asked.

"No longer than three weeks. As soon as we can get the boat ready we'll move on."

"There's no hurry, you should be undisturbed here. The Lady Sun has been impatient, waiting for news about your arrival. I'll send her a message letting her know you're here... she'll want to see you. And tonight my refugees wish to welcome you to the camp—there will be a bonfire on the beach and dancing. Will you come?"

He said he would.

Alice left him at the door. "I'll go now and settle your refugees." She turned to Mae Ling, who stood with the rest of the new arrivals. The living quarters in the boat shed consisted of a single open bamboo platform, and she wanted to separate this girl from the four men. "Help me with them," she told Mae Ling, "then I'll find you a place to stay."

Mae Ling had no choice but to follow Alice.

FIFTH STREET was the first to enter the shelter, clearly surprised at the sight—set on a cradle of crudely hewn wood trestles was a lean, seventy-foot-long World War II gunboat. He reached up and touched its flared bows that had obviously been designed for speed, then ran his hands along the smooth planing surfaces. He had heard about these vessels but had never seen one before. He knew that in their day they had operated as the surface gray wolves of the English Channel, hunting in packs in the dark, maneuvering skillfully through enemy waters. When fully throttled they were a threat even to the great cruisers and capital ships... but that had been long ago. He wasn't certain of how an old boat like this would match today's craft...

"What the hell type is it?" Fifth Street said to Nicholai after circling around the boat.

"A Vosper seventy-three-foot, type-two MGB. Sold off as war surplus stock and shipped out to Hong Kong from England in 1947. I got hold of her in the fifties. She's served us well."

"What's she made of?"

"Hard chine, double mahogany, plywood frames, half-inch plywood deck."

Fifth Street prowled along the side of the boat, running his hands over it, searching for toledo worm that often riddled boats in tropical conditions. She was narrow. "Beam?"

"Nineteen foot, four and a half inches."

He thought so—she'd be a bitch in heavy seas. "Draught?"

"Forward, two foot eight inches. Aft, five foot seven."

"Displacement?"

"Forty tons when she's stripped down."

Fifth Street walked over to the stern, where he surveyed the triple brass propellers that gleamed in the dim light, obviously well cared for. "What kind of engines have you got in her?"

"Three Packard marine engines, fourteen hundred brake horsepower each."

That sounded like the original engines to Fifth Street. "What kind of speed could you get out of her?"

"Thirty-five knots. She can go four hundred eighty miles at twenty-five knots."

Fifth Street looked up at the empty gun turrets on either side of the bridge.

"Armament," Nicholai said, "used to be two point-five-inch Brownings on pedestal mounts."

"Have you still got them?"

Nicholai nodded. "They've been well greased and carefully hidden. Keng Po will pick them up in a couple of days."

After inspecting the boat Fifth Street returned to the bows where he'd started. Above his head, written in Chinese characters, was the boat's name.

"We called her the *Teng Eung*, the *East Wind*," Nicholai said. It was obvious that this boat meant a great deal to him. "What do you think of her?"

Fifth Street sat dejectedly on an upturned drum. When they'd told him they had a craft that would match the *Scimitar*, he'd been expecting something modern and fast, a hydrofoil at least. As he sat considering what this meant for them, he became aware of the others watching him.

"You guys have got to be out of your minds if you think you're going to take a boat that's come out of the ark and try and break through one of the toughest blockades in the world... you know as well as I do that even if we can get this tub out of Macau waters we'll have to cross Communist waters and then the British will be waiting for us. They've got radar and hovercraft, and the *Scimitar*. Hell, even their police launches can do seventeen knots. What are you trying to do? Commit suicide?"

He paused for a moment, rubbing his eyes, hoping to relieve some of the tension he felt building. They didn't seem to be getting the message. "Times have changed. You're out of date with this tub. Get a new one or forget it."

"I know my boat," Nicholai said quietly, confident that the rest of his crew backed him. "I understand what she can do. And I know this coast. I know every rock and every sandbank. I know where a hovercraft can't turn and I can. Radar is only as good as the people who operate it. Your job is to make this boat go faster than the *Scimitar*. The engines are there. Simple question: can you do it?"

Fifth Street eyed him. "I don't know." He realized nothing he could say was going to change Nicholai's mind about his precious boat. "I'll need to take a good look at them first."

157

Wen Yuan came to the boat shed and approached Nicholai. "Take my junk on to the Inner Harbor of Macau and wait there until I contact you," Nicholai told him. Wen Yuan nodded and left.

THAT NIGHT by the firelight the refugees sang and performed the graceful swaying dances of their homeland for the Snake Boat Man's crew. In the distance they could hear the rhythmic clanking from the camp's water pump and the diesel thud of the leprosarium's generator.

Throughout the evening Fool Boy kept leading his friends one at a time up to Nicholai. The children would advance shyly from behind, touch him lightly on the shoulder, then run off into the darkness.

"What's he doing?" he asked Alice, who was seated next to him.

"Fool Boy's charging them for the privilege of touching you. They believe you'll bring them luck."

Overhearing this Udo jumped up, looking around for his son. "The little devil, I'll beat the hell out of him," he began, shouting for the boy.

"Leave him alone," Nicholai said. "He shows some real initiative." He was smiling.

A woman with no hands served him a bowl of food, managing with only her wrists.

"My leprosy patients are the most rewarding to work with," Alice told Nicholai. "Their disease makes it easier for them to accept life in a community that must exist outside the mainstream of society. They live in the next bay. They have their families to come and stay and their children learn not to concern themselves with their parents' disfigurements. It's the refugees who are my main problem...they are disoriented, frustrated, frightened people with no common bond except that they all feel their lives are being wasted here."

She had observed the refugees' unusually animated faces in the firelight. "Tonight is a special occasion," she told Nicholai and Fifth Street, who was seated on the other side of her. "Normally it's a struggle for me to get them out of their lethargy. They're very excited, not only by your arrival but because the host nation selection teams are due here again soon and naturally they all hope to be chosen."

"Will many of them leave then?"

"Fewer each time, I'm afraid," Alice said to Fifth Street. "So far nearly one and a quarter million refugees have fled Indochina since the end of the Vietnamese War, and the world is finding less and less room for them."

"Why don't they get work and do something with their time?" Fifth Street said, his voice tinged with impatience. He knew what it was to be down and out and had always managed to survive.

"The local villagers are hostile toward us. They're afraid that if given the chance the refugees will work harder and for less pay than they will. And in that, at least, they're right. See that man?" She pointed out a middle-aged man with a broken arm and a severely bruised face who was shuffling painfully through the dance steps with his family near the fire. "He and three other men off the same boat recently tried to get work at the fireworks factory in Taipei. The villagers caught them and beat one man so badly that he died of his injuries. In the past they've reacted to the slightest provocation by attacking the camp, molesting the women and looting the shelters."

"What about the police?" Fifth Street said.

"They do nothing. They rarely if ever visit this side of the island. Until three generations ago it was the main pirate stronghold for the whole of this coast. The local clans are pirate stock. They're a violent, insular people. Most of them are recruited for the Macau Syndicate. I meant to warn you about them this afternoon... please," Alice said, her voice low, almost pleading, "do nothing to antagonize the local islanders. This camp is on their land and they barely tolerate us as it is."

LATE THAT night Nicholai and Alice walked back along the beach under the stars. "It's good to have you back," she said. "Macau wasn't the same without you."

She stopped suddenly, staring out at the dark sea. "Listen to me, Nicholai. You've brought your fit, fighting men among my poor, broken-spirited people. Your people can protect themselves, mine can't. I want no recriminations from the villagers or the Syndicate because of your presence here. Believe me, I'll do anything to protect my refugees. Do we understand each other?"

Nicholai smiled at her worried look in the starlight. "Alice, relax. Your refugees are safe with us here. Besides, in a way we are more like them than not. Do you understand?"

She nodded, and squeezed his hand.

CHAPTER 14

THE *NAM SHAN*, a two-thousand-ton ferry, lumbered steadily along its midnight path from Macau to Hong Kong. Below its waterline third-class passengers slept in packed dormitories. On the deck above, gamblers played one-armed bandits or shuffled counters in the mah-jongg rooms. On the topmost deck, behind the bridge in the luxuriously appointed owner's suite, three men sat around a green baize table.

The first was Thomas Wu. On his right was Fang Choy, known as Billion Dollar Choy and reputed to be the wealthiest self-made tycoon in Hong Kong. Across from them, slouched in his chair, was Smallpox Kang, a ruthless man whose reputation equalled that of Dr. Sun in his day. He was the lodgemaster of the 14K Triad, which controlled most of the crime in Hong Kong.

Billion Dollar Choy, owner of the Chung Choy Bank of Prosperity, was suspected by the secretary for security—and with good cause—of maintaining close links with the Triads.

Until Choy, no Chinese had ever considered attacking the Princely House, which had always been the single most powerful institution in Hong Kong. But times had changed for the Princely House. Billion Dollar Choy found its weakness, and it was he who had carefully laid plans for its destruction.

"I estimate it has cost the Princely House a little over nine hundred million dollars so far to fight us off," he said. "We know that their cash assets must be exhausted by now and they've pledged all other assets they own to protect Asian Land." The taipan of the Princely House had put up a far fiercer fight than any of them had expected... Choy stirred uncomfortably in his chair under the level gaze of the others as he explained.

"I had not thought that the taipan would have been able to raise so much money to back his shares, which is why it's taken longer than expected to reach this phase in our plans. However, I believe that his house has now been weakened sufficiently." He turned to Koa Kang. "The time is right for your Triad to launch their labor strikes against the Princely House. I guarantee the stock exchanges will panic and its shares will plummet." A faint look of satisfaction crossed his face.

If Choy's scheme was carried out, the whole overheated economy of Hong Kong could crash, creating a bloodbath for its investors, large and small. But this was of no concern to the men gathered there... what mattered to them was who ruled Hong Kong into the next decade.

"What of the other British *hongs?*" Thomas Wu asked.

"They won't lift a finger to help the Princely House," Choy said. "Their jealousy and greed has turned them into a wolf pack waiting for the Princely House to fall so that they can be first to claim the spoils."

"And we will not allow them to do that," Wu reminded the others. Day after day he and Fang Choy had bought into Asian Land and sold Asian Trading short, manipulating shares they did not own. "This has cost us a great deal more than we bargained for. If we were to fail now it would almost certainly break us. I agree that the time has come to instigate the strikes. The market is nervous anyway about China's intentions concerning the lease. Labor unrest in the companies owned by Princely House is all it needs to send their shares plunging down."

Koa Kang, master of the 14K Triad, hadn't yet spoken. His grizzled head was set on huge, hunched shoulders. He wore a crumpled safari suit, more fitting for the lower deck than the company he kept tonight.

But he was a man who cared little for appearances...

The Triad that Smallpox Kang represented differed markedly from the Macau Syndicate—it was based in Hong Kong and originally organized according to semireligious principles. The Macau Syndicate had no pretensions to being anything other than a criminal society governed by internal laws similar to those of the Mafia.

Triad history traced itself back to the seventeenth century when five Buddhist monks, trained in the martial arts, organized the defense of the Ming Dynasty against the Manchus. The secret society, the Triad that they formed, was pledged to the protection of the emperor. After the decline of the Ming dynasty the Triad fell into disuse, and was not resurrected until the late 1930s, by General Koi Sui-heong, who used it as a secret information source for the Kuomintang. The general found sanctuary in Hong Kong after the Nationalists led by Chiang Kai-shek had lost the civil war to the Communists. He then set about reorganizing the 14K in order to have a base for the eventual return to China of the right-wing Nationalists. But during their years in exile the Triad's original goals were forgotten and along with the six other ruling Triads, of which the 14K was the largest, they too descended into a Mafia-style criminal and terrorist organization.

It was the Triads who inflamed and exploited the disastrous riots of 1956, which led to martial law in Hong Kong. Their members touched off the looting after popular opposition to the ferry-fare price increases in 1966, and they assisted in the Communist-instigated rioting of 1967 when they made and threw bombs for the Communist Party they had once been organized against, killing and maiming more Chinese than *gwilos*.

The police struck back in an attempt to break the Triad's grip on Hong Kong by forming a special anti-Triad department. The lodgemasters, thinking themselves all powerful, had grown complacent, and in a short while the police had assembled a gallery containing photographs of over 50,000 known Triad members. They launched a purge, arresting or driving out the lodgemasters, and the Triads—without the iron discipline imposed by their leaders—splintered into commonplace underworld gangs that engaged in a violent and self-defeating rivalry.

Then Koa Kang, a refugee from China and a longtime Triad member who had worked his way from a forty-nine, or common soldier, through the ranks of red staff and white fan to vanguard, seized power. In three brief years he had reorganized the 14K, reintroducing its rigid code of initiation and discipline. And now he was the single most powerful figure in the Hong Kong underworld. His lodge members were especially well represented in the labor unions. Which was where—as in the riots of the fifties and sixties—he proposed to use his power.

"Everything you have asked for is in place," Smallpox Kang said to Thomas Wu. He had finished nearly a bottle of Remy Martin and his eyes were half closed. "Except you have forgotten one thing"—he raised his head, the menacing look on his face reinforced by his smallpox scars— "my lodge hasn't received one ounce of gold yet."

Kang knew that Thomas Wu was using the gold as a means of squeezing Crystal Lily out of Macau, and had accepted Wu's promise that his Triad would not suffer any losses as a result of the power struggle. He approved of Thomas Wu's succession as head of the Macau Syndicate—certainly the Macanese would be easier to deal with than some chit of a girl. "Even so," Kang said, his tone a warning, "the gold has been intercepted first by you and then by the British. So far it is they who prosper, not us."

"She has managed to tip the British off whenever I've tried to pass a shipment on to you. We stalemate each other—"

"She's a child. Can't you finish with her?" Kang demanded.

"Soon," Wu said. Though Kang was on his side, for convenience' sake, he wasn't to be crossed. "Very soon now. As you know, the debt she owes your lodge falls due on the last day of this month. I can assure you she will not be able to make the delivery. She will have to default—"

"And if you then remove her, who guarantees this debt to me?"

"I will." Koa Kang was striking a hard bargain, but Wu was left with no choice. "I guarantee the debt owed by Dr. Sun to your lodge."

"And you?" Koa Kang turned to Billion Dollar Choy. "Our arrangement is that this gold is to be my Triad's investment in the Princely House. Before I proceed with the strike I want a guarantee that, for our part in this, we will receive the value of our gold in shares in the Princely House. Do you guarantee this to me?"

Choy nervously caught Thomas Wu's eye. Both men knew there was no way back from a debt to a Triad, that they were both irreversibly in it now. The only escape would be death—and a very unpleasant one. "Agreed," he said.

"Then I will make sure the Princely House comes crashing down." Koa Kang was clearly delighted with himself. "Imagine," he said, mocking Billion Dollar Choy's well-known social pretensions, "as a major shareholder in the Princely House the British governor might have to give me a knighthood, too."

Choy thought it politic to join in with Koa Kang's amusement, even though it was at his expense... unaware that Denning's successor as taipan of the Princely House, appointed by Koa Kang—the newly arisen kingmaker—was Thomas Wu. The result would be the joining of the underworld of the Two Sisters, Macau and Hong Kong. It was an old dream that had yet to be realized, and the man who achieved it would wield more power than anyone beyond the realm of China. It was possible that that time had now come...

On the bridge of the ferry the captain, a Welshman, spotted the lights on the tip of Lantau Island that marked the boundary of Hong Kong waters. In crisp whites, his cap respectfully tucked under his arm, he made his way along a passage filled with lounging bodyguards and knocked on the door to the owner's suite. Thomas Wu looked up. "We'll be in Hong Kong waters in another ten minutes, sir." For all his years on the South China Sea the captain's Welsh accent was unmistakable.

"All right. Call my boat alongside," Wu said as he got up. The captain's interruption had been timely—Wu had no intention of allowing Hong Kong Special Branch and immigration authorities to identify him in the company of the other two just yet.

"Monday then," he said to Koa Kang. They had agreed on the first day of the following week as the date the strikes against the Princely House would begin.

"Monday," Kang nodded. "And see to it that you control that she-cat in Macau." He got up, ready to leave Billion Dollar Choy to his stateroom so that he could mingle inconspicuously with the third-class passengers below before the ferry docked in Hong Kong.

The captain escorted Thomas Wu to the head of the gangway. A high-speed launch waited alongside to carry him back to Macau.

It had been a difficult, but successful... he hoped... meeting.

IT WAS the siesta hour in Macau. Crystal Lily rested on her bed, drifting uneasily between sleep and wakefulness. Her mind wandered back to more peaceful times in Hawaii. Her amah had spied on her there for her father and bodyguards watched her every move, but in the relaxed American atmosphere guards could be evaded, and she had lived a life that seemed almost normal.

She remembered with a tug of regret the earnest doctor she'd made light of to Nicholai, a man she'd nearly fallen in love with. Their romance, of course, had to end badly... She hadn't been fair or honest

164

with him, going to great lengths to disguise her true background. It was bad enough for his rich Episcopalian parents that he wanted to marry a *Chinese*—if they had known who she really was, she thought wryly, they would have suffered a joint stroke. In Hawaii she was always hiding, waiting in limbo for her father to die or disinherit her... Her thoughts now drifted to the Irishman who had pursued her near the end of her stay... he, on the other hand, knew about her father and something of her past... he wouldn't dare follow her here. She smiled...

"My lady," the comprador called to her from outside her bedroom door... he'd had to climb the stairs in a hurry, causing a shortness of breath. "My lady, Thomas Wu is here—"

She was alert instantly and all thoughts of her past life were pushed aside, now abruptly unreal. "Has he come alone?" She tried to will herself to lock her fear of Thomas Wu in the back of her mind.

"Yes, my lady, he wishes to speak with you in private, I've shown him into your father's room."

Lily got up and checked her appearance in the mirror. She ran a brush through her gleaming waist-length hair, was about to place it more formally on the top of her head when she stopped, leaving it down. It made her face softer, her whole appearance more fragile. It might give Wu some false confidence.

"Watch us," she instructed the comprador as they parted at the bottom of the stairs, and he promptly made his way to the small cubicle where the spy grill had been worked into one of the cabinets.

Wu had seated himself in her father's ornate chair at the head of the table in the Crystal Room. His tall figure was lean, his long face sallow, with a pampered skin and heavy jowls. His whole being seemed to radiate his malevolence.

He stood as Crystal Lily entered the room and came toward her, his lips in a bloodless smile.

"Why have you put your guards around my palace?" she said quickly, stopping his approach.

"We haven't yet discovered who was behind the attack on you," Wu lied. "Chang has merely been instructed to protect you—"

"Who gave Chang his orders?"

"I did," Wu said, and immediately regretted rising to the bait.

"I still lead the Syndicate, not you." She seated herself in her father's chair. "And when I am ready to do so I will instruct Chang in matters concerning my personal safety."

"Why must we quarrel?" Wu said, attempting to recoup. "My only thought was to defend you from harm." She's afraid, he thought... the attack seems to have had its effect...

He pulled up a chair facing her. "The reason I have come to see you is because you are young, and alone, and surrounded by real danger. Whether you know it or not, I have cared about you very much ever since you were a child." Even now he couldn't camouflage the lust he felt when he was with her... his long-fingered hands had begun to drum restlessly on the table, and she had to restrain herself from flinching when he reached out and touched her. She waited, apparently passive, for what would come next. Inside she felt only a deep loathing for this man, her earlier memories of him now awakened...

Thomas Wu had served her father like a dog. His position as private secretary gave him access to their living quarters within the palace and on several occasions as a young girl she had looked up from her bed to find him standing in the doorway, watching her. He stalked her, trying to fondle her when no one was around. She had heard stories, whispered by the amahs those times when she'd crept to their quarters for comfort, about Wu's sexual perversions, his fondness for visiting certain houses in the Street of Happiness where men sought the child virgins to arouse their jaded appetites. His face was frequently the subject of her nightmares... Her mother had died before she was three and her father's concubines considered her a potential enemy. So there was no one in the palace with enough power or interest to protect her on a particularly horrible night when Wu came to her bed. She was nine years of age. She fought him silently with her nails and her teeth, and although he almost suffocated her, in the end he did break away and creep out of her room. She'd gone immediately to her father, told him what had happened. Wu indignantly denied her allegations and, as he expected, no servant dared go against him. By this time her father was growing old, his power was declining and Wu was, he felt, too useful to destroy on his daughter's hysterical word. Encouraged by this, Wu mistakenly tried to bargain with Dr. Sun for his child's hand in marriage. She'd begged her father not to consider such a match. It wasn't necessary. Dr. Sun had no intention of allowing his daughter to marry his secretary, and though he teased her, convinced that such treatment was a legitimate means of sharpening her character, he nearly ended Wu's life. Not for his assault, but for his presumption. Wu became appropriately humble and even more ingratiating, biding his time. In the end it was Nicholai who persuaded Dr. Sun to send his daughter away...

The years had helped to heal many memories, but Thomas Wu was reminding her of the worst of them once again.

"I offer you my protection in marriage," he was saying. "You would remain here in your own home. You would continue to live the life you are accustomed to, and you would have all the advantages of a loyal and dutiful husband—"

"Provided, of course, I pay him wifely duty by turning over everything I own?" She well understood that he was proposing a bloodless way for him to take power, her power in the Syndicate.

He shrugged. "You would be protected. Is that not a husband's duty...?"

Crystal knew that once married to Wu and stripped of the protection of her palace and her guards she wouldn't last more than a few months. The man seemed to have forgotten the lessons he and her father had taught her as a child. She applied one of them now.

"It's true that my inheritance has become a burden," she said, seeming to open up to him. "I have, in fact, considered taking a husband... my comprador has mentioned Rocky Lee..."

"Has he approached you?" Wu's voice was sharp. Worried in spite of himself.

"Not me, of course." She shrugged. "But my comprador does speak of him from time to time." She almost smiled at him.

What was Yu Shik Lieu up to now, Wu thought, and disliked the obvious answer. "Lee is a womanizer. I assure you he would bring you nothing but trouble and pain. And such a marriage would serve no purpose—he doesn't command the respect of the others, they would prefer to be led by me—"

"I assume this is something you've already discussed with them?"

"Your marriage?" Wu stayed calm. It would, he thought, be a pleasure to tame her... "Yes, it seemed a sensible means of safeguarding the Syndicate. Your sex and education... your father never meant you to have this life. No man would wish it for his daughter—"

"You're mistaken. He made me his heir."

"At the end his mind was no longer able to reason. No one dared approach him on the subject of his successor—"

"Even so, he appointed me."

Wu understood the cards she held. She knew that he needed access to the gold and the lists of bribed officials, debtors, bank account numbers held inside the palace, that it was impossible for him to operate the Syndicate without them. The time had come, he decided, to remind her of the consequences should she refuse his offer.

"There are methods other than marriage by which an inheritance such as yours can be transferred. I am sure you recall what happened to your mother... Now I fear for your safety even within this palace. One never

167

knows when one can be betrayed by those one most trusts."

She understood he was telling her that there were traitors close to her. He'd managed to touch on her point of greatest weakness.

Maintaining her control, Crystal Lily got up slowly. "I appreciate the value of your proposal," she said, abruptly all feminine and vulnerable as she searched for a way to buy herself time, "but I have no family to draw support from. I will need at least a short while to prepare myself for the prospect of marriage—"

"How long?"

"Not long."

"May we consider ourselves betrothed?" After the failed attack he needed something concrete to help consolidate his position inside the Syndicate.

"No, not yet..." She smiled to soften the words, and as she passed him, she forced herself to let her thigh brush lightly against his arm. And added, "But perhaps we are on the way to becoming allies?"

She personally saw him to the door.

The comprador came up behind her after Wu had left, proud of his pupil. "You did very well—"

"I doubt I really fooled him," she said as she watched the chauffeur open the door of Wu's car.

"The Snake Boat Man is on the move," the comprador said, trying to encourage her, "and we know of Thomas Wu's meeting with Billion Dollar Choy and Koa Kang."

But she wasn't easily reassured. "Make contact with the taipan. Tell him that we will help him in his fight to keep control of the Princely House. We need an ally in Hong Kong. You'll have to reach him yourself... I've put myself into a corner," she said, thinking aloud. "If I fail there will be no escape from a marriage to Thomas Wu..."

They were both aware of the consequences of that. Crystal Lily had grown very pale, except for the traces of red that colored her high cheekbones, showing her feelings. "All I want to do," she said quietly as she remembered Wu's hands on her, "is to kill him."

"In the same situation, your father would tell you to wait patiently and watch the channel," the comprador advised, "and eventually the bodies of your enemies will float by."

"And did they for him?"

"They did, my lady. Unfailingly."

But am I, she thought, my father's daughter?

168

CHAPTER 15

JOSS DENNING stood alone in the ballroom at the Peninsula Hotel attired in evening clothes. This was an important event in Hong Kong's social calendar—the charity ball organized by the governor's lady—and tonight, to protect his face when the Princely House was in trouble, he had to attend. As the music played and the beautifully dressed people filtered by, Joss wished himself anywhere else...

Dina Maplin broke away from the group gathered around her husband and she approached Joss. She was a pretty brunette, some ten years younger than her husband, and already a little drunk.

"Taipan, where's that gorgeous wife of yours tonight?" she asked, though of course she knew the answer. Hong Kong's gossip missed nothing. Dina was merely testing to see how the taipan would react in the role of cuckolded husband. She should have known better—Joss Denning was a far tougher man than his sensitive looks suggested. His marriage was a private heartache. He offered no excuses for his wife's absence. "As you can see," he said, firmly, shutting off further questions, "she's not here."

"Well, don't you worry, darling, everybody loves a sailor, but sooner or later this one's got to go back to sea." Years ago she had wanted Joss herself and was still jealous of Clair, who behaved as willfully as she liked in spite of the rigid codes of Hong Kong's colonial society. "By the way, why don't you throw her out, or is it her shares?"

His answer was unspoken... It's because I loved her, Joss thought. I don't grieve for the marriage that's ending. I grieve for the love we lost...

To Dina he now said, "Clair votes her own shares, you know that." He smiled graciously, about to turn away when she took hold of his arm, stopping him.

"I know I'm a bitch for saying that, but damnit, Joss, I care about you—"

Dina's husband, tall, suave, graying appropriately at the temples, spotted his wife with the taipan and crossed the room to join them. As Dina quickly linked her arm possessively through his, Joss couldn't help wonder just how much Maplin really knew about her...

Hugh Maplin, something less than in control of his own wife, was chairman of the Kowloon Peninsula Bank, the biggest and by far most influential bank in the colony. "I've been trying to reach you these last two days," Joss said to him.

"I've been meaning to get back to you," Maplin stalled, but Joss was determined to use the opportunity to press him before he could move on. "I know this is no place to talk but I need an answer to that plan I put to your board." Dina, not interested, spotted someone she wanted to speak to and left.

"Ah, yes." Maplin nodded. He knew that the taipan's plan represented a last-ditch attempt to save his company from defaulting on its debts by using a ninety-day bridging loan from his bank. To secure the loan, he was prepared to offer every available asset his company had left, but it was still far from enough.

Maplin studied Joss for a moment, relishing his ability to destroy a man he felt had no right, in any case, to occupy the position of a taipan. "I would have preferred to have told you this in my office," he said. "Unfortunately we can't assist you. Normally we would protect our clients' confidence, but in view of the long and special relationship our bank has had with the Princely House, I will advise you that we are now acting for Billion Dollar Choy."

170

Joss was stunned, though he immediately knew he shouldn't have been. Still . . . the Kowloon Peninsula Bank and the Princely House had an association that went back to the very beginning of Hong Kong. They were partners in an untold number of ventures. Maplin had information about Princely House's borrowings and corporate structure that was known only to members of the board . . . and now he was coolly telling him that he was switching sides.

"Sorry, old boy," Maplin said, his voice hardly apologetic, "but you know how tough it gets in this shark's pool. The old order giveth way to the new. Got Chinese on my board now who want me to support men like Fang Choy over the old British *hongs*. More and more it's the Chinese firms that hold the financial power here, and banks like mine have to recognize that fact of life if we're to survive in Hong Kong. No hard feelings, I hope. You'll try the other banks—?"

"You know damn well that if the Kowloon Peninsula, which knows more about my companies than anyone else, doesn't back me then no one else will."

Maplin smiled, shrugged and moved away. As he did, the secretary for security waited until he'd joined his wife, then helped himself neatly to two glasses of wine from a passing waiter's tray and handed one to the taipan. "Just been listening in on some gossip being passed around by your colleagues," he said, fixing his shrewd eyes on Joss's face. "Can you stand some more bad news?"

Joss assumed it would be about the Kowloon Peninsula switching sides. "I think I already know—"

"Not about this, I'm afraid. Your directors have called a board meeting for nine o'clock tomorrow morning."

Joss didn't bother to reply; that was already common knowledge.

"They're going to try and vote you out."

"They can't do that—"

"Don't be too sure," Trevelyan warned. "The word in my ear is that your wife has been persuaded by her various cousins to withdraw her voting proxy from you. If her family has anything to do with it, the notice from her lawyers will be on your desk by start of business tomorrow. Without the support of her shares you know as well as I that you'll find yourself voted down."

Trevelyan gave the taipan a moment to digest this news, then asked, "Have you any more information for me from Macau?" The taipan hadn't been in touch since the tip-off about the sampan carrying General Li Ch'en.

"I've nothing new," Joss told him, wanting badly to get away. "No one in Macau is talking. Even old friends"... are there any left, he wondered?... "of the Princely House seem afraid to open their mouths."

"I'm getting much the same reaction here in Hong Kong," the secretary for security said. He spotted his wife beside the governor's lady signaling him over to meet some visiting VIPs. "God knows why I let myself be dragged to these charity bashes, I loathe them." He knew why Clair Denning was absent tonight, and he was impressed with the way the young taipan was handling the situation. "Good luck for tomorrow," he said, touching Joss's arm before he drifted away. He was one of the few men in that room who meant it.

Joss reached into his pocket and found a message there, slipped to him by one of the hotel doormen when he'd arrived earlier that evening. It gave a time and a place for a meeting, and the chop mark was familiar. He had been less than strictly honest with the secretary for security about his contacts in Macau. He waited another twenty minutes and then left.

It took Joss forty minutes to cross the harbor and drive over steep, winding roads to Stanley village, which was situated on a southern peninsula of Hong Kong Island. He parked his car and walked down the narrow lanes of what, before property prices soared, had been a thriving artists' colony.

It was two A.M. on a hot night. A thick wet mist curled in over the harbor from the sea. He stopped once or twice, listening for the footsteps of anyone following him, but was cocooned from the night sounds by the mist. Soon he reached the area that in daytime was a colorful tourist market. He found the address he had been directed to and waited in a shop doorway.

Nothing stirred in the village; even the dogs aboard the junks were silenced by the mist. Joss felt ill at ease. There had been no time to check the authenticity of the message... he caught a glimpse of a face pressed against the glass shop door, studying him. He heard the catches being drawn back, the door opened and a handsome middle-aged woman signaled him to follow her into the shop. Quietly she closed the door and led him through the gloom into the back.

The shop, squeezed unobtrusively between a trendy boutique and a hi-fi center, was owned by a Chinese apothecary. It was narrow and dusty, smelled of musk, ginger, seaweed and incense. In the gloom he could just make out, on top of tall cabinets, glass jars containing pickled bears' claws, scaly anteater, otters' penis and snakes' gallbladders. Within each cabinet were housed countless tiny drawers that must have held

172

many of the two thousand traditional remedies used by the Cantonese to prolong life and vigor.

The woman ducked under the counter, leaned her weight against one of the tall cabinets, which rolled back smoothly, revealing a trapdoor. She opened it and signaled Joss to climb down. As he did so his nostrils caught the distinctive sweet, clinging scent of opium. He found himself in a softly lit cellar. Red silk paneling covered the walls, a thick carpet the floor. On a low divan at the far end of the cellar, propped on silk cushions, lay Crystal Lily's comprador, Yu Shik Lieu. The old man had been dreaming under opium fumes to ease the pain in his lungs. He opened his eyes. "Welcome, taipan," he said. He lifted an arm, indicating the woman who was now crouching over a spirit stove in a corner of the room. "My number three wife," he added, vouching for her.

Joss guessed that the old man was too sick to venture far without a nurse. "I hadn't expected to find you in Hong Kong," he said.

The comprador gave a dry chuckle. "Neither would my enemies. An old fox keeps more than one lair. But I confess, the journey becomes too dangerous, this will be my last visit for a while."

Things were beginning to fall into place for Joss now. "It was you who sent me the information that allowed the police to intercept that sampan?"

"Yes." The comprador nodded. "A gesture of our good faith."

Third wife brought tea, kneeling to present the steaming, fragrant pale amber liquid that would refresh her husband.

The comprador watched Joss in turn receive a bowl from third wife. He looked into Joss's intense eyes and wondered at this man's sensitive face that seemed more suited to a poet than a great taipan of the Princely House. Yu Shik Lieu considered if he could trust him, if he had made the right decision to come here. But his lady's instructions had been clear.

Joss waited for the old man to speak.

"I hear that the Princely House is in danger, taipan," the comprador probed. "Your enemies have caught you at a most vulnerable time. They are forcing your shares down, daily reducing the amount of collateral your company can offer to renew its loans. When do these loans fall due?"

"The first of them, on the fifteenth of September."

Nearly five weeks. Time enough to help, the comprador thought.

"What interest do you in Macau have in this?"

"Our houses have been allied in the past. Now that we face a common enemy, they can be again." Yu Shik Lieu was referring to the days when the Princely House bought gold on the London market and shipped it to the Syndicate. Some of the more respectable directors of the Princely House, he realized, would rather forget the past...

"How can you help me?" Joss asked cautiously. He had met Yu Shik Lieu briefly years ago and remembered that the comprador's mind was like quicksilver.

"Two nights ago a meeting took place between Thomas Wu of the Macau Syndicate, Billion Dollar Choy and Koa Kang, master of the 14K Triad."

"How do you know this?"

Yu Shik Lieu shrugged. "The captain of the ferry is loyal to us. Thomas Wu has trapped my lady's fortune in Macau at a time when the Triad are pressing her to repay a debt to them in gold. That is our concern. But why should they be meeting with Fang Choy, who is in a battle with you for the Princely House? Unless"—the comprador answered his own question—"Fang Choy and Thomas Wu have gambled all that they own and are now ready to use the Triad as a means to ensure they win against you."

"Why should the Triad help them?"

"What if, in return, the Triad use the gold to buy a portion of the Princely House?"

Joss was there ahead of him. "With the lease on Hong Kong running out, there would be no better way for them to spread their power out of the east."

Yu Shik Lieu looked up, pleased to find that Joss possessed a shrewd mind. His lady was right. Properly handled, this young taipan could prove a useful ally.

Joss understood now why Yu Shik Lieu had risked this meeting. "But if you fail to deliver the gold, then the danger the Triad represents to the Princely House falls away?"

"My lady has no choice but to honor her debt to the Triad. Failure to do so would cost her her life."

"Then if she wins, I fail."

The comprador raised himself on his cushions and clicked his tongue impatiently. "If our interests had conflicted to such a degree, would I have advised you of our intentions? There are ways of discharging a debt," he went on quietly, "that will bring no benefit to the Triad, Thomas Wu or Billion Dollar Choy. We will use this gold to destroy our enemies. And as soon as my lady is free, she is prepared to loan you sufficient monies to tide you over your debt-repayment date."

"And in return...?"

"In return you must see to it that the Snake Boat Man's craft, carrying our gold, is allowed through Hong Kong's defenses. Also, if she chooses, my lady may leave Macau and be granted full resident status in Hong Kong."

"That's impossible," Joss said, his voice sounding his disappointment... he had no hope of meeting such conditions. "The governor isn't going to take a risk on my word or yours that the gold will not reach the Triad, *and* he has all the force he needs to stop your boat."

"The Princely House is still a very important pillar in the British establishment. Put our proposal to the governor," Yu Shik Lieu urged. "Show him why he cannot refuse, and when you have an answer bring it to Macau. My lady wishes to see you herself. But I warn you, in return for her aid she will require nothing less than an assurance of free passage directly from the governor."

Joss stood. "I will do all I can, but tell your mistress that the Princely House, unfortunately, carries less authority than it used to."

The interview had tired out the comprador, he wanted to rest. "This meeting with your directors tomorrow," he asked suddenly as Joss climbed the stairs, "can you win?"

For a moment Joss was caught off-guard by the comprador's knowledge of his affairs, then reminded himself that the Syndicate would have kept a paid informer in the Princely House from the days when they traded together. "Put it this way," he said, thinking of his wife, "I've not lost yet."

The comprador liked the man's spirit. "Neither has my lady lost her fight yet," he told Joss. "Bring word soon to Macau. Together we may still hold off our enemies..."

CHAPTER 16

JOSS SLEPT for an hour over the wheel of his car, then drove to a beach house near Shek O. He and Clair had built it soon after they were married. It had been a special place for them . . . a hideaway where they could go to be alone, to swim naked in the private cove and make love long into the night. Gradually, as their marriage broke down, they stopped going. Now Clair used it as a place to meet her lovers.

Joss climbed out of his car and in the hot, harsh light of the dawn walked down the steep driveway. His tie was unknotted, his crumpled dinner jacket slung over his shoulder. He knew he looked like hell but he could hold off no longer. He had to be back in the city by eight A.M.

He rang the bell, heared it chime inside the cool, white cottage built over the rocks just above the tideline. When there was no answer he rang again. Clair kept late hours and none of the servants were about yet. Then he heard bare footsteps padding across the tiled floors, and the door of his house was opened by the dark-haired American naval commander, naked except for a ridiculous sarong around his waist that Clair must have lent him.

"What the hell...?" the American began, then recognized Joss, and the sleep left his eyes.

"May I come in?" Joss said, moving past the American into his house. He looked around, his eyes meeting all the familiar objects. He'd been expecting Clair to have company, but still he felt the sharp stab of pain. He walked down the steps into the sunken drawing room. Records lay scattered on the floor, along with empty brandy glasses and a bottle. He could almost feel Clair in this room from last night, curled up on the floor with a cushion, listening to music...

The naval officer followed him. He had recovered some of his self-confidence now. "I guess I should introduce myself—"

"I remember you," Joss told him. "Please call my wife." He felt the room closing in on him. He had trouble breathing. He walked quickly through the french doors to the wooden balcony with steps that he'd built himself leading down to the sea.

Clair came now, on bare feet, wearing a thin robe that clearly limned her figure, showed the dull gold suntan beneath.

Joss had been leaning against the wooden balustrade staring at the sea. He straightened when he heard her, tried, without success, to keep the strain and weariness from his face.

"Poor Joss," she said, studying her husband with eyes that held a hint of pity in them.

"Why did you bring him here? I preferred it when you used hotels."

"I've been meaning to find you and tell you," she said. She nodded back in the direction of the American waiting somewhere in the rooms behind them. "This time it's serious—"

"You've said good-bye and hello to a dozen men on a dozen ships... what makes this one different?"

"I'm getting old," Clair said. "Perhaps you haven't noticed, darling, but others have. To be young and beautiful and rich is to be forgiven everything in Hong Kong—but it's no place for a woman to grow old. Given half a chance the society matrons are going to crucify me. I'm thinking of leaving before that happens."

"And the Princely House?"

"I'm not sure yet. You cared enough about Asian Trading to lose me. Why should I help you?" She leaned against the balustrade. "Any regrets, Joss?"

"What's the point?"

Typical puritan Joss, she thought. He never bent no matter how much he needed her. That was a good part of their trouble... she'd never owned him, possessed him, and that made her horribly insecure... "I don't think you can win, poor darling. Are you going to keep on fighting?"

"Yes, I'm going to keep on fighting."

"Well, good luck this morning."

"Will you be there?"

"I may be."

"On which side?"

"On my own, darling. Surely by now you must know that."

JOSS REACHED Hong Kong's Central District in the snarl of the morning traffic and took the private elevator to the taipan's suite on the fifty-first floor of the Asian Trading building. He showered and changed, then went down a floor to his office. His secretary, Connie Ching, was there arranging the workload on his desk. She was a well-groomed, marvelously efficient Eurasian who had worked loyally for Joss since he'd become taipan.

She indicated an envelope on top of the pile. "This came from your wife's lawyers," she said. "I had to sign for it." They both knew what it contained. Connie's face showed clearly that she was sharing much of the strain Joss was under.

"I've been expecting it," he said.

"The board meeting's still scheduled for nine A.M.," she reminded him dully, as though somehow she had hoped it had been canceled, or just disappeared.

"Have you checked the latest line-up of directors?" He knew Connie had her own sources of information in the building.

"The majority are against you," she said. "Some of the senior staff came in very early this morning, taipan," Connie added. "They'd like to see you before the meeting." Joss glanced at the piles of urgent telexes at his elbow waiting for his attention. "It's important..."

"All right," he said, "show them in."

The majority of the men who entered his spacious office were Chinese. He was surprised at the number, some thirty in all. Men he had promoted to senior managers over the strong racial bias of his conservative-minded board to revitalize the struggling Asian Trading subsidiary companies. On the whole they were succeeding, but to turn around their companies' fortunes had taken time, and money.

"What can I do for you, gentlemen?" Joss had guessed that they were there to seek reassurance from him over their futures with the Princely House. It was a human enough reaction from men who'd reached the stage in their careers when it would be difficult for them to find equivalent senior positions in a rival *hong*.

Their spokesman, John Chan, stepped forward. One of the most talented managers in the Asian shipping arm, he handed Joss a slim folder. "Taipan," he said, "this contains the resignations of every man in the room. We understand better than anyone what you have done for our great *hong*. If at this morning's meeting the directors choose to force your resignation, then we will go with you."

Joss hadn't been expecting this and was stunned. He was also deeply grateful.

"Are you suggesting that I blackmail my board with these resignations?" He smiled.

"Let's just say that we know the strength of the opposition you're facing and we're offering you a small edge, taipan."

It was more than that, much more. They were throwing him a lifeline and he knew it. "If you back me in this way and I still lose, none of the other *hongs* will ever employ you—"

"None of us want to work for the other *hongs*, sir," Chan said quietly. "We're of the Princely House, and so, for most of us here, were our fathers before us. You are perhaps the finest taipan we've had since our founder. We wanted you to know that you are not alone in this fight. Nearly all your staff are behind you."

"Thank you," Joss said, more deeply touched than his reserve would allow him to show. The wreck of his personal life, combined with the weariness and loneliness of being taipan of a company under siege, had begun to undermine his determination. Now the knowledge that his managers stood solidly behind him shored up his confidence. He only wished he had words to tell them how much their gesture was appreciated, but of course they already knew... "Thank you for your support, I'll do my best to deserve it," he said, and the managers withdrew.

Connie remained behind. Joss knew someone must have spent a frantic weekend drumming up support and committing those men to him, and he need hardly guess it was she. "Is your resignation in here with the others?" he asked, touching the folder.

"Of course, taipan," she said. "As a matter of fact, mine was the first." To her surprise and intense pleasure he crossed the room quickly and kissed her.

"Bless you, Connie, how long have I got?"

She glanced at her watch. "Another thirty minutes."

"All right, leave me and see I'm not disturbed."

"You know"—Connie turned to him by the door—"the staff didn't give a damn about you not being born a Tiernan. They accepted you as taipan a long time ago. Fight for us all this morning, our faith is with you."

HALF AN hour later Joss walked down a carpeted corridor and entered the boardroom. The others were already assembled. Only the taipan's chair at the head of the table was vacant.

His eyes found Clair. She had come after all. She was dressed in a smartly tailored two-piece suit with a wide-brimmed hat and, as always, she had managed to make herself the center of attention. She smiled at Joss—her funny, sad, down-at-the-mouth smile that told him her vote was against him.

Around the walls of this imposing paneled room hung the portraits of the previous taipans, reminding Joss that here lay the center of power of a great company with tentacles reaching into every corner of the marketplace and affecting the tide of business throughout the Orient.

The taipan brought the meeting to order. There was only one item on the agenda. "I know that your shares and your individual fortunes are committed to the Princely House, alongside the futures of thousands of our staff who have looked to their livelihoods from this company for generations. I tell you now that as taipan it is my firm resolve not to sell. We are not even going to negotiate with Fang Choy and the rest of his wolfpack. We are going to fight them."

"Taipan, we've no choice." Lord Angus McEwan, his face still a blustery red from days spent shooting on his Scottish estates, was the first to attack. He and Clair's other cousins had flown in from all over the world especially for this meeting. "The first loan repayments are due in five weeks. We can't meet them, that's common knowledge now, and the banks won't extend. The Princely House shares have been driven so low that we can't raise any more collateral and the market won't take a public issue in the present climate. We're beaten. We have to sell now while our shares still command a price—"

"What has Billion Dollar Choy offered you?" Joss asked Angus quietly, knowing that Choy would have already approached the cousins individually.

180

"Fifty percent over present market price," Angus said, not even sounding uncomfortable. "That's a very fair offer in the circumstances, to my mind."

"The Princely House has been in your family for five generations," Joss reminded him.

"That doesn't count now," Cousin Willie interrupted him. He had stock brokerage interests in London, and no doubt Billion Dollar Choy had guaranteed to keep the Princely House business going loyally in that direction. "What matters is that since you were made taipan you've continually committed this company to an overborrowed situation. You rode your luck as long as the market stayed high, but now in a recession, and with debts to repay, you've let our enemies choose this moment to catch us truly between the frying pan and the fire. If you and your local directors had behaved more responsibly in the first place, we wouldn't be sitting here now."

"When I was made taipan the Princely House was running down," Joss said. "The reason I was elected over you gentlemen was because something had to be done to stop the slide, and fast, and none of you was prepared to take that responsibility. As you well know, I was obliged to borrow money to capitalize our companies, and if you look at our balance sheet rather than at what you see happening to our shares on the market, you'll see I've been successful. We've turned the corner and we're coming up again. Billion Dollar Choy is exploiting a temporary weakness—"

"Can you guarantee that you'll find the money to repay these loans as they fall due?" Cousin Charles demanded. His branch of the family had set up in Canada dealing in oil leases. "Because if not, I can tell you Fang Choy is already bidding the institutions for our shares and, longtime loyalty or not, if you don't come up with some announcement soon that stops the stock market slide in our shares, the institutions are going to sell. Before that happens, taipan, and we've got nothing left to offer, we want you to approach Billion Dollar Choy and sell our company to him at the best price you can get for us."

"It's no bad thing to be selling now," Angus told Joss. "Our forebears had the best out of Hong Kong. The lease expires in less than sixteen years. We'll do well to get our money clear before then, and let Choy and his kind deal with the damned Communists."

"I happen to believe Hong Kong has a future," Joss said with emphasis. "Beyond the expiration of the lease." He was Hong Kong born and cared deeply about its future, whereas the cousins were all descended from the

181

female line of the family and had long since moved away. "It has survived war and occupation and the Communist takeover of the Mainland. It will survive beyond nineteen ninety-seven when the lease runs out. Our companies' roots are buried deep in the bedrock of this colony. We know the trade, we've made our profits here, and the livelihood of our share-holders and our employees depends on our decision today. I hardly need tell you that even Billion Dollar Choy can't afford all of the Princely House. No individual can. He'll have to strip its assets and sell them off to pay for what he keeps. I can guarantee you nothing, gentlemen, except that we still have five weeks left to raise new bridging loans. And at the pace business moves in Hong Kong, that is a long time. Don't sell out."

"Look, we're not here to argue with you." Cousin Angus's voice was more a growl. "We've already discussed this among us and we're here to vote. If you decide to go against the majority vote, then we'll elect another taipan to negotiate the sale to Billion Dollar Choy."

Joss looked at Clair. She was silent, she was going along with her cousins. So would most of the other directors. Among them, the family held the largest bloc of voting shares and when it came to the crunch, they held the power.

"Before you take this vote, there's something I wish to clarify," Joss said. "Billion Dollar Choy's offer to you is to pay fifty percent above whatever the market value of the shares are at the date of sale. Am I right?" He gambled that Billion Dollar Choy would have phrased his offer in this way so as to exert maximum pressure on the majority share-holders to sell before the market dropped further.

"You're right," Angus said.

"Well, then, I can't agree to sell," Joss said, and slid the folder down to the center of the polished table. "In there, gentlemen, you'll find my resignation, to take effect immediately together with the resignations of the majority of the senior management of the Princely House. You can imagine at this time the effect such an announcement will have on the value of your shares. Now, I have a good deal of urgent work to get through. I'll leave you to deliberate and give me your decision."

Angus had reached for and was leafing through the folder even before Joss had left the room. "He's got them right enough," he announced shakily to the other directors. "Nearly all the senior management will go with him."

"Damn him. If he does this to us," Charles put in, "he's finished in Hong Kong. And what about the countless minority shareholders he's always whining about? They'll suffer too."

"Angus, go back to Billion Dollar Choy," Willie urged, "see if he'll do a deal for our shares at today's market price."

"No, Choy will have got a sniff of these resignations before we've left this room. He'll wait for the market to panic and then he'll buy us out at the bottom. He'll clean us out. Wouldn't you? We'll get nothing for our shares."

Clair listened contemptuously to her bickering relatives. "*Cousins* Willie, Angus, Charles, you convinced me that for the good of the family Joss had to go. Instead it's clear, dear cousins, that *he's* got *you* by the balls. And I have to tell you"—there was a special gleam in her eyes—"that it's a distinct pleasure to see you soft foreign bastards squirm in Hong Kong. Face it," she told them, "he's left us no alternative but to stick with the Princely House. You try and bring it to the vote, dear cousins, and I'll side with him."

Clair, as the only direct descendant of the founding Tiernan, held the largest single bloc of shares, and the others well realized that if she switched to her husband's side, with the powers already invested in the taipan, there would be no contest.

JOSS WAITED in his office. He was looking up at the portrait of the man who had founded the house. Half pirate, half genius . . . the face no longer intimidated him now.

"Taipan," Connie called him. "They'd like you to return to the board-room."

Joss felt it in the air. Everyone in that room, except Clair, avoided his eyes. "Taipan," she said, and this time she used his title respectfully, "the board has just given you a vote of confidence."

Joss nodded. Clair, whatever else she might be, was a considerable woman. "Before you leave here," he now said, "I remind you that in accordance with the founder's instructions to the family you can vote your shares but you cannot sell them without the taipan's permission, and I will not grant you that permission until this house is clear of its problems."

Joss waited as the others stood and silently left the room. Clair, on her way out, stopped by her husband's chair. She leaned over him, with her cheek brushing so close to his it was like an invitation. He smelled the cool perfume on her skin. "Well, you won," she said softly, "but I don't think the cousins are ever going to forgive you."

"I'll worry about them when the five weeks are up," Joss said.

Connie let the taipan's wife out, then closed the boardroom door and swung around to Joss. She was among the first of the fiftieth-floor staff to hear the news. "The directors have just dictated a press release promising you their full support." She was clearly excited and pleased for him.

Joss leaned back in his chair and closed his eyes. "Thank God for that," he said. "At least for a while I don't have to fight on two fronts."

The telephone on the table by his side began to ring. Connie snatched it up. "I told you, no calls," she snapped at the switchboard operator. Then, with a muttered apology, she handed the phone on to Joss. "It's the secretary for security..."

Trevelyan's voice came on the line sharp and worried. "Trouble at your factories," he told the taipan briefly, never a man to waste words. "I've just seen the first police reports. It's looking serious. You'd better get down there fast."

Joss glanced at the calendar. It was Monday, the fifteenth of August. The first of the loans were due for repayment on September fifteenth. War had been declared.

CHAPTER 17

FREDDIE CHEN, a minor ex-customs official and now a successful fence in Hong Kong's underworld, waited anxiously outside the entrance to the Far Eastern hydrofoil jetty on Hong Kong Island. Parked across the street from him was a squadron of riot police Land Rovers, making him acutely aware of the mounting tension in the city.

A taxi squealed to a halt at the curb nearby, and a tall, handsome European climbed out. His name was Michael Ansty. There was much of the Irish gypsy about this man, all charm and dark fire and a wildness in his ice-blue eyes. He turned back to the taxi and drew out two identically wrapped packages, flat and each roughly fourteen inches square. He handled them with great care.

"We're late," Chen told him. He reached in and picked up Ansty's last piece of luggage, a brown canvas hold-all. "Hurry, or we'll miss the hydrofoil."

Ansty looked back in the direction he'd just come from. In the canyonlike spaces between the office blocks and waterfront of central Hong Kong a buzz rose like the warning hum of angry bees. "I thought that mob was going to turn over my taxi. What's going on back there?" He spoke in an unmistakable Irish brogue.

"Strikes," Chen said, "against the Princely House lighter and wharf companies. They're refusing to unload the ships." The noise was growing louder, moving their way. The police Land Rovers drove into position to block off the streets.

"Seems more like riots in the making than strikes to me," Ansty murmured, surveying the scene with a practiced eye. "The way those people were squaring up to the police, they could teach the Irish a thing or two about strikes."

"Thank God we'll be out of here before it starts," Chen said, knowing how quickly violence could spark in these hot, overcrowded streets. "I have the tickets."

They took their seats aboard the Boeing jetfoil that in less than fifty minutes skimmed the passage between Hong Kong and Macau, expressly for the benefit of wealthy gamblers and businessmen.

The engines whined as the craft was backed out of its berth. It turned and raced across the harbor like an aircraft on takeoff. Then all sensation of travel over water ceased as it rose high on its foils above the waves and streaked for Macau.

Chen was a nervous passenger, but once the craft had risen smoothly onto its foils he relaxed and leaned back in his seat. He was a small man beside Ansty, who was well over six feet, and he was dressed more conservatively in a gray suit and wore thick tortoiseshell-rimmed glasses. In his last years Dr. Sun had invested in fine objets d'art. Chen had acted as his agent, and when the old man died he'd worried that he would lose a major part of his income.

"Are you sure the Lady Sun will honor her father's obligation?" Ansty asked.

"She'll honor it," Chen told him. "I have evidence that there was a bargain made between you and her father. She would cause eternal disgrace to her ancestor if she didn't. But make certain you hand over the right picture." Chen glanced at the identical packages in Ansty's lap. "She's certain to have someone there to check."

"Sure now I know the right one," Ansty said, smiling at Chen, who was squirming like a frightened puppy. "All that's required from you is to supply the introduction, and God knows, you're being paid well enough for that. Anyway, it's my experience that rich folks who buy stolen paintings are naturally suspicious and inclined to check their purchases very thoroughly. As long as the new owners don't realize when it's switched, they get along quite happily with the fake."

"You're taking this too casually," Chen said, alarmed by the Irishman's attitude. "Macau is not like Hong Kong. It's a very dangerous place to do business in. Nothing must go wrong."

"Ah now, we're dealing with a chit of a girl reared for most of her life in a convent," Ansty said confidently, stretching his long limbs. He had spent a hectic night in the bed of a very energetic lady. "Her father was a different proposition, I grant you, but she'll be no problem to me. You've never met her?"

"No, there's been no time since her return from Hawaii. Have you wondered why her father named her Crystal Lily?"

"What's that supposed to mean?"

"A lily is gracious and lovely, but crystal is one of the hardest substances on earth—names are very important to us Chinese. From the days of Confucius down we are told to name things rightly. For this girl to be so named, I warn you she will have earned it."

"Holy Mother, don't I already know that," Ansty said beneath his breath, but the hydrofoil was docking in Macau and Chen didn't hear him.

Chen made a telephone call from a room rented in the Lisboa Casino Hotel. In the hotel's safekeeping they left the canvas hold-all and the second painting... "A car is coming to collect us," he told Ansty.

The two men waited in the morning sunlight on the steps of the Lisboa's tiger's-jaw entrance. The streets behind the casino were strategically lined with pawnbrokers so that unlucky gamblers could pawn their possessions for a ticket home. A black limousine pulled up to the steps. Ansty had noticed that it rode low on its wheels, but only when inside did he realize the vehicle was armor-plated. Which discovery sobered him a little. His brash confidence was further undermined when they drove in through the palace entrance and were thoroughly searched by armed bodyguards.

"This place is a fortress," Ansty muttered to Chen. He swung around, contemplating the odds, and caught a glimpse of the guard dogs patrolling the walls as their car moved through the checkpoints.

"The security is greater than I have ever seen before," Chen said, suffering another attack of nerves. "Much has changed, it seems, since the death of Dr. Sun..."

They were shown into the long drawing room, where Ansty's attention

187

was immediately captured by a display of early Chinese ceramics. He promptly moved across the room to inspect them. "Could that be genuine Tang dynasty?" he asked, pointing to a vase.

"Some of the ceramics in this collection are two thousand years old," Chen told him. "I procured them for Dr. Sun."

Ansty let out an awed whistle, and at the same time an unholy glint appeared in his eyes. "These pieces alone must be worth a fortune," he calculated. "Now do you understand why I've made you bring me here? And they represent just a small part of the wealth stored in this palace. Perhaps I should put up the price of my picture?"

"Don't change the terms of the agreement," Chen said nervously, "or we may lose everything. Be sure to address her as 'my lady,' or 'Madame Sun,' and be most careful or her comprador—"

The door opened. Crystal Lily walked into the room escorted by her aged comprador and another younger, modern-suited Chinese who had worked for Sotheby's in Hong Kong.

Ansty was intrigued by the aloof grace of this girl, and he used the gently mocking lilt in his voice to say so. "You're just as lovely, I see, as the day you left the U.S. of A."

"You two know each other?" Chen was appalled.

"I told you not to follow me here." Crystal Lily did not extend her hand to Ansty.

"Indeed?" Ansty said. "But we're old friends..."

"Was this the man who bothered you in Hawaii?" the comprador asked.

Crystal barely nodded. "I understand now that he used me only to make contact with my father—"

"I'll have him thrown out," the comprador said quickly, but Chen's jitters escalated as the old man raised his arm to summon the Manchu.

"Lordy, have you no fond thoughts left of us as we were just a few months ago?"

"I am not an American. Whatever I was there I have left behind," she told him. "However"—she stopped her comprador—"I have inherited an obligation." She turned back to Ansty. "I believe my late father entered into an agreement with you through Chen to procure a certain work of art?"

"He did, my lady." Ansty played along, addressing her as he'd been coached.

"Are the owners of the painting aware that it's missing?" she asked.

"No, nor are they likely to be unless something stirs their suspicions. I replaced it with a very fine reproduction."

188

Her art expert had by now unwrapped the picture and examined it. "I believe it to be genuine." It was a pronouncement.

"My comprador tells me that a price of eighty-seven thousand dollars was agreed."

"That's so, my lady." Ansty figured the sum would be little more than petty cash to her. "It's worth five times that on the open market," he added, leaving room to bargain upward in spite of Chen's warning.

"There's no such thing as an open market for a stolen painting," Crystal Lily told him. "If you wish to find another buyer, do so."

He'd not been expecting her to be quite so sharp. Shut up, he told himself.

"My comprador will pay you half in gold and half in American dollars, as you asked."

Ansty felt Chen's arm nudge him. He needed to get a look at the rest of the rooms in the palace, particularly the Crystal Room. "I've carried this picture a long way and cared for it," he said, using all his charm in his surrender. "Before I leave, would you let me hang it for you?"

She shrugged. Actually she had no interest where it went, had scarcely glanced at the painting.

"It's an early Monet landscape," Ansty said. "One of the finer examples of the great artist's work—"

"Put it in the Crystal Room." She turned to Chen. "I want no more stolen objets d'art brought to me. If in the future I want something, I'll buy it legitimately."

Chen tried to object. "Some of the pieces your father collected were simply never placed on the open market—"

"Then unlike my father I have no need of them. I suggest you don't linger in Macau with that much money. Good day to you both."

"YOU FOOL." Chen nearly spat at him as their car drew away from the palace. "You could have got us both killed. Why didn't you tell me that you knew her?"

"Ah, that was in America. A fine-looking girl with a proud spirit in her. I never tamed her," Ansty said wistfully. "She was treated like a princess there too, with her guards and her servants, and always as cool as you like. I never had the chance to get really well acquainted."

"Will you still go back tonight?" Chen asked, thinking that Ansty might have changed his mind.

"Nothing's changed... Now, I suggest we gamble at the high-stakes table until a couple of hours before the last ferry leaves, then I'll get my painting back and anything else we can steal."

THE COMPRADOR rejoined his Lady in the Crystal Room. He knew men, and he'd read in Ansty's lean, hawkish face the character of an arrogant and bold man who would not surrender as easily as he'd pretended. He speculated about the extent of their relationship, and he probed... "I will see that this man Ansty doesn't trouble you again, unless, of course, you wish it..."

The name apparently did not register. She was looking at the Monet. "My father had never been further than Thailand to inspect the poppy crop. Why did you let him squander his money on pieces of western art that can't possibly have had any meaning to him?"

"Because by then he was old, my lady, and half mad and surrounded by enemies. He thought that the gold in his vaults, and if not that then his objets d'art, would protect him from the poverty he'd known when he was young."

She changed the subject abruptly. "Why hasn't Nicholai come to see me yet?"

The question made clear her real preoccupation. "He's working on his boat, he's sent word that he'll come tomorrow."

"I know what's delaying him in Coloane," she said with a sharpness that surprised him. Her spies, of course, had reported the presence of the beautiful refugee girl Mae Ling. Crystal's eternal jealousy about Nicholai was clouding her mind at a time when she most needed to act and think clearly...

She paced the room with the quick, impatient steps of a girl who'd been held a virtual prisoner in the palace too long and was charged with an energy no longer able to be suppressed.

"What now?" she demanded.

"As always, the next move is to wait, my lady. Our time is coming—"

"Wait? Wait?...I could explode."

"FOUR QUEENS." Ansty glanced around at the players in the private gambling room on the second floor of the Lisboa. The game was poker, and Ansty had the devil's own luck with cards. He'd even beaten Chen so badly that the fence thought seriously before warning him. Nonetheless, as much for his own safety as for Ansty's, he leaned across, his eyes blinking nervously behind his thick glasses. "They don't intend to let you leave with their money. The man in the center of the table is Ho Li, number two to Chang, the enforcer of the Macau Syndicate. Three of the other gamblers at this table are *fàan-yans* too. They'll be armed, so just leave all your chips on the table and back away toward the door."

"And if I don't?" Ansty asked softly, the smile dying from his face.

"Then I would remind you that there is only one way out of Macau, unless you mean to visit Communist China, and that's by the ferry. And we won't make it."

Ansty eyed the six men at the table. He had to admit they were as fine a bunch of thugs as he could wish to meet. He probably should have known better than to crash a private high-stakes game with strangers in this town. "What about the croupier?" he said, weighing the odds.

Chen shook his head imperceptibly. "He's got to live in Macau."

"All right, cash in my chips and bring the money back here." Chen returned and placed a pile of high-denomination American dollar bills in front of Ansty. "You can leave now," Ansty said, not taking his eyes off the other man. "Pull the door to but don't close it. I'll meet you outside."

"Give them their money back," Chen urged in a whisper before he left. "Don't try anything crazy."

Ansty lifted the green cloth bag that the casino had supplied to carry his chips and stuffed the money inside it. Ho Li lifted his hands onto the table among the scattered cards and stood up—a silent warning to Ansty to leave the bag. The others came to their feet with him.

Ansty, shrugging at them like a good-natured loser, put his hand into the pocket of his white linen jacket and pulled out a cylindrical, stainless steel antipersonnel grenade. The size of a small orange, it was light, easy to carry. He rolled the grenade down the green baize table toward the croupier. "Keep the change," he said.

He gathered up the bag and swiftly crossed the room. The last he saw of them, they were frozen over the table, watching the grenade roll toward them. He slammed the door shut and pressed himself against the outside wall just before it exploded. The casino guards, guns drawn, pounded toward the explosion, passing Ansty as he walked down the stairs. He crossed the foyer, collected his canvas hold-all and the picture from safekeeping with Reception, then joined the jostling crowd of gamblers who were frantically pushing their way out through the main entrance.

He found Chen in the shadows by the steps.

"What's going on in there?" Chen, of course, had heard the explosion, as well as voices inside shouting for ambulances.

Ansty held up the bag. "They decided they didn't need my money after all."

"You *fool*. I told you they worked for the Syndicate. They can identify us. They'll circulate our descriptions. Now we'll never get out of Macau—"

"Those men were standing over an antipersonnel grenade when it exploded," Ansty told him. "They're not going to be in shape to do any identifying." He glanced at his watch. "We've got plenty of time left to do what we came for... And by the by, you can run out on me if you want to, but you'll get nothing. Anyway, all I need you for now is to watch the street while I go in."

Chen didn't answer as they made their way up the hill to the old quarter and reconnoitered the palace walls. He had noticed a darkened car parked at the curb. "It seems that there are some others watching this palace."

"Just its entrance and exit gates," Ansty said. He'd spotted the watchers long before. He pulled Chen into a dark alleyway that ran below the west wall. "You're safe enough here," he said as he judged the climb to the razor-sharp shards of glass-and-iron barbs that protected the top of the twenty-foot wall. "Now go over the geography of this palace again for me."

"To the left," Chen said, "when you scale the wall, you will see a three-story building set on its own in the corner of the compound. That is the bodyguards' quarters. Next to it in the west wing of the palace are the comprador's quarters. The east wing is given over to the Lady Sun's private quarters. A passage leads from there to the kitchens."

"And that's where I go in," Ansty decided. He had knelt and was unzipping his canvas hold-all.

"Make your way in along the ground floor and remember the rooms we're interested in lead off to the left," Chen told him.

"What about burglar alarms?" Ansty asked as he slipped on a pair of black overalls, then soft-soled shoes and gloves.

"None that I know of. Dr. Sun had more confidence in his bodyguards than electric devices, and with good reason."

"A piece of cake," Ansty said. He took out the second picture from its wrapping and placed it in a zippered square of cloth, then turned to Chen to fasten its straps to his back and place the tightly rolled half-inch-thick rubber groundsheet onto his shoulders.

192

"Apart from the picture," Chen said as he worked, "make sure you bring me the Tang dynasty ceramics. I can sell them for a fortune."

Ansty took a long silk rope out of the hold-all, one end of which as protected by a length of steel trace and fastened onto a three-pronged hook that flashed open on a spring. He circled the hook above his head until he'd gained sufficient momentum, then aimed it at the top of the wall, leaving the first four feet of steel trace unaffected by the barbs and glass shards.

"I'll be back in thirty minutes," Ansty said.

"I'll wait as long as I can," Chen told him, "but we have a reservation on the ferry that leaves at two A.M. and I intend to catch it. After what you did this evening, it's not likely that either of us can ever come back to Macau."

"Who in the hell wants to?" Ansty took up the slack in the rope, swung his legs up to give his rubber-soled shoes a purchase in the joints of the brickwork, and began to walk up the wall.

At the top he threw his groundsheet over the glass and barbs and stretched out on it, blending his profile with the wall until a guard with a dog on a leash had passed by below on his rounds. Now Ansty stood, circled the hook over his head, paying out the line, and threw it again. The hook landed on the ridge of the roof over the servants' quarters. He tightened the rope, then swung down off the wall, describing a stomach-swooping pendulum, and landed silently on all fours on its curved tiles.

He slid down the steep pitched roof, leaned out over the edge, opened the window directly above the topmost landing and wriggled headfirst through it. He proceeded through the kitchens and into the palace, following a long, high-ceilinged passage until he entered a large, dark room. Its wooden floorboards creaked softly beneath his feet.

His flashlight beam picked out shelf after shelf of finest crystal, but he wasn't interested, not yet. He moved on down the room to his painting and lifted it reverently from its position on the wall. He shrugged off the cloth bag on his back and was busily unzipping it when the lights blazed on.

Crystal Lily stood in the doorway holding a wicked-looking automatic pistol and aimed it at him. She held the weapon professionally; there was no shake in her hand. Ansty lifted his arms clear of his sides and took a step away from the Monet. He thanked God he'd gone for his painting first and not the ceramics. If she could be made to see his motive in a slightly better light than just that of a thief, it might help...

Crystal Lily said nothing. She wore a silk nightgown embroidered with golden dragons. Her fine black hair was loose and fell past her cheeks and over her breasts.

Her silence was worse than a challenge. It would take all his blarney to talk himself out of this one... "My lady, you may well wonder what I am doing here, and I must tell you the truth... I was on my way to declare my passion for you." His brogue deepened. "I've never seen a face so beautiful, eyes like the inner stars of a sapphire—"

"You're both a damn fool and a liar. You came to steal my painting." Her dark eyes seemed to cut through him like lasers.

Retreat, he told himself. He indeed might be a fool, she clearly was not... "That's so." He shrugged. "You have so many paintings on these fine walls that mine would be lost among them. For you this is just another possession. To me it is as valuable as my only child. I confess I see in it the storehouse of all the artistic talent I once tried to find, and that wasn't in me. What more can I say...?"

"You've obviously done this before."

"This painting is my only capital. I persuade myself to part with it when I need money to live. Then I switch it on its new owner with a perfectly adequate reproduction. Sure," he challenged, "didn't I just about warn you this afternoon? Until now I've never been caught, which tells you that rich people rarely appreciate a painting once they possess it, whereas I appreciate mine all the time. So, I'm caught. Congratulations to you. I'll just buy my painting back and be on my way. I imagine you don't want trouble with the police, and of course neither do I."

She had listened to him quietly, and now she moved out of the doorway to make room for two large, gray-haired men who followed her into the room. "I doubt if you'll leave here alive, Michael Ansty," she said, the anger gone from her voice. "Certainly not if I allow my comprador and my Manchus to have their way. I warned you things would be different in Macau."

"Ah, surely you wouldn't murder me for a painting?"

"The painting isn't important. The fact that you broke into my palace, unfortunately for you, is."

The comprador came into the room, resting on the arm of his wife. "I'd half-expected to see you again," he said, fixing his eyes on Ansty. "I remember you went to great efforts to see this room. You've been a fool." He said it like a judgment. He turned and bowed his head in apology to his lady. "I'm sorry you were disturbed. Lao Ta and I will attend to this."

Crystal had no difficulty in seeing through Ansty, but at the same time the cool courage of this man intrigued her. "See that he spends the rest of the night where he can do no harm," she ordered, indicating to Yu

Shik Lieu that at least she did not want the Irishman executed immediately.

As Ansty was led away between the Manchus he glanced down and spotted an electronic eye cunningly worked into the paneling of the doorway. He turned to Crystal Lily, still trying to keep up his mocking humor in spite of the predicament he was in. "And I was told your father had no faith in electronic devices."

"That's what he wanted people to believe...well, goodnight, Mr. Ansty. And pleasant dreams."

The guards took Ansty off into the cellars deep below the palace. They passed the great time-locked vaults that stored the gold and continued on along a stone-flagged passage to where a series of narrow cells had been tunneled into the rock below the foundations.

The cell he entered had not been used for some time, but it retained a smell of death about it. The comprador had taken the private elevator down to the cellars. He entered Ansty's cell followed by a squat, bull-necked man with small bloodshot eyes and a drooping moustache. "This is Lao Ta, head of the Manchus," the comprador introduced the silent man to Ansty. "If you refuse to answer my questions truthfully Lao Ta will take over, and you will surely tell him. He has ways to make even the rocks speak."

"Jesus, I'm an art thief. I came here to steal my picture back. I told her the truth. What in the hell are you all getting so excited about?"

"We live in dangerous times here in Macau, Mr. Ansty. It's important to us to know that the theft of the painting was your only objective in breaking in here. Now the truth, please, starting from the beginning, and remember we have contacts in most parts of the world who can run a check on your story."

Ansty glanced up at Lao Ta's face. "I'll save you the trouble," he said wearily. "I'm no bloody hero. What do you want to know?"

A Manchu abruptly summoned the comprador from the cell. He returned with Ansty's canvas hold-all. "My guards have checked the palace perimeter and this is all they've found. Where is your accomplice Mr. Chen?"

"If he's any sense," Ansty said, "he'll be on the two A.M. ferry back to Hong Kong, which means you're too late to stop him now."

"I think perhaps not," Yu Shik Lieu said quietly. "News has reached us of the disturbance at the Lisboa tonight. You and Chen were not found among the dead and injured in that room. Perhaps, after all, you are the luckier man. Chang, the enforcer, has his soldiers watching the ferries."

* * *

FREDDIE CHEN had made his way down to the Praia Grande. He hailed a taxi outside the Sintra Hotel and had it drop him opposite the ferry terminus in the outer harbor with only minutes to spare. As he crossed the street he recognized the Syndicate's mobsters checking the passengers who were filing into the terminus. Midway across the street he hesitated, then he turned away, seeking the shelter of darkness along the seafront wall. On his left was the lighted building of the jai alai stadium, ahead the road ended in the reservoir that had been built out into the sea.

He heard footsteps following him. He increased his pace. Parked nose to tail in the dark along the curb were three cars. A voice called out from behind. The car doors opened, blocking him. Chen's heart seemed ready to explode as he pounded along the pavement, and then a paralyzing sickness clutched at his belly. He was a rabbit mesmerized by a snake. Chang, the enforcer, whose reputation for sadism was legendary, was coming toward him, head hunched in his rounded shoulders, wearing a smile that on his face seemed grotesque. Chen felt hands from behind seize him and pinion his arms. The enforcer opened Chen's jacket and found wads of bills stuffed into every pocket. Greed over the money had left Chen with no excuses. "So," Chang said, "at least you've had a successful night's gambling."

Freddie Chen understood that he was going to die. As the men surrounded him his voice was little more then a despairing cry that echoed out over the empty waters of the reservoir.

CHAPTER 18

STARLIGHT LANCED through the bamboo-plaited walls of the boat shed on Coloane Island, tiger-striping the rakish hull of the old gunboat with light and shadow.

It was shortly before dawn. The four men had been working on the boat with hardly a break. The strain showed, particularly on Fifth Street. He worked the hardest to block out the loss of his woman and child, and his nerves were stretched nearly to breaking point.

Udo hefted a heavy truck battery down the ladder into the engine compartment of the boat. Fifth Street lay sprawled out on his back under the number one engine, with a fading handlight trying to strip and check the gleaming gearing to the propeller shaft.

Udo switched the leads onto the fresh battery and immediately the light under the engine became brighter. "That's better," he rumbled. "The Snake Boat Man said to tell you he'll have a power line rigged from here to the camp's main generators by tomorrow." He moved along the narrow catwalk between the number one and two main engines toward Fifth Street. "You want anything else?"

"You fat bastard," Fifth Street suddenly screamed in pain. "You fucking great mountain of shit, *move.*"

"What in the hell's eating you now?"

"Your goddamn foot's on my hand."

"It's dark in here, I couldn't see," Udo said, coming as close to an apology as he was capable of. He swung his weight off the metal rung that ran along the edge of the catwalk.

Fifth Street snatched his hand away and checked his bruised knuckles to see if any were broken. "Get out of my engine room, will you," he shouted at Udo. "Just get the hell out of here. You're too damn fat to fit—"

"I've had enough of your big mouth," Udo lashed back, and faster than Fifth Street thought possible, the big man lunged at him.

Fifth Street rolled out of Udo's way, grabbed the lamp and smashed it against the gear casing, plunging the engine room into darkness. "All right, you fat bastard," Fifth Street whispered, feeling for the heavy steel wrench that he'd been using. "Now you're goin' to get yours." Actually Fifth Street was grateful for the opportunity for the sheer physical release. He'd kept his miseries bottled up too long. Udo was big and powerful and popular with the others—everything Fifth Street was not. The time had come to settle with him.

Fifth Street squirmed under the propeller shaft, through the warm oil that dripped from the gearbox and wriggled out into the narrow catwalk on the other side next to the hull. He intended to come up on the fat man unawares. The heavy wrench he carried rasped softly against the metal of the engine, which was all the sound he made.

He listened for the sound of movement the big man surely had to make in the cramped space between the engines . . . he sensed rather than heard a presence loom in the blackness behind him—but before he could defend himself Udo's massive arm went around his neck, twisting his head almost at right angles.

In a red haze of pain Fifth Street hit out with the wrench, but Udo almost effortlessly lifted him by his neck off his feet, swung him hard so that he crashed against the engine casing, knocking the wrench from his grip and the remaining breath from his lungs. And then he hung him feet down over the bilges. The arm around Fifth Street's neck gripped like a band of steel. The more he struggled the faster he strangled himself.

198

Moments before he passed out his flailing feet kicked over a drum, sending it crashing down into the bilge. Alerted by the noise, Nicholai and Keng Po came sliding down the engine compartment ladder. Nicholai's torch beam stabbed through the darkness and shone full into Udo's face. "Let him go," Nicholai ordered. "We *need* him."

Without a word Udo dropped Fifth Street, letting his body crumple into an unconscious heap on the catwalk.

Nicholai knelt beside the man.

"If he lives," Keng Po said, glad it had come to a head at last, "then perhaps this little set-to with the Bear will have taught him a lesson."

Nicholai felt a pulse beat. "Get out of here," he told the others. He opened Fifth Street's mouth and breathed air into his lungs. "Come on, you crazy bastard, don't give up on me now," he whispered.

Fifth Street opened his eyes, and Nicholai proceeded to drag him up on deck. The stars through the bamboo were fading, heralding the coming dawn. Nicholai sat with his back against the bridge opposite Fifth Street, waiting for him to get back his breath. "You all right?"

"Sure," Fifth Street croaked. His throat felt crushed, his back and the knuckles of his right hand throbbed. "What about the other guy?" he asked hopefully.

"You didn't lay a finger on him."

"Yeah, I remember now. He moves pretty fast."

"You're very lucky to be alive. When I met Udo he was a professional fighter. He took on all comers on one of the hulks in the Inner Harbor— akido, kung fu, karate. In those days it was just called street fighting, and Udo lived by it."

"Where is he?"

"I told him to get some rest."

"Next time tell that fat bastard I'll use a gun—"

"There will be *no* next time. You were looking for a fight and you got one. Now listen to me... I need Udo, and I need you. Here"—Nicholai offered a flask. His voice was quiet without losing any of its authority. Fifth Street felt unaccustomedly at ease with this man. "Drink this."

Fifth Street sniffed at the liquor inside. "What is it?"

"It's a local rice liquor. You look like you could use it." Nicholai's voice had softened. "You're still grieving—"

"That's no damn business of yours..." But the fight had drained much of the anger out of him at least for a while, and the liquor soothed him. Now he needed to talk, to try to explain a little of the pain and the guilt he felt...

199

"Way I grew up in what they like to call institutions," Fifth Street began, "no one wasted time giving a damn about anybody. Hell, I knew I had nothing to offer, but that woman and kid... they were something special, for sure. She stuck by me no matter what I did. They were my only kin, the two people in this world I ever let care about me, and I've failed them, just like I've failed myself every time..."

"This time it's going to work... now what about my boat?"

"I've checked the electrics, the hydraulics and the engines and so far I haven't seen anything I can't fix," Fifth Street said quickly, glad to retreat onto firmer ground. "You and Keng Po have been checking the hull. What have you found?"

"Some decay, nothing too serious." Nicholai's hand reached out and touched the deck of his boat. "She's good for one last run."

"How much gold will we be carrying?"

"Just under five tons."

Fifth Street made a quick calculation. "Add that to the weight of fuel we'll have to carry and we've slowed this old boat down to twenty-seven, maybe twenty-eight knots." He looked up at Nicholai. "We're not going to make it to Hong Kong in this boat the way she is now, and you know it."

"I can do it," Nicholai said, "if you make sure the engines don't fail me."

"I can do better than that." Fifth Street had realized he was stuck with the old MGB, and over the last few days he'd already been thinking through a radical change in the boat's design. "If you'll let me, I think I can give you an edge."

"How?"

"First, by stripping out the propellers and rudders and replacing them with aquajets."

"No," Nicholai said instantly, wary about any changes in his boat. "I know how she performs now, I know what I can do with her—"

"Let me finish," Fifth Street interrupted. He might be beaten down and bitter, but he was sure of himself when it came to machinery. "Loaded, this boat will draw nearly six feet at the stern. With aquajets I guarantee to cut her draught to three feet or less. It's one thing taking on the limeys, but you've got to get out through the damn shoals surrounding Macau first. When I've finished with her you'll be able to go right over the mudbanks and through junk that would tear your propellers off."

"But I'd lose on the turns—"

200

"Bull. With the modern aquajet you can divert the thrust of all three engines into whichever way you're going. You'll be able to stand a boat like this on her tail as long as her hull can take the strain."

"What about speed?"

"Look, with no bubbles from the propellers, especially in shallow water, and no drag from the rudders, and if I strip out the generators and auxiliaries and all the other useless weight, I bet I can give you another five to seven knots... I worked with aquajet boats on the Mekong River during the war in 'Nam. I know what they can do."

"We've got less than two weeks," Nicholai said. "Can you make your changes in that time?"

"You get me the equipment and I'll make the changes... there's something else we were working on during the war," he added, not sure how to broach this far-out notion to Nicholai. "It was to help our river boats when they got trapped by the Vietcong in the Mekong."

"What are you talking about?"

"We figured out a way to sink a boat in up to forty feet of water and then refloat her."

"That's impossible," Nicholai said, "the hull would twist—"

"Not if the boat went down even, and it would have to be onto a sand or mud bottom."

"And the crew?"

"They could survive on the bottom with the boat. The engine-room compartment of this MGB is steel-lined. We can carry enough compressed air to pressurize it to a depth of thirty feet and keep it watertight as long as it's not holed. The crew can live up to an hour in there. I wouldn't count on any of the electric stuff working, and we'd have to get the engines firing on a cartridge start, but that's not hard."

"How would you bring her up?"

"Pump liquid nitrogen from cylinders stored in the engine room through the bulkhead into salvage inflation-bags placed along the keel. It's a volatile gas, but it expands so fast that even if some of the bags are punctured it'll still bring the boat up."

"Did you ever get it to work?"

"The war ended before we had the chance to test it out, but I really believe I can do it. If you'll let me try."

Nicholai couldn't help but be intrigued by the idea of his seventy-foot-long boat playing possum on the bottom, especially if they were trapped in some channel or inlet by a superior force. "Where do you want to store the gold, on deck?"

"No, I'll need to keep all that weight in the bottom of the boat and as close as I can get it to the engine room to make sure the boat settles evenly. I don't want to risk hanging at ninety degrees to the seabed with my ass out of the water on account of all the extra buoyancy we create by the airtight engine compartment..." He grinned at Nicholai, pleased with his own argument.

Nicholai measured him. "All right, I'll go along with you, the aquajets, all of it. It's crazy, but so are we. Give me a list of what you want."

"One last thing... I need permission to put two big life-raft cannisters back there on the stern. They won't weigh much, the cannisters will be empty apart from some oxygen rebreathing equipment. I figure we might have to abandon this boat at high speed, and at least some of the crew may be able to make it to the cannisters, climb inside and operate the release mechanism I plan to fix up in there. Then instead of knocking themselves unconscious trying to dive unprotected into the water, the men inside those cannisters can drop into the wake and stand a pretty good chance of getting away. Especially since at forty knots, by the time those cannisters get to the surface again the boat and everyone chasing it will be a country mile away. I'm trying to think of most everything that can go wrong..."

Nicholai went along. Why not? It was the most ingenious idea he'd ever heard...

The door to the boat shed opened a crack now and Mae Ling slipped through. In the light of the breaking dawn she could just make out the silhouettes of the two men up on the deck of the boat. She climbed up the ladder to them, balancing gracefully on the rungs. On a pole across her shoulders she carried a kettle of green tea and a pot of rice in shrimp gravy that she intended to heat for their breakfast. She took one look at Fifth Street's gray hurting face and swollen neck and stopped. "What happened?" She came and knelt in front of him and put her cool hands on his inflamed flesh. "He should see Dr. Alice," she said to Nicholai.

"It's nothing," Fifth Street told her.

She knew that he was painfully shy and had quickly figured out by the atmosphere in the boat shed and the absence of the others that he'd been in a fight that night. Her exquisite face was directly in front of him. He thought he saw in her eyes some compassion, and he was amazed that a woman like this would care about him. Her curved lips parted over remarkably white teeth. He caught the soft fragrance of her scent as her fingers gently worked their way into the muscles of his neck. He knew she belonged to Nicholai, and felt a rush of jealousy. He couldn't

202

handle this... couldn't look at her. He closed his eyes, and savored her touch.

"There," she said after a while, "I've relaxed all the muscles I can reach. Put a cold compress around your neck, it will bring down the swelling."

He assumed she wanted to be alone with the Snake Boat Man and got unsteadily to his feet. "I'll go heat this food," he muttered awkwardly.

Mae Ling waited until Fifth Street had disappeared below the level of the deck, then turned to Nicholai and said with elaborate indifference, "I hear you will go to Macau today to see the Lady Sun."

"Yes."

She turned her appealing eyes on him. "Take me with you."

"Why?"

"I have heard she's very beautiful. I want to see her—"

"That's impossible, you can't leave here."

"I cannot stay much longer either. I'll go mad—"

"You've only been here a few days."

"You have no interest except this old boat. I work in the hospital with the doctor. You know what this camp is? It's for the no-hopers. The ones who are too old to be chosen to go to a new country, or who are diseased. It's for young children without parents who cannot find foster homes. These people are defeated, they have almost lost hope. They are accustomed to being refugees, to living in squalor in tin shacks. They frighten and sicken me. Don't you understand? If I stay here I could easily become one of them..."

"No." He drew her against his chest to calm her. "I've promised you that."

"And the Lady Sun? What does she say?"

"Who's been talking to you, Mae Ling?"

"No one. But I hear things. I believe she's dangerous. I don't want you to go to her—"

"I have to see her. She happens to be the reason I'm here. And you," he said, lifting Mae Ling's face so that he could look at her beauty before he kissed her, "have to go back to work. Help Dr. Alice prepare to receive the refugee selection teams that are coming today, and who knows, this time a few more may find countries that will take them."

"When will you leave?"

"Soon, before the selection teams arrive."

"When will you be back?"

"This evening, probably very late."

203

"I'll wait all night under the trees on the west side of the beach," she said. "Come to me as soon as you return."

AT DIM SUM that morning, with Nicholai gone, Udo and Keng Po waited to see what Fifth Street would do. What he did was not back down. If he did, he knew he was finished with them. He waited without eating until the rice bowl was empty, then said to Udo, his aching throat making his voice especially harsh, "Okay, fat man, you've proved you can lick me, but if you want to get this boat on the water I'll call the shots. Clear?" Nicholai had already talked to Udo and Keng Po. They dutifully nodded, hating it all the way. "All right," Fifth Street told them, "to begin with, I want the partitioning above the keel forward of the engine room stripped out and all the sharp edges that could puncture the inflation bags taken off..." He had to force back a smile. He was enjoying this.

MAE LING spent the day working with Alice Van Heffelin. The sun burned down on the miserable collection of tin shanties, and in Alice's infirmary the refugee selection teams from six host nations, seated behind rickety home-built interview desks, sweated through their work.

Outside the refugees lined up patiently, brushing to no effect at the clouds of flies and clutching precious diplomas of education, much folded and refolded and travel-soiled. Mae Ling knelt by three small children whose parents had been buried at sea. They stood there in bewilderment outside the office, hand in hand, looked after by Fool Boy. Mae Ling filled in their forms as best she could and brought them before a representative of the host nation. The children had already been turned down by three nations, but still they lined up in the faint hope that they would find a chance to start a new life on the other side of the world.

"This is the camp we hate the most to visit," a young fair-haired Australian refugee selector confessed to Alice as they stretched their legs during the lunch break. "You do your best, of course, but Coloane attracts all the losers."

"What would you have me do? Send them back to sea?"

"No, no, I only wish I could do more for you."

"How many can you take this time?" she asked. The wealthier nations like America and Australia had the largest quotas for refugees, but they took their pick of the best—the ones who were relatively healthy and with skills and some education. The lesser nations took their rejects, and so on down the line until it came to a camp like Coloane that gave shelter to the people nobody wanted.

"I can take three families this quarter," the selector said, "and a few singles who can pass the physical—"

"Each time you take less and less," Alice said with some annoyance, "but every month brings more and more boatloads of refugees."

The Australian shrugged. "Orders from home. We'll help, but we're not about to have the unwanted of Asia dumped on us." They had walked to the edge of the low cliff, where he noticed the long bamboo shelter half-hidden in the vegetation above the beach. "That's a new building..."

"It's part of the leprosarium," Alice said casually. "We put it up to house a new batch of refugees we suspect might be contagious. Would you like to visit them?" She watched his face closely.

"No, no, no need..." It was hot, and the path down the cliff was steep. "I'm sure you've got everything under control down there." At which point the bell on the lepers' church began to toll, recalling them to the interview tables.

"How can you stay out here year after year on the edge of nowhere?" he asked as they retraced their steps, thinking of the unrelenting misery of the lepers and refugees.

"They need me," Alice said.

CHAPTER 19

NICHOLAI, DRESSED as a coolie, rode in the rickety villagers' bus from Coloane, the most distant part of the entrepôt, to the city. He sat by the window, the hot moist air buffeting his face, the peasant women crowded beside him, their chickens and squirming piglets trapped in wicker cages between their feet.

The bus rumbled over the long spindly bridge that spanned the expanse of silted water between Macau and Taipa—the Ou Moon, gateway to the Sea Mirror Bay. Junks with fish-fin sails journeyed from the Inner Harbor through the narrow deep-water channel that ran below the central span, serenely ignoring the hydrofoils and jetfoils that raced to and fro the forty-five miles from Hong Kong.

Nicholai debarked from the bus in the Praia Grande, and taking precautions not to draw attention to himself, made his way to the palace.

The situation had grown worse since he'd last been there... the palace of the Lady Sun was virtually under siege. He was forced to wait until a street accident between a lorry and a taxi fortuitously distracted the attention of the Syndicate's thugs before he could gain entrance...

"My lady," the old amah said as he came to her door, "he is here."

Crystal Lily had no doubts who it was. She'd been prepared... She had changed into a *cheongsam*, the discreetly provocative thigh-slit dress. She moved to the mirror and glanced at her reflection, wondering if he would prefer her with her hair up or down. Up, she decided. It made her look older, more sophisticated.

"Where is he?" she asked, trying to keep the eagerness from her voice.

"He is with the comprador."

"Prepare a room for him, he may want to stay the night. And tell the kitchen staff to prepare a special meal."

The amah nodded. "When he would come here long ago he would eat Szechuanese food with your father... they both liked their dishes hot and spicy."

"Can you remember what he particularly liked?"

"Slivers of baked duck on noodles with chestnuts and lotus leaves," she said, delighted with her ability to remember.

"See to it."

The amah hurried away and Crystal went to her comprador's office... "Nicholai... what are you two arguing about?"

The comprador slumped back in his seat. He gestured to the list of equipment being requested by the Snake Boat Man. "I was under the impression, my lady, that he already had a boat, not that he wished to build a new one."

"I've found an engineer," Nicholai quickly told them, "who has persuaded me that he can redesign the propulsion unit of the *East Wind* and so cut its draught by a full three feet and give me an extra five or seven knots. I believe in this man's ability. Besides, he is our best hope... what he proposes can make the difference."

"Then it must be done." She turned decisively to her comprador. "I can't believe it will be a problem for our agents to find the equipment in Hong Kong. What next?" The demure girl had quickly changed into her father's daughter.

"In nine days," Nicholai told them, "I will move the *East Wind* to the Inner Harbor. You must have the gold ready then to load onto my boat—"

"How do you propose we get it out of the palace?" the comprador put in, less than delighted with Nicholai's high-handed manner. "You know we're under siege. A road convoy carrying the gold to the harbor would not get past the gates."

"You have fifteen bodyguards. I have my crew and the guns of the *East Wind*. I'll come up with a way to break you out of here and protect the convoy. The gold must be aboard the *East Wind* by eleven-twenty P.M. on the night of the thirtieth. At that time the full moon and the spring tide coincide. I will start my run then."

"But that means leaving it to the final day before my debt to the Triad is due..."

"It's true the Syndicate and the Communists will be watching the deep-water channel under the Taipa Bridge and can block it almost at will," Nicholai told her, "but the extra eighteen inches of water then should make it possible for my boat to cross the Bay of Ou Moon and escape to the sea through the neck between Mainland China and Coloane. Your ChrisCraft will act as my decoy... it will use the channel and make the run as far as it can go."

"We can't protect your boat while it's in Coloane. You must bring it here sooner," she said.

"You can't protect it here in Macau either. All Thomas Wu's attention will be on your ChrisCraft. He won't be expecting the *East Wind*."

"He's right," the comprador said quietly. "Listen to me. You are both weaker than the Syndicate, and your meager forces are divided between Macau and Coloane. If Thomas Wu chooses to attack either of you, you could be destroyed. I think we have persuaded Thomas Wu that he can afford to wait until you are forced to deliver your gold from the vaults in this palace to your ChrisCraft. That is the moment when he will strike. The Snake Boat Man must survive the next nine days, everything we have depends on him..."

Crystal turned from the window, where she had been watching Ansty exercise between two guards in the garden below, and as he looked up at her and waved she put aside the decision she'd nearly come to about him... She looked at Nicholai, now concentrating on the matter at hand. "Our strategy should be to make you seem as unthreatening as possible to Thomas Wu. He and his Syndicate supporters must be made to think we're mad for having put our trust in you... Your having been away from the sea for fifteen years, and being just a touch older..." She smiled... "well, that's all to the good if it makes them overconfident. It would also be a good idea if you were seen in Macau drinking again. Let them think your nerves are cracking... and even if Wu's spies do find out where your boat is hidden, it should only confuse them... how

208

could he and they believe I'd choose you and your old boat before the ChrisCraft—?"

Nicholai had heard enough, as she intended.

"No, damnit—"

"It will work." The comprador rushed to counter Nicholai's expected resistance. "No one will expect the Snake Boat Man voluntarily to humiliate himself in public. The deception, though dangerous, should convince. Meanwhile my lady and I will attempt to weave our own web from within the palace and draw Thomas Wu into it. We will divert his attention from your boat by every means possible, but you must help us." Before Nicholai could explode the comprador hurried on, "We must be the bird that pretends a crippled wing in order to lead the snake away from its nest. Our enemy believes himself all-powerful. We shall encourage him in this, as we already have begun to do. But when this bird has drawn the snake safely away from her young, she will not fly away." He caught Crystal Lily's eye. "On the night we leave, we shall combine forces. We shall settle accounts with the Syndicate." It was a promise. "Does my lady have your support?"

Nicholai could do little else but go along. He made clear, though, his displeasure.

When the comprador had left Crystal Lily turned to Nicholai, her cool and businesslike manner deserting her. She had missed him, missed him very much... and she was afraid of losing him now. "Stay with me here"... her voice not much more than a whisper... "and when this is over, share all I have?"

He shook his head. He'd been hurt even more than he'd shown by the role she expected him to play... in too many ways it was too close to the truth.

"I need you—"

"I'm with you, I always have been—"

"Then stay."

"No."

Her face changed and she moved away. "Could it be Mae Ling, the refugee? You can't wait to get back to her—?"

He'd be damned if he'd reassure her... not now... "That's no business of yours."

"Oh, but it *is*. On account of her you've made enemies in Hong Kong, and they will find you here. And for *what*? Some refugee girl who's captured your fancy? Send her back. You're risking my life now, not just yours—"

Well, he thought, my lady is a jealous lady. He was almost flat-

209

tered... "No, Crystal, I have given this girl my protection. As soon as I can I'll send her to safety, but—"

"They tell me, Nicholai, that she bears an uncanny resemblance to your wife. Do you know anything else about her, this girl who claims your protection?" She knew she was overstepping the bounds, but she couldn't help it... not with this man she'd loved from as far back as she could remember.

Nicholai looked at her, not reacting. "Her past is hardly important to me—"

"You put too much faith in her," Crystal Lily warned. "I know you still think of me as a young girl... believe me, I am not. I ask you, though, at least take me seriously when I suggest you learn more about who she is."

"I'll leave you and get back to my work," was Nicholai's answer.

She saw him to the door, furious at him and not wanting... or able... to take her eyes off him. "Remember," she said, "the countdown of days has begun. We must do all we can to confuse and divide our enemies. Our position of weakness must be made into our strength... and you must play your part."

He nodded without speaking, and when he had left, it was as though the air around her had turned suddenly cold.

THE COMPRADOR found her alone in the Crystal Room studying Ansty's painting. "My Lady, has the Snake Boat Man gone?"

"Yes." She turned to Yu Shik Lieu, and it was the first time he had ever found her so near to tears. "Why do I always fight with him when I want him so badly? When I was a girl in the convent in Hawaii he was the only one who cared enough to write to me. I would read each word in his letters, probing them for the secret of how much he loved me. I would crawl down my bed to the window at the end of my stifling cubicle and look up at the moon and whisper his name. Whisper it to nobody, to everybody. I was young and a very lonely girl, and he was already a legend, but at least I knew he cared about me... Why else would he have protected me? Why else would he have gone on writing to me when my father ordered that there not be any contact from here?"

"Unlike the rest of us, my lady, he was never afraid of your father. But don't demand too much of him now. You've grown older, but then so has he, and perhaps he still remembers the girl he befriended and doesn't yet see the woman..."

"He's angry... he recognized my father in me today. I meant to tell him I intended to turn the Syndicate into a legitimate business when I get control, but he never gave me the chance—"

"Perhaps it's *joss*, my lady. Your father would tell each man only as much as he needed to know and trusted no one with his innermost thoughts."

"But I chose him long ago for my husband—" she was letting her hurt show plainly now. "He has every quality in a man that I want. He *is* the man I want—"

"There is an isolation for those who wish to rule, my lady..." When he received no answer except her sharp, annoyed look, he switched from philosophy to more mundane matters. "My lady, Ansty has admitted that before he met you in America he worked as a mercenary. He is more dangerous than he seems. We should kill him."

"I can use him." Her eyes seemed to crackle with a cold, angry fire. She would use Ansty to make Nicholai jealous... "I'll send him to the Snake Boat Man."

"No, no..." The comprador's warning had produced an entirely different result from the one he'd intended. "Ansty will try to set himself up as a rival, will challenge and perhaps even usurp the authority of the Snake Boat Man—"

"Fine," she said, thinking of Nicholai going back to Mae Ling that night. "I'll make myself two captains... the younger one to rival and stir up the blood of the older... Send him to me now."

Ansty was brought to her apartments.

"Leave us," she told her amah and comprador. "Alone." There was an obvious edge to her voice.

Ansty waited self-confidently, his dark gypsy good looks and startling blue eyes lit with arrogant amusement. She had to remind herself that this man had once earned his living as a cold-blooded mercenary.

"I'm sorry to tell you," she said as the door softly closed behind them, "that your... your associate was found murdered a few hours ago."

"Ah, poor Chen," Ansty said lightly, refusing to accept her opening words as a threat. "I had the feeling he had it coming."

"The police found him blindfolded and tied to a stake by the sea reservoir. He choked to death in the oncoming tide."

"Well now, that's not a pleasant way to die, is it... I take it, then, he must have run into Chang, the Syndicate's enforcer?"

"I would imagine so. Chang's looking for you now." She watched the cocksure humor leave his eyes, and changed the subject. "You've traveled a long way just to rob me?"

"That wasn't all I came for and you know it. I'd hardly recognize you now, you've changed so."

"What was I before?"

"Just a spoiled, rich, all-American bitch who was trying to get her master's degree and would answer none of my messages. But at least in Hawaii you didn't expect to be treated like royalty..." Ansty decided to go down like a man.

"You can hardly complain, you were less than honest with me."

"When could I have told you about myself with any sort of hope that you'd understand my past? We never had the chance to be really alone. It was always at some *occasion* that we met."

"That part interests me. How did someone like you get into all the best houses in Hawaii?"

"Oh, I forged myself some impressive introductions and I had a fine way with the hostesses on the register. The Marquis of Dunbrody is a distant cousin of mine. I felt he would have no great objection to my borrowing his title in a good cause."

"And then you used the island's social affairs to choose your victims." Crystal Lily remembered the physical attraction she and Ansty had had for each other... but there had been no opportunity to get better acquainted. Her father was dying, she had other preoccupations. "My comprador has found out that you were a mercenary—"

"Did he also tell you that I gave up that life before I tried to enter yours?"

"Why?"

Ansty shrugged. "Because I got tired of always being on the losing side. Grand theft seemed an easier living, and after all, I was well qualified for it." He was recovering his humor.

"Would you fight again?"

He shook his head. "I lived by the gun in Ireland and Africa for five long years. I want no more of it."

Crystal Lily heard him but didn't believe him. Truth in telling was not exactly his long suit, for all his charm and good looks. "I have a boat that shortly will be making a run between here and Hong Kong. People will try to stop it. If the boat gets through, its crew will be very well rewarded."

"How well?"

"You said your painting represents all the capital you have. Do you want it back, along with your life?"

"Is that your best offer?" He said it with a straight face.

"How much is your life worth to you?"

His defenses slipped, and for a split second he looked at her with something like respect... This woman seemed very different from the girl he'd known in Hawaii... from in fact, any *woman* he'd ever known. Her face at one moment was cool, seemingly carved from ivory, the next her dark eyes traveled up the scale from freezing to white-hot heat. What man could avoid responding to her challenge...?

He had no time for drawn-out decisions. "Well, it seems I'm your man, then." He held out his hand to her. "Let's make a bargain on it." His blue eyes, once arrogant and mocking, had changed as he became increasingly aware of the honey-gold thigh that showed through the slit in her *cheongsam*, of her small, taut breasts jutting against the silk. They would fit snugly in the palms of his hands, he thought, and, damn her, he'd bet she could read his thoughts in his face.

"Much more than the value of any painting," he said, close to her now, "should I prove out to be your very loyal servant, what reward might I expect?"

She turned away, leaving his question nicely unanswered. He watched her cross the room, her body gliding with the suppleness usually found only in trained dancers. Her small hands, with their tapering fingers, gestured with impatience toward the table set for two. "Have you eaten yet?"

He hadn't touched food in the last thirty-six hours. "To tell you the truth," he said, "I'd been hoping for a few scraps for my last supper... especially after your guards assured me I'd never see tomorrow."

She lifted the lids from exquisitely decorated ceramic pots on the hot tray, tempting him with the steaming fragrance of the food inside. "I can offer golden carp fresh from the cold lakes of the Yunan, and then baked duck cooked in honey." She was enjoying this.

She filled a bowl and served him. As he ate she lifted circlets of white jasmine and miniature white orchid blossoms from the porcelain saucers on the table, dipped her fingers into the bowl and splashed droplets on the petals. The pungent, heavy scent of the flowers slowly filtered into every corner of the room.

Ansty looked up and found her watching him. Her eyes had a strange double light in them, the whites clear as fine porcelain.

"Aren't you going to eat?" Ansty asked, seeing her push her bowl away untasted.

"Food doesn't seem to interest me..." Outside the moon filtered through the humid night. She got up and opened the french doors leading down steps to a garden patio. He left the table and followed her into the tropical night, along a gravel path, past tangled beds of flowers and climbing bougainvillea, their fiery colors darkened by the moonlight. The perfume of the night scented with magnolia and jasmine, the scream of cicadas, most of all the beguiling, shadowy figure leading him on had brought his desire to a fever heat.

She waited for him on a wooden bridge that stood above the lotus ponds, their blossoms floating on reflecting pools. "This is the moon-viewing platform I once told you about in the States. We stand here on the nights of the moon festivals to watch the moon rise. I have very few friends," she said, looking up at the slim, golden sickle that was whipping through a necklace of stars. "That eternal night light is one of them . . . it never fails—"

Ansty took her face between his hands and kissed her. She was prepared to allow him that much, then would cut it off . . . but before she could he'd scooped her up in his arms and set off back to the house. He'd misunderstood the game . . . or rather was playing it out in a fashion she didn't quite intend. She was a princess of Macau, she would dictate the terms . . . she'd only wanted to make Nicholai jealous, she'd not intended to have Ansty make love to her. She'd done her job too well, she realized. A strong corrective was in order . . . her nails raked his face, and as he raised his arms to protect himself she squirmed out of his reach. "Another time and that could cost you your life." She wondered if her own fear came through as she said the words. The comprador had warned her . . . this man would not be easy . . .

"Call the guards," he challenged.

She kept silent as she recouped her inner composure, reached up and brushed her lips over the weals on his cheek. It was a tiger's kiss—a promise . . . a warning . . . "Perhaps," she said, considering him now with her dark eyes, "some other time when you have proved you are indeed loyal . . ."

She raised her voice and called out the name of her personal bodyguard. Hei Ta-hau, a large dark-skinned Manchu, materialized out of the shadows. "He will see you back to your quarters. Tomorrow . . ." She turned before Ansty could sort that out and went quickly back through the french doors.

Hei Ta-hau's face was split by a gold-toothed grin. He ran his knife-point lightly across Ansty's throat. "You lucky man, *gwilo*," he said, still all smiles. "Lucky not dead. Maybe next time."

* * *

214

THE AMAH was waiting in her lady's private quarters as Crystal Lily stepped out of the shower and sat down at her dressing table. The amah loosened her hair and let it fall, then took up a hairbrush and with long, slow brushstrokes began to draw some of the tension out of the girl.

Crystal's eyes were half-closed. "Amah, do you ever think about America?"

"Many times. We were safe there. Here in Macau among these barbarians of the Syndicate, our lives are worth nothing." She paused in her work. "My child, I have always tried to give you good advice. Please listen to me now. You must not put your faith in the Snake Boat Man or this wild *gwilo*, Ansty, whom you have encouraged tonight. They do not have the power. Thomas Wu does... put yourself under the protection of Thomas Wu—"

"How can you of all people ask that?" Crystal Lily spun around angrily from the mirror to face her. "You know how he has treated me... how he has worked to undermine me..."

The amah occupied a privileged position in Crystal Lily's life. True, she was vain, often weak, and had accompanied Crystal to America to spy on her for her father. But she also was all the family Crystal had. "A woman with your beauty... even Thomas Wu can be managed... If you wish to remain in Macau, you must have his protection. The comprador will die soon, he has his family to concern him... are you so sure you can trust him?"

She then bustled into the adjoining room and turned down the sheets. "This is not America. The East is still a world for men. A wise woman chooses the strongest ally. Think of what I've said tomorrow. Now rest," she whispered, "relax, child, or you will not sleep. Neither of us has closed our eyes properly since we returned to this accursed place."

CHAPTER 20

THAT EVENING as Nicholai walked along the Praia Grande in the direction of his old home, a coolie dozing on the seat of his pedicab spotted him and rode up alongside. "Lord, no walk, people think you no have face."

"*Ngŏh shik k'ui*, I know you." Nicholai spoke in Cantonese as he looked, with the help of the street light, into the coolie's work-worn face. "You carried me once before to the Inner Harbor?"

"Yes, lord," the coolie said, pleased that the great man had recognized him. "Get in, I take you that place you want to go."

"There's a house not far from the old fortress of Barra," Nicholai said, seating himself in the pedicab.

The coolie nodded. "I know."

The coolie let Nicholai off some ways before the old fortress on the sea road. Nicholai walked across the street and stopped, staring up at the two-story building on a forty-foot ridge above the sea. It was a gracious, uniquely Macanese blend of Mediterranean and Chinese architecture with a steeply pitched roof and balconies to each bedroom. The house was empty, as he had left it, and desolate now, with a view across the bay to the islands and China. Nicholai's eyes were fixed on the paint-peeled balcony of the top-floor master bedroom...his thoughts going back to the last time he had seen his wife, Li Wen...

Her servants had carried her onto the balcony so that she could watch his departure from the Inner Harbor. She had accepted the cancer that brought her death and had wanted her husband to stay with her. But he'd fought against losing her, couldn't face losing her...When he'd come back from Japan with the special drug secured for him by Dr. Sun, he'd found his household in deep mourning and his wife dead—

"Lord, what you do?" The coolie's words broke his reverie.

"I'm looking at my past," Nicholai told him. Crystal Lily's words still taunted him...that he could expect to be mocked, to be considered too old for action more appropriate for younger men who hadn't been away from the sea for fifteen years. He couldn't surprise them if he were seen in Macau drinking heavily again...Well, at least he could be convincing in his role...

"*Saa san* watch us," the coolie was saying.

Nicholai had expected to be followed. Wanted to be. It suited him now for the Syndicate to know where he was. "How many and where?" he asked without turning his head.

"Two Syndicate gunmen, back there under the banyan trees. You have gun, lord?"

"No."

"Then we leave this empty place," the coolie urged. "No good lord stay here now night time and close to sea."

Nicholai walked back to the coolie's pedicab. "What news do you hear from the waterfront?" he asked casually.

The two men following watched closely.

"All say you try run boat, Thomas Wu make stop."

"Who do they say will win?"

The coolie swung on to his saddle and kicked the pedal up to start. "All bet plenty *patacas* you no win. *I* bet for you win."

At the moment, feeling as he did, full of memories of his dead wife and of the depths he'd once sunk to, Nicholai wished he could be as confident. Well, get on with it, he told himself, and climbed into the pedicab and directed the coolie to take him back to the Bella Vista Hotel.

* * *

SPECIAL BRANCH Superintendent Malloy found Nicholai at a corner table
on the veranda of the Bella Vista. Nicholai chose to drink here in this
decrepit but lovely old hotel with its wooden floors, creaking fans and
peeling paint because somehow it still felt real to him . . . a habitation fit
for humans against the modern concrete and plastic buildings that were
overtaking Macau. The familiar sights and sounds of Macau after so long
were crowding in on him, making him feel his time was past; that the
world had moved on to more efficient machines and younger men and
he was a damn fool to try to come back.

"May I?" Malloy pulled back a chair. He hated the Snake Boat Man,
had never forgotten or forgiven the beating he'd received so long ago.

"There are other empty seats," Nicholai said as he looked up at Malloy's
pockmarked face, "or is this an official visit?"

"I have a word for you from the secretary for security in Hong Kong,"
Malloy said, sitting down. "He knows you're going to try to make the
run. He can't understand why you'd be fool enough to get involved, you
can't need the money. But he says to tell you that Sun's daughter is no
better than her father, so let her take what's coming to her and stay out
of this. If you drop it, he's prepared to overlook your recent indiscretion
with the refugee girl . . ." Malloy, thinking of Mae Ling as he spoke,
could barely stand to talk about her . . . "He wants you back in Hong
Kong now, and under his eyes."

"And if I choose not to return?"

Malloy was waiting, with pleasure, for just that challenge. "Then we
will withdraw your Hong Kong residence permit, you'll be stateless again.
You'll lose your house. We'll freeze your bank accounts. That's only a
sample of the pressure we can apply. Don't make the run."

"I've already moved my assets out of Hong Kong's jurisdiction," Nicholai said, "and tell the secretary for security that as for my Hong Kong
residency, I'm moving on when this is finished anyway. Still, I appreciate
his sending his messenger boy all this way to warn me."

Malloy was predictably infuriated by the Snake Boat Man's tone and
even more by the thought of his possessing Mae Ling . . . "For my part I
wouldn't waste my time warning you off. You're all finished here, but
it seems it's going to take this run to teach you that. When you try to
cross into Hong Kong waters it's going to be my very great pleasure to
drown you. And, if I can't manage that, I'll put you in Stanley Jail for
the rest of your miserable life."

Feeling less confident than he hoped he sounded, Nicholai reminded

218

Malloy of what had happened before... and saw by the expression on Malloy's face that he indeed did remember and only too well his week spent in the black hold of a junk. "All right, now get out of here or I'll break both your arms again..."

Malloy stood up, pushed Nicholai's glass and half-empty bottle of whiskey toward him. "Times have changed, I guarantee you... make this run and it's going to be my turn..."

MAE LING waited under her tree on the beach. The lapping of the waves had lulled her into a fitful sleep. She heard footsteps on the sand, a figure loomed over her. She tried to get up but a hand pushed her back. She fought down her panic. "How did you find me here...?"

Malloy was smiling in the darkness. "My lovely," he said squatting beside her, "don't ever forget a refugee camp is full of informers... it's the nature of the beast to survive at any cost, and I've had my people out looking for you from the moment you slipped away." He reached out, took her by the jaw, brutally drew her face close to his. "Well now," he said, pleased by her show of fear, "where's my warm welcome? Surely you remember how hard you used to try to please me—?"

She wrenched away. "He's coming, he'll find you here—"

"I've just left *him* indulging in a spectacular drunk in Macau. He won't be back tonight. This great legend was so pickled in alcohol by the time he retired from the wars that it's taken him fifteen years to dry out. And now he's back on the juice and that'll be the end of him... At least I'm a man, he's a booze-soaked imitation of one. You made a bad choice, my lovely, when you ran out on me."

She remembered that sickening glare in Malloy's eyes and knew he was going to hurt her.

"You tipped him off—"

"*No*, he knew. Somehow he knew. I tried to hold him where he was, I did all I could—"

"Lying bitch," Malloy said, but didn't hit her... he was reserving that pleasure.

"And you?" Her courage flared in spite of her situation. "Weren't you lying when you said you'd get me to Singapore?"

"Look where you are now," was Malloy's answer, the threat of violence still in his eyes. "You're no closer to getting there with him. Instead you're on the losing side of a fight that's about to rip Macau apart. Her Highness pulled the Snake Boat Man out of mothballs because he's all she's got left, but never fool yourself that he can keep you from me, or from the Macau Syndicate. Look over there"—he pointed west across the rocky headland to the moonlit hills of China—"your friends are less than half a mile away. At low tide they can just about walk across the channel to collect you."

Malloy let her think on that for a moment. "I know who you are... one word from me, and nobody in Macau can stop them from picking you up and taking you back, and you'll follow the same route to the firing squad as your father. Are you beginning to understand your situation...?"

She nodded slowly.

"Say it, damn you."

"I... understand."

"You *sure*? You're not going to cross me again?"

She shook her head.

"All right, now you stay here and you work for *me*. I'll set you up a message drop in the village. I want to know everything he does. I want to know in advance when he's going to leave and what route he's going to take—"

"He won't tell me..."

"You'll find a way. And as a reward I'll get you away from here before his enemies destroy him and everything collapses."

"To Singapore?"

"To Singapore..." He looked into that exquisitely beautiful face, into her lovely, expressive eyes that could lie so convincingly. He still wanted to punish her, to beat her with his bare fists for running out on him... but another even deeper urge took over... He reached out and took hold of her breasts, then slowly, never taking his eyes from hers, one by one undid the buttons of her dress and slid it down. His mouth was dry, his heart pounding. He gazed at her naked body. His hands went on down, spreading her thighs, and she no longer flinched from him. "There's a good whore," he whispered to her. "I knew I could count on your watching out for your own skin first."

Mae Ling was terrified and fascinated by the primitive lust and brutality of this man. His rough but skillful fingers opened up her body to his, and a soft hot flame began to throb, kindling the small of her back, licking up her loins, leaping up below her navel, burning with an ever increasing intensity until he drove himself into her and the flame burst into wildfire. She had experienced this with him before. And now it made her feel exultant, revived her sense of her power over men, especially Malloy, whom, even as he threatened her, she felt she could enslave...

220

* * *

FIFTH STREET had left the boat shed to get some air and was now walking down the beach. Fool Boy, who was fishing just above the high-tide mark, dropped his line and ran at the sight of him. "You don't have to do that," Fifth Street called after him. "I've got nothing against you, boy, it's your father I can't stand... Goddamn," he said aloud when the boy didn't respond, and then he remembered that Fool Boy was dumb, a human disaster like everyone else in this damned camp.

Malloy, hearing Fifth Street, nervously said, "Who's that?"

"One of the boat crew," Mae Ling told him.

By now a thin line of crimson colored the horizon. "Time I was going," Malloy said, figuring that if he moved fast enough he'd make the early morning ferry back to Hong Kong. He turned and dug his fingers into Mae Ling's arm. "Now you be sure to remember, my lovely, whose side you're on... and who's on yours..."

Fifth Street saw a man's figure rise from under the trees at the far side of the beach and walked toward him, but the man disappeared quickly into the gloom. He watched as Mae Ling came out from the shelter of the trees, then tried to hurry past him. He recognized the look of deep trouble in her face... hell, he thought, if anybody knew that look, he did... He reached out, took hold of her arm. "Listen, I'm your friend," he said, not mentioning that he'd seen the other man with her. "Anything I can do to help, you tell me. Okay?"

"It's none of your business," Mae Ling told him brusquely and pushed past him.

She came across Fool Boy by the start of the cliff path. "Come here," she ordered. When he did she reached out with both hands and gently lifted his shy face to hers. It was only on very rare occasions since his mother had deserted him that he'd felt a woman's touch and his eyes rose adoringly to Mae Ling's. Yes, she decided, noting the boy's infatuation with her, he'd do well enough for Malloy's messenger. Fool Boy would have followed her then, but she turned him back.

Fifth Street noticed Fool Boy hovering nervously at the top of the beach wanting to get back to his fishing line. "Go on, boy"—Fifth Street waved to him—"catch us some breakfast." He sat down on the sand, well clear of Fool Boy, and watched the dawn break, especially enjoying the cooler air in the knowledge that in a few hours' time the air and the sand would burn.

Now a gray-haired couple walked hand-in-hand down the beach wear-

221

ing black coolie work clothes. The woman had carefully rolled up her cotton trousers above her knees as though she intended to wade in the sea. She and her husband had calm, wrinkled faces and the bright, sparrow-eyed look of old people who slept badly. Other than that there was nothing remarkable about them. Fifth Street dismissed them from his mind and turned inward to his own thoughts.

The old couple walked on down and into the sea. They went right in up to their necks, and then they began to swim down the rippling path of the sun, or rather the old man swam in a labored breaststroke and the woman, her arms trustingly about his neck, floated beside him—she could not swim.

Fool Boy dropped his line, jumped up and down waving his arms and pointing to attract Fifth Street's attention. Fifth Street looked up... in time to see the bobbing gray heads disappear. He ran down the beach kicking off his slops and tearing off his shirt, and plunged into the sea, swimming strongly for the spot where he'd seen them go down.

Almost immediately Fifth Street felt the strong undertow dragging him down too. The tide was on the ebb, and the current flowed out of the bay past the headland. He fought hard against it, reaching down every few moments with his hand to try and feel for the old couple's bodies. "Get help," he shouted to Fool Boy. "Get the others." Fortunately Fool Boy understood and raced off for the boat shed.

Fifth Street felt his strength failing against the current and, reluctantly, struck back for the shore. Udo and Keng Po came hurrying down the beach, the slanting glare from the sun burning the sleep from their eyes. Fifth Street staggered, exhausted, out of the water. "Get me a rope," he gasped. "There's an old couple out there drowning themselves."

Keng Po narrowed his eyes and scanned the empty bay. "There's nothing you can do for them now," he said. "If they're caught in the undertow their bodies will probably come back this evening and end up in the Taipa causeway... where most of the refugees' bodies end up, if the sharks haven't got them first..."

They left Fifth Street lying on the sand like a stranded fish, his skinny chest heaving. Later when he had regained some of his strength he stalked up the path to the doctor's surgery. "I saw a couple drown themselves," he told Alice from the door, his stomach screwed up into a tight ball of anger. "Why did they do it? Or don't you care?"

Alice had already gotten the news, and had no good answers to satisfy this man. She ran her hands wearily through her gray hair. "They have a son who shows great promise," she told Fifth Street more calmly than

222

she felt. "He's been accepted by several nations while they've been turned down. The family, or what was left of the family, swore they'd never be parted and the son has refused to leave his parents. There was no longer any hope of them all leaving the camp together, now his parents have freed him from his oath... I've put the boy under sedation... at least he'll live to honor his parents' sacrifice. That's why they did it. As for whether I care... I won't answer that," she said with a tinge of anger in her voice.

"Well, *shit*." Fifth Street punched with impotent anger at the door. Life here among these people was too much a reflection of his own life... "I hate this place... *hate* it, you understand me... ?"

Alice did, better than he imagined. "Mr. Fifth Street..." she paused, wanting to answer him seriously, but the name she had to call him by was a joke... "Surely you must have another name?"

"Yeah, I do, and I don't like it," he said, refusing to have anything to do with the name chosen for him out of an orphanage telephone book.

Alice realized she'd better get used to it. "Well then, Mr. Fifth Street, our greatest problem is that after a while hope becomes more and more difficult to teach these refugees, and without hope they cease to survive as a community or a family unit. It's impossible to motivate them. They stop teaching their young the ways of their culture. They just rot. To put it very plainly, that is what's happening here, and without more help there's nothing I can do about it."

He eyed her closely... "I'll help you, do what I can—"

"I understand you're already putting in more than double the others' working hours on that boat of yours."

"I'll find the time. You tell me what I can do."

"Well, you and your colleagues have a certain amount of authority in this camp," she told him, signaling Mae Ling to bring in the first patient of the day, a teenage girl with an abscess under her arm. "These people respect you. Maybe *you* could get them motivated again. It'll help a great deal when they go before the American and Australian selection teams if they can already speak some English. Also, back up my demands on hygiene, and we need to get a school going again for the children with someone to teach in it. Lord, we need so many things, anything you can do is a start..."

NICHOLAI RETURNED to the camp in time for *dim sum*. He avoided Mae Ling. His face was drained of color, his eyes were bloodshot. He said

223

little to the others, refused food, crawled into the hull and wearily tried to work.

Keng Po found him there, whiskey on his breath. "I don't know what happened to you last night in Macau," he said, obviously worried, "but don't go back on the booze again. Udo and I have followed you because we still believe in you. Don't fall apart on us."

Udo now crowded his huge bulk into the compartment. "Is it remembering what happened before?" He himself remembered all too well their last run and how after it Nicholai abandoned the boat and left Macau . . .

"You mean, have I lost my nerve? The truth?"

"The truth," both men demanded.

"I don't know." Nicholai shrugged, having no trouble playing his role, his head fuzzy with alcohol.

"Then why are you doing this to yourself?" Keng Po said. "Why are you even bothering to make this run?"

"Because it seems I'm more afraid of dying forgotten than I am of dying of old age. They said I was the best once. I need to be again. One last time, so I will know it."

Keng Po looked at him, nodded and turned to go.

"Do the boat people remember me as a drunk?" Nicholai asked, collapsing back against the hull.

"No," Keng Po told him. "They've forgotten because they never wanted to believe it. You're remembered the way you were before Li Wen died. You're still a legend. And you're alive. Don't disappoint them."

MICHAEL ANSTY was brought to Crystal Lily's quarters before breakfast. He had borrowed a razor and taken great care about his appearance. She was working at her desk in her study, and this time he waited silently for her to notice him.

"Ah, Mr. Ansty," she said, taking her own good time to acknowledge him. She wore a soft clinging dressing gown, her black hair tumbling down over her shoulders. "I've had an interesting request concerning you . . . Thomas Wu wants you. He wants to interview you about some incident at the casino. Naturally . . . for the time being . . . I've denied all knowledge about your whereabouts. Thomas Wu, though, has spies in this palace. He knows it's a lie, but can't do anything about it until you go outside these walls."

"How do you intend to get me to Coloane, then?" Ansty wasn't exactly encouraged by her news. He should, he told himself, have stayed in

Hawaii... or anywhere but this damn hornet's nest. As usual, he was ruled by what was between his legs, and as usual it bid fair to be his undoing...

"Tomorrow morning, early, a Red Cross truck carrying provisions for the refugee camp leaves Macau. You will be in it. We will also put in your care several crates for delivery to the Snake Boat Man."

"Why send me to Coloane at all? You need me to protect you here, and God knows," he argued earnestly, "I'm trained well enough for that—"

"My Manchus are enough protection for me, but you're right," she agreed with more courtesy than she had used before, "I need your skills— in Coloane."

A scratch at the door, and the comprador entered her study. He glanced sharply at Ansty, not bothering to hide his distrust of the Irishman. "Leave now," Crystal told Ansty. "I've business to attend to. Tonight I want you to dine with me again. And this time"—she smiled—"I'll see you're not hurried over your meal."

The comprador was growing more and more uncomfortable about his mistress's relationship with this ex-mercenary. "I don't *trust* that man," he said as the door closed on Ansty. "Remember what he did in the casino, my lady. I know his type... he'll sell himself to the highest bidder, which may not be you."

"I grew up seeing such men around my father. I know what to expect. But behind a gun and on our side he can make a difference. So I shall treat him as a good fighting animal and hold him on a short leash. As for trust, I trust the Snake Boat Man..." She looked with her intense, dark eyes straight at the comprador, making him flinch. "At least as much as I trust any man. Now, what bad news do you bring me this early in the morning?"

"I am sorry to tell you that it is now certain that the governor of Kwangtung Province has alerted his coastal patrol craft and will try to intercept the gold himself."

She shook her head. "Thomas Wu allies himself with such a greedy and corrupt Communist official? But can the governor use his coastal forces to steal from us without Peking knowing?"

"The governor's patrol boats are already little more than licensed pirates who intercept the smuggling junks carrying consumer goods into China, then sell them at a profit and pay the governor a heavy squeeze, which he stores up in hard currency accounts overseas. Such men cannot last forever, but as for Peking interfering now"—the comprador shrugged, quoting an old proverb of the Kwangtung Province—"'Heaven is high and the emperor is far away.' The gold, all of it in one boat on open water, is too rich a prize for him to resist."

Crystal Lily's spirits plunged. "We will just have to send a warning to Nicholai that the thirty miles of the Pearl River estuary between the boundaries of Macau and Hong Kong is no longer neutral territory. That it is, in fact, enemy territory..."

CHAPTER 21

ANSTY FOLLOWED Mae Ling down the steep cliff path to the boat shed, where the crew were at work in the boat. To find them Ansty and Mae Ling had to descend on down the ladder into the cramped engine compartment. A jerry-rigged lightbulb cast its oily gleam over three hulking Packard marine engines that took up nearly all the space in the forward area. The nearest or number one engine was placed against the midships bulkhead, within which could be stored two-and-a-half thousand gallons of fuel in triple tanks. Engines number two and three lay side by side toward the stern, a narrow catwalk between them.

Ansty's curiosity was stirred by what he saw in the space behind the engines—the propellers, rudders and all their connecting gear had been ripped out, and three rectangular holes had been cut into the bottom of the craft to accommodate water inlets. Similarly, three holes to accommodate the thrust nozzles of the aquajets had been cut through the stern.

For the moment the crew were too absorbed in their task of dismantling one of the two generators to pay any attention to Ansty. "How are you going to fit a block and tackle in there?" he asked, impressed by the weight of machinery that had to be lifted out of an impossibly tight space.

A scrawny black man wriggled out from underneath the generator, a wrench in hand. "We don't need a block and tackle, man, whoever you are... Okay, it's free as it's ever going to be," he then said to a huge man in an oily, sweat-stained shirt.

Udo squatted down, took the weight in his thighs, kept his back straight. He concentrated for a moment, then, with a grunt, he unleashed all his power in the lift. The heavy generator came off its bed. As he swung it out the others grabbed hold and helped him hustle it along the narrow catwalk to a spot where it could be lifted out through the deck hatch by a mechanical winch.

"Honky gorilla," Fifth Street jeered at Udo, his face, like the others', streaming with sweat. "Now I *know* you belong in a zoo."

"All right, take five," said another man. Ansty rightly assumed, by the authority he seemed to wield over the others, that this one was Nicholai, the Snake Boat Man.

The crew climbed wearily out of the oven-hot, steel-lined engine compartment and gulped in the cooling breeze on the deck. Udo tasted the salty tang in the humid air and glanced up through the bamboo slats at the sun, which was now partly obscured by cloud. "Storm coming," he said with the foreknowledge of a man who had lived his life on this part of the coast. "Maybe a full typhoon." He considered their flimsy bamboo shelter. "If it hits we're going to be in deep trouble."

Ansty felt very much the outsider. These people all had something in common... "I've been sent by the Lady Sun," he said, and quickly noticed the effect that name had on Mae Ling.

"We heard you were coming." Nicholai turned to him. "Who are you?" The others pointedly waited for Ansty's reply.

"You need a gunner"—Ansty shrugged—"and if I do say so myself, I have a way with guns." And women too, he thought, as he glanced at and quickly away from Mae Ling.

"We were told that you have a military background..." Keng Po said. He'd been watching Ansty closely, not missing how he took note of Mae Ling.

"I was trained by the Irish army," Ansty said, thinking he'd seen a slight warning shake of the head from the girl... "and I left it with the

228

belief I could earn my living doing what the army taught me. I had a bit part in some small wars, mainly in Africa, and I was with the Rhodesian forces from nineteen seventy-six to seventy-nine—"

"What as?" Nicholai put in.

"A helicopter gunner."

"Could you operate a point-fifty-caliber machine gun from a boat?"

"I said I was good with all kinds of weapons. From a helicopter, over a range of four hundred yards, I figure I could hit a man running through rough terrain within a spread of, say, four rounds. A boat should offer a better target."

"And after Rhodesia?" Fifth Street asked.

"There was some foolishness in Somalia." Ansty was silent for a moment, not wanting to elaborate on that fiasco. "It was then I decided I'd had enough of supporting losing sides." He looked over the raffish collection of men on the deck and was reminded of how often he'd seen groups like these before. "I thought I was finished with working with guys with crazy nicknames who swallowed pills for courage—"

The doors of the boat shed opened just then and a file of refugees struggled in carrying two long wooden crates. "Oh, these came on the supply truck for you," Ansty said into the hostile silence that followed his last remark. "The *Lady* Sun has advised that the rest of the machinery you need has been located and will be delivered in the same way over the next few days."

Nicholai waited until the refugees had gone, then got a crowbar. "This should interest you," he said to Ansty as he pried the lids off the boxes. Inside, carefully greased, wrapped in oilcloth and in as perfect condition as when they were lowered into their hiding place in Macau fifteen years ago, were two .50-caliber machine guns.

Ansty recognized the Brownings. "They're air-cooled, recoil-operated, belt-fed. A hundred ten rounds to a belt. Rate of fire, five hundred and seventy-five rounds per minute. They used 'em in Spitfires in World War Two. Which is about the vintage of your boat, if I'm not mistaken. Well, lucky for you, even old machine guns are my specialty."

"Yes, we're grateful to the gods for your presence," Nicholai said straight-faced. "And since you're such an expert, you've got the job of stripping the grease off these. Clean and reassemble them, then check that they fit on their pedestal mountings on both sides of the bridge. When the time comes you'll operate one gun and Udo the other."

"What's the opposition got?"

Nicholai looked at the Irishman and half-smiled. "More than we have, so you'd better hope it never comes to a straight fight."

"Sounds more and more like every fight I've ever been in," Ansty said. Nobody bothered to answer that.

AFTER THE evening meal Ansty sought out Fifth Street, figuring the Negro would be the outsider he could manipulate into giving the information he was after. "They're a right strange bunch here, no mistake, I'm sure you'll agree," he said, sitting down on the beach beside Fifth Street, noting that a little way along from them Fool Boy was fishing in the surf. He lit a cigarette and offered one to his presumed new buddy.

Fifth Street shook his head. "Don't smoke."

"I do like it better, can do a better job when I know who I'm working with," Ansty said. "Give me a rundown on them?"

Two weeks ago Fifth Street wouldn't have talked to the Irishman, but now that he was steadily more involved with the boat and its crew, he wanted the run to succeed and would do what he could, even if he disliked this smart-assed Irisher. "Keng Po is the little guy who got together the guns and most of the equipment on this boat. He's always figuring the play two steps ahead of everyone else. Udo ... they call him the Bear around here ... he's strong as he looks. Don't mix with him. I tried him once ... He's also probably the closest of all of us to the one they call the Snake Boat Man. They go back a long ways."

"And the Snake Boat Man? Is he still living on his past reputation or does he still earn it?"

"He earns it, all right ... hey, he's older now, and the booze has got to him a little, but I'd follow him. I trust him." From Fifth Street that was rare praise and Ansty knew it.

"What about Mae Ling?"

"She's his, if she's anybody's. I'd stay clear of her if I were you."

"What about living arrangements?"

"Suit yourself. You can either stay out here on the beach, or if you want company find yourself a spare mat on deck. Now if you don't mind, man, I've got to go."

"Where? Don't tell me you've found some social life in this dump."

A real charmer, Fifth Street thought as he went off to see the refugee families waiting for him.

LATER THAT evening Keng Po slipped into the boat shed and announced to the others, "That crazy bastard, he's gone clean out of his mind. This is something you've got to see..." He led them up through the shanty huts to a converted schoolroom.

"Now you listen to me," they heard Fifth Street's harsh voice rasp out over the refugees who were gathered silently on benches before him, "because I'm here to help you get *out* of this place." He waited for Alice, who was acting as interpreter, to finish.

At first the boat crew gathered in the dark outside the glassless windows were disbelieving of the scene they were looking on.

"Tonight we're working in the kitchen." Fifth Street signaled to a teenage girl, Mary Hung Hei, on the front bench. She was a Christian Vietnamese who had come to the infirmary when he was there to have the sores on her arm treated, and she was special to him... she wasn't, after all, much older than his daughter would have been... She held up a utensil and turned to the others so that they could put a name to it. They tried, then spluttered into a shy silence.

"Kettle," Fifth Street prompted. "*Say* it." The refugees, as though hypnotized by his fierce intensity, struggled with the foreign sounding word. "No, goddamn it, sound the *k*."

This *ferang*, the assembled immigrants decided, seemed ready to ram the English words down their throats.

"Jug," Fifth Street said as Mary held up another chipped enamel vessel.

"W-u-g," they chorused.

"No, *j*. Say the *j*, goddamn it."

"Go-dam," the refugees parroted, and winced at Fifth Street's annoyed shouts for silence.

"Okay, okay," he muttered, taking a deep breath, "nobody ever said this was going to be easy."

Only then, during this break, did he pick up the snorts and grunts of muffled laughter coming from the men outside. He walked to the doorway.

"Okay, you jokers... laugh all you want, and then either you come in here and help or you fuck off. Which is it?"

They drifted away, only Nicholai stayed and came into the room.

"Thank you," Fifth Street said stiffly, his speech clipped to hide his gratitude. "These people have respect for you. It should help with you alongside me."...

At the end of the evening Fifth Street made his way back along down the cliff path to the boat shed, while Alice stayed behind to talk to Nicholai.

"That is a committed man," she said.

Nicholai told her about the war Fifth Street had been in, and the loss of his wife and child... "He's trying to pay back a debt to these people."

"Why don't you let him stay on and work with me here? I could use his help—"

"When he's finished the run he'll be free to do whatever he wants."

Nicholai left her by her infirmary, where she occupied a cramped, airless room in the back. "You mean *if* you ever do finish this run," she called after him. "Dear God, I pray it's over soon."

Nicholai, not one for praying, mouthed a silent amen.

THE SKY was leaden gray, the wind howled and the sea churned with whitecaps. Malloy had made the uncomfortable journey in a police launch across Hong Kong Harbor to the tip of Tsim Sha Tsui on the Kowloon side. The ground felt like it was rocking under his feet as he hurried up the steps of the gracious three-story Victorian building that housed MAR-POL, marine police headquarters.

A policeman on duty at the reception desk glanced at his identification. "Yes, sir"—he lifted a telephone—"the D.P.C. is expecting you."

"I know the way," Malloy told him, then crossed the hall. On his right was a closed door leading to the joint navy-police crisis room, continuously manned against emergencies in the colony. He turned the brass handle to the large wooden door on the opposite side of the passage.

John Carey had just been appointed divisional police commander of the marine wing. He was a heavy-set, bluff-faced seaman with broad shoulders and ginger hair thinning to a shiny bald patch on top. His braided peak cap and cane lay on the desk in front of him. "Well,"—he greeted Malloy cautiously—"it's not too often a senior member of Special Branch trudges all the way out to Tsim Sha Tsui. Must be important business that brings you here."

"What news do you have about the typhoon?"

"She's veered off into the South China Sea again," Carey said with obvious relief. "All she's left us with now is the rain."

"Good," Malloy murmured to himself. "That'll help cool down striker protests in the streets, but it won't stop him..."

Carey didn't intend to let Malloy conduct a one-sided interview in his office. "By *him* I take it you're referring to the one they call Snake Boat Man?"

"Do you think I'd waste my time coming here if I wasn't?"

Carey remembered Malloy's clash with Nicholai. "Harry," he advised, "don't let the chance of catching him throw you again, because long after you and I are dead the people we've tried to protect will put up a statue to that man and the birds will compete with one another to unload on his bronzed shoulders."

"Not if he doesn't make it. What's the saying? 'The green grass of a man's reputation can't flourish under the gallows.' Death in a cell or at the end of a rope will make bloody sure there's no monument to that bastard. I want to make certain that if he breaks out of Macau your boats can stop him."

Carey got to his feet. "Well, I'd say the odds must be around seventy to thirty in our favor, but ask me for my gut instinct and I'll tell you they're a damn sight less, even with the new boats and equipment I've got."

"What if I tell you the date he'll be making the run?"

"That'll help."

"And with radar..."

"Radar makes a difference," Carey agreed, "but look at the map." Malloy followed Carey across his office to a large wall map. His launches were divided into north, south, east and west sectors, and they covered the sea and all the coastline within the Square Boundary of Hong Kong.

"There are two hundred and thirty-five islands within the Square Boundary," Carey told him. "Most of them uninhabited, and as many islands again, Communist-owned, around the Boundary's edges. Now look closely at the kind of coastline I have to defend. Every inch contains a bay or a cove or a rocky headland where small craft can land... the Royal Navy patrols the Square Boundary and can cross into international waters where my launches can't go according to our lease agreement with China. If Snake Boat Man can get past the navy, then even if we're following him on radar, at the speed he'll be traveling we'll be left with little or no time to intercept. In the old days he'd keep two or three fallback landing places in case we managed to head him off from reaching the first one." Carey tapped his cane thoughtfully on the board. "Nobody knows this coastline better than he does. Better than modern boats and radar are the old police methods of knowing your enemy's *modus operandi* and deducing from that what landing place he favors. You don't by chance have anyone with that kind of information, do you?"

"Not yet, but I may—"

"I doubt it. He wouldn't tell that to just anybody... it would have to be someone he especially trusted..."

"Did you ever come across an old marine policeman called Lao Ch'en?" Malloy asked while studying the map.

"Yes... he was the deck sergeant on my very first launch. Now there's a man who understood this coast almost like the Snake Boat Man, and damnit, he nearly got him a couple of times... but he's been retired so long I wonder if he's still alive, or if so, where he is now."

"I know," Malloy said.

MALLOY MADE his next stop the Tsz Wan housing area. The closely packed towers of concrete were a streaming, rain-wet, sullen gray. Banners of washing had been withdrawn from the balconies, and the canvas roof of the produce market flapped like a loose sail.

Malloy laboriously climbed the seventeen stories to Deck Sergeant Lao Ch'en's apartment. The whole building swayed under the force of the wind. Malloy hated to think what it would be like to live here in a typhoon.

He knocked on the door. Eventually a wispy, gray-haired old woman opened the door a crack and peered suspiciously through. "*Mat-ye shi*, what matter?"

He showed her his Special Branch I.D. "Fetch your husband," he ordered.

Lao Ch'en's face appeared. He recognized Malloy and his heart sank. He had been expecting a visit by the police ever since he'd heard of their raid on the Snake Boat Man's house. He shrugged fatalistically and unlatched the chain from the door.

His wife slumped back against the wall and began to wail that they'd be turned out into the streets to starve, the family was destroyed, her husband would die in jail and his pension would be stopped...

"Be silent, woman," Lao Ch'en told her. "You wish me come station?" he asked Malloy with all the dignity he could gather.

"If I was going to arrest you, I'd have sent the uniformed police. I don't relish climbing... I want to talk to you alone."

Lao Ch'en signaled to the rest of the clan to leave them. His apartment was so tiny that a whisper could travel from one end to the other, which meant his family now had to wait outside in the draughty passage, where the old woman's sobs alerted the neighbors, who promptly closed their doors and windows to shut her out.

"I've a deal for you," Malloy told Lao Ch'en quietly. "The Snake Boat Man is going to make a run. No one knows this coast better than you do, and after all those years spent hunting him, you even know his mind. I want your help to stop him."

234

"I cannot do that..."

"Why? Would you rather spend the rest of your life in jail?"

Lao Ch'en looked Malloy straight in the eye. "I cannot help you."

Malloy's instincts warned him he was handling this stubborn old man all wrong. He needed another lever... He strode across the room, flung the door open and summoned Lao Ch'en's wife. "You have harbored a girl you knew to be an illegal immigrant," he said coldly. "I have the say-so of the taxi driver who took your husband to the Snake Boat Man's house. And if need be I have no doubt I can soon squeeze from your neighbors a witness who remembers your sheltering her..."

The deck sergeant did not try to lie. "One piece girl from my clan. I must give help her."

Malloy was momentarily taken aback. "You were a policeman, you know the law, you know the penalty for breaking it."

"Then arrest me, sir," Lao Ch'en said.

Malloy ignored the challenge. Now it was he who had to backtrack. "I'm prepared to destroy all evidence of your husband's crime if he will help me catch the Snake Boat Man," he told Lao Ch'en's wife, "but it seems he would prefer to sacrifice not only himself but you and his whole clan as well. Perhaps you can talk some sense into him..."

"Fool," the old woman hissed at her husband with such venom that Lao Ch'en, who'd stood rock solid against Malloy, physically flinched. "Take what the gwilo offers." And then to Malloy: "Lord"—she changed into a halting English—"Snake Boat Man my husband hunt all career. Now old fool. When can have chance finish life here he want go jail."

"I owe him a debt," Lao Ch'en told her stubbornly.

"Husband promise Snake Boat Man thirty thousand Hong Kong dollars," she told Malloy, "he take Nui Macau. I tell old fool, why must repay debt to outlaw?"

"For my face." Lao Ch'en was an old-fashioned man with old-fashioned values, and on a matter of face he was unshakable.

"But if you repay him"—Malloy began to see a way out of the impasse—"then the debt is canceled?"

Lao Ch'en shook his head. "Sorry, no have money."

"I can advance you the money out of Special Branch fund," Malloy said. "The secretary for security is placing a reward of two hundred and fifty thousand Hong Kong dollars for information leading to the capture of the Snake Boat Man. If you're in the control room at MARPOL on the night he makes the run, I'll see you get a share of the reward and with that you can repay the fund. Is that honorable enough for you?"

"Take," Lao Ch'en's wife hissed at her husband. "Take. You gave word to repay, more nothing than that. You were policeman, he outlaw. Take money, cancel debt.". . .

All that night Lao Ch'en lay awake fighting with his conscience. The next morning he went to Special Branch headquarters and collected the money. Malloy made him sign for it. When he had done so the deck sergeant drew himself up with dignity. "Thirty-five years I gave all my duty to police," he told Malloy. "I break law only because my clan law is higher."

"Of course," Malloy said, showing him to the door, "just another honest cop. You stay close to home where I can reach you in a hurry. You're going to be my best insurance in case the Snake Boat Man gets past the navy."

AH CHUEN had finished packing the furniture in the Snake Boat Man's house on the Peak and limped restlessly through the empty rooms. He was caretaking the house only until the end of the month when the new owners would arrive. The intercom buzzed. He went over to the console and pressed the switch. The face of Lao Ch'en flickered onto the screen. "I have something for the Snake Boat Man," Lao Ch'en barked in nervous Cantonese, knowing that Malloy's men could well be watching him.

"Go away," Ah Chuen told him, fearing a trap. "The Snake Boat Man no longer lives here." But Lao Ch'en insisted that he come to the door.

"See this." Lao Ch'en held up a bulky package. "It holds thirty thousand Hong Kong dollars. Take to your lord, and when you give to him be sure to tell it from Lao Ch'en, the deck sergeant. Tell him all debts now paid."

Which was as far as Lao Ch'en could go to warn Nicholai that he was back on the side of the police.

CHAPTER 22

NICHOLAI WALKED in the dark across the beach to their meeting place under the trees. Mae Ling reached up to him, and he knelt down beside her. His fingers stroked her face as he kissed her. His movements were gentle, springing from a sureness with her—the opposite of Malloy. Mae Ling felt a stab in her heart... she actually cared for this man, more than she had for any other man, and she didn't know how to cope with this new, untrusted feeling—

She noticed the package. "What is that?"

"It's from your uncle... thirty thousand Hong Kong dollars to repay his debt." Nicholai had too much on his mind to think about the significance of the message that had come with the money. "It's for you, I never wanted his money."

Mae Ling took it. "Did Ah Chuen bring my papers?"

"No... the police and the Triad have your description and they've cracked down on the forgers in Hong Kong. I'm trying in Macau but right now nothing moves there without the permission of Thomas Wu."

"So I'm trapped..." It was what she had feared most.

"No," Nicholai told her, "I'll get you your papers, I have promised you that..."

The moon moved out from behind a black devil cloud. She used its light to look into his face. Nicholai had enemies as powerful as hers... he was in no position to make such promises... "What bothers you?" she asked in a quiet voice. "Your spirit is so low since you've returned from Macau. You've told me nothing about your meeting."

"There is nothing to tell."

He was lying, and she knew it. And was she to risk everything on him as her deliverer? "Is that so? I hear that the Lady Sun has also put Ansty under her spell."

"You imagine too much. We are commissioned by her to do a job, that's all."

Mae Ling blazed with jealous resentment of Crystal Lily, who had wealth, power, who she imagined was invulnerable, while she had nothing, and needed the acceptance of men for her very existence... "If you believe that is all, then ask Ansty what he was doing on the nights he dined alone with her. Ask him to tell you about the decorations of her private suite, or about the moon bridge over the lotus pond. Or do you know that already?"

"*Enough*," Nicholai told her.

Knowing she had hurt him, Mae Ling changed her tack. "I love you," she now said with a convincing tenderness. "Once Ah Chuen told me that I looked very much like your wife, and I was flattered to resemble, even in a small way, someone who held so much of your love. But now you frighten me because I cannot reach you. Is it that devil woman in Macau... or has someone else been telling you evil things about me? Tell me so that at least I can defend myself."

She was reaching him more than she knew... more than he'd intended. "Mae Ling, I've been empty a long time." He took her into his arms. Have faith in me. Ask for no more explanations or promises." She felt his body's hardness against her. His lips found hers. With his hands, his lips, his mind, his whole being, he began to make love to her, gently at first, then demanding. He pulled her sarong away, she stretched her hips up to meet him...

Later, as they rested with her arms pillowing his head against her heart, she said softly, "Nicholai, you are a very special man. In China we were taught nothing of love or God or beauty. Only to seek our own survival under the terrible power of the State. You ask me to have faith in you, but understand I have no conception of such a trust. I understand only that people are driven before the winds of their fate like clouds across the moon. They have no choice—"

"What are you trying to tell me?" Nicholai asked sleepily, hearing only one word in three.

"Nothing," she whispered, deciding not to break the spell. She brushed the pulse spot on his temple with her lips, wishing he hadn't left her that night under these trees to Malloy.

THE SUPPLY truck brought in the aqua propulsion units, which had to be broken into component parts, then carried, swinging from bamboo poles, down the steep path to the boat shed by files of refugees.

Fifth Street waited, everything in his engine room readied to receive them. He immediately set to work reassembling the aquajets, which he linked through Z drives to the main engines.

"Steering's worked by twin-balanced deflector plates aft of each nozzle," he explained to Nicholai. "I'll mount one set of controls for all three engines on the bridge. To stop or go astern, the deflector plates drop behind the nozzles and back up the thrust. It's simple and easy to operate. You can beach this boat now if you have to, or run over fishermens' nets without problems. But if plastic sacking or some such debris chokes the water inlet, then the loss of power on that engine will register on vacuum pressure gauges on the bridge. What you do then is keep checking the gauges and I'll fit you a hydraulically operated backwash gizmo that'll spit out any debris from the protective grills."

Nicholai was impressed.

"Wait till you try this old boat," Fifth Street said with deep pride, "no one's going to believe what she can do."

Fifth Street worked on with Nicholai and the others until it was time to go up and give his afternoon class, which lasted through the siesta hour when everyone else slept. "You coming?" he asked Nicholai, wanting his support.

"I'll look in later."

Each afternoon and night class found fewer and fewer refugees attending, unless Nicholai was quietly sitting there by the desk, and then they came mostly out of curiosity to see the Snake Boat Man. Fifth Street had tried being less demanding in his teaching, but it made little difference. Most of the refugees simply did not believe his efforts would really make any difference in their chances of success with the selection teams.

Fifth Street now entered the schoolroom and greeted the small gathering of hopefuls who had stayed with him, then noticed Mary Hung Hei was missing. "Where is she?"

At first nobody answered, then her brother, who was nearly ten and her only surviving relative, shyly put up his hand. She had given him a part of the advance money but he couldn't keep silent... "Lord," he burst our nervously, "she's going to work in Macau—"

"Oh my god," Alice groaned as she interpreted this for Fifth Street. "The pimps have got her."

"What do you mean?"

"The *pimps*, for God's sake. Youths from the local village that owns this land, they're always preying on the young girls here. They promise to protect them from prosecution as illegal residents if they work in the Macau brothels."

"Can't the authorities do anything to stop it?"

"They don't even look. A fresh girl is worth a lot of money, and since they're supported and protected and don't last long, nobody cares."

"Her brother said she's going. Does that mean she hasn't left yet? Where is she now?"

Alice questioned Mary's brother, then reported: "She's outside the main gates waiting for the pimps to collect her. I've seen it all too many times before. It's a state of mind... she's made her choice. She's gone from us now as surely as if she'd walked into the sea. There's nothing we can do—"

"Like hell there isn't." Fifth Street couldn't just forget about a scared fifteen-year-old girl. She reminded him of too many others from his own past. "We can at least try to change her mind, or are you ready just to let those damn pimps pick her off—?"

"You don't understand. The villagers are too well connected with the Syndicate for even the police to interfere, let alone us. They only barely tolerate this camp as it is."

"So what happens to Mary?"

"It's her life, I can't stop these people killing themselves and I can't stop them selling themselves. All I can do is stay with the survivors and try to hold them together—"

"What for? What in the hell are you doing this for?" Fifth Street was shouting now. "No wonder they don't want to learn, they figure everyone's given up on them—"

"Not true," Alice snapped back. "Look, I have to protect them all, one individual can't count against the rest—"

"She does to me."

Alice guessed what he was going to do. "Don't interfere, you'll only bring punishment down on the rest of them..."

But Fifth Street had already ducked through the door, was running up the path that led over the brow of the red earth hill toward the entrance gate that was set in a wire fence that surrounded the camp.

A flight of concrete steps led down to the narrow, potholed coast road. Mary Hung Hei was sitting there on the bottom step, all her possessions held at her side in a small wicker carrier bag.

A car drew up. Two pimps in their early twenties were in the front seats. One of them got out and motioned to Mary. She got up and slowly crossed the road to him.

"Mary," Fifth Street called to her as he took the steps three at a time. "Mary, *stop*." She turned, hesitated, impressed that this man cared enough to try to stop her. The pimp took her elbow and nudged her toward the back seat of the car.

Fifth Street knew she had learned enough English to understand him... "Mary, don't go with them, don't do it, *please*..." The second pimp got out of the car, and they both squared up to him. In a practiced display their wrists blurred in unison as each drew from his pocket a glittering knife blade. Fifth Street didn't back off. "It's your choice," he told Mary. "Say the word and I'll stop them." Or at least try to...

He heard a sound behind him, too late to turn and face it.

"Why is it, crazy man," a steady voice said with friendly sarcasm, "that when all this time I've been wanting to break your ass, I find myself having to save it?"

"Get lost," Fifth Street told Udo, but his face betrayed his relief at finding that the big man had come to help.

"You go alone against these two and they'll cut you to pieces," Udo told him. "Now tell the girl to come to us. If she doesn't, we back off."

Mary, perhaps understandably, in her naïveté had visions of the good clothes and good food she'd been promised once she got to Macau. And who knew, the pimps had told her, within a few months a rich man might well buy her out of the brothel and she could send for her brother... Mary had to compare such a future in Macau with the refugee camp. Nothing could be worse than life here, she thought, and got into the car.

The pimps sidled backward, opened the car doors and got in. Mary was promptly, brutally locked into the back seat. Her eyes were on an

241

ugly wart growing on the neck of one of the pimps. She felt nauseated. The car began to move. The pimps ignored her as though she were already so much parceled meat. The full realization of what she was doing burst on her. No doubts now. She screamed out the window, calling out to Fifth Street.

It was all he needed. He ran across the road, made a grab for the back door handle. But the car accelerated away, dragging, then tossing him, bruised and winded, onto the side of the road.

The driver executed a tight three-point turn just past the gates. As he did, Udo spotted a refugee on his way back to camp with a cartload of chopped wood. Udo crossed over to the woodcutter, wrenched the long-handled axe from his hands and, holding it across his chest, blocked the narrow road.

As the car came along the road the driver spotted Udo and considered him no threat. After all, one man, even this huge one, against a speeding car... He drove straight at him. Udo moved out of the car's path at the last minute. As he did so he swung the axe high over his head and, using every single ounce of force he could muster, he struck the blade edge against the windshield directly over the driver's face. It shattered and collapsed inward, showering glass over the people inside. The driver lost control as the blade shaved his face, swerved off the road into the ditch, and the car turned over. Udo stooped, picked up the axe, which had been torn from his hands, and wielding it purposefully, strolled toward the wreckage. The pimps, banged up and bloody, nonetheless scrambled from their car and ran off before Udo got to them.

"Thanks," Fifth Street muttered as he moved quickly past him. He was badly bruised and covered with red mud.

"I think we're going to be in plenty of trouble now," Udo said, watching the pimps leave. Nicholai and Keng Po would be furious. Still, it had been worth it.

Fifth Street looked at him with new respect, then helped Mary climb out through the window. She was cut some from the flying glass and pale with shock. "It's all over now," he said, trying to reassure her, took her arm and led her back through the camp gates. . . .

Keng Po was furious at them when he met them at Alice's infirmary, where Mary was having her cuts treated. "What have you done to us?" He turned to Udo. "You... you were sent by the Snake Boat Man to keep this crazy one out of trouble, not start it." . . .

Later that evening Alice, leaning wearily against one of the bamboo supports in the boat shed, addressed the crew. "The Heung Cheung, the headman of the village, has sent me a message," she told them. "He

242

wants the girl back. That was to be expected, but he also wants Udo and Fifth Street for punishment. It's a matter of saving his face here on the island, and he won't be talked out of it."

The others kept silent, waiting for the Snake Boat Man to speak. "That's out of the question," Nicholai said.

"What about the girl?" Keng Po asked.

"Nothing doing," Fifth Street answered him quickly.

"You can't keep her here—"

"Why not?"

"Because they'll have made a contract to deliver her to Macau."

"Well, damn 'em, they'll just have to break it—"

"Do you know what you two have done?" Mae Ling broke in. This girl, she felt, had brought nothing but trouble down on them, *and* made her especially vulnerable... "Do you really think the headman will let this pass? No, he will bring all the men in his village and they will punish you, me, everyone in this miserable camp. Send the girl back now before it's too late. At least then maybe we can make a compromise with him for the lives of Udo and Fifth Street—"

"Have you any idea of the sort of life this girl was going to?" Fifth Street put in, seeing a side of Mae Ling that was new to him. Not too pretty, he thought.

"She knew," Mae Ling said. "She made the choice to leave here. What better life can any of you offer her? All you've done by interfering is make things worse for those of us who are left here."

Keng Po backed her up. "It was crazy to draw attention to us like this. The villagers can attack the camp at any time—"

"What would you have done?" Fifth Street looked to the Snake Boat Man for help. "Would you have let them take her?"

Nicholai was staring into the fire. He made his decision and lifted his head. "The girl stays," he said. "If they come, we'll fight them off."

"What with?" Keng Po had to challenge him.

"The refugees."

"They won't fight," Mae Ling said contemptuously. "They're like cattle in a slaughter pen—"

"They will if we lead them," Nicholai said quietly.

"Wait a minute," Alice interrupted, unable to believe her ears. "You can't be serious. You promised when you came here you wouldn't get involved with my people. You would just work on your boat and move on. Now you actually want to lead them into a confrontation with the Heung Cheung? Mae Ling and Keng Po are right—"

"Alice," Nicholai said, grim-faced. "Your people have no life as it is.

243

You know that. At least let us try to teach them to fight back. Let me talk to them, see what they decide..."

The refugees were gathered with their families around a fire on the beach. In the distance was the clanking sound of the water pump. This time there was no welcome as Nicholai and his men stepped into the circle. He hadn't expected it. The refugees ignored Mary. She stood to one side holding her brother's hand, already an outcast.

"The damage is done," Nicholai said, his voice low and resonant. He had the force... the charisma to make them listen, to draw them toward him. "No matter what happens now, the Heung Cheung will send his men. They will loot what few possessions you have left and molest your women—"

"We cannot stop them." It was the tired voice of an old man. "They have attacked us as they pleased ever since we came here."

"If they drive you out of here, where will you go... into the sea?" Nicholai tried to challenge them. "By now you must have had enough of cringing to the authorities in Macau, to the selection teams, to the Heung Cheung and his villagers. This time when they come, fight back. We'll show you how."

"Lord," the old man said, his voice firmer now as he stepped forward, responding to Nicholai and his crew, "we were not always like this." He turned to the refugees. "All we have left for our pride, my people, is to fight." It was the women who began to mutter in a gathering tide, urging their men on. "Show us what to do," they said.

Nicholai issued terse instructions to his crew. "Each of you choose ten men or sturdy women. Arm them with pickaxe handles or whatever you can find. But don't use guns—"

"*Ach*," Alice interrupted, swept along by her refugees' desire to fight back, proud of them, in fact. "This is madness, but give me some men to lead and I'll fight too."

Nicholai smiled his gratitude at her, a warm, seductive smile, and she felt herself responding to him. She understood why men still followed him.

Michael Ansty, who had said nothing, now turned and walked back in the direction of the boat shed.

"What about you?" Nicholai's question stopped him.

"I'm contracted to make a run, not involve myself in some village war over a bunch of refugees—"

"You're part of us, Ansty," Fifth Street told him. "I don't give a damn what you signed on for, you're going to go along or—"

244

"Wrong. If you want to get your heads beaten in over a bunch of refugees, be my guests—"

"Let him go," Nicholai ordered. He turned to Keng Po.

"Well, it's madness... but when have I not supported you?"

It was enough. "How many men in the Heung Cheung village?" Nicholai turned to Alice.

"About a hundred and fifty, maybe more."

Nicholai proceeded to set the refugees into defensive positions around the perimeter of the camp....

Mae Ling found Keng Po alone as the others waited through the night. He was watching the main gate to the refugee camp. "Stop him," she said. "You have the sense to see what will happen if news of this reaches Macau—"

"I can't"—Keng Po shrugged—"he won't listen to me."

"Find some way, make him listen or he will bring disaster down on us all."

"Once he's made up his mind he won't change."

"Then he must lose," she said miserably.

"Perhaps." Keng Po nodded.

"If you feel that way then why do you stay here?"

"Because, girl, I love him... he cares about things the way few men do... he will take on odds that others won't even attempt... he'll fight for the life of a refugee like you, who maybe doesn't even deserve it..."

She ignored that last. "And if he loses because his enemies are too powerful and too clever for him?" Mae Ling asked. "When his end comes, where will you be?"

"Where Udo will be, by his side. At least I hope I will have the courage to be there too."

She realized her best answer to that, at least for now, was to say nothing.

"You see," Keng Po went on, "all my life I have weighed everything twice. I doubt myself too much, but this man has made me better than I am. I can't help you."

MAE LING slipped out of the refugee camp and made her way to Coloane village. A Syndicate-owned car waited against the curb. Mae Ling, relieved to see that it was unoccupied, opened the driver's door and dropped a message onto the seat. Up to now her messages had been for Malloy, and Fool Boy had been her messenger. But this message was not for Malloy. With it she was playing her last card for survival. Her father the

245

general had established contact with Thomas Wu prior to their escape from China. It was Wu who had secured their place in the sampan bound for Hong Kong, which had been intercepted by Malloy.

Mae Ling had avoided going to him before this because she had no wish to put herself under his protection, and, of course, to be used by still another man. But now she felt she had no choice left. She could not trust Malloy and she had lost faith in Nicholai's ability to help her... though she still felt for him. She was gambling that Thomas Wu was about to win control over the Macau Syndicate, whose territory she was in. Once on top he could smooth over her problems with the Syndicate's sister organization, the 14K Triad in Hong Kong. Clearly he had liked her well enough when he last saw her with her father to want her for his mistress. The prospect was hardly an attractive one, but she had been alone and hunted for so long that she could harden herself to almost any prospect... and cold logic said that an alliance with Thomas Wu was the best way she had left to insure that she soon got out of this awful place. . . .

From the square she made her way to the Tam Chim temple and sought out a Fung Shui man. "I am from the mainland, I do not know how to appeal to the gods. Tell me my future with the one I love and teach me how to pray."

Under the Fung Shui man's direction, on good-luck paper spangled with gold, Mae Ling composed with brush and ink a love spell to bind Nicholai to her and prayed for the cunning and strength with which, even as she betrayed Nicholai, she could protect him from harm. Then she burned incense sticks to the lord Buddha, whose image was canopied in crimson and seated above the altar. She threw the half-moon-shaped clappers given her by the Fung Shui man on the ground in sequences of three and five times, shook the joss sticks in the cylinder. The future foretold by the sticks that fell out was unfavorable to the lovers. She felt her heart freeze over as she was shown their paths dividing.

DAWN BROKE. The Heung Cheung still hadn't brought his villagers to attack. "There must be a reason," Nicholai said, more concerned than he showed. "Someone's been holding them back. But they'll be coming tonight."

CHAPTER 23

LORD ANGUS McEWAN and Billion Dollar Choy were shown into the taipan's suite on the fiftieth floor of the Asian Trading building. Rain lashed the windows, which were level with the cloud base over the harbor.

"Bloody rain," McEwan complained. "Seems it'll never stop, but at least the typhoon's given us a break and hit further up the coast."

Fang Choy helped himself to a seat. Joss Denning, who had been working at his desk below the portrait of the founder, looked up. "I thought you'd gone back to your grouse moors in Scotland."

"I've too much at stake here." Joss noticed that Clair's cousin had lost some of his normally ruddy complexion. Too many late nights closeted with Billion Dollar Choy trying to figure out how to save his share of the family fortune, Joss thought with satisfaction.

"We've got a proposition to put to you." McEwan got straight to the point.

"I thought you might have."

"Sell me Asian Land." Billion Dollar Choy put it like a demand, not a question or even a request.

Asian Land was the plum cash-generating company in the whole Princely House complex. Joss immediately saw through the offer. "Out of the question."

"Why, man, for God's sake?" McEwan burst out in frustration. "Choy here will give a fair price and the cash the sale generates will buy us breathing space on our loans. He's offering you a way out. Don't be a fool. Take it."

"You know as well as I," Joss told McEwan, "if I sell Asian Land to Choy, then through the interlocking structure of our companies he'll gain enough shares to put two of his directors on our main board with a blocking vote. And from there on he'll own us within a year. Conceivably it might give the family time to bail out, but what about our staff, our minority shareholders? No, sir, I don't sell."

"Hold out against me," Choy warned, "and it's only a matter of weeks before all that you own comes down. I *promise* you that..."

"Damnit," Lord McEwan said to Joss, no longer caring if he humiliated him in front of a stranger, "your father was a *clerk* in this company. You should never have been allowed to climb past the fortieth floor. When this is over and you find yourself kicked out on the street without Clair's money to back you, I'll see you never work in Hong Kong again—"

"Taipan"—Connie's voice on the intercom fortuitously cut through McEwan's tirade. "Your appointment with the governor is in fifteen minutes."

Joss promptly showed Choy out. "Wait," he said to McEwan, and closed the door. "I can't order you to go back to Scotland"—there was a hard note of authority in Joss's voice that McEwan had never been exposed to before—"but I can order you to have no more dealings with Choy behind my back, and *if* I find that you choose to ignore my instructions I'll have your resignation as a director of the Princely House on my desk within twenty-four hours."

And then he did shut the door on McEwan, who never got out another word.

THE MEETING took place in the governor's study. On hand were the secretary for security Trevelyan, Joss Denning and Sir Howard Caley.

"What about these strikes against your companies?" the governor asked

Denning. "I hear you went down to the wharves the other day, faced them and tried to talk to them. That took some guts, I must say."

"It was an act of desperation," Joss said. "With the wharf companies out of action, nobody is going to advance my house a penny. I got nowhere. The Triad is making damn sure the strikers don't get the chance to think for themselves."

"We may be able to help you there," Trevelyan put in. "The police have picked up a strike agitator and are holding him in connection with the murder last year of one of our police constables. He's facing a hanging offense and may just be willing to identify the Triad leadership for us. If so, the police snatch squads will go to work picking them up, and the strike should fall apart."

"That could take more time than I've got."

"You know, of course, that this Smallpox Kang is behind it all," the governor said, "and it's no longer hard to guess at his link to Choy...Billion Dollar Choy, I believe he's called...except we've not a shred of hard proof. I'm sorry," he said and meant it, "that we can't be of more help."

"There is a way I can raise the money"—Joss had decided to put his cards on the table—"which is why, sir, I've asked for this meeting. In five days time the Lady Sun has to repay the debt owed by her father to the Triad. If you will let her boat carrying the gold through into Hong Kong, she will guarantee to dissolve the Macau Syndicate and she will help you destroy the Triad. She also wants the right to reside in Hong Kong and permission to move her fortune here..."

"The daughter of Dr. Sun expects us to believe that she's ready to turn her operations legitimate?" The secretary for security had to smile.

"She's asking that, yes. I tend to believe her, though I confess to a self-interest," Denning said. "Once she's safely reached Hong Kong, she'll lend me sufficient moneys to tide me over my loan repayment dates."

"How much gold are we talking about?" the governor asked.

"We calculate that she owes the Triad something close to one hundred million Hong Kong dollars. Her own fortune is difficult to estimate."

The governor thought about possible consequences. One of the most successful means of fighting corruption in Hong Kong was the right to check into bank accounts and living standards of all government employees. He was thinking of how that quantity of untraceable gold bullion could be put to use in the hands of the Triad...to bribe officials, pay for more enforcers. With it the Triad could become the single most powerful force on the wrong side of the law in Hong Kong. Which was what the 14K Triad had been trying, unsuccessfully, to achieve since the founding of the colony. "Does this young lady really expect us to take her at her word?" he asked, echoing Trevelyan. "What if it's all a hoax and the gold does reach the Triad?"

"The consequences would of course be disastrous," Trevelyan said firmly. "We're already facing widespread strikes... put that with the rise in power of the 14K Triad and the fragile balance of power we now hold would be destroyed. We can't take the risk. The boat must be stopped from landing here at all costs."

"I'm afraid I must agree with the secretary," the governor said. "I've no objection to your keeping in touch with her," he added, never one to break off contact unless he was absolutely certain he'd won, "but you can't hold out to her any hope of a deal with us."

"I see," Joss said, getting up slowly.

"What will you do now?"

"Making a deal with Sun's daughter may be the only chance I have to raise the money," he said, his face tight, "and I have no intention of being the last taipan of the Princely House. Draw your own conclusions." ...

The governor returned to the secretary for security after seeing Joss out. "At first I never understood what a woman like Clair saw in him," he said, "but I'm beginning to like that fellow. How long's he got?"

"The first of his loans falls due on the fifteenth of next month, Your Excellency. He's desperate enough to go against us. I think he'd bear watching."

BY THE time Joss returned to the Asian Trading building it was deserted. Everyone on the fiftieth floor had gone home, or almost everyone. Connie was still waiting for him. She didn't have to ask about his meeting... he was too tired to keep from his face that it had been unsuccessful. "Your wife is waiting for you in your office," she said.

"The servants tell me that you never come home"—Clair turned as he entered his office—"so I had to come here to say good-bye." She was standing by the window in the shadows, lit by the reflection of the harbor lights. She looked lovely, and in spite of everything he felt the familiar ache start in him.

"I saw the destroyer squadron leave the harbor this morning"—he felt his mouth go dry—"I didn't think you'd be one to follow the fleet."

"He's going to marry me," Clair said, not so much challenging as asking for understanding. "Joss, I can't lose this one."

"Good luck to you, then."

Clair shook her head, impatient with Joss's lack of response, or at least the one she'd hoped for. But then, Joss understood her in ways no one else did. "I'll need it, so will you. Hong Kong's in for a stormy ride with China. You'll never leave, will you?"

"I belong here, regardless of what some may think, and I believe Hong Kong will survive, one way or another."

"My lawyers are going to contact you for a divorce. Will you contest it?" She was almost hopeful he would.

"No."

"I've told them to offer you my shares in the Princely House."

"Why sell?"

"Because you're going to need all the stock you can get hold of to fight off my cousins. Anyway"—Clair raised her chin and said in the old mocking tone he knew so well—"when you've paid me what I'm worth I'll be rich enough to buy my sailor out of the navy and give him his own bloody destroyer to play with." She came to him, put her arms around his neck and kissed him with something of the passion they'd once had. "'Bye, darling," she said huskily.

After Clair had left, Joss crossed the darkened office to the window and stood facing the harbor, the taste of his wife warm on his lips, silent tears on his face. He couldn't live with her—but he didn't know if he could live without her.

Connie gave him ten minutes alone, then tapped on his door. "Can I get you some coffee?" She knew he'd touched nothing all day. "Or send out for some food?"

Joss stood by his desk leafing through the urgent telexes. "No," he answered her distractedly. "Thanks, Connie, that'll be all . . ."

Connie guessed that he intended to spend the night in the office again. After a moment he looked up and saw her hovering in the doorway trying to get up her courage to say what she felt. And then she did . . . "Taipan, would you like to come home with me tonight?" Home for her was a very small apartment in Pok Fulam. There was no question of her offering him a place on the couch, and there was room for only one bed.

Joss gave her a grateful smile. He felt utterly alone and it showed on his face. Her heart went out to him . . . at that moment she thought him the most sensitive, the most desirable man she had ever seen . . .

"Thank you, Connie," he said, and she knew he meant it, "but I have got to stay here and work." She had half-expected to be rejected. Clair was the kind of woman who knew how to leave her mark, he would need

251

time to get over her. But she was glad that she'd made the offer. "Good-night, taipan," she said, and walked off—

"Connie..." Joss called after her.

She hurried back, hoping against hope, along the carpeted corridor to his office.

"Do you have anybody on the Chinese side of your family you can trust absolutely?" It had to be a Chinese, a Eurasian like Connie would attract attention.

She needed a moment to collect herself, then managed to get out, "My half brother, I would trust him..."

"All right. I want a meeting with the Lady Sun. Send your half brother to Macau... he's to tell her to set up a safe place..."

STORM CLOUDS veiled the moon over Coloane, but as yet no rain had fallen. The heat was oppressive. The sullen, leaden sea hissed over the rocks at the bottom of the cliff.

A perfect night for the Heung Cheung to lead a small army of his men into the refugee camp, just as Nicholai had predicted. They tramped through the fence ten abreast, armed with staves, clubs and knives, eager for their work... they had raided this miserable collection of shanties before without reprisal, taking pleasure in the women and the bits of loot they had managed to squeeze out of the refugees.

The road through the camp narrowed to no more than a red earth path that snaked through the shanties, obliging the Heung Cheung's men to spread out into single file, hemmed in as they were on either side by tin walls. The camp was deserted, the only sound coming from the tramp of a hundred and thirty men's sandals on the earth, punctuated by the occasional burst of drunken laughter from those who had celebrated too much before the raid.

The Heung Cheung kicked down door after door of the shanties. Inside, cooking pots lay freshly scoured, the families' spare clothes on a line in one corner and in another the sleeping mats were laid out ready. He looked for signs in the earth floor where they would have dug out their valuables, and finding them, he turned disgustedly to his men. "They've run off," he shouted. "Light your torch brands and fire the shanties—"

A curious sort of singing sound—and a man beside the Heung Cheung abruptly put his hands to his head and crumbled. Another, and then another man in the file, with hardly a sound, fell to the ground. The Heung Cheung spun round, trying to spot the source of this, until a

252

stone hit his arm with tremendous force, making him scream out with pain and drop his long machete.

And then, fired by sling or catapult, pebbles collected from the beach came whistling down in lethal showers on his men caught on the steep path with no protection against them.

Another stone caught the Heung Cheung in the ribs. Another brought down his bodyguard, who had held the blazing torch brand. The Heung Cheung, nearly doubled over in pain, hurried forward. The path twisted sharply to the right and down. He followed it, and found it blocked by a six-foot-high barricade. From behind it the distinctive voice of a *gwilo* issued an order, followed by a fresh cloud of angry, whining stones. "Back," the Heung Cheung bawled at his men. *"Back."* His men had become disorganized... those at the back were still trying to press forward while those at the front were trying to retreat up the hill away from the punishment they were taking at the barricade. What most unnerved them was that there was still no sign of a single refugee. The refugees knew intimately the sloping, cluttered topography of their camp and were using it. From every direction came the incessant angry hum of stones, followed by the cries of men falling to the ground.

Led by their Heung Cheung, the villagers broke formation and ran, every man for himself, ducking and crawling into the narrow spaces between the shanties, trying to get away from the terrible rain of stones.

The Heung Cheung and six of his men who had stayed with him kicked down the back wall of a shanty and stumbled out into the maze of narrow paths behind. Each shanty looked like the next, and once away from the main path they became disoriented.

It was then that the refugees in groups of ten, no longer able to use their stones effectively in the melee between the shanties, attacked with clubs and axe handles, taking a merciless revenge for all their past humiliations.

The sound of a gunshot... none of them carried firearms but the refugees were too preoccupied to pay attention to it. Sporadic bursts of shooting, then silence, and finally the piercing call of Nicholai's whistle, signaling that the battle was over.

Reluctantly the refugees rounded up those of the villagers who could still walk and herded them to the open space on the cliff edge that was to be used as a holding point. Keng Po's and Alice's groups were the last to arrive... and found Nicholai and Udo, their hands on their heads, surrounded by armed men who, from their well-fed look and the better cut of their clothes, were obviously Syndicate gunmen. Fifth Street lay on the ground, blood leaking from a bullet wound in his leg. Alice, ignoring the guns leveled at her, hurried over to him. The leader of the gunmen quickly checked that everyone was there, then signaled to a man hidden by the darkness further up the path.

He came toward them now, a slight figure immaculately dressed, stepping delicately over the rough ground. The gunmen moved respectfully aside to let him pass. Thomas Wu paused, looked directly at Nicholai. "So it's true," Wu said. "You did come back." He studied Nicholai closely. "You've grown careless, you wouldn't have let me win the advantage so easily in the old days... but then, I hear you're still drinking heavily. How else could you have allowed a foolish young girl to flatter you into coming out of an honorable retirement to *this?*" His disdainful glance took in the refugees and shanties, the boat shed above the beach. "The years can't have been good to you. And I was really to believe that you would provide the decoy vessel for the ChrisCraft? Could you and the Lady Sun have been so foolish to think you could trick me? Never mind, it's over now. Burn the boat." He signaled in the direction of the boat shed and three of his men carrying blazing torch brands hurried down the path.

Wu then turned his attention to the Heung Cheung. "Without my help you would have been defeated by this scum. Get out, go home."

As the villagers filed away Wu turned to Nicholai: "You will accompany me part of the way to Macau. I will allow you an honorable death. The rest of you," he said to the crew, "you are finished here. Leave the enclave. Now."

Wu turned and began to walk up the hill as his remaining guards moved in on Nicholai, motioning to him to come with them. For a moment they failed to notice Udo edging forward, but they didn't fail to hear, and be shocked by, the reverberating crash of heavy-caliber machine gun fire from the boat shed. The bodyguards turned toward the sound, knowing that their colleagues down there had no such weapon. As they did Udo chopped the arm of the man nearest him, raised again the cutting edge of his hand and broke the man's neck. As the man fell Udo wrenched the gun from his nerveless fingers. It had taken no more than a few seconds. Meanwhile Nicholai had disarmed the man next to him. The third and fourth gunmen spun around looking for Keng Po, who had gone behind them. Now he gripped an axe handle, flicked it first one way and then the other against their heads, and brought them both down...

Thomas Wu heard the heavy-caliber gunshots, saw no sign of his men following him. He increased his pace, saw no point in turning back to find out what had happened. His own neck was his priority. The Snake Boat Man would be taken care of in due course...

He reached his car and got quickly inside. His chauffeur glanced around, looking for his bodyguards. "Never mind, drive out of here," Wu ordered.

He sighed and turned his attention to the figure sharing the back seat with him. As the car moved away he reached up and switched on the interior light so that he could savor Mae Ling's loveliness. He liked the irony of that face that seemed to shine with such purity, all innocent. The effect put an edge on his jaded appetite. "I received your message," he said to her... "you're a smart girl to have chosen me to protect you. You know I helped your father all through those years when I was his contact outside China. Now I have the power to help you, the Snake Boat Man does not—"

"You didn't kill him? He's still alive...?"

"No, not yet. Don't worry about him, he's through... But now you... the people who might still have helped you at home have been wiped out in the latest purges. China is moving away from its revolutionary past. You're one of the few supporters of your mistress Madame Mao Tse-tung to escape. I advise you to destroy whatever documents you've managed to smuggle out of China. And put away any thoughts of re-igniting the Revolution. All you can hope to' do now is reach safety and keep free—"

"I intend to do that, make a new life."

"Where?"

"Singapore... I must get to Singapore."

As the car sped over the long metal spans of Tai Pei bridge Wu spoke through the intercom to the chauffeur. "The ferry terminal."

"Am I leaving?" Mae Ling asked hopefully.

Wu brushed his fingers above her knee. "No, my dear. Not yet, not yet..."

The car drew up on the other side of the road from the ferry terminal and Mae Ling spotted a bald, barrel-chested man dressed in a light safari suit, whose neck was so thick his ears seemed to join his shoulders.

"My enforcer Chang," Thomas Wu told her, following her gaze. "Ah," he said with obvious satisfaction as Chang stepped forward to greet two squat men dressed in plain suits and carrying briefcases. "Koreans... some claim they're the best assassins in the business. And no one in Macau expects them or knows their faces. The others in the Syndicate are prepared to wait, but I don't like taking unnecessary risks. It's time to go directly to the heart of the matter...time to kill the Lady Sun."

Chang, though, was annoyed as he came up to the car window. "Why do we need foreigners?"

Wu appeased him with, "Sun's daughter still has a few loyal retainers. This way they'll have no reason to carry on a feud with me if strangers are the cause of her death."

He leaned back in his seat, well-satisfied with himself, looking forward to the night, and Mae Ling.

"HEAVE THOSE bodies into the sea," Nicholai ordered. "The current will take care of them." He was referring to the four blasted corpses that lay in front of the open doors of the boat shed. "The police won't ask questions and the Syndicate will pay off their families."

He stepped through the doorway. Michael Ansty was still up on the deck of the boat crouched behind his gun. Now he swung the barrel and leveled it at Nicholai.

"You bastard..." his voice carried down through air that reeked of cordite. "You knew damn well if they came in here I'd have to fight—"

"Yes, and now the Syndicate has four more good reasons for finding you," Nicholai said, allowing him a smile. "Keep that in mind if you ever think of changing sides..."

The others came crowding into the boat shed, followed by the refugees who wanted to stay with the crew.

"Mae Ling?" Nicholai asked.

His men avoided his eyes. No one wanted to be the one to tell him. Finally Alice did. "I saw her...she's gone off with Thomas Wu."

"You knew she was going," Udo reminded his old friend. "Fool Boy brought you her messages."

Still, Nicholai had been hoping that in the end she'd decide not to leave.

"She'll tell them everything she knows about us," Ansty said, climbing down from the deck and pleased to be getting back at him a little. "They'll be back, and they won't depend on handguns next time. They'll bring in their own artillery."

"Then we'll have to hurry," Nicholai said quietly, and from the expression on his face the others knew not to mention Mae Ling's name again..."How's your leg?"

"I'll live," Fifth Street said, "it's a flesh wound. Lucky...we all were."

Alice came up to Nicholai now, almost as unhappy as Ansty. "So you won tonight, but what happens to my refugees? When you go you'll leave us at the mercy of the villagers again. You can imagine what that will mean for us."

"Alice, how would you like to get all your people out of here?" Nicholai said.

"And go where?"

"Hong Kong, they can come with us to Hong Kong."

She looked at him disbelievingly.

Keng Po leaned over to Nicholai. He had followed him for a long time and knew he was capable of some remarkable, even reckless, decisions, but now he drew the line. "What are you, mad or drunk?" he whispered. "We can't fit all these people on our boat."

"They won't be going on our boat. Crystal Lily owns the biggest junk fleet in these waters. On the night we leave they'll provide a radar shield for us from the British navy. The refugees can travel over with them. And at the same time they'll help create a diversion for us—"

"What happens when, *if*, they get to Hong Kong?"

"They'll have friends or relatives there to help them. Some will get caught, but many of them should make it. The worst that can happen is that they'll be sent back here."

"What do you say, Alice?" Fifth Street put in. "Let them come with us. Hell, it's worth the risk. What have they got to lose?"

Alice shook her head. "*Mein Gott*, if I thought my people could get just one day of freedom, well, it would be worth it." She'd made up her mind. "Take them with you, Nicholai. And the night you leave I won't be here. I'll find some reason to spend it in Macau." And it better be a good one, she told herself.

INSPECTOR REM CHOY reported the bad news to Malloy early the following morning. "That refugee girl in Coloane, the one whose messages you've been relying on, sir..."

"Well?"

"She didn't make the scheduled letter drop yesterday. I checked it out...I'm afraid the information I've received is that she's now placed herself under the protection of Thomas Wu—"

"*What?*" Malloy was furious, almost as much with himself as with Mae Ling. He'd underestimated her. He also quickly realized how much she could now hurt him. He had to get her back from Thomas Wu if only to insure that the fact he'd helped her escape didn't reach his superiors. At the moment he felt something in common with Nicholai . . . she'd double-crossed them both . . .

"We'll no longer have any advance warning when the Snake Boat Man leaves, sir," Rem Choy added uneasily.

"It doesn't matter—we'll know soon enough. I'm betting the Syndicate never lets his boat out of the harbor . . . All right, where's the taipan?"

"He's on his way to Macau. We've put a tail on him as you ordered—"

"Do your men know the enclave well?"

"No . . ."

"Well then, I wouldn't count on them staying with him." Malloy vented his rage on Rem Choy. "Unlike you, Denning's no fool."

CHAPTER 24

JOSS DENNING walked out of the ferry terminal into Macau's humid sunlight. He spotted the car that had been sent to collect him and climbed in. As the limousine nosed into the stream of traffic. Joss glanced behind and watched two men scramble for a taxi. "We're being followed," he said quietly to the driver.

L'eung Heung, one of Crystal Lily's bodyguards, looked up at his rearview mirror. "*Ho-la*, master. I take care." He turned the car sharply into a road behind the Lisboa Casino Hotel, throwing Joss off balance. Then, in quick succession he expertly directed the powerful vehicle through a series of narrow, crowded sidestreets until he satisfied himself that no one still followed them.

"Is okay now," L'eung Heung announced. He was a burly gunman appropriately nicknamed Bad Man. They crossed at a more sedate pace

259

to the west side of the city and parked. L'eung Heung led Joss down a busy street and stopped in front of an unobtrusive doorway set in a high brick wall. L'eung Heung knocked to gain admittance, and as he did Joss read the plaque above the arch: "Protestant Church and Cemetery of the English East India Company, 1814." The door was unlocked from the inside by the caretaker. He had heard of this little cemetery in Macau but had never visited it before. The door closed, blocking out the noise of the city, and the din that had been hammering in his ears was abruptly replaced by silence. He stood looking out over a space of shaded green lawns splashed with the bright colors of frangipane and bauhinia. Steps led down from the small chapel to the cemetery, which was squeezed between high brick walls.

L'eung Heung stood guard by the door and announced his lady would be coming soon. Much of the turbulent history of Macau was engraved upon the headstones of this deserted cemetery. Joss walked past the tombs of famous merchant adventurers, missionaries, English and American sea captains. He turned along a path to the left of the stairs, at the far end of which was a monument to the talented artist George Chinnery, who had fled to the East to escape his wife; some wondered whether his deserted spouse had had a hand in designing his tomb with a blank door.

Joss, hearing voices by the chapel, turned from Chinnery's vault to see the Lady Sun walking down the steps, dressed in western clothes, including a wide-brimmed hat shading her exotic face. He watched in fascination as she moved through the lush gardens toward him with a supple, unself-conscious grace.

"Thank you for taking the risk in coming here to meet me," she greeted him as she came near. Her voice, he noted, carried a hint of an American accent. "It seems I can no longer speak in my own palace without risking being overheard by those plotting against me."

It was her first meeting with the taipan of the Princely House. It's true what they say, she thought, his eyes are as blue as sapphires . . . slim and deceptively frail-looking, his face and hands were sensitive as those of an artist. Hardly what one would expect in a taipan. She continued to study him . . . could she trust him? And if so, had he the authority to deliver what she needed?

On his part, Joss was impressed by her air of cool self-assurance, suspected that for all her youth and femininity she would be as courageous, and perhaps tough to deal with, as her father had been. Instinctively he liked her.

"Well," she said to him, "what answer do you have from Hong Kong?"

"The governor won't agree..."

Her eyes darkened. "He won't accept my guarantee?"

"He won't take the risk."

She shrugged, trying to hide her disappointment. "Then we have nothing more to discuss." She turned to walk back up the steps.

"Wait... it's a bad setback, no question, but we're not closed out yet. If your boat can break through the blockade—" Joss knew he was urging her to break British laws—"rather than let the Triad have the gold, Sir Howard Caley will have to make a deal with you. But above all, you must prevent the gold from falling into the Triad's hands."

"Land the gold in Hong Kong and then prevent the Triad from taking it? That's almost impossible... but if I did find a way to do it, I'd then hold all the cards. My terms would be much more... demanding."

"Such as?"

"I intend to leave Macau, whatever happens. I need a place to go *to*."

"I've told His Excellency that, but why do you want to leave here? After all, Macau has reached its accommodation with China, Hong Kong's future is still uncertain."

"Macau is too small... it's only six square miles *and* it's on the mainland of China. That's nothing to bet your future on. Hong Kong has the great harbor and the support structures to go with it. No matter how bad things look for it now, I believe it will survive... after all, it's the gateway for trade with China. Like you, I have faith that it will be prosperous again. I want to be part of its future..."

"And the Syndicate? Are you really prepared to give up its power and influence to live like an ordinary person?"

"I don't want to spend the rest of my life the way my father did... a prisoner guarded by palace walls and bodyguards. I *also* have no intention of seeing my enemies... his enemies... get their bloody hands on everything he left me. So the Syndicate will be dissolved, permanently, and when I move to Hong Kong I'll start my own *legitimate* trading *hong*. Like yours. I realize I'll need more than money. I'll need a power base to build on—good companies in Hong Kong with strong management and potential... I'm talking about some of your own companies..."

Joss looked at her. She certainly was her father's daughter. Her appearance, though, was incredibly deceptive... as, it occurred to him, many people thought his was...

"I want to buy Asian Air Carriers"... a booming freight company that would open up trading links for her all over the East... "and then I want Asian Wharves and Godowns. I know it's been weakened by strikes but it owns development land that I can start building on right away. And Asian Technology that owns the worldwide agency for Saturn computers... I'll buy that one from you too..."

Joss was impressed... she'd done her homework. "It so happens," he told her, "those are three of the Princely Houses' most valuable assets. I might as well make a deal with Mr. Billion Dollar Choy—"

"He wants *everything*. I'm at least leaving you the Princely House. The money I'd pay for the companies would let the Princely House get rid of its debt, put it in a position to be on top again—"

"It would also position you as one of my chief competitors."

"Oh, I've so much to learn about trade."

Joss had to smile. "Well, never mind, I'll welcome the competition. Hong Kong is going to need people like you."

"Thank you. I hope we both get our chance."

"I can't make promises," he told her, "except, as you know, I'll do anything to save the Princely House... Land the gold, keep it from the Triad and leave it to me to blackmail Sir Howard Caley into admitting you to Hong Kong."

"And if the British manage to intercept the gold?" Crystal Lily made herself face the possibility.

"Then you'll be left with nothing to bargain with, and I'll lose the Princely House."

"My comprador said I could trust you... the next forty-eight hours are crucial to me. Keep in close touch through my comprador. He'll contact you as soon as I've landed the gold. After that you'll have to persuade the governor to accept my terms right away... I'll have very little time to deal with the Triad... deal with them in a way to earn me my residency in Hong Kong."

Joss nodded. "The thirty-first of August, then?"

"In Hong Kong," she said, sealing the bargain.

She left him at the foot of the stairs. Her personal bodyguard Hei Ta-hau ushered her into the back seat of a car. The windows were dark-tinted; no one could see in. Even so she leaned back nervously, feeling exposed in streets controlled by the Syndicate. Her hands gripped the armrests as Hei Ta-hau followed the one-way traffic system up to the Rua de Thomas Vieira, from which he'd planned a different route back to the palace.

The late afternoon shadows were lengthening. Pedicabs, cars and shoppers thronged the narrow streets as the car inched its way through, then picked up speed just before turning south at the main road junction.

Suddenly an old woman, balancing two wicker baskets filled with chickens on either end of a pole across her shoulders, stepped off the pavement right into the path of the car. Crystal Lily heard the old woman scream as the car struck her, its front wheels coming to a halt over the pole and crushing a basket of chickens. The old woman slipped off the hood and crumpled onto the road, a patch of blood already beginning to stain her *samfu*.

The old woman's body lay only a few yards from the car. Acting on instinct, Crystal Lily opened her door and went to the woman's aid. Hei Ta-hau's arm swung out to stop her but he was too late. "Come back, my lady," he called after her, holding the door open from the inside.

Crystal Lily was already on her knees beside the old woman, and as she bent over her, felt the shock waves of a bullet that just missed her head and ended splintering a rotted wood post behind her.

At the sound of the gunshot the old woman opened her eyes, and before Crystal Lily could react she'd gotten nimbly to her feet, dropped the sponge with which she had so effectively bloodied herself, and darted off into the crowd.

The shot also had its effect on the milling onlookers who'd been attracted to the scene. Hei Ta-hau watched as they now backed away, leaving his mistress exposed on the street at the place where the old woman had fallen. He figured the direction of the shot and, taking out his gun, ran from the car to shield her. He'd taken only a few steps from the car when one of the assassin's bullets struck him in the back above his left shoulder blade, another passed through his upper stomach. He staggered, then gathering up his last reserves, came toward her, arms outspread, still trying to protect her. There were two assassins, one on each side of the street. If Crystal Lily tried to get back to the car she would present them with an easy target.

"Get back," Hei Ta-hau called our hoarsely to her, "stay with the crowd." But the street, as if by magic, had quickly emptied. Crystal withdrew into a shop's open doorway. Hei Ta-hau had almost reached her now. "Through the back," he panted. The owner of the shop and his family had taken refuge under the counter. No one lifted their heads as Crystal Lily and her wounded bodyguard retreated through the shop into the airless, unlit recesses of a shanty-built storeroom behind.

Hei Ta-hau kicked open the flimsy door at the back that led into a deserted lane. Across from it was another doorway providing access to the shop from the next parallel street down. Hei Ta-hau crossed the muddy lane and kicked in the opposite door, then came back for Crystal

Lily. As he reached out to help her a bullet fired from further down the lane struck him, and another ricocheted past Crystal, who ducked back into the doorway.

The last bullet, again in his back, nearly destroyed Hei Ta-hau. He grabbed at the wall to support himself, then using both hands to lift his gun, he twisted painfully around and sent half a magazine of bullets in the direction of the assassin. The blood was draining from his face and he could barely get out the words... "We don't have much time..."

One gunman was coming through the shop while the other had anticipated the lane and had moved quickly to cut off their escape. Hei Ta-hau labored for breath, cold sweat trickling down his face. "Cross the lane, I can't follow you, I'll try to hold them off... Go through the next shop and turn west. Get to where there are the most people, hide among them until you can get word to the comprador to send help..."

Crystal Lily had known this huge, wonderful man all her life. He was her friend as much as her bodyguard. Now she reached up and kissed him, knowing that she was saying good-bye.

He fitted a fresh magazine into his gun, fired a burst into the shop, then staggered out into the alley and sent another long burst ricocheting down either wall. "*Now*," he said, "run..."

Crystal Lily darted across the lane and through the door. Hei Ta-hau tried to follow as far as the doorway, figuring to hold off the assassins long enough to give her a chance to escape. His eyesight was fading; his body was so numb that he hardly felt the bullet that came from the gunman inside the shop. The force of it knocked him down, but he managed to crawl through the mud to the doorway, and tumbled over the sill...

The gunman crouching in the lane listened for movement, decided Crystal Lily's bodyguard was either dead or too badly wounded to be any threat. He went in fast through the doorway, jumping over the body and firing down as he did so.

Hei Ta-hau was waiting for him, his back propped against the far wall, his gun arm painfully steadied across his knees. Sight had all but gone from his eyes now, but he could sense the blurred figure of a man hurtling through the doorway. The two of them fired at the same time... and Hei Ta-hau had the satisfaction of knowing, before he died, that his bullet had mortally wounded the gunman, whose body fell across his legs.

The second gunman called in a whisper for his partner. When there was no answer he came through the doorway, saw Hei Ta-hau crumpled against the wall, the gun slipping from his nerveless fingers. Better be sure, he thought, and emptied nearly an entire magazine into Hei Ta-hau. Next he put a soft-nosed bullet into the face of his partner, making sure that he would not be recognized . . . and then he went after the Lady Sun.

JOSS DENNING had left the cemetery a few minutes after Crystal Lily. He noticed that the street ahead was swarming with people. And then he saw the abandoned car, its doors wide open, its front wheels over the crushed chicken coop. He asked his driver what had happened.

"I not know," L'eung Heung told him, moving steadily forward in first gear and climbing up onto the pavement to avoid the car. The police were slow in coming, and he soon spotted faces in the crowd that he knew meant trouble. "Down, down, sir . . ."

"Is it her car?"

"Yes."

"We must help her," Joss told him when L'eung Heung made no attempt to stop.

"Too late," L'eung Heung muttered. He had seen no sign of bodies on the road or damage to the car so he as able to assume Crystal Lily and Hei Ta-hau had escaped the ambush. His job now, he felt, was to get the taipan off the streets to safety.

"I take you ferry," he spoke firmly over his shoulder. "You go Hong Kong, Macau too dangerous now. Lady escape, I think . . . Thomas Wu shoot taipan if stay here. You go, *heya?*"

"At least get me to a telephone," Joss demanded. "We've got to warn the comprador so he can send help—"

"Telephone at ferry terminus." L'eung Heung nodded vigorously, then sent his car speeding through the traffic—

"*No,* damnit, we'll be too late. Stop here. *Now.*"

Joss found his way into the upstairs foyer of a restaurant, bribed the manager to let him use the telephone. He got through to the comprador in the palace, in a few words sketched out what he knew, then offered to stay and help.

"L'eung Heung is right," the comprador said, the shock coming through clear in his voice. "Thomas Wu has struck at us sooner than I thought . . . understand that as long as my lady is alive, Wu will make an attempt on your life. You should leave Macau at once . . . but may I ask a favor before you go?"

"I'll do what I can."

"As soon as Wu learns that the Lady Sun is still alive he will seal off the palace to prevent her from returning—he will probably move to cut off our telephone too, so I will be brief... After this call I will try to contact the Snake Boat Man. Should my message fail to get through, I ask you to tell him that I will hold this palace at all costs until I learn for certain whether my lady is dead or in the hands of Thomas Wu. The Snake Boat Man has the only force outside these walls that we can now depend on. He must find my lady and get her safely back to the palace. If the telephones are cut, then he will have to open up another line of communication. Please check with me again from the ferry terminal. If there is no answer, send L'eung Heung with my message to the Snake Boat Man in Coloane. It is vital the Snake Boat Man know I can hold this palace. Otherwise there would be no reason for him to continue to resist Thomas Wu..."

Joss called from the phone booth in the ferry terminal, from which a jetfoil was about to depart for Hong Kong.

The comprador's line, as feared, was dead...

In the palace the comprador dropped the useless receiver and spun around as Manchu came hurrying toward him.

"*Lao Ta*," the Manchu reported in near panic, "he's gone."

"Who else is missing?"

"The amah."

Lady Sun's amah... so that was how Lao Ta had got his information out of the palace. No one suspected the old woman closest to Crystal Lily.

Rumors of Crystal Lily's death would be circulating like wildfire among the servants in the palace. Clearly morale was about to collapse if the comprador did not act swiftly to restore it... "They will both die," he promised. "Close the gates. *No one else leaves.*"

L'EUNG HEUNG drove swiftly to Coloane and was promptly taken down the cliff path to the boat shed, where he reported to Nicholai.

Nicholai called his men together. "Thomas Wu has sent his assassins after the Lady Sun," he told them. "The comprador thinks she's still alive and hiding somewhere on the streets of Macau. We've got to get to her before they do. Alice"—he turned to the doctor who'd hurried down the path—"I need all your people down here to help launch the boat."

The bell on the lepers' church rang out minutes later summoning the inhabitants of the camp. The wide doors to the boat shed were pulled down.

"But I'm not finished," Fifth Street protested as a human chain of refugees worked to lay greased logs for the slipway side-by-side down the beach. "I need at least another twenty-four hours—"

"You'll have to work on her in Macau," Nicholai told him. The boat's cradle was attached to a crude winch. "Let her go," Nicholai called out.

Udo knocked away the chocks that held the cradle, then went to help the refugees on the winch take the strain. The seventy-foot gunboat inched out of the boat shed and then down the beach to the sea. The crew worked in the water up to their chests to float the boat free from its cradle.

Nicholai said to Ansty, "Will you risk going back to Macau?"

"I will for *her*," Ansty told him, making it clear where his loyalty lay. By now Ansty had learned something of the long and deep relationship between Nicholai and Crystal Lily, and was jealous of it... even considered himself Nicholai's rival.

Nicholai had no time to worry about such feelings. He needed Ansty's special talents. "Find some two-way radios. Get one of them to the comprador in the palace. You had better plan on going in over the wall, the same way you did before, or you'll run up against Wu's men."

"Udo," Nicholai now ordered the big man, "go with him. L'eung Heung will take you in the car to Macau. Then find Da Costa, tell him I'm moving my boat to his harbor tonight instead of tomorrow night. I'll be there before midnight. Have my old boatman Wen Yuan meet me at the harbor. As soon as I arrive I'll work the waterfront. Keng Po will come with me and search the old quarter of the city where Crystal Lily was last seen... we may still have some old friends left there who'll help us." To the refugees gathered on the beach, he said, "Tomorrow at sunset the junks from Lady Sun's fishing fleet will collect you and take you to Hong Kong. So be ready."

Alice took Nicholai by the shoulders and hugged him. Her eyes were bright with emotion. "You are a splendid man. You take this little force to Macau to fight the Syndicate and you expect to win. I will not see your like again. Good-bye, my friend..."

Nicholai waded out to his gunboat and swung himself over the side. Fifth Street was already supervising the pulling of camouflage-painted canvas over wood frames to disguise the *East Wind*'s sleek hull, transforming it to pass in the dark as a bare-masted motorized junk.

Before the gunboat got under way, the car with Ansty, Udo and L'eung Heung inside it sped toward Macau.

Nicholai felt numb, as though to protect himself from the cold presentiment of what might have happened to Crystal Lily. Keng Po, never one to avoid reality, voiced his thoughts... "We'd better face it, the chances of her surviving Wu's killers aren't good. In all her sheltered life she has never even set foot on the streets of Macau without some protecting escort..."

Nicholai had no answer for him. He started the engines of the *East Wind* and proceeded as fast as he dared for Macau. He did, though, make himself... and her... a promise—when he got there, he personally would see that Thomas Wu paid.

Because, after all, for Nicholai it was never so much his "face" that had mattered, nor a last run that would revive his reputation. It was her.

CHAPTER 25

CRYSTAL LILY slipped through a second row of shops and found herself in a narrow slum street. Immediately she began to attract attention, finding herself as she did among the poorest people in Macau—coolie laborers with workworn faces, bandy-legged fishermen off the junks, stall owners, beggars—and all of them were staring at her. No woman dressed as she was would be seen on foot in these streets. She realized she had to find something less conspicuous...

The Syndicate gunmen were sealing off either end of the street. Among them she spotted the bald skull of Thomas Wu's enforcer, Chang, listening to an explanation from a squat, flat-featured Korean.

Rickety wooden stalls lined the sides of the street, offering soft drinks, cigarettes, Chinese snacks. Between two of the stalls was an entrance— no more than a hole in a high wall and almost hidden. Crystal Lily ducked through it and found herself at the top of a winding path that led to an open courtyard. A plaque informed her that in better times this had once been the compound of the great merchant Chen. The path led past narrow house fronts, where his retainers would once have lived, and then on into the dark gaping mouth of a larger building. It was cool in there, and once her eyes accustomed themselves to the gloom she realized the house had been converted into dormitories for the poor. Leading off either side of the narrow aisle were tiny wood-partitioned cubicles, each with a thin cotton curtain to cover the opening. These cubicles were sleeping areas for a whole family and the cotton screen provided their only privacy.

Crystal Lily hurried down the aisle and on into another courtyard that was open to the sky. At the far end two large taps gushed water, and shafts of evening light streamed down on the women who sat on the steps before them working at their washing. She glanced up at a two-storied building that framed all four sides of the courtyard, its ornately carved wooden verandas and window shutters inlaid with mother-of-pearl. She had not realized these ancient compounds, styled in the architecture of imperial China, still existed in Macau.

Opening off the far end of the courtyard was another arched entrance. She went quickly through it in the hope of gaining the street, but instead found a flight of stone steps that brought her down into a dark, cavernlike room. Its windows were coated with grime. Along the entire length of one side was a cooking range of glowing coals, with great ovens below. A powerfully built, bald-headed Chinese cook was at work there. He was naked except for an apron wrapped around his loins. Rolls of fat hung from his chest and stomach, and his skin, shining with sweat, reflected the red glare from the fire. He was making sweetcakes on top of the range and roasting pigs on spits below. He sensed rather than heard Crystal Lily's presence in the room and turned to her.

"I am the Lady Sun. Please help me," she begged. Whether he believed her or not, he believed what his eyes saw . . . her rich clothes, jewelry. He reached behind him, his hands grasped the cleaver. She heard the chink of metal and then he was swinging the cleaver over his head in a glittering arc, slashing down at her. She flinched rather than ducked, the large chopping blade missed her by a fraction and buried itself in the table. He grabbed hold of her arm with his free hand while he tried to wrench the cleaver free, and she took the opportunity to rake his face with her nails and pull loose from him. Finally he managed to free the cleaver from the table and lumbered after her, now convinced she was who she'd said she was, calling out in his pain to nobody and everybody that he'd caught the Lady Sun, that he, Wang the cook, claimed the reward...

Crystal Lily heard his cry being taken up in the dormitories behind her. She ran up the stone stairs, brushing past a youth who came bursting through the entrance in answer to Wang's call. "After her," Wang roared at his assistant, "catch her, Thomas Wu has put a price on her head..."

Crystal ran back through the courtyard, past the women at their washing, who kept their eyes down and made no move to stop her or help her. Behind her the hue-and-cry warning of her presence had already reached the street, and in a few moments, she realized, Chang's gunmen would be in the courtyard. Which way to turn, which way to go... nobody would help her—

"Here..." a hand motioned to her from a doorway in the north corner of the courtyard. "Come, this way..." She had no choice but to risk it. The hunched figure of a street beggar turned as she approached and limped hurriedly on ahead of her, showing her the way to another almost hidden opening in the wall that surrounded the ancient compound of the house of Chen. She followed him through it and down a long flight of slippery wet, worn stone steps. The beggar turned a sharp corner and plunged on down again. He was leading her into a maze of crumbling derelict cellars that extended warrenlike beneath the buildings of the old quarter of the city.

Finally they stopped, waited, trying to catch their breath in the semi-idarkness, listening for signs of anyone coming after them.

"Do you know me?" she asked.

"Yes."

"Can you tell me what's happening at my palace?"

"They say your comprador has barred the gates and won't negotiate with Thomas Wu."

She felt some relief to hear that... at least *he* hadn't betrayed her, and as long as Yu Shik Lieu could hold the palace there was still hope. "Can you use the telephone?"

"Yes, but I have no money."

And Crystal Lily carried no money. She slipped off her ring, an heirloom from her father, then realized that such a valuable piece of jewelry in the hands of a beggar would attract attention. She gave him one of her earrings.

"Give me the ring too," he demanded. He had a hunger-pinched cunning face, a whining voice. She found it difficult to trust him, but clearly had no choice.

"When you come back..." she said, trying to stall.

"You may not be here. Give me the ring now, and then I know you will reward me well when you are safe."

What else could she do? She gave him the ring that bore the carved emblem of the house of Sun. "Don't show it to anyone, it will attract attention... and I need less conspicuous clothes."

The beggar grinned. "No one will see it, wait here. I'll bring help.

She crouched down in a dark corner of a crumbling cellar. The seconds passed like minutes, the minutes like hours...

WHEN THE beggar reached the street above, night had fallen, and he limped off hurriedly in search of enforcer Chang...

Chang stood in the second courtyard, fat Wang sprawled senseless in front of him, blood trickling from a blow to his bald head. Chang knew that he had lost her, and that the blame for this would again be put on him. He was at his most unpredictable, most violent... none of his men would, if they could help it, approach him when he was like that. They tried to stop the beggar from annoying their master, but he was persisting.

The gunmen told him that "every coolie is claiming the reward for knowing where she's hiding. We've followed each informer, we haven't found her. If you care about your miserable life don't lead Lord Chang on another fool's errand."

The beggar clutched the ring in his hand. "Please... take me to Chang and I will give him *proof* that I know where to find her."

When they finally did the beggar told the enforcer, "My lord Chang"— he opened his hand, showing the ring—"I swear I can lead you to her. I claim the reward..."

SOME TWENTY minutes had passed—without a watch it was difficult to tell. Crystal Lily stood up. A faint gleam, reflected from the city lights, filtered through a broken part of the ceiling. She used it to look for a safer place to hide. She knew if she went deeper into the warren she would soon become lost and might miss the beggar's return... if he returned... Abruptly she saw the flash of a carelessly guarded torch beam strike against the wall of the passage beyond, followed by a rush of feet.

The beggar had betrayed her... Crystal Lily climbed up a pile of rubble, pulled herself onto the ledge of the wall as Chang's men rushed the opening, the beggar crushed between them. "There," he pointed dramatically to where he had left her, and three powerful torch beams focused on the empty spot. Empty. The sound of a blow, then a cry of pain from the beggar. "Search," Chang ordered. The torch beams tracked the cellar, probing into every corner. Nothing.

"She was here..." The beggar was on his knees now. "She can't have gone far, she would fall down in the darkness. There are holes in the floors, old wells and sewers, she wouldn't know where they were."

Crystal Lily pressed herself against the ledge as Chang walked into the room below her. A torch beam flickered up the wall—and caught her foot. "There she is..."

Crystal crawled along the lip of the wall on into the next cellar, and then the crumbling masonry gave way beneath her and she tumbled down.

"Follow her," the beggar was screaming, afraid his reward was slipping out of reach.

"She's trapped," Chang said. "There is nothing more we can do until first light. If the rats haven't attacked her, or she hasn't broken her neck, I'll send the beggars in to pick her up then. How many exits?"

"On this side, two," the beggar told him. "On the west side by the Inner Harbor there are more, but she wouldn't dare cross the cellars. Too dangerous..."

THOMAS WU'S limousine drew up in the Rua Felecidade, Macau's once-famous Street of Happiness. The days when merchant adventurers and sailors had jammed this narrow cobbled street, and every second doorway led to a house of pleasure, were gone. A few discreet establishments still catered to rich men with jaded tastes, but mostly the street now offered the finest restaurants in the entrepôt.

Outside these restaurants in wire cages stacked one upon the other were bedraggled, whimpering puppy dogs and wide-eyed monkeys set on top of cages imprisoning poisonous snakes. The narrow mesh warned of the venom of the snakes inside. In the past aggressive gourmands had poked their fingers through the cage in order to test the flesh of the snake. The restaurants found their reputations damaged by foolish westerners who collapsed in their doorways, stricken with the poison spreading from their punctured fingers.

Thomas Wu held a special Chinese appreciation of the reptiles

273

...believing that the more poisonous the snake, or more intimate the portion of an animal eaten, the more potent the dose of virility it contributed. Which was why he had brought Mae Ling to Mog Wok's restaurant. He would have need of its specialty to satisfy himself with her.

Mae Ling got out of the car. She wore a flowing white silk dress that set off her honey-gold skin. From her ears dangled an early present from Wu, teardrop jade earrings, and fastened around her slender neck was a broad choker blazing with white diamonds set in coral, each stone weighing at least one carat.

Seated around a circular table in the restaurant were the other leading members of the Syndicate, and when Mae Ling entered, all their heads turned. How could they not?... she was so extraordinarily beautiful. Her hand resting lightly on Thomas Wu's arm, she was led to the chair beside his at the head of the table, Wu obviously proud of the attention she attracted.

An ancient, wrinkled amah and a fierce looking old man with small bloodshot eyes and a drooping nicotine-stained moustache waited uneasily to be identified. They were Crystal Lily's amah and Lao Ta, once chief of her Manchus. "They have served me well, and tonight they will dine with us," Wu said. "Make a place for them at the table."

The amah and Lao Ta bowed respectfully, and one by one the Syndicate men rose and bowed to Thomas Wu's new lady. The last was Chang, and Wu was reminded that this celebration was premature.

"What news?" he asked abruptly.

"She's hiding in the warren that runs under the old quarter of the city," his enforcer told him.

"The beggars' quarter...well, tell them to find her."

"They will at first light. If they sweep the area now they could miss her—"

"I will increase the reward," Wu said. "She'll find every hand in Macau against her. Damn her...she should have accepted my offer. I can imagine that tonight, in the cellars of the beggars' quarter, that spoiled bitch wishes she had." He turned to Mae Ling at his side. "It must give you satisfaction," he said, his free hand caressing her thigh, "to remember that you were once chased through the streets like an animal and tonight, while you dine here with me, it's *her* turn... Now," he said expansively, "I have ordered a special delicacy for us." He signaled to the restaurant owner, who had been rushing about to insure that all was in perfect readiness for the very important, and powerful, personage.

274

First a jar of boiling oil was wheeled forward on a trolley. Beside it was placed a large razor-sharp cleaver. With a flourish a waiter pulled away the white tablecloth, revealing a hole in the center of the table through which was thrust a monkey, its arms strapped tightly to its sides. The monkey's wide eyes were pierced through with fear, and as its head rose above the level of the table it opened its mouth wide and screamed, a sound like that of a terrified child. Thomas Wu, with an expert flick of the cleaver, severed the crown from the monkey's head. Immediately the boiling oil was poured over its brain and the diners surged forward with their long-handled spoons to dig out the still-quivering delicacy.

Mae Ling used the next monkey's piercing cries as an excuse to run out of the restaurant. As a matter of course two of Thomas Wu's bodyguards got up from the table and followed her. A pedicab rider waited in the street just behind the car. He had tracked her down on Nicholai's instructions. She'd noticed him watching her with more than ordinary interest when she first arrived. With her back to the guards, and leaning against his cab as though fighting down her nausea, she took her life in her hands. "Old father, tell me quickly, do you know the Snake Boat Man?"

The coolie's expression did not change. "Who does not?"

"Then take this message to him. Tell him the person he seeks is hiding in the cellars beneath the old quarter of the city. She has until morning. Go quickly. And tell him, be certain to tell him Mae Ling sent you . . ."

As Mae Ling returned and sat down at the table Thomas Wu looked at her and smiled. "I can't imagine you of all people being squeamish," he told her, his damp fingers gripping her thigh.

"It was a passing malaise—something I must have picked up in the camp. I'm much better now," Mae Ling assured him.

THE GUNBOAT nosed into the Portuguese harbor in Macau. Its crossing from Coloane had taken place without incident, the Syndicate's attention having been diverted by their hunt for the Lady Sun.

Da Costa, the chief of police, Udo, Ansty and L'eung Heung stepped out of the shadows.

"Well?" Nicholai asked as the boat drew up against the stone jetty opposite the ChrisCraft.

"She's still alive," Da Costa told him. "A pedicab coolie has brought a message for you."

275

CRYSTAL LILY, her shoulder badly bruised from her earlier fall, inched her way in the darkness along a passage. Each time she thought she might have found a way out of the warren she came across some movement or sound warning her that that exit was being guarded. Now she was trying to cross the cellars to the west of the city and the Inner Harbor.

Fear of the dark, of the slimy footing, of the squeak and rustle of rats—and the knowledge that where rat colonies flourished there would be snakes to prey on them—all served to stretch her nerves to the breaking point.

She would have preferred to stay where she was and wait for morning when she could at least expect some light to filter through into the cellars and show her the way, but she had heard Chang's threat to send the beggars into the cellars at first light to find her.

To avoid the rats she kept as high up in the cellar system as she could, risking another fall. In doing so she had stumbled across a route that the beggars normally used to cross from one side to another. Planks of wood, rescued from the debris, had been placed across the crumbling walls between the cellars and over holes where dislodged stones continued to rattle down. Balancing with her arms outstretched, she forced herself to cross them, one hesitant step at a time.

She caught the sound of water trickling along the passage, then felt the floor beneath her suddenly dip. She missed her footing, fell and slid down a slippery smooth stone funnel into a conduit built centuries before to carry away the runoff from the monsoon rains. Her fingernails tore as she struggled to seize a purchase in the joints between the flagstones. She flung her arms and legs out and tried to grip the walls with her fingers and toes, but still she couldn't stop the slide. She went down and down, heard the stones she had loosened falling into the water far below. Her descent into the conduit was growing steeper. She could not stop herself—her arms and legs, fingers and toes too bruised and weary to keep their grip. She could feel herself gaining speed and then came a tearing of material and her slide came to a halt. Her skirt had snagged on the rusty bolt of a sewer pipe that emptied out into the conduit at this level.

She lay there against the cold, slimy flagstones and sobbed out loud with relief. She stayed that way for a long time, trying to regain her nerve and rest, then worked the bolt loose and used its flattened rusted edge to gain a hold in the joint between the flagstones above her. With the aid

276

of the bolt to take her weight, she inched herself back up over the lip of the conduit and collapsed, her muscles, unaccustomed to such exertion, a fiery mass of pain. She might have given up then, but the thought of the beggars sweeping through after her, and what Chang would let them do to her, made her stagger to her feet and drive herself on.

The whole area was no more than a quarter of a kilometer wide, but it took her nearly the rest of the night to cross it. She came up to the ground-floor levels of the western side just before dawn—in a state of exhaustion, clothes torn, shoulders throbbing, face bloodied. But in the darkness ahead she saw the flickering light of a fire. She crept up a flight of steps that led into a huge room. In the center, crouched around in a circle with the leaping flames reflecting off their half-naked bodies, were some twenty beggars. They were gambling, shouting out their bets as the dice fell, the winners hurrying to finish the game before the light became strong enough to start their search.

At the far end of the room was an open doorway, and through it Crystal Lily caught a glimpse of the lightening sky. She skirted the room in the shadows by the walls and made for the door. She was within a few feet of it when Chang barged through with orders to start the search—and saw Crystal Lily. No one, including Chang, had expected her to reach the western edge of the cellars. He quickly overcame his surprise and reached out to grab her, and at the same time the Korean close behind stepped back to block the doorway. He was too late. Crystal Lily had ducked past Chang's arms and wriggled through the doorway out into the street.

Over the roofs of the buildings she could see the masts of the junks riding in the Inner Harbor. The street was already astir, with owners sleepily rolling up the blinds of their shops and hawkers brewing breakfast on the pavements. Behind her were the gunmen and beggars. She hadn't the strength left to outrun them, and judged from the sound of their voices that, in another hundred yards, they would run her down—

The sound of a bicycle bell shrilled urgently behind her. When she didn't turn her head the coolie rode his pedicab right up beside her. "Get in, my lady, get in... I friend for Snake Boat Man." She literally threw herself into the back of the pedicab, feeling it sway and jolt as the coolie raced down the street. Only when they had gone some distance did she risk pulling herself up. "Where is he?" she managed to get out as she tried to regain her breath and some composure.

"I take you main jetty, Inner Harbor, my lady. Snake Boat Man has boat ready for you escape. Everything okay now..."

*　*　*

CHANG'S HASTILY summoned car rounded the corner, tires screeching. The doors opened and Chang and the Korean climbed in. "Where will she go?" the Korean asked.

"She'll head for the Inner Harbor. She has no place to hide in Macau so she'll try to board a junk. We'll catch her there. Put men on each of the jetties. It won't be hard to spot her."

*　*　*

ONCE SURE he had shaken off pursuit, the pedicab rider cautiously doubled back on his tracks toward the Inner Harbor. He saw the limousines had arrived there before him and were parked along the curb. "*Mo hó,*" he said, "everything not okay."

"What can I do?"

"Must go end jetty," the coolie said firmly. He'd been well briefed by Nicholai.

"Chang has an assassin..."

"Snake Boat Man savvy, you trust him. I make accident, turn pedicab across pavement, crash against guards. When that happen you jump out, run end of jetty."

Crystal Lily nodded, glanced up at the sky and braced herself. "Quickly then, before the light breaks."

The pedicab rider picked up speed. "May all the gods protect you," he muttered in the traditional salutation.

"And you," she answered as she pressed herself far back in her seat. The gunmen patrolling the entrance to the jetty saw a pedicab lurch out of the traffic toward them and flung themselves out of its way. The coolie promptly rode on through the gap they left and stood up on his pedals...

Chang was the first to understand what was happening. He nodded to the Korean. "Shoot him."

The Korean raised his heavy-caliber automatic and shot off two rounds in such quick succession that the echoing reports flattened into each other. His aim was on-target. The bullets entered the coolie an inch apart through his chest, their impact lifting his scrawny body off his saddle. His handlebars were wrenched out of his already lifeless hands, and the pedicab turned over, spilling Crystal Lily on to the wooden planks beside his body. She was instantly on her feet and running, as he'd told her, for the end of the jetty. Knots of workers from the sampans, who were landing the night's fishing catch, backed out of her way. The gunman took three quick steps into the center of the jetty, raised his gun, tracked the running figure and took aim.

Crystal Lily somehow willed her exhausted legs to go faster. She was panting, drawing air in sobbing lungfuls. She knew very well that to a professional like the Korean she presented an easy target. She felt her back crawling as she waited for his bullet.

A man showed himself briefly in the second floor window of a godown overlooking the jetty, the barrel of a rifle edged over the lip of the window, a trigger was squeezed. The long burst on full automatic cut the Korean almost in half. Chang threw himself to the ground as another burst of fire brought down two of the gunmen closest to him and tore the planks by his head to splinters. "Shoot," he ordered to his bodyguards, who poured fire into the window of the godown as Chang, cursing, crawled on all fours to what he hoped was a safe spot.

"TIME TO get out of here," Keng Po called out to Ansty, pulling him back from the window.

CRYSTAL LILY heard the shots, and in a final effort to save herself... she had no idea who'd fired them... she dived over the rail of the jetty into the water. It was blood-warm... down, down she went, felt the thick silted mud on the bottom sucking at her feet. She kicked free, air bubbles bursting from her lungs as she fought her way back to the surface. Her head broke the reeking water amid the garbage and the jetsam from the fish-catch. She felt hands grab her, tried to fight them off but was dragged over the side of the sampan and put under its canvas-covered shelter.

She lay still, uncaring now, too exhausted to move. As the sampan began to move through the water, driven by the powerful sweep of its stern oar, she felt strong hands gently lift and cradle her head, felt lips brush against hers. She opened her eyes.

"Didn't I tell you she still lives?" Wen Yuan, the boatman at the oar said gruffly.

"Thank God," a deep husky voice answered.

She knew that voice... looked up to the face she loved framed in the battered conical straw hat of the boat people. "Nicholai... Nicholai..." It was all she could manage, but it said all she felt.

"You're safe," he said quietly, intensely. He held her trembling body right against his chest. "You're safe now."

* * *

"SHE DROWNED, I'm sure of it," a gunman said to Chang. "I saw her go to the bottom, I swear it—"

"Then who killed the Korean?" Chang had been tricked and he knew it. "Search the sampans." The whole of the Inner Harbor was choked with them. It would take hours. He understood that too. Which made him even more furious, and desperate. She was alive, and he'd better find her, before Thomas Wu put him where she should have been . . . at the bottom of the harbor, forever.

CHAPTER 26

CRYSTAL LILY lay very still, in the aftermath of shock. She felt an overpowering weariness, her bones seemed to be pressing painfully down through the rush matting onto the deck. But before she could sleep there was something she had to know, although hating the notion of a positive answer.

"Was it my comprador? Did he betray me?"

"No," Nicholai told her. She tried ineffectually to help him as he stripped off her torn wet clothes and replaced them with the black cotton *samfu* of the boat people. "He had even rallied your remaining Manchus. He's holding your palace against Thomas Wu."

The sampan was so small and narrow that from where she lay she could reach up and touch the woven rattan roof. Through the opening she could see Wen Yuan's muscular legs on the raised stern as he stroked the oar.

"Thank God it wasn't him," she said. "Who then?"

"Lao Ta."

She showed no surprise. "An ambitious man. I suspected him... Who else?"

"Your amah."

Crystal Lily was shaken. "Not her. She was as close as a mother to me."

"The only family blood ties she has left are in China. To save them Lao Ta persuaded her to betray you."

Crystal lily winced as Nicholai bound her bruised shoulder. "Rest," he urged.

But she was too keyed up. "No wonder Thomas Wu felt confident," she said bitterly, "with my amah and my chief bodyguard ready to sell me out. Even so, I'm surprised Wu didn't wait for Lao Ta to kill me." She seemed deadly calm as she said it.

"You made him impatient. He expected less resistance—"

"His arrogance will cost him," she promised, some of the old fire coming back into her eyes. "And Ansty?"

"He did well. It was his skill with a gun that saved your life."

She nodded, then asked about Mae Ling. There was no softness in her voice when she did. "Even when we argued I always felt we were close, always would be. Except I admit I was afraid of her... well, when the time comes I'll take care of her, for what she did to you—"

"No—"

"You defend her, even though she betrayed both of us? You don't understand, she's a witch, especially with men. She'll betray you again—"

"She sent me the message that saved your life."

Crystal Lily shook her head in annoyance. "Don't you see *why*...? She did it to save herself... if by some unlikely chance I happened to survive, she would be able to claim the debt from you. I told you she is a witch, and a damn clever one—"

"She's no longer important to us," Nicholai said, trying to calm her. "She told Thomas Wu what we wanted him to hear, and because she deserted me for what she took to be the stronger side, he'll believe her."

Just then Wen Yuan put his head into the shelter. "You've done quite a job... all of Macau believes you are a drunk, a failure with women..."

Nicholai pretended not to be bothered. "They believe it because I wanted them to. It will be different when I take my boat to sea... what do you want?"

282

"We've reached the Communist side of the river. I've seen Chang's men searching the sampans along Macau's Inner Harbor, but the Hokolo people are for you. Chang's men will get no help from them. What do you want me to do—?"

"Has the *East Wind* gotten to the Portuguese harbor?" Crystal Lily interrupted.

"Yes," Nicholai told her, "but we won't make for it in daylight and risk attracting attention. We're safe for now where we are. We'll cross back to Macau after sundown."

Wen Yuan drew down the curtains and left them. As soon as he had gone she turned to Nicholai, knowing how proud he was, how much he valued his name... "Nicholai, I know the shame I've made you suffer for my sake—"

"I decided to come out of retirement." He would not put any blame on her. "I did it for my own reasons. At least I feel alive again. And for that I have you to thank..."

Beyond the spidery spans of the Taipa bridge, waiting just on the edge of Macau's waters, were the low gray silhouettes of Communist-owned *hoi kungs*—the fast, heavily armed coastal patrol boats manned by crews from the mainland sea communes.

"Look at them," Crystal Lily said, peering through a hole in the rattan shelter. "The governor of the Kwangtung Province has his boats gathering out there like hungry sharks."

"They've smelled five tons of gold that will be on the water. Like everyone else tonight they're going to chase us from here to hell to get it."

Crystal Lily shivered. "Everything is against us..."

He sensed she was touching bottom, drawing on the last reserves of her courage. "I've set a trap, with you as the bait. My men are assembling a convoy in the Portuguese admiralty harbor. When we go to collect the gold from your palace we'll be taking the *East Wind*'s guns along with us. No one in the Syndicate will expect to meet that kind of firepower. The last few moves should belong to us... Rest now, you'll need all your strength for what you'll have to do." He reached forward to part the curtain—

"Stay with me. Please. Hold me..."

And when he did, she relaxed, and told him, "If we somehow win this I'll finish with the Syndicate and transfer my holdings to Hong Kong. I've already been in contact with Joshua Denning. Once the gold is on British soil the governor will be persuaded to let us enter on our terms.

In Hong Kong I'll make a career as a legitimate businesswoman." She smiled. "Maybe then you will approve of me, and marry me..." She put her finger to his lips, drew it away and kissed him. "And don't tell me you're too old," she said. "I already know that."

"So you'll be a respectable pillar of society, a member of the Jockey Club, the governor's council...you won't want to attach yourself to a smuggler—"

"Be quiet, smuggler. You once told me that a woman who pursued power couldn't commit herself to any one man. You may be right...with one exception—you. You wouldn't be jealous, or need to compete. You, Nicholai, are too much of a man. I also happen to love you..."

"What about Joss Denning?"

"The taipan of the Princely House? I respect him, and I'll honor my part in our bargain. But don't you see? Denning will become my number one rival in Hong Kong. From the moment I establish myself there I'll be his main competition...and he, mine.

"My father left me Macau as an inheritance. With you I hope to make the House of Sun the greatest trading house in the East. You hated to see me head of the Syndicate. After tonight, if we're successful, the Syndicate will no longer exist, and I promise to do everything I can to make sure nothing like it ever happens again in Macau."

Nicholai looked at her and smiled. Her sudden optimism was catching. "We've been fighting for our lives these past few weeks," he said, "when did you find time to decide all this?"

"While I've been shut up in the palace I had too much time...to realize that this would be the only way we could have a future together. At least it's a good dream, something to hold onto?"...Both of them knew without saying it that before they could have any future together they first had to get to Hong Kong, and the odds were growing longer against them every minute.

But Nicholai would not spoil her mood. "The Lady Sun and the smuggler," he said, holding her tightly.

"We'll become so *very* respectable when we live in Hong Kong," she promised him gravely, then laughed. "Except when we're alone...then I'll long for rainy mornings."

Nicholai kissed her, all his reservations gone, and she could believe, at least for the moment, that Mae Ling didn't exist..."It's not just a dream," she murmured to him before falling asleep in his arms. "I've already bought your house in Hong Kong, before the British could confiscate it."...

He woke her when it was almost dark. The sky over Macau was the color of a purple bruise, and there was a slight chop on the water. Outlined on the ridge above the Inner Harbor were the gutted ruins of the great cathedral. Wen Yuan used them for his landmark as he cautiously rowed his sampan back across the center of the river. Minutes later he spotted the dark gray outline of a waiting Macau police launch and nudged his craft up against it.

"Who sent this boat—?"

"Da Costa," Nicholai told her as he lifted her on board. "I called on the chief of police for the favor he owes the House of Sun. He's agreed to help us tonight."

The police launch engines started up again, leaving the sampan with Wen Yuan bobbing away in the wake. The launch took Crystal Lily and Nicholai swiftly to the stone-walled Portuguese harbor situated on the southern tip of Macau. As the launch rounded the dog-leg entrance that protected the harbor from a view from the river she saw, under the arc lights on one side of the mole, her gleaming white ChrisCraft; and on the other, painted a light blue-gray and looking sleek, grubby and purposeful, was Nicholai's *East Wind*.

"Why that color?" she asked.

"At night a vessel blends with the horizon, not the sea," Nicholai told her, looking over his boat, assessing its state of readiness, "and we'll be running down-moon to Hong Kong."

She walked now beside Nicholai down the jetty between their vessels, holding herself erect, trying to hide the pain and the stiffness in her bruised body. Her crew, in white T-shirts and bell-bottoms, were lined up beside their craft for her inspection. On the gunboat Udo and Fifth Street rose from their work, their faces dirty and tired, their clothes sweat-stained and streaked with oil.

"Fifth Street, my engineer," Nicholai said, introducing him to Crystal Lily, "and Udo you know."

Udo grinned and took her hands warmly between his massive paws. "We've got this far," he told her. "We'll win this yet."

"What's the weather forecast for tonight?" Nicholai asked.

"Good," Udo told him. "Winds northeasterly, force two or three. Sea calm. Moonrise at eight-forty P.M. High water eleven-twenty P.M."

"Any fog?"

"Yes, over the northwest of the New Territories. It could keep some of Hong Kong's aircraft grounded."

"Good." To Fifth Street Nicholai said, "If all goes well we'll be back with the gold a little before eleven P.M. Can you finish with the engines by then?"

"I'm finished now," Fifth Street said wearily. "I'm coming along with you."

Nicholai saw that both the .50-caliber machine guns were missing from their turrets on either side of the bridge. "Are Ansty and Keng Po ready?"

Udo nodded in the direction of the five-ton canvas-backed vehicle that was parked at the end of the mole beside a police car. "Fifth Street's done all the hard work, the others are just finishing up."

"Da Costa's help again?" Crystal Lily was asking about where the vehicles came from.

"Yes," Nicholai said. "There he is now."

Da Costa had climbed out of the driver's seat of the police car and was coming toward them. He looked unhappy, and his jowly face shone with sweat. "I should not be here," he told Crystal Lily. "If I had any sense I would be in my headquarters dreaming up an alibi and praying that you win. Otherwise I'm going to be called on to account with my life to Thomas Wu and the rest of the Syndicate for the help I've given you tonight."

"You're an honorable man," Crystal Lily said. "I thank you."

"Your father paid for my children's education in Portugal. Now I pay back my personal debt to your family... and tonight I'm risking my position, my pension, my life for the future welfare of Macau, if you mean what you've said about disbanding the Syndicate—"

"I mean it," she said. "You've no reason to think otherwise—"

"I know that, I did not mean to imply—"

"Of course, I'm glad to hear it... but now we must get on with our business." A nervous man, she thought. But then, he had some good reason... as did they all this night...

Ansty jumped down from the truck, leaving Keng Po to finish lacing up its back flap. "Well, all's ready," he said, "and I can promise you someone's in for a mighty surprise." His blue eyes crinkled into a smile, ignored Nicholai and Da Costa as soon as he saw Crystal Lily. "It's good to see you safe," he said to her in his soft Irish brogue.

"I believe I owe you my life."

"So you do"—the smile broadened—"and you can pay me for it later."

Keng Po joined them. "There's the telephone"—he indicated a small office by the end of the mole—"I've kept Thomas Wu sweating through the last hour waiting for your call. Has Nicholai briefed you?" Crystal

Lily nodded. "Don't talk for more than ninety seconds or he may be able to trace the call."

Crystal Lily sat in front of the desk watching Nicholai dial the number Keng Po had given him. "Do you think this can work?"

"The Syndicate is like a wolfpack. Wu can't be confirmed as leader until he's gotten rid of you, and by now he must be coming under great pressure from the others for failing to do that." He let the number ring once and handed the receiver to her. "You've got ninety seconds to convince him..." He looked at his watch. Behind her Da Costa sweated in silent agony.

"Thomas Wu," a voice answered abruptly.

Crystal Lily's knuckles whitened on the receiver. She closed her eyes for a split second and concentrated on clearing her mind of the hatred she felt for this man. "This is Madame Sun...I have only a limited time to talk. We have come to a stalemate again—"

"Not so. I control Macau."

"Except for my palace."

"I have the force to take it whenever I want."

"My Manchus are still loyal to me. You would create war that would disrupt the whole city, frighten the tourists and gamblers away for months. The others would hardly let you do that."

Silence, then... "What do you suggest?"

"I am prepared to give up my leadership of the Syndicate, on certain conditions."

She caught the sound of relief, and surprise, in Wu's voice, and knew that Nicholai had guessed right. The rest of the Syndicate had become angry at the disruption to their profits and Wu was under pressure from them to settle.

"And those conditions? Remember, your position is weaker now. Nothing, not even a mouse can reenter that palace. The streets around it are sealed tight by my men—"

"My conditions are that my servants and I be allowed to leave Macau tonight and that I may take with me the gold owed to the 14K Triad. I will sign over all instruments of authority willed to me by my father. You will receive bank account numbers, lists of officials in our pay, agents, dealers, everything you need to run Syndicate business. But if we fail to reach an agreement, then I have nothing more to lose and I will instruct my comprador to destroy my palace, and *everything* in it." She caught Nicholai's eye. He was signaling to her that the time was up. "I will call you back for your answer."

"There is no reason to stop," Wu said quickly, "you should know we have no system for tracing telephone calls in Macau." But he was talking to a silent receiver.

Chang now replaced the second receiver linked to the telephone exchange, through which he had been trying to trace the call. "Nothing," he reported. "Not enough time. There is no doubt that it was her?"

"None. Who helped her escape?"

"The Snake Boat Man. We underestimated him—"

"Did you check the refugee camp on Coloane?"

"It's deserted. His boat has left and so have his men."

"Then they're in Macau."

"Another twelve hours," Chang promised, "my men will find them all."

Thomas Wu was thinking of Rocky Lee with his own force of drug smugglers rubbing their hands over his and Chang's failure to destroy Crystal Lily, and seeing this as an opportunity to renew the struggle for leadership... "Too late"—Wu shook his head—"we've no time. She was right about one thing... I can't risk the destruction of the palace, all the Syndicate's records—"

"So you will give her safe passage for the gold?"

"Why not... if we get the palace?" Wu leaned back in his chair and pressed his slender fingers against his temples. "She will not, of course, leave here alive. Her boat will get no further than the end of the Macau channel, where our craft and the Communist *hoi kungs* are waiting. The water there is less than twenty feet deep. We can dredge the gold up, pay a small portion to the governor of Kwangtung Province, pay back some to the 14K Triad and keep the rest ourselves. It could work out..."

The phone rang again, he reached for it. It was Crystal Lily. "I agree to your terms," Thomas Wu told her.

Her voice was brisk. "As a guarantee of my safe passage I want not only your word but the word of each member of the Syndicate, no exception. Are they all in Macau?"

He knew there was no point in lying, it would be too easy for her to check. "Yes."

"Then you will wait for me outside the entrance to my palace. Once my comprador has confirmed that you are all there, I will surrender myself and my Manchus to you. But I will do so in the open street, in full view of witnesses."

"What witnesses?" Whom had she gone to for protection?

"The police."

288

Smart bitch... "Accepted," Wu said after only a moment's hesitation. "Where is the Snake Boat Man and his crew?"

"They'll stay with their boat. You have one hour. At nine P.M. tell your guards blocking the streets to let me through." She handed the phone to Da Costa, who proceeded to try to finalize the details, barely able to hold the phone steady, under the firm prompting of Nicholai.

"...For the peace of Macau... and the safety of all its citizens I will bear witness... Tell your men to expect one car and a heavy vehicle to carry away the gold—"

"Da Costa"—Wu said the name with undisguised anger —"you should not have got involved. You will regret this..."

Da Costa lowered the receiver. He'd lost all his color, his fat jowls tensed. "Mother of God," he said to Nicholai and Crystal Lily, "don't fail."

"CONTACT THE other members, have them meet outside the palace," Thomas Wu instructed Chang. "Tell them she has surrendered, that this time we can't fail. Her little sojourn in the beggars' cellars seemed to have had its effect..."

Once Chang had left, Wu turned his attention to more pleasant matters. A lamp cast a rich pool of light over his desk; the rest of his study lay in dark shadow. Mae Ling, who had been sitting silently on a cushion against the wall, now rose, moved sinuously toward him.

"Superintendent Malloy of the Hong Kong police would sell his soul to get you back," he told her. "He's willing to come here to Macau right now to offer me any favor I want."

"What did you say?" Malloy or Thomas Wu... what a choice...

"That I will not trade you." Not yet, he added to himself. "I have a surprise for you." He reached into his desk and put before her an American passport, birth certificate, Social Security card and driver's license.

She took up the passport, turned immediately to the page with her photograph, read on down and to where it said she was born a Hawaiian Chinese. The other forgery was perfect too. The documents could be her salvation. She was stunned, and for an unguarded moment allowed herself to believe him.

"You have your freedom. I mean that. These documents will establish you anywhere in the world... Or," he said, raising her hand to his lips, "you could marry me and, after tonight, the Sun palace and all of Macau will be yours."

"Thank you for offering me my freedom first," she said, quickly realizing her momentary trust had been self-delusion and knowing her only option now was to fall in with his charade, appease him. But she understood he had no intention of letting her go.

"You are a new kind of woman for me... I would not even want to buy you. You are different..."

And you are a damn liar, she thought, but said, "May I come with you tonight? I'm curious, I would like to see her."

"No, this is Syndicate business. The others would resent it." He scooped up the passport and identity documents. "What is freedom, after all," he said, returning them to the drawer, "when all Macau can be yours?"

Mae Ling took care to lower her eyes submissively, and noted that the future head of the Macau Syndicate apparently felt so secure in his power over her that he had neglected to lock the drawer.

CHAPTER 27

IN THE harbor office the signal light flashed to life on the small two-way radio on the table beside Crystal Lily.

"My lady"—it was the voice of her comprador speaking from the palace wall—"I have identified all four members of the Syndicate. They wait here for you."

"We're leaving now."

Nicholai looked at his watch. Nine P.M. He signaled to his men to get into the truck.

Ansty, face blackened and a crimson scarf tied around his head to keep the sweat out of his eyes, jumped onto the tailgate and disappeared into the dark recesses of the truck. He was followed by Udo, Keng Po and Fifth Street. L'eung Heung, dressed in a policeman's uniform, swung up into the driver's seat and started the engine. Four of the crew from the ChrisCraft, also dressed in police uniforms and carrying rifles to act as an escort for Da Costa, followed Nicholai into the back of the truck and pulled up the tailgate. Their faces and uniform caps were all that remained visible through the partly open canvas flap.

Crystal Lily got into the car beside Da Costa. The chief of police flashed his lights at the guard on the dock gates who swung open the heavy gates. The car, followed by the truck, bumped over some potholes, turned right and then accelerated away. "We've reached the street," Nicholai was told as he swayed with the others in the darkness to the motion of the truck.

"THEY'RE LATE." Thomas Wu paced nervously beside Chang outside the palace, avoiding the impatient glares of the others.

Chang's lieutenant, with responsibility for the streets to the east of the palace, caught the sound of vehicles being driven hard up the hill. He radioed Chang.

"Can you identify them?"

The lieutenant checked as the vehicles came over the rise. "I see Da Costa and a woman in the first car, and four of his police in the back of the truck. I'm going to stop and search—"

"No, she's here—that's all that matters now. What harm can she do? We've got thirty armed men on the streets."

The car and the truck drew up opposite the palace gates. Crystal Lily got out, passed very close to the side of the truck.

"Remember," Nicholai whispered to her through a narrow hole cut into the canvas, "walk slowly. Draw them to you. As though you were about to take their picture. I want them *all* in it."

She proceeded to walk very slowly across the street. Da Costa climbed down out of the car and leaned against the door to show himself. The sweat of fear was pouring off him, his legs were shaking too much to hold him up unaided.

Apart from Da Costa, she was alone. As soon as the Syndicate men had assured themselves of this they relaxed and, edging away from the protection of their limousines and bodyguards, formed a knot to meet her.

No more than thirty paces to go, she thought. Nicholai was cutting it too fine... her heart pounded against her chest. Each step she took into the no-man's-land in the middle of the brightly lit street would, she was certain, be her last. She saw Thomas Wu, a smile of relief on his face; behind him was Chang, the man who murdered her mother, with his bald dome and fleshy lips. Beside him stood Rocky Lee in a loud Italian suit and an even more vulgar tie—the playboy of Macau. They were all there, except for Chen Kitung. Where was he? And then she saw his round Buddhalike figure step into the frame that Nicholai had helped her to fix in her mind—

Nicholai's voice shouting to her, finally... she threw herself face down on the street as behind her the canvas sides of the truck fell away.

Thomas Wu, the others from the Syndicate beheld an extraordinary sight... bolted onto a platform on the back of the truck were the gunboat's two heavy-caliber machine guns. As they took this in the wicked snouts of the guns spat fire. Shells loaded alternately with high-explosive and armor-piercing ammunition capable of destroying a tank or a small ship were hurtled at close range across the street, sweeping every man in their path into bloody bundles of rags.

Ansty and Udo operated the machine guns while Keng Po and Fifth Street fed in the ammunition belts.

Crystal Lily felt the concussion of the shells split the air just above her head. The shock effect was like a series of fingers snapping deep inside her brain. This was followed instantaneously by the even more terrifying explosions of the projectiles landing on their targets. Fragments, chips, splinters from the destruction showered down on her. She had been lying outstretched, trying to press herself into the tarmac, but now she raised her hands to her ears to drown out the mind-shattering roar set up by the guns. Her movement drew the attention of the Syndicate gunmen behind a limousine parked further down the street. Their bullets kicked into the heat-softened tarmac around her. Ansty promptly directed his machine gun against the car. The armor-piercing shells punctured the gas tank and the high-explosive shells did the rest of the work. The long black limousine shuddered, then blew up, sending great black-and-orange gouts of flame skyward, raining down burning fuel on those who survived the blast.

Nicholai crawled toward her. She felt his hand grasp her leg. "Stay down and follow me." She wriggled on her belly after him, back across the street.

The answering fire died. The machine guns on the truck became silent when they could no longer find targets. Nicholai went to Da Costa's car, tapped on the side. "You can come out now."

Da Costa wriggled his bulk out from his hiding place under the car, saw with astonishment the burning cars, the ragged bodies blown apart in the street. There could be no survivors.

"Mother of God, what a destruction," Da Costa said, shaking his head.

"The gangsters have moved on to smaller weapons and assassins' bullets, they've forgotten you still had those terrible guns..."

The gates of the palace opened and the Manchus came running out. "Have them check the bodies, collect their guns and close the sidestreets," Nicholai told Keng Po. "We don't want any surprises when we leave. The rest of you stay with the truck." L'eung Heung had already begun to back it through the palace gates. "We'll start loading up the gold immediately."

The comprador and Crystal Lily led the men down to the vaults. Crystal Lily operated the system of combination locks that opened the doors. Inside, stacked along the length of the steel-lined room, were tier upon tier of gold bars. "Five tons—a fortune worth seventy million dollars. Well, don't just stand there looking at it," Nicholai told an awestruck Ansty. "Load it onto the trolleys and take it up to the truck."

"I've some personal things to attend to," Crystal told Nicholai. "When you've finished we'll drive in convoy to the boat." She signaled her comprador to follow her....

As soon as they were alone she told him to send men to scour Macau, to find Lao Ta, her amah and Mae Ling. They had all been under Thomas Wu's protection—worthless now. "Bring them to me, I'll be in my rooms."

While she waited Crystal Lily showered and changed her clothes, gave instructions to her servants, then sat at her desk sorting through her papers, putting those she needed to take with her in a leather briefcase and discarding the rest.

SHE HEARD the comprador's familiar scratch at the door. "Come in."

"They are here," Yu Shik Lieu announced. She steeled herself to use, possibly for the last time, the power given her by her father. She got up and followed the comprador into the next room. "Wait by the door," she said to L'eung Heung, who was guarding them. She had meant to concentrate first on her amah and the disloyal Manchu, and then on the girl, but her curiosity overrode her and she stole a look at Mae Ling. She was more beautiful than Crystal Lily could have imagined. No wonder Nicholai had been attracted to her. What man would not be?

Well, she had been betrayed by each one of them. She would take her revenge, once more her father's daughter. "You, my most trusted chief bodyguard..." She turned to Lao Ta. "You swore a sacred oath to my father and then to me to protect the House of Sun.

"And you," to the quaking amah. "It was into *your* arms I crawled for

294

comfort as a child. I could forgive your lack of courage when you didn't protect me then. But not this time. The punishment is death." She made an end of it quickly, the pulse spots on her temple throbbing. "See that their bodies are discovered in the gutters of Macau, let people learn why they died.". . . If, she reminded herself, she were to let them live the remnants of the Syndicate would take courage at her weakness, follow her to Hong Kong and strike at her when she was defenseless.

"And now you"—she turned back to Mae Ling, who understood her end had come. "You were not only unscrupulous but a fool to have betrayed the Snake Boat Man. Didn't you love him enough to protect his life from a man like Thomas Wu?"

"You talk of love?" Mae Ling countered angrily. "We are not so different, you and I. We are women on our own in a world owned by men. I could not protect myself any more than you could. I had to choose a man. As one failed I used another—just as you have done."

Which had its effect. . . "I love him, I would *never* betray him—"

"And I loved him as much as I could afford. I have spent months in hiding. I have known my share of betrayal and terror. I have learned to live each day for my own survival. He has lived longer and harder than you, he would understand. . . Where is he now?"

"He's gone," Crystal Lily lied. "He can't help you."

"He won't allow you to kill me." She had one card left to play. "If you do he will find out, and you will lose him."

Crystal Lily looked at her with a certain respect. Nicholai probably would not approve. . . "All right, you live, but only as long as he lives. So pray for him to whatever gods you know. Tonight you come with us. Your life rides on the *East Wind* to Hong Kong with Nicholai and me. If he dies, you die. Now take her away," she ordered L'eung Heung. "Tomorrow, if we're free in Hong Kong, release her. But there is one condition," she added before Mae Ling left. "You never again even try to see Nicholai."

"I *accept*," Mae Ling said quickly. "On my life, be it."

"On your life, yes."

Crystal returned then to her room, sat down heavily, slumped over her dressing table.

Yu Shik Lieu followed her and closed the door.

"You did well," the comprador told her. "You could not allow them to live. . . Did you expect me to betray you too?" the old man asked softly.

She looked up at his reflection in the mirror. "I could not be sure, even of you."

Yu Shik Lieu was silent.

"Don't be angry with me—"

"I'm not angry," the old man replied. "I was thinking that you have acted exactly as your father would have done. Are you sure, now the path to succession is open to you, that you still wish to give up mastery of the Syndicate and leave Macau?"

"Nothing of that plan has changed."

"My lady, I have not much longer to live. I do not think I will transplant well in Hong Kong."

"Comprador, don't abandon me. I need your wise head to guide me until the end. After I reach Hong Kong I still have to destroy the Triad and lay the blame for its destruction at the door of my last enemy, Billion Dollar Choy." She sat there at her dressing table with no makeup, in jeans and an open-neck shirt, looking as young and vulnerable as she had the first day she returned to Macau.

She is clever, Yu Shik Lieu thought, knowing that she knew he would be touched at the thought that she still needed him... Suddenly he caught a whiff of smoke. "Have you given instructions to burn the palace?"

"Yes. Tonight I end my ties to my father and all he stood for."

It was done, then. With the destruction of the fortified palace, the era of the beggar's House of Sun in Macau was finished. Yu Shik Lieu sighed. It would take him a longer time than he had left to adjust to a law-abiding life.

She got up from her chair. "Give me your arm, comprador, it's time we left."

She helped him descend the staircase. They had made their exit none too soon. Smoke billowed through the huge ground-floor rooms. Curtains flared. The remaining servants ran frantically about. "I've given instructions for all the stolen art to be handed over to the city fathers of Macau. They can return them to their rightful owners or keep them. It will be out of my hands." The comprador privately had no doubt as to what the city fathers would do. "The furnishings and everything else can burn." She shivered. "When I was a child I hated this place."

She stopped by the Crystal Room door. A servant darted out carrying her father's precious begging bowl. "Give me that," she told him. She held up the famous hand-carved dragon boat. "This is the one possession of his that I will keep," she said. "I'll use it as the emblem of my Princely House in Hong Kong."

She stepped into a waiting limousine. Yu Shik Lieu got in beside her. The eleven remaining bodyguards, who were to accompany them, followed in vehicles behind the truck that held Nicholai's crew and the gold.

"Where is your wife?" Crystal Lily looked for Yu Shik Lieu's third wife.

"She will follow with the other servants if indeed we are able to become established in Hong Kong," the comprador said.

The convoy reached the Portuguese harbor without incident, but the comprador well understood that this dangerous night had only just begun...

THE MACHINE GUNS and the gold were lifted from the truck and carried across the quay to the *East Wind*. Fifth Street worried about the boat's stability. "I want that gold laid right along the transom. Pack it in tight so it can't move." While the work went on he checked the moorings of the large escape cannisters placed side-by-side at the stern of the boat.

"Do you think they'll work?" Udo asked dubiously.

"I don't see why not, but I sure as hell hope we don't have to find out." He turned and hurried back below deck. . . .

As soon as the loading was finished he laid the inflation bags over the gold and connected their hoses to the cylinders of nitrous oxide in the engine room. "If anything happens and these things start to inflate, get out of here fast," he warned the others. "In sixty seconds they'll squash you to death against the hull."

The ChrisCraft's engines were turning over, giving out a deep diesel throb. On its deck fast Zodiac rubber dinghies were being readied for escape.

"Have you got your instructions clear?" Nicholai asked the captain.

He nodded. "I break down the channel under the bridge and head for the open sea. I draw the Communist *hoi kungs* and Wu's craft after me and then I abandon ship."

"I'll need a mile start, that's all," Nicholai told him. "By then I'll be in shoal water where they can't follow me." Nicholai glanced at his watch. Seven minutes left to high water.

Da Costa waited by the gangway for Crystal Lily to board the *East Wind*.

"What, have no other senior members of the Macau administration come to bid farewell to the House of Sun—just the Honorable Da Costa?"

Irony, or detection of same, was not Da Costa's long suit. "My lady, you understand none of this could ever be official—"

"I do," and suppressed a smile.

Da Costa was awed by the flames on the hill, reddening the sky over Macau, consuming her palace. She had left herself no possibility of going back. "You kept your word to me," he said seriously.

"As you did to me. The Syndicate is all but destroyed. At least mortally wounded. The city you and I have loved will prosper without being sucked dry."

"It's good to know that after thirty years as a policeman I have done my duty. I will retire and be forgotten, but you will go on, your journey is just beginning. God bless you, and keep you safe tonight."

The comprador and the Manchus who escorted Mae Ling were filing across the gangplank onto the MGB. Before she joined them Crystal Lily turned back to Da Costa. "Will you see that the governor of Hong Kong learns of what has been done tonight, that we have destroyed the Syndicate? It should help convince him that Dr. Sun's daughter has turned legitimate."

"I will do that." Da Costa waved a pudgy hand. "I will take special pleasure in communicating the truth to those officious British bastards as soon as you've safely landed the gold."

CHAPTER 28

THE EXHAUST note from the ChrisCraft's engines rose to an angry howl, the noise reverberating off the enclosing stone walls of the small harbor. At Nicholai's signal it leaped free from its moorings and, accelerating, banked sharply to round the narrow right-angled entrance to the harbor mouth. By the time it met the rippling waters of the Inner Harbor it was rising on the plane, sheets of spray shot through by moonlight flying from its bows.

Nicholai ran up the stone steps to the top of the harbor wall. From there he could see the ChrisCraft start its run down the narrow, deep-water passage, past the Praia Grande with its neon-lit hotels and gambling casinos, through the central span of the Taipa bridge. It banked sharply now to starboard, following the one-and-a-half-mile, flag-marked channel that provided Macau's only deep-water access through the mud shoals to the sea.

But the ChrisCraft never had a chance of reaching the sea—blocking the end of the channel were three Communist *hoi kungs*. While the ChrisCraft was still in Macau waters they opened fire. Nicholai watched brilliant streams of tracer fire travel lazily across the sky and straddle the skimming ChrisCraft. Pinpricks of light, like giant matches being struck, glowed all along its hull. Smoke began to billow from its stern. Now, Nicholai willed its captain... enough, abandon the boat...

As if its captain had heard him the ChrisCraft slewed out of control, ran out of the channel and beached itself on the mudbanks. A Zodiac dinghy dropped astern, racing the captain and the skeleton crew of the ChrisCraft back to Macau. The Communist gunboats had bought the decoy—which was all Nicholai needed to know.

He ran down the steps of the jetty and boarded the *East Wind*. "Cast off forward, cast off stern," he shouted. Keng Po on the deck jumped to his order. Nicholai took the wheel. "Get down below with the others," he told Crystal Lily. "You'll be safer—"

"No," she said, gripping the bridge rail, nearly deafened by the savage chant of the gunboat's triple engines. "I'll stay here, with you."

Ansty and Udo, on either side of the bridge, had strapped themselves into their shoulder harnesses and were swinging outboard their .50-caliber Browning machine guns.

As the *East Wind* pulled away from the jetty Fifth Street below deck issued last minute instructions, his eyes avoiding Mae Ling's. "Everybody... take care not to damage these," he warned again, pointing to the salvage bags placed carefully on top of the gold, "and if a stray bullet hits the cylinders and these bags start to inflate, you've got less then sixty seconds to get out of here. So keep the hatches open." He left the Manchus, the comprador and Mae Ling huddled in the stripped-out shell of the hull and climbed back through the watertight hatch to tend his engines.

The gunboat shot from the protection of the harbor, its aquajets lifting the bows and hull clear of the water for a full third of the boat's length. Keng Po, working forward, was pitched off his feet by the violent surge of acceleration and scrambled for a hold on the steeply lifting bows.

The estuary was shaped like a bottle with the deepwater channel through the Taipa bridge its neck. But to the southeast of the estuary was an escape route, a narrow channel that led between the tip of Coloane and the Communist mainland. To reach it the gunboat had to cross five miles of treacherous shallows and mud flats, covered in many places by less than three feet of water. It was thought impassable by the Communists

300

to all but the shallowest draught vessels. But the aquajets could operate in less than thirty inches of water, and with the moonlight and his knowledge of this estuary Nicholai possessed the skill needed to thread a passage through the shoals.

THE COMMANDER of the *hoi kungs* felt a growing sense of disquiet as his vessels gingerly approached the beached ChrisCraft. There was something wrong . . . the ChrisCraft carrying that weight of gold should have settled deeper into the mud. Then his attention was riveted to a high plume of wake left by the *East Wind* as it streaked across the estuary, and he realized which boat must be carrying the gold. He called out a warning over the radio, ordering his boats to disengage from the ChrisCraft. His *hoi kungs* had too deep a draught to follow the *East Wind* across the shallows, but he could alert the lightly armed militia junks that patrolled the channel. If they could hold the gunboat long enough for the *hoi kungs* to round the seaward side of Coloane and cut it off, then all was still not lost.

FIFTH STREET, huddled in the engine room, listened to the troubled chant of his engines. Beneath his feet he could feel the keel grate on the bottom and knew mud and sand was being sucked up through the jets. He hurried forward to the frightened, seasick Manchus and urged them to move toward the bows. He used their weight to trim the boat, lifting as much of the stern out of the water as possible so that the gunboat hung on her aquajets.

On the bridge Nicholai and Crystal Lily heard the engine note hardening, rising to a thick solid howl as the jets took hold. The whole boat bumped and shuddered as Nicholai drove it onward. Ahead now lay the channel. But it was less than three hundred yards wide and their way was blocked by the moon-drenched silhouettes of the Communist militia junks. Flashes of light began winking from their bow guns, tracer fire arched toward the *East Wind*. Nicholai sounded the fire bells. Udo and Ansty's guns immediately trained on the lead junk and opened fire. Their shells flew dead on-target, tracer fire from the *East Wind* seeming to hit the sturdy junk in one solid thunderclap. There was a brief glow, then with a brilliant flash she disintegrated, her main magazine and fuel tanks blowing skyward, leaving the surface of the channel pockmarked with splashes as bits of timber from the junk fell back into the sea.

The other junks still tried to block the way. Nicholai chose the spot between the Coloane shore and to the left of where the lead junk had been. "Hold on," he ordered as he saw the sandbanks that had been shifted across his path by the currents. The gunboat hit the first sandbank, rose into the air, came down in deep water on the other side with a crash, sheets of spray soaking everyone on deck. It hit another sandbank, twisted in the air as Nicholai fought to keep control, and came thumping down again. Below, Fifth Street and Mae Ling held on to the comprador, trying to give him some support, while the Manchus who had failed to find handholds were tossed into groaning heaps.

The MGB burst through the blockade before the rest of the startled militia junks could respond. But the way to the sea was still contested. Communist artillery emplacements in the hills above the channel opened up, raining down shells on the gunboat. Nicholai banked and weaved his craft, leaving a cloud of smoke from the exhausts hanging livid in the moonlight to obscure the battle area.

A forty-knot slipstream seared Crystal Lily's cheeks. The engines bellowed, shells whined and cracked with near-sonic booms as they whipped close overhead. She glanced astern, seeing the wake rush away into blackness like a cliffside cataract. But she felt an exhilaration from the speed of the *East Wind* and the violent scene around her.

Nicholai's senses were fine-tuned. Every detail of his boat was clear in the moonlight. The rush of wind and water, louder than the engines, brought him the adrenaline-charged thrill of action that he'd hungered for in his retirement. Now he shed those empty years. He was a vibrant force again, felt more alive than ever before. Nothing could take the place of it. Nicholai the Russian, the legendary Snake Boat Man, was once more breaking out of Macau . . .

A Communist gun emplacement on the shore engaged the *East Wind* at close range. Udo and Ansty went to work. Streams of tracers from the *East Wind*'s Brownings now filled the air and made the opposition's fire seem less. The gun-emplacement flashes provided Udo and Ansty their aiming points and they concentrated on them. The enemy fire halted, then lifted high overhead as the Communist gunners seemed to lose their nerve.

The shore-gun emplacement was the last Communist barrier to the channel. The *East Wind*, barreling through the moonlight, left behind a cacophony of exploding guns and a night sky lit with tracers. Nicholai had gained the freedom of the South China Sea, outpacing the pursuing *hoi kungs* steaming around Coloane to cut off his escape.

Ahead lay Hong Kong. Malloy, with all the British forces at his disposal, waited for Nicholai there. The odds were against him, he knew, but when had they not been . . . ?

JOSS DENNING, escorted by the secretary for security, hurried up the steps to the marine police headquarters at Tsim Sha Tsui. Malloy met them as they came through the door to the operations room. "Sorry to disturb your evening, sir," Malloy said with more relish than he meant to show to the secretary, "but I've just heard that the Snake Boat Man's broken out of Macau."

"How in hell did he manage that?"

"I don't know, but nothing gets you ten he's on his way here."

"Have you alerted the coast watchers?"

"Yes, sir. I've also acted on your authority to claim this as a police operation."

"I know," the secretary said. "I've had the navy on to me already."

Malloy blocked Denning's way. "This is a security area."

"It's all right"—the secretary for security passed Denning through the door—"he's here at the governor's invitation. The taipan of the Princely House has a vested interest in tonight's events . . . if the opposition wins we may be forced to intercede through him with the Lady Sun rather than risk her gold reaching the Triad."

Malloy followed the secretary and Denning into the harshly lit control room. In the center, facing each other across a table, sat two duty controllers—one from the police and the other from the navy. The Hong Kong police operated greater numbers of men and patrol vessels, but the Royal Navy, largely responsible for founding Hong Kong in the eighteenth century as a base for its China squadron, still jealously guarded its traditional superiority—which, of course, had become a constant source of friction between the two forces.

One wall of the control room was covered by a map detailing the islands, the coastline of Hong Kong, the Square Boundary and its sea approaches. Above the map was a large old-fashioned clock, its hands pointing to twenty-five minutes past eleven. Carey, the D.P.C. of the marine wing, stood in front of the map. He positioned colored markers to indicate the navy and police patrol vessels with which he intended to block the western sector of Hong Kong's territorial waters. The other end of the room was partitioned by a soundproofed wall to chest height, with plate glass above. "That's the crisis room," the secretary for security told

Denning. "It's for the use of senior officers in the event of a threat to the colony." Inside was a conference table, one of its places already occupied by the senior naval officer of Hong Kong. In front of him was a telephone hot line that linked the crisis room directly to the governor.

"I see you've pulled the Royal Navy's minesweepers off the Square Boundary," the secretary said to Carey, following closely the disposition of his forces on the map.

"They're too slow to catch him, sir," the D.P.C. said, "but they've got heavy guns and if it comes to a fight I want to use them in-shore to back up my lightly armed police launches."

"I can't authorize your men to open fire unless Nicholai fires first or seriously endangers the lives of your crews."

The D.P.C. nodded. Hong Kong followed British law and he knew its limitations.

"What's the weather forecast?"

"Full moon and a clear night out at sea, sir. Northwest of the New Territories and most of Kowloon are cut off by a belt of fog."

"Sek Kong, the RAF's airfield, is fogged in solid, sir," Malloy said. "That bastard has chosen a good time to invade Hong Kong's waters."

"Helicopters?"

"We hope to use some of the RHKAAF's stationed at Kai Tak if the fog lifts," Carey said. "Until then we'll have to hunt him with our surface vessels... Sir, everything depends on whether he's going to make for Hong Kong along the north or south side of Lantau Island."

Malloy pointed to the map and told the secretary, "We've placed the R.N. hovercraft at the Lam Chau beach, that's right in his path from Macau. West sector police launches are below Shek Tse Po, and south sector's launches are blocking the Lantau channel. We should get him either way he goes."

"Yes... he may be able to outrun my police launches, sir," the D.P.C. put in, "but he hasn't got a hope in hell of outrunning the hovercraft."

"But if it's a clear night as you say out at sea, then in all the clutter set up by the islands and other vessels he'll be able to see almost as far as your radar," the secretary said, not convinced. He also sensed that he and Denning were getting in the D.P.C.'s way. "I'll leave it to you," and he led Denning into the crisis room, where through its intercom and glass partitioning they could monitor everything inside the control room.

"Evening, Captain Simmonds," he greeted the naval officer, a stiff, dark-haired taciturn man in starched whites. He nodded to the taipan. "You two know each other."

"Have you come to see how your side is doing?" the navy captain jibed at Denning.

Until then Joss had been careful to keep silent. "I admit," he said quietly, "my interests lie with the Lady Sun and the Snake Boat Man—"

"Then, sir, you're going to be out of luck."

The secretary for security summoned an aide. "Try to rustle us up some coffee, will you." He shared none of the confidence of his police force and navy. "If the Snake Boat Man has broken out of Macau under the noses of the Communists," he said to the captain, "it seems to me we could be in for a very long, long night..."

THE EAST WIND ran down the path of the moon to Hong Kong, spray rising upward and outward, higher on either side than the combing of the open bridge—sheets of silvery white water pierced through with moonlight falling away in spectacular lunar rainbows, and astern the high white-plumed wake boiling and seething, dripping phosphorous cold fire.

Fifth Street came up on the bridge now, exchanging the diesel fumes in his lungs for clean salt air, shaking his head to clear it of the clamor of his engines. "How fast are we going?" he shouted to Nicholai above the slipstream.

Nicholai glanced down at the rev counters. "We must be touching forty-two knots."

"How does she feel?" Fifth Street asked anxiously.

"She's handling better than I could have believed possible," Nicholai told him.

Udo leaned across, grabbed Fifth Street affectionately with his free arm and hugged him. "You bloody number one engineer," he shouted. "Somehow you've taught this old boat to fly."

"You're okay." Keng Po from his place at the helm nodded to Fifth Street. It was the highest praise he could offer, it meant final acceptance.

For Fifth Street it was a new sensation... for the first time in his life he'd found people to *belong* with. "Don't count your chickens, you crazy fucking bastards," he told them, also silently warning himself not to go sentimental... still he wouldn't have traded his place on this boat tonight for anything. "We've got a long way to go yet."

Ahead, under the shadow of Lantau Island on the boundary of Hong Kong's waters, winked the lights of the Lady Sun's fishing fleet.

* * *

HIGH UP on Shek Tse Po on the tip of Lantau Island was a Royal Navy coast-watching station used mostly to check on Communist shipping movements in the Pearl River estuary and to spot smugglers coming in from Macau.

Chief Petty Officer Simpson in charge of the station paused now on his rounds to glance over the shoulder of a rating whose eyes were fixed on the radar screen.

"It's a big fishing fleet," he commented as a cluster of echoes lit the screen. "Whose are they?"

"Not ours. They've been drifting in from the west all evening, chief."

"Are they sweeping?"

"Looks like it."

"Must be the moon. I hear it brings the fish to the surface."

"Do you want me to report it?"

Simpson made a quick calculation. The junk fleet still had a little way to go before it reached the Square Boundary. Before then no doubt it would turn and sweep back. "No, we've got enough on our plates tonight." He moved on. He hadn't got far before the rating called him back. "Chief, I've picked up a contact moving in from the southwest, range ten miles."

"How fast is it going?"

The rating studied the white blip on his screen. "It must be making forty knots."

"*That's* our man." He reached for the telephone to alert the operations room.

"Chief," the rating warned without taking his eyes from the blip, "the reason I never picked him up sooner was 'cause he was sheltering behind the Niu-T'ou Islands... and now he's headed straight for that fishing fleet..."

The navy controller relayed the message to the D.P.C., who quickly plotted the contact's position on the map. So the Snake Boat Man was going to run south of Lantau, Carey thought. It made sense—more sea room, more islands to hide behind.

"Radar's lost contact again, sir." The navy controller lowered his telephone and called the operations room. "He's disappeared among a fishing fleet on the border."

"Send in the hovercraft to flush him out," the D.P.C. ordered.

His voice was relayed over the intercom system to the secretary for security, who asked, "How long will it take to intercept?"

The captain saw in his mind's eye the hovercraft lifting off the beach at Lam Chau. "Ten minutes. The hovercrft can make fifty-five knots and is equipped with sophisticated radar," he told the secretary and Denning. "Once she's on his tail," he added, "he won't shake her off."

CHAPTER 29

THE *EAST WIND* drew alongside the swiftest junk in Crystal Lily's Macau fleet. The refugees were already scattered among the other junks that formed the outer shield. Fifth Street spotted Mary and her brother with Fool Boy, waving furiously to him across the water. Hesitantly, and then with increasing confidence, he waved back, deeply relieved to see they were safe. "Engineer, engineer," they called excitedly to him. "Good luck."

Nine of Crystal Lily's bodyguards and Mae Ling transferred to the junk, and as she did so she gave Nicholai such a beseeching, pitiable look that he felt obliged to follow her over to the other vessel. The comprador, L'eung Heung and two others stayed behind with their mistress on the gunboat. Crystal Lily now drew her comprador to one side... "The Triad are waiting to receive the gold at Tai Tam Harbor.

Contact them there. If we don't reach that landing place, lead them to the next one, and so on if we fail again, to the last one... Only you will show the landing places, and only my men will be armed in case they try to cheat us."

"My lady, leave this boat and come ashore with me," the comprador pleaded.

She shook her head. "No, my life, or death, rides with the Snake Boat Man and his crew tonight." She also looked across to the junk where Nicholai was talking with Mae Ling. "Remember," she told her comprador before he too crossed over to the junk, "if we fail, it's the girl's life for Nicholai's."...

Mae Ling faced Nicholai on the sloping deck of the junk in the shadow of its sail. Her eyes pleaded with Nicholai to keep her with him. Words were superfluous.

"You will be safe—"

"For as long as you live. No longer."

"I will try my best to live. For both our sakes."

"Do not hate me for what I did?"

"No."

"You understand... the position I was in... I had no choice—"

"I understand." And in a way he did. "I too was a refugee once."

"That's not easy to believe about you," she said. He seemed too strong to understand the total vulnerability of a refugee. "I have done things, bad things, but I know how to love... and I love you Nicholai. Believe me."

And for a moment he almost did. Almost... He said nothing, but took her face between his hands and kissed her good-bye.

"Nicholai—" Keng Po's yell of warning reached him from the gunboat's bridge. "The hovercraft..." He had spotted it streaking in from the tip of Lantau.

It was forty feet long, twenty-five feet wide and painted in the dark blue color of the Royal Navy. It made an impressive sight as it converged on the fishing fleet at fifty knots, fine spray, like smoke, blasting up from the air cushion it rode on.

The *East Wind* was positioned up-moon, which gave it an initial advantage; it lay in an outer ring of darkness looking toward the light, and the clutter of junks made the hovercraft's radar useless at close range. But the hovercraft, instead of circling, burst in among the junks, searching out the gunboat.

Nicholai leaped back onto the deck of the *East Wind* just as its triple engines burst to life. With a full-throated roar the gunboat jumped, then began to rip forward, the bows lifting, spray whipping upward and outward. Nicholai took the helm and commenced to weave, for a gap in the outer ring of junks. The *East Wind*, heading south for the shelter of the Soko Islands, was making thirty-five knots when it flashed past the junks. The chase drew the hovercraft and the slower south-sector police launches after it, leaving those junks carrying the comprador, Mae Ling and the refugees an open passage to Hong Kong.

Spread out to the north and south of Lantau Island and across the border, the comprador's junk signaled to the junk fleet. "We'll try to cause British as great a distraction as possible.". . .

"God, what I'd give for some helicopters now," the D.P.C. said as he saw that the junk fleet was splitting up and scattering all along the colony's western coast. Any one of them could be carrying the gold.

"What about the fixed-wing aircraft?" Malloy asked.

Ordinarily the D.P.C. would not have wanted to operate fixed-wing aircraft alongside helicopters, but he now said, "I'll take anything you can get into the air." And then to his controllers: "Move south sector's launches around to reinforce west sector . . . put all police units that can be spared on the ground along the western coast to intercept the junks when they land."

"RHKAAF at Kai Tak say the weather's lifted enough for them to get two helicopters into the air. Sek Kong's still fogged in tight," Malloy reported from the communications net he was operating on the controller's desk.

"I'll take them," the D.P.C. said. "Have the helicopters concentrate on the junk fleet. We know where the Snake Boat Man is . . ."

Over the radio into the brightly lit operations room came the faint howl of aero engines followed by the hollow, amplified voice of the hovercraft's captain. "Contact range one mile and closing . . ." He paused, uncertain whether or not his eyes were playing tricks on him. He was sitting on a padded chair on the bridge that looked similar to an aircraft's flight deck. "Contact looks like a Second World War MGB, except that's got to be impossible. And I can't believe the speed it's traveling. It must be making over forty knots."

"The crazy bastard must be using the *East Wind*—his old boat," Malloy said.

"Contact's going into the Soko Islands. Range closing to seven cables," the hovercraft captain reported. "I'm going in after him.". . .

Crystal Lily watched Ansty swing his Browning astern and take aim at the pursuing hovercraft.

"No," she called out, reached over the bridge rail and grabbed his shoulders to stop him. "Don't shoot."

"Why the hell not?" Ansty yelled at her above the slipstream. "Can't you see that hovercraft's gaining on us?"

Crystal Lily turned to Nicholai. "The guns served their purpose helping us escape from Macau, but you can't use them now. If you fire on the British they'll *never* let me into Hong Kong. You must understand that..."

Nicholai did... "Udo, Ansty, don't fire unless they fire first."

"Then we might as well give up," Ansty snapped in frustration, "because if we don't stop that hovercraft she's going to run right up our wake."

"The hovercraft's fast," Nicholai agreed, relieved that the British had sent the hovercraft after him first, not the *Scimitar*, "but she can't turn, can't weave. We'll shake her off." He hoped...

The rocky spines of the Soko Islands showed ahead in the moonlight, the sides tumbling steeply down to the sea. Nicholai drove the gunboat through the channel that divided the two closest islands, searching for something he'd spotted when he'd made his practice run through here. And then he found it... three hundred yards out from a beautiful half-moon beach was an outcrop of rock that jutted just above the water-line.

Nicholai spoke through the voice pipe to the engine room. "Fifth Street."

"Yeah."

"Do you still claim you can make this boat stand on its tail?"

"Don't drop the revs," Fifth Street said. "She'll turn on her jets."

"Then hold on." Nicholai spun the helm, the MGB banked violently, the hull bucking under the strain as all three aquajets bit deep into the water. The gunboat carved a tight circle around the rocks, throwing up steep, churning waves in its wake.

The hovercraft tried to follow... the captain brought his vessel around in a controlled skid. He thought he was going to make it, then in the toughest point of the turn he hit the steep waves set up by the MGB's wake. The hovercraft kicked out of control, skated sideways and rode up on the rocks. Its rubberized bumpers that controlled the cushion of air were ripped to shreds, and it just managed to limp the three hundred yards to the beach without sinking....

When the news that the navy hovercraft had wrecked itself was radioed through to the operations room Captain Simmonds let out a startled oath. "Did they fire on it?"

"No," the D.P.C. told him, "your man's error..."

Twenty minutes later the slower police launches reached the Soko Islands and reported no sign of the Snake Boat Man.

"Maybe he's gone back to Macau," Captain Simmonds said, not really believing it.

"He's hiding in the Communist islands across the Square Boundary," Malloy said, knowing he should have anticipated that the Snake Boat Man would use something like the junk fleet as a diversion and that the hunt for him was only just beginning. "He'll be back..."

"How about letting my police launches go after him across the Boundary?" the D.P.C. said to the secretary for security. "You could smooth it over later with Peking."

"No." The secretary shook his head decisively. "It would create a precedent. In similar circumstances they would cross our border and that's something neither I nor the governor want to encourage. It seems to me, gentlemen," the secretary told his people, "that we've missed our chance of picking him up at sea. Now we'll have to concentrate on catching him when he comes in-shore to land his gold."

"I think in that case," Captain Simmonds spoke bleakly to Malloy, "the next move is up to you."

"So it is," Malloy agreed. In a way he was glad it hadn't ended too soon. He wanted the Snake Boat Man to know who was responsible for destroying him. Malloy lifted the telephone and pressed the button that connected him with the MARPOL switchboard. "Send in Deck Sergeant Lao Ch'en."

Two police constables brought Lao Ch'en into the operations room, the old man looking uneasy in his shabby civilian clothes among the military-looking men in the room.

"Who's this?" the secretary for security asked.

"He's a retired deck sergeant in the marine police," Malloy explained as he left the crisis room to join the D.P.C. and the deck sergeant. "If anybody can stop the Snake Boat Man, I think he can..."

Lao Ch'en recognized the D.P.C. "I good again see you sir," he said in halting English, then bowed with old-fashioned courtesy and shook Superintendent Carey's hand. The deck sergeant insisted on greeting every man in the operations room with the same courtesy. All the frustrations of age and feeling useless in retirement had been replaced by a renewed excitement at being part of something. He was very conscious of his importance, that all attention was on him. At last his moment had come. He turned to the map. "He in which place?"

"Somewhere down here"—the D.P.C. pointed to a chain of islands on the map—"south of the Sokos."

312

"What boat use?"

"We believe his old one, the *East Wind*."

"No can." Lao Ch'en was astonished, but Malloy nodded.

The hovercraft captain said, "He's mocking us. He wants to prove nothing's changed and he can still make monkeys out of us—"

"Still can run faster than police?" Lao Ch'en asked.

"Yes."

"Your job," Malloy reminded the deck sergeant, trying to keep his voice even, "is to try to figure out where he's going to land the gold. *We'll* worry about catching him."

Lao Ch'en stared up at the map, made a play at concentrating, but the whole of Hong Kong's rugged coastline with its steep cliff faces, rocky bays and reefs had been etched into his mind over his forty-five years with the force. He fairly glowed within. All these important *gwilos*, and they *needed* old Lao Ch'en. Because he knew exactly where he would land the gold shipment if he were the Snake Boat Man. "Here," and he stabbed up at the map with a long wooden pointer.

The D.P.C. followed the pointer. "Tai Tam Harbor? That's impossible, that's right in the heart of Hong Kong Island—"

"No impossible, this one piece person"—he indicated Malloy—"tell me know Snake Boat Man carry many tons gold. Must land close for road for vehicle carry 'way gold. All other places no so good, Triad can't catch gold. Snake Boat Man use Tai Tam many times old days. British never believe, never catch him."

The D.P.C. caught Malloy's eye, asking if this crazy old man was to be trusted.

Malloy had begun to have doubts, but he nodded. "We've no good alternatives. Let's give him a try."

The D.P.C. shrugged. "There are thirty or forty places he can land along this coast and I reckon that's the longest shot on the boards. But"— he pointed to a bay to the east of Stanley village—"just in case I'll put a couple of launches in there—"

"No can put there," the ex-deck sergeant interrupted impatiently.

"Why not?" The D.P.C. was somewhat taken aback by Lao Ch'en's vehemence. "They can sweep the whole of Tai Tam Bay with their radar."

"Bright moon south sector tonight," the deck sergeant said, trying to make his case. "Snake Boat Man choose where he can see. Your boat wait here, he go 'way. You not catch him. You put police launch here"— he traced with his pointer the length of Tai Tam Bay to the small harbor at its end—"he land there, you catch him."

The D.P.C. studied the map. Lao Ch'en was pointing to a small pier

313

twenty yards away from an access road. The Snake Boat Man would need the devil's own arrogance to go in there among the anchored pleasure craft and unload his gold. It was only slightly less obvious than steaming into Aberdeen or Hong Kong Harbor and announcing himself to the police.

But Lao Ch'en didn't back down.

"All right," the D.P.C. said. "I'll put two launches in the harbor... Move north sector's launches down to cover the area between Cape Collinson, Tung Lung Island, Clear Water Bay and Inner Port Shelter," he ordered his controllers. "The old man better be right," he muttered to Malloy. "I'm stretching my reserves very thin. Not to mention what I'm doing to my neck..."

OUT AT sea the helicopters were harassing the junk fleet. The crew of a fleeing junk heard the heavy beat of rotors hover just above the mast, turning the air into a solid gale that threatened to rip their sails to shreds. Spotlights blazed down on the junk's canting deck. "*Lap jeck ten ji*, immediate stop," a disembodied voice boomed from a loud hailer above. The captain, his junk plunging out of control, yelled an order to his crew, which pulled down the sail in surrender.

The police launches, summoned by the helicopter, surged alongside, and a boarding party of armed police leapt onto the deck of the junk....

Closer to the western coast of the colony, seeking shelter where the fog belt began, the junks that had managed to escape the net found police ground forces waiting to arrest them as they ran ashore. But with so many junks sailing for Hong Kong, some of them made it...

The comprador's junk, escorted by four of the swifter junks, reached safety further south at Wah Fu on Hong Kong Island. On the southern coast there was no fog, just a light sea mist where the land met the sea. No police had gotten there yet, but the junk commanders knew that they had arrived with only minutes to spare. The comprador proceeded to issue instructions to the refugees who had accompanied him... "Those of you who cannot find relatives to help you and still have survived, in two week's time find my Lady Sun. She may again be in a position to offer you her protection on behalf of the Snake Boat Man. Now go, scatter quickly before your presence is reported to the police." He turned to Mae Ling. "Untie her," he ordered his guards. He had decided that this girl was going to be too much baggage to take along, and he could not spare men to guard her.

Mae Ling rubbed her wrists. He's going to kill me, she thought resignedly. So be it... she couldn't find any mercy from those pitiless old eyes. She'd fought for her life, made all those sacrifices for nothing... she waited for a bullet to bring her end.

What she got was the old man saying, "I do not wish to start my lady's new life in Hong Kong with a crime. Go, you are free, but should my lady and I survive this night, do not let us find you here..."

Mae Ling walked slowly through the circle of bodyguards. She had been deceived before, and still waited for a bullet in the back. When it didn't come, she staggered a little with relief, then slipped off into the night and began to run.

Crossing the muddy fields, she made for the nearest road, hoping to flag down a car. She had taken her passport and money from Thomas Wu's desk, but she had only the hours of darkness left to reach Kai Tak Airport and leave Hong Kong before Malloy or the Triad found her.

To the Manchu bodyguards gathered around him the comprador muttered, "Help me." They hurried him to the waiting vehicles, opened the lead car door and placed him carefully in the seat beside the driver, a member of the 14K Triad. "Has your master placed his men in position?" the comprador asked.

"Yes, lord." The cars moved away.

"And they know the signal?"

"Yes, lord."

"Hurry then, we're already late."

315

CHAPTER 30

THE *EAST WIND*, having made its way down to an uninhabited island in the San-Man chain south of Lantau, lay tucked tight against a cliff face in a small inlet, waves gently lapping against its chines.

The crew waited on the bridge as the rhythmic beat of powerful diesel engines approached and a Communist *hoi kung* steamed past the entrance to the inlet. Its searchlight played along the shoreline, the tip of its beam touching the bow of the MGB. The gunboat's light camouflage, though, blended with the rock face . . . the searchlight hesitated, flashed away and the *hoi kung* went on to search the nearby island of Heng-Kang Chau.

Nicholai waited for the engine noise to fade into the night, then eased the gunboat away from the cliff face and out through the entrance to the inlet. The *East Wind*'s lean hull climbed onto the plane, the defiant thunder of its engines whipped back in the wind. The *hoi kung,* even if it had spotted the gunboat, had no chance of catching it now. Ahead, less than twenty kilometers away, the lights of Hong Kong Island glowed against the sky.

The *East Wind* roared unchallenged over the Square Boundary. The lighthouse on the tip of Stanley Peninsula flashed a warning as it rounded the sheer rock headland and surged into Tai Tam Bay. "The wind off the sea has hemmed the fog in the north over Kowloon," Nicholai said, "leaving us clear visibility along the southern coast. It happens at this time of year, especially at full moon."

Crystal Lily felt her stomach twist into knots—she would have preferred a less bold entrance to Hong Kong. Still, she trusted Nicholai's judgment.

On the left of the bridge appeared the grim white walls of Stanley Prison, and Udo said above the slipstream, "Nicholai, they've built the walls higher. Do you think they can hold us?"

Nicholai grinned at his old friend. "I'm betting they'll never get the chance to try." The lights of Stanley village appeared set into the hillside, and on the right rose steamy, dark cliffs scarred by open-cast quarrying known as the Dragon's Back.

Five kilometers in and the bay narrowed sharply. As Nicholai slackened off the throttle, the bows of the gunboat floated down and kissed the water like a landing swan. He scanned the Obelisk, which, thanks to the bright light of the moon could be seen with the naked eye. The danger signal was to have been a white shroud at its base... white, the Chinese color of mourning. There was nothing. Dark bush and rocks covered the sides of the steep hills that trapped the open water of the harbor. The pier that Nicholai was looking for was invisible, until he rounded the corner. Pleasure boats at anchor came into view. The pier was hard on the left. Car headlights on the road above the pier now did begin to flash an urgent message of warning, but Nicholai had already spotted the police launches edging forward from their hiding places among the pleasure craft to cut off his escape.

He opened the throttles wide and spun the *East Wind* in a crash turn. The gunboat banked so steeply that it nearly capsized, the sea flowing over the deck, the thin hull vibrating and bucking, the dark bush and rocks of the headland a blur, inches in front of its bows. Then the gunboat streaked out of the harbor, racing back down Tai Tam Bay, outdistancing the pursuing police launches.

Keng Po clambered onto the bridge from the deck, soaked through with seawater. "How could they have been waiting for us?"

"Damned if I know," Nicholai shouted to him. The boat was listing over at an angle. "What about the gold?"

"Fifth Street says it's moved. He and Crystal Lily's Manchus are working to restack it now."

"WHY WASN'T the warning signal given sooner?" the comprador, from his car parked above the pier, asked Koa Kang, the master of the 14K Triad.

"No one spotted the police launches until it was too late," the most powerful man in the underworld of Hong Kong told him, not accustomed to being challenged this way.

The comprador was hardly intimidated. "Move on to the next landing place," he ordered. "Have your men follow me."

MALLOY TURNED away from the communications net in the operations room in Kowloon. "We've *lost* him, and the Triad was there waiting. We could have got the whole damn lot of them."

Lao Ch'en found it impossible to conceal his delight at being proved right.

"I never for a moment thought it possible that the Snake Boat Man would use Tai Tam," the D.P.C., whose confidence had been severely shaken, admitted. He left Lao Ch'en and walked through the door to the crisis room, where he sat, shoulders hunched wearily over the conference table in front of the secretary for security, Denning and Captain Simmonds. The bald patch on the top of his head glinted in the light. "Well, at least we know for sure who's carrying the gold now, and it's not the junks," the D.P.C. said. "I can't begin to guess what kind of engines Nicholai's put in that old boat of his, but it's so damn fast he's running away from my police launches and your minesweepers. We may yet have to use your good offices to intercede with the Lady Sun," he added dryly to Denning, voicing the thought no other man there was willing to admit.

"What about the *Scimitar?*" the secretary asked. "Surely the *jet* boat can catch him?"

"Yes," the D.P.C. said, "*if* I knew in which sector to base her. I've got four hundred miles of coastline to protect, and I can no longer guarantee to stop him with just my boats. I need more support. What can you give me?"

"Twenty-eight Squadron's Wessex helicopters are still fogged in at Sek Kong, along with nine scouts from Six-sixty Squadron Army Air Corps," the secretary told him, privately cursing the cutbacks that had robbed the

318

colony of most of its air defense and restricted those aircraft it had to one military airfield. "All I can offer you is use of the RHKAAF."

"They've only got three Dauphin helicopters," the D.P.C. said, "and they've been flying two in the air and one down for refueling since this began."

"They're an all-volunteer unit, the best we've got. Use them," the secretary ordered, "until they tell you they can't go on."

The D.P.C. turned to Captain Simmonds. "Can the navy come up with any more men? Mine are stretched out all along the western coast."

"I can give you an additional six eight-man teams of royal marines on high-speed rigid raiders," Simmonds said. "At the moment they're operating against illegals crossing Deep Bay. Your helicopters can lift them in from there..."

Deep Bay, the D.P.C. reflected, was on the western frontier with China, and the marines' raiders were capable of operating only in sheltered waters...but anything should be tried now. He moved back into the operations room. The clock above the great wall map showed two A.M. He reached for the telephone on the controller's desk and rang through to the RHKAAF duty room.

The auxiliary air force was a unit owned and financed by the Hong Kong taxpayer to deal with emergencies inside the colony. Like the police it was restricted to operate within the territorial boundaries of the colony. A young executive with the Kowloon Peninsula Bank was the duty pilot officer at Kai Tak, where a modern headquarters housed the unit.

"Can you boys keep flying?" the D.P.C. asked him.

"As long as the weather doesn't close in over this part of Kowloon again," the pilot told him.

"Visibility still too bad to get any commercial fixed-wing aircraft off the ground?"

"Yes, we're taking out choppers up through a hole over the harbor."

"How long to get you and your other two choppers over to Deep Bay to pick up a detachment of marines?"

"The other two will have to come in to refuel...allow about forty-five minutes."

"Right. Call straight through to this operation room on channel six when you're airborne."

When Malloy came by, the D.P.C., feeling increasingly frustrated by the minute, was looking hard at the wall map. "Who'd have thought he'd have gone to Tai Tam... Trouble is, he thinks like a damn Chinese and I don't."

"You've caught other smugglers—"

"Not like him. The police have never caught him, and he's proving again he's still the best at what he does that this coast has ever seen—"

"Bullshit, he's just lucky. Have you asked the old man where he'll try the next landing?"

"He mentioned three possible sites, but he thinks our man will land here," and the D.P.C. pointed to Shek O on the eastern side of Hong .Kong Island.

Malloy looked surprised. Shek O' was on the Tathong channel, right within the approaches to Hong Kong Harbor.

"Lao Ch'en was dead on the first time. I'm ready to risk seeing if he can call it right again."

"Well, if the Snake Boat Man tries to land there," Malloy said, "we've got him."

"I've ordered the *Scimitar* to Tathong Point." The D.P.C. moved a marker across the channel. "If the Snake Boat Man comes into Shek O, the *Scimitar* will cut off his escape route back to the sea."

"I want to join her."

"She's already left station."

"I'll have one of the helicopters lower me onto her," Malloy insisted. "I've been after the bastard for too long to risk his slipping through my fingers now. If he does enter the trap I want to be damn sure it's sprung tight . . ."

A RHKAAF helicopter lifted Malloy off the runway at Kai Tak and climbed steeply up through a hole in the fog over the harbor. At two in the morning the harbor was still awake and working like some gigantic fairground, its brilliant confusion of lights penetrating the fog with an eerie glow.

The sky cleared as the helicopter passed over the eastern neck of the harbor at Lei Yue Mun and into Junk Bay. Malloy went forward to speak with the pilot. "Don't you carry guns in this thing?"

"Afraid not."

"Well, then, don't get too close to the Snake Boat Man."

When they picked up the *Scimitar* steaming from her previous patrol position in Clear Water Bay, Malloy told his pilot, "There's no time to rendezvous ashore. Can you lower me onto her deck?"

The pilot signaled his intention to the *Scimitar*, which slowed and turned her searchlights inboard to floodlight her superstructure. The pilot lined up with Waglen Light, the shipping lights at Tathong Point and Cape Collinson, and using his radar altimeter, inched the helicopter into position. At his signal the jump doors of the helicopter opened to a howling blast of air. The technician adjusted the clip on Malloy's harness and tapped his shoulder. Malloy closed his eyes, stepped out of the door and found himself falling slowly through a gale, the beat of the rotors above his head deafening. As he began to spin someone on the deck of the *Scimitar* grabbed his legs to stop him from going over the side. The jet boat rose and plunged in the easterly swell coming in from the South China Sea. Malloy, as his feet gained the deck, felt the familiar nausea of seasickness start, but compared to hanging below the helicopter from a harness, he almost welcomed it. He made his way awkwardly to the bridge as the helicopter lifted away into the night.

The captain of the *Scimitar* welcomed Malloy to his bridge. "I take it your being here with us tonight means the Snake Boat Man's coming this way?"

"If he does, do you think *perhaps* you can get him this time?"

The captain remembered all too well his past humiliation at the hands of the Snake Boat Man when he'd almost lost one of his crew. "You're in the same kind of boat, same builders—except that this one's forty years more up to date. Where would you want to put your money?"

THE *EAST WIND* rounded Cape D'Aguilar. Nicholai then brought the gunboat in as close as he dared beneath D'Aguilar Peak and raced toward Shek O. Keng Po and Crystal Lily stood on either side of him on the bridge, searching the coastline ahead. On the left the village of Shek O snuggled into the folds of the cliff; below the sheer cliff face was a sandy U-shaped beach lined with luxury homes. Access from the beach was up steep flights of wooden steps to the road on the top of the cliff, where the comprador and Koa Kang had only just arrived. A few hundred yards out from the beach were two small islands, uninhabited rock hills jutting out from the sea.

"It's clear ahead," Keng Po said.

But Nicholai didn't slacken off their speed; instead the wake of the *East Wind* curved away from its path toward the beach back out to sea, leaving the islands to port.

"I don't like it," Nicholai said. "I'm going to make a run past. If it's clear we'll only have lost a little time."

If Nicholai was uneasy, it was a bad sign. Crystal Lily raised binoculars to her eyes, scanned the beach and cliffs as the *East Wind* raced by. She

concentrated then on to the two small islands—and spotted the bow
silhouette of a minesweeper. "*Nicholai*, turn away, it's a trap . . ."

"NOT SEE minesweepers," the old deck sergeant insisted as the radio
report burst on the operations room. "He just *smell* trap, like always
before."

"Well, if he's passing Shek O Point he'll sure as hell spot the minesweepers now," the D.P.C. said, amazed that Lao Ch'en had got it so
accurately again. "Order all our launches in the area not to try to give
chase but to close the channel and cut off his escape to the sea. Which
way is he turning?"

The navy controller glanced up from his communications net to the
plot on the map. "He's turning east around Tung Lung Island."

"We can still get him." The D.P.C. bunched his fists excitedly. "Tell
the *Scimitar* he's all hers." . . .

Malloy was standing beside the young captain when the message was
broadcast to the *Scimitar*'s bridge. "You heard that, we've got the bastard
trapped. How long before you catch him now?"

"Not long," the captain promised. "Close down diesels"—the *Scimitar*
was running on slow-speed diesels to conserve fuel—"Flash up port, flash
up starboard turbines," he ordered. The hot breath from the fuel that
powered the Rolls-Royce turbojet engines flowed back across the open
bridge in black clouds of cloying smoke. A sixty-foot-long orange ball of
flame erupted from the exhaust ports at its stern. Ten seconds of orange
flame, then Malloy heard the turbines whine and engage the propellers.
The boat trembled with power as it rose on its stern and set off down the
Tathong channel on an interception course with the *East Wind*.

THE WAY back to the sea was blocked by police launches and the
minesweepers. The only way out of the trap lay through the narrow Fat
Toung Mun reef. Nicholai looked over his shoulder and saw the *Scimitar*
round Tung Lung Island, its black bows lifted on a welter of spray.
Someone in Hong Kong was responsible for setting this trap . . . someone
who understood him too well . . .

And the answer flashed into his mind . . . it lay in the thirty thousand
Hong Kong dollars returned with the message he'd ignored. After all
those years of trying, the temptation to catch him must have been too
great for ex-deck sergeant Lao Ch'en to resist . . .

322

Ahead, pulling slowly through the two-hundred-yard-wide gap in the Fat Toung Mun reef, was a rusted old tugboat; behind it on a long towline lumbered a heavily laden sand barge. The tug was just one of a long convoy taking advantage of the light night traffic to use this quicker route to reach Hong Kong. Between them, the tug and barge blocked the gap in the reef. Nicholai gauged the distance between them to be about four hundred yards; he gauged the draught of his boat... it was just possible... He spoke into the voice pipe to Fifth Street. "I know you've been nursing these engines of yours, but we've got to pass between a sand barge and a tug up ahead. Open the throttles, give me everything you've got."...

The jet-powered boat chased the *East Wind* through Joss House Bay, both vessels making well over forty knots. "He's headed for the gap in Fat Toung Mun reef," Malloy reported over the radio in the operations room.

"Tell them he's as fast as we are," the captain shouted in disbelief to Malloy. He was watching the *East Wind* through light-intensifier binoculars. "Good God," he said abruptly as Fifth Street in the MGB poured on the power, "he's pulling *away* from us..."

"Well, get this tub moving after him."

"I'm already running the turbines at maximum compressor speed."... It was then that the captain spotted the sand barge pulling across the channel through the reef. "Look," he called to Malloy, "look ahead..."

The *East Wind* didn't falter; it went straight through between the tugboat and the barge, over the towing wire.

"If he can do it so can we," the captain insisted. "That old boat draws as much as we do."

He held his course.

But Malloy thought of the gunboat's extra turn of speed, and the means it must have used to break out of Macau past the Communist *hoi kungs* without using the deep-water channel. "Turn away," he shouted. "*Stop.* They must have made some modifications to that MGB."

But it was too late. The jet boat followed the MGB's wake across the steel dragline. And though the tugboat had stopped and the towline curved ever more deeply into the water, it was still enough to saw along the hull of Malloy's boat and rip off both of its propellers.

Malloy was thrown violently across the bridge. He heard the snap of his collarbone breaking. Pain pierced his chest, spreading with a fiery sensation. Below, the tearing noises of breaking turbines and machinery ceased, and the *Scimitar* drifted, listing and leaking.

The captain, face bleeding from cuts, helped Malloy to his feet.

"My collarbone's broken," Malloy muttered. He put his good arm on the bridge rail to steady himself, stared far into the distant moonlight. He could just make out the defiant white plume of spray from the *East Wind* as it threaded through the reef and escaped out to sea. He said nothing. The bitterness he felt was too great for mere words.

Helicopter rotors beat overhead. "What about this boat?" Malloy asked as the damage reports came in.

"We can keep it afloat, I'll take a tow from one of the police launches," the captain told him.

"Tell the helicopter to pick me up." He surveyed the listing shambles of the jet-powered boat: "Forty years more advanced...I should have put my money on the *East Wind*."

After he was winched from the deck of the stricken *Scimitar* to the helicopter, Malloy made his way to the flight deck. "Follow the *East Wind*, hound it back out to sea," he ordered.

"Sorry, no can do," the pilot told him. "I'm already low on fuel—"

Malloy abruptly snatched the radio headset from the co-pilot. "Patch me through to the D.P.C.," he ordered the operations room controller... "Carey, it's Malloy. Confirm the two other helicopters are airborne?"

"Yes."

"Divert them from Deep Bay. Have them hang on the bastard's tail. Chase him back over the Square Boundary. I'm coming in."

"I'll have a doctor standing by for you," the D.P.C. said dryly. He had already received the *Scimitar* captain's report...

The secretary for security turned to Captain Simmonds. "Don't put too much blame on your young captain. He couldn't know that that MGB had been so modified."

Simmonds hardly heard him. He was white-faced with anger. "That's the second of my boats this man's wrecked." He turned to Denning. "Just who in the hell *is* this bastard? Superintendent Malloy assured me that he and his old boat were all washed up."

MAE LING had reached Kai Tak, too relieved to notice that the lights of the airport gloomed through the fog and the engines of the wide-bodied aircraft off the runway were silent. She pushed open the doors into the brightly lit departure hall and waited in line at a Cathay Pacific ticket desk. When her turn came she blurted out, "I must get to Singapore on the next plane—"

"I'm sorry," the Cathay desk clerk said, "but the fog's grounded all our planes."

"When will it lift?"

The girl shrugged. Through the night she'd fielded that question from a hundred stranded passengers. "We have no information yet."

"Can I buy a ticket to Singapore on the first plane to leave, I have urgent family reasons..."

Must be a death or serious illness in the family, the girl guessed from the ashen look on Mae Ling's face. She felt sorry for her. There had been plenty of flight cancellations from passengers returning to their hotels. "Why not," the Cathay girl said helpfully, "then you can go through and wait in the departure lounge, it's less crowded in there."

It was also safer for Mae Ling. She bought her ticket, then presented her passport at immigration control.

The immigration officer leafed through it. "Where's your visa that entitled you to enter Hong Kong?" he asked suddenly.

Mae Ling, of course, had no answer. She hadn't realized when she entered Hong Kong illegally that there would be a stamp missing from her passport. She knew under questioning that she could never pass herself off for long as a Chinese-American. "My husband," she improvised, "he took care of our passport when we came. I'm going to join him now in Singapore. He went ahead..."

The official kept her passport and pressed the buzzer below his desk, summoning his superior. "Wait here," he told her.

Mae Ling froze in panic. They're going to find out, word will reach Malloy, he'll find me here...

CHAPTER 31

"**WHAT TIME** is sunrise?"

"Six-oh-eight."

"Then it's nearly dawn, surely it's over now," Crystal Lily said, breaking the silence. She could ask no more of the men.

Its engines stopped, the *East Wind* wallowed in the deep swells of the South China Sea, where it had fled to shake off the helicopters. Its crew rested, exhausted, at their guns or propped against the bridge rail. The physical strain from the boat pounding against the sea, the constant harassment... all had extracted their toll. Fifth Street climbed up to the bridge with a thermos of hot sweet coffee. The crew shared the same mug, sipping from it and passing it on in deep and wordless comradeship.

"We've time and fuel enough for one last try," Nicholai finally said. He saw spirits wavering. "Fifth Street, after all that you've made of my boat I owe you the right to speak first. What do you say?"

326

Fifth Street looked up. He was beginning to love this man. And he understood that he had pledged himself, his life, to finishing this run for Crystal Lily, whose whole future depended on him. It was a crazy, noble kind of thing to do, and it was catching. "What the hell," Fifth Street said with more confidence than he felt, "I say, do it."

"Ansty?" Nicholai turned next to the Irish ex-mercenary.

"Well, we can't go back to Macau. Can we reach the Philippines?"

"We've burned too much fuel."

"Well, then"—Ansty tried to manage a reckless grin to impress Crystal Lily—"I'm with our friend here. Let's go for it."

"Udo?"

"You know what I think," the big man rumbled. He had no loyalty other than to Nicholai. "Go."

"Keng Po?"

The shrewd bright eyes that met Nicholai's didn't hesitate, though Keng Po believed that by now they must surely have used up all their luck. "I'm with you."

He turned to Crystal Lily. The final decision was hers.

"We make the final attempt," she said, grateful to them all, then voiced a question that had been troubling them all. "The British have been waiting for us at each landing place. How could they know?"

"Malloy's put someone in his operations room who understands too well how I think."

"Who?"

"Lao Ch'en, an ex-policeman who hunted me years ago."

"Can we change the final landing place?"

"It's too late now. The comprador and the Triad will be almost there, and not even Lao Ch'en can guess right three times in a row." Or so he hoped and felt compelled to say.

"We've still got a card to play that the British can't begin to know about," Fifth Street said. "If there's no way out, then this old boat's going down. Ditch the guns and make for the engine-room hatch. You won't have long . . ."

They understood.

Nicholai started the engines and brought the *East Wind* around in the direction of Hong Kong. The night was almost gone. The crew knew this had to be the last run . . .

The moon was down, a light mist was on the sea, and the *East Wind* barreled through it like a lean, dark surface shark, leaving a wide wake behind.

North sector police launches stationed at Fung Head picked up the

327

gunboat as it closed in on the New Territories coast and gave chase. Two police seventy-footers tried, and failed, to intercept it further south at Ke Kok Tau.

"They were expecting us to go into Mirs Bay," Keng Po called out, finding new hope in the apparent lack of opposition. "We're faster than the police boats, we can outrun them..."

Ahead, providing eastern access to Rocky Harbor, loomed the channel of Sau-si-Mun, so named by the Chinese because it was shaped like a key and difficult to navigate. Nicholai was betting that the pursuing police launches wouldn't follow him through here in the dark. Neither could the British operate their helicopters until the sun burned away the fog that had blown inland.

On the hilltop above the channel lay the ruins of the monastery reputed to be haunted by ghosts. Nicholai picked the white warning markers painted on the rocks on the left of the entrance. The full force of the swell bore down through the channel, causing the waves to build up to a crest in the center and making a journey from the entrance a terrifying ordeal.

At full speed, the spray from the bow wave drenching the white-foamed rocks on both sides, Nicholai navigated the channel with only feet to spare. He held the helm hard over to the right until the *East Wind* seemed to brush the rocks, causing Crystal Lily to give out a scream of warning, sure that they must wreck themselves. And then, at the very last moment, Nicholai spun the helm and his powerful gunboat responded, driving through the current to the center line of the channel. They crossed to the left, spray lashing over the bridge, engine exhausts booming back from the rocks, then banked steeply right around a jagged promontory... and came through into Rocky Harbor.

Here was a natural inland waterway that Nicholai had scouted in his practice run, and in an empty area of the New Territories—silent, deserted, stretching for five miles like a flooded valley with just the tips of the mountaintops showing. Islands to the south were scattered like mist-shrouded jewels in a silver-dark sea. The landing place they were headed for lay up the coast behind Urn Island in the tiny bay of Tsen Chu Wen. And the way to it was clear of British police and navy vessels.

Keng Po, ever skeptical, the most suspicious of them all, actually began to cheer. And the others took up his cry, whooping and yelling, the long night of tension and exhaustion giving way to a burst of exhilaration at what they'd accomplished.

"We're clear, Nicholai." Keng Po clapped his old friend on the back.

"We're through, we've made it."

Four miles, three miles... The *East Wind* closed the distance on Urn Island—

Disaster struck. From seemingly out of nowhere came the sonic boom of an overshot, a hundred yards astern of the gunboat a high-explosive shellburst, kicking up a great gout of dirty white water...

In the operations room at MARPOL there was celebration to match what moments before had gripped the *East Wind*. "You've got him"— Malloy pounded the old deck sergeant's shoulder with his good hand— "you've *got* him, by God..."

"Bloody marvelous," the D.P.C. said in his most British fashion. "God knows how you guessed it, but you did, you were right."

Lao Ch'en was so excited that he could not stop his ancient feet from dancing a kind of jig in front of the huge wall map on which they had been plotting the *East Wind*'s course. He had gambled and won. Thanks to him a token force had been placed in Mirs Bay, and his trap was sprung in Rocky Harbor. He would be famous now, he would become revered in coastal legend as the man who finally caught the Snake Boat Man...

Two more shells screaming out of the night sky exploded directly in front of the *East Wind*, making the sea erupt. "Minesweepers." Keng Po's sharp eyes picked them up as they crept forward from the shelter of Urn Island. "Two of them. How did Lao Ch'en outguess us?"

Nicholai knew... it was his fault... his vanity, his overriding need to recover his pride... In planning his last run each landing place he'd chosen tonight had been the scene of an earlier triumph of his, and humiliation for the police. Lao Ch'en, of course, had remembered. And now he had run out of time, out of fuel. There was no turning back. The minesweepers were armed with 40/60-caliber Orlikons. They had twice the range and many times the hitting power of his guns.

But he held his course. He had one trick left in his pack. "Fifth Street," he called through the voice pipe to the engine room, "I'm sending everyone below. Open the forward hatches, stand by to open the seacocks."...

Over the radio into the operations room came a crisp warning from the lead minesweeper's captain. "He must be making forty-five knots and he's holding a course that's going to take him right between our vessels..." In the background of the radio broadcast the men in the operations room could hear the minesweeper's gunnery officer counting off the range.

"The minesweepers have got to stop him," Malloy said to the secretary for security. *"They can't let him through."*

It was a decision only the secretary could make. No British vessel had fired its guns in anger in the colony's waters in nearly fifteen years.

"He's armed and he's endangering my ships," Captain Simmonds warned. "I demand permission to open fire on him. There's too much at stake."

"Very good," the secretary said quietly, avoiding Denning's eyes. "Open fire."...

The minesweepers quickly found the range. Shell splashes bracketed the *East Wind*. The others had already left the bridge, only Nicholai remained holding the *East Wind* on its course. Fifth Street left his engine room and came back for him. "Get out of here, you crazy bastard, she's going down."

The bright flash of a shell exploding against the bridge...the force of it lifting Fifth Street, hurling him against the deck...He rolled over once, curled himself up into a tight ball of pain.

Crystal Lily's worry about Nicholai had made her return too. Momentarily blinded by the flash, she crawled to Fifth Street's side through the acrid stench of high-explosive fumes.

Nicholai got there first. He pulled Fifth Street onto his back, and Crystal Lily saw the blood welling through the shrapnel wound in his chest. "If we move him," she said quietly, "he'll die."

Fifth Street opened his eyes. "The hell I will." He put his arm around Nicholai's neck so he could be lifted. "Get me below. Hurry, I've opened the seacocks, she's going down..."

The *East Wind* stopped, began to settle in the water as if she had been mortally hit. Through his night glasses the captain of the lead minesweeper could see a fire burning on deck and unmanned guns pointing at the sky. The *East Wind* settled very fast, then slid, bows first, to the bottom...

The news that the *East Wind* had been sunk in a gun action was received in MARPOL with fierce yells of victory. Amid the shouting and the flurry of congratulations Malloy noticed the old deck sergeant standing alone in front of the wall map. He was no longer capering about with excitement. Instead, tears dribbled down his wrinkled face. The adrenaline that had sustained him through the hunt was gone, its place taken by a profound hurt...he hadn't counted on his victory bringing the Snake Boat Man's death...

The D.P.C. looked up at the clock. "Dawn in forty minutes," he announced. "We know where the gold is now. Leave the minesweepers to guard the wreck and send all other police and navy boats back on patrol. Stand down the marines in Mirs Bay and tell the minesweepers we'll fly out divers to begin salvage operations at first light. Any survivors yet?"

"None reported, sir," the navy controller told him, "but the mine-sweepers are still searching."

THE LODGEMASTER of the 14K Triad stood at the end of the short pier at Tsen Chu Wen, the hamlet Nicholai had found two miles north of Urn Island where an old vehicle track ran directly down to the water's edge. Hidden within its small bay he could not see into Rocky Harbor, but he had heard the rolling thunder of heavy-caliber gunfire. He turned and walked stiffly to the comprador's car. "It's over," he said, his heavy, fleshy face tight with anger, "the British have intercepted your famous Snake Boat Man. He's not coming—"

"Wait," the comprador told him.

"For what? You have failed us. You had better pray that your lady is dead."

"She instructed me that no matter what the situation appeared to be to wait until dawn. If you want your gold, be silent and wait..."

THIRTY FEET down in Rocky Harbor the East Wind was settling onto the mud bottom. Its crew were crouched in the watertight compartment that Fifth Street had constructed in the steel-lined engine room. Thin jets of pressurized water spurted from shrapnel holes high along the starboard side. The air was dank and acrid, smelling of hot engines and diesel oil. Nicholai caught the glint of rising water in the bilges. "It's filling up," he said to Udo, "find something to plug the holes, anything that will slow down the water."

By the glow of one weak overhead light—all the power they dared drain from the battery—Crystal Lily worked to stanch the flow of blood from Fifth Street's wound. And all the while the propellers from the minesweepers pounded overhead in their search for survivors.

The East Wind groaned a low shuddering protest along the whole length of its hull, then settled at a further angle to port. "Easy, easy," Nicholai fairly crooned to his boat.

"What's going on?" Ansty asked nervously. He was hunched in the dimly lit machinery spaces beside Keng Po, trying to fight down his claustrophobia.

"It's the pressure equalizing."

"Is it going to work?"

"It will, with luck," Nicholai tried to assure him—and himself—and crawled over to Fifth Street, who was propped below the ladder by the number one engine.

"What's the damage?"

"Not too bad," Nicholai told him. "She should rise and run, provided the shrapnel hasn't pierced the inflation bags in too many places."

"Anyone else hurt?"

"We lost one of my bodyguards when the shell hit the deck," Crystal Lily told him, still working on his wound. "He never came down with the others."

"L'eung Heung?"

"Still here, master," L'eung Heung, who had taken over as chief of Crystal Lily's Manchus, permitted himself a grin. He was ripping his shirt into bandages that Crystal Lily bound around Fifth Street's chest.

"I'm sorry I can't help you anymore," Fifth Street said, wincing. "Look after the *East Wind*, she's going to need you to get us out of here..."

Nicholai motioned to Crystal Lily and moved aside. "How bad is it?"

"He's losing a lot of blood, and I can't seem to stop it..."

"Keep pressing it with fresh bandages, bleeding should slow down." Should...

"Udo"—Nicholai indicated a lever by the forward bulkhead—"take that hydraulic jack and close the seacocks that Fifth Street built into the hull. Get to work...Now listen to me," he said to the others, "we've maybe twenty minutes before the water rises and we've no air left." He paused, the noise overhead had abruptly ceased as the minesweepers abandoned their search. Then clearly, through the thirty feet of water separating the *East Wind*'s engine room from the surface, came the rattle of anchor chains descending. "They've buoyed us," Nicholai said in the silence that followed. "Now they'll wait up top for the helicopters to bring out salvage divers from Hong Kong. They won't arrive until after dawn. Before then we should be gone...When I open these"—Nicholai pointed to a rack of cylinders laid against the bulkhead—"liquid nitrogen is going to flow into the inflation bags we've put forward along the keel. The gas will expand with terrific force inside the bags, displacing the water that's flooding the hull through the forward deck hatches. The boat will then regain buoyancy, bow first, and rise to the surface. There is, though, one problem—"

Ansty groaned. "I knew it."

"As we leave the bottom," Nicholai said, ignoring him, "we have got to restart the engines. With the minesweepers right above us, if we don't get the engines started, then all we've accomplished is to save the British the trouble of salvaging us. Ansty, Keng Po—Fifth Street's rigged up each engine to fire from a shotgun cartridge. You take engines one and two, Udo'll take three. When I give the signal bring the hammer down hard on the firing pin. When you hear the engines kick over, start swallowing to free your ears. Pressure is going to drop fast as they burn up what's left of the air in here."

Nicholai moved Fifth Street up against the ladder...the water was already creeping toward the first rung. "Hold him up," he told Crystal Lily and L'eung Heung. He knew they had little time. He spun open the valves on the rack of cylinders, listened to the nitrogen gas hiss through the pipes. "Ready?" He glanced quickly through the dim light to each man standing by the engines. The hull groaned. He hung onto a pipe as he felt the bows lurch free of the mud. The inflation bags were working.

"Now!"

CHAPTER 32

IN MARPOL headquarters Malloy, who had been on his feet for twenty-four straight hours, was bone-tired and his collarbone throbbed. "There's nothing further we can do here until the salvage teams report on the wreck," he told the others. "I'm going home for a shower and change of shirt."

Taipan Joss Denning, seated across the table, never wanted to go through another night like this one... an observer watching impotently while everything he had spent his life fighting for seemed to be slipping away. "Yes, it seems that's the end of it," he said quietly. He had lost the Princely House. Billion Dollar Choy would now have a free hand to dismember it. He rose from his chair and made his way to the operations room, feeling as he looked... frail, weary.

"A successful night's work, I'd say," the secretary for security said, congratulating Malloy. "I'll phone the governor with the news." He glanced at Malloy. "You've been working hard for this, yet you don't seem pleased."

Malloy didn't know how to explain the peculiar emptiness he felt. Lao Ch'en . . . he'd already gone home . . . would have understood. When you've hunted a man as long as I've hunted this one . . . well, his death takes a little of you with him . . . He couldn't tell them that. Instead he asked about survivors before leaving the operations room.

"No, sir," the navy controller in contact with the minesweepers told him. "Not a single body, alive or dead."

Which worried Malloy . . . He caught up with Denning at the top of the MARPOL steps, and they made their way through the deserted parking space to their cars. The first violet traces of dawn were showing in the sky. "No survivors . . ." Malloy muttered to himself, breathing in the humid predawn air. In the distance came the growl of traffic.

"Fog's lifting," Denning said as he spotted the glimmer of lights along Nathan Road. He walked stiffly, holding his despair tight inside himself, not willing to let Malloy see how he was feeling.

Actually Malloy took no notice, his mind concentrated on the *East Wind*. "No bodies at all," he muttered again to himself. And then suddenly a realization struck him . . . he turned abruptly from Denning, ran up the steps and into the operations room.

"Don't you understand?" he shouted at the startled men still there. "There had to be some men on the *East Wind* decks. At the helm, at its guns. When it went down some of them must have floated free— even if they were all dead there had to be bodies . . . Patch me through to the captain of the minesweepers."

But Malloy was too late. Out in Rocky Harbor the *East Wind* was rising to the surface . . .

AT NICHOLAI'S command Keng Po brought his hammer against the cartridge start of the number one engine. It kicked under the impetus of the explosion, coughed, caught, and the fourteen-hundred-horsepower engine roared to life. The number two engine fired successfully, and the already acrid air reeked with the stench of burned cordite. The number three engine fired and the noise of all three escalated to a shattering roar.

Every bit of available air was sucked into the engines. Forty, sixty, eighty seconds passed as the boat regained its buoyancy; and then the aquajets, building to full power, blasted it off the bottom, and everyone in the cramped compartment was screaming above the engine noise in an attempt to relieve the agonizing change in pressure against their eardrums.

The boat broke the surface. Nicholai had cut his timing very fine; another thirty seconds and there would have been no air left. Keng Po scrambled to release the hatch. Water flooded in, and with it a gale of fresh, salt-tainted air.

The power of its engines lifted the bow section and the first third of the *East Wind* clear of the sea. Nicholai, followed by Keng Po, hurried along the deck to the bridge and took control of the helm. A rush of spray drained from every hole and hatch in the hull. Leaving a cloud of exhaust smoke and with her distinctive high-pluming wake forming behind, the *East Wind* dug in her stern and took off again under the very bows of the surprised minesweepers.

By the time the navy vessels could raise their anchors and give chase, the *East Wind* was lost from sight around Urn Island...

"Go *after him.*" Malloy sounded hysterical responding to the garbled report that came over the operations room radio. He turned to the D.P.C. "They can't follow him, he can hide in any one of the shallow bays to the north of Urn Island..."

The D.P.C. traced the last sighting of the *East Wind* on the wall map and shrugged. "Our minesweepers draw too much water to go after him, and our smaller craft are useless."

"If the helicopters left now, how long would it take them to reach the area?"

"Fifteen, twenty minutes, but they'd have to search each bay—"

"We'll use the marines on their rigid raiders, maybe they'll winkle him out of there..."

Denning had just come back to the operations room to see what the commotion was about, and heard from the secretary for security that Nicholai had broken through...

THE *EAST WIND* was a sorry sight...battle-scarred and reeking of nitrogen gas, she glided quietly into the bay of Tsen Chu Wen.

Udo, wearing an oxygen mask, emerged on deck carrying the last of the now-deflated buoyancy bags and tossed it over the side. He tore off his oxygen mask, and it followed the bag into the water. He had left all the hatches open to blow fresh air through the hull. "With normal breathing you'll be able to reach the gold in a couple of minutes," he reported to Nicholai on the bridge. "There's about three feet of water over the keel, and I've found the body of the Manchu... poor bastard must have been trapped in the hull when the boat went down. What do you want done with him?"

"We've no time to bury him, leave him with the boat."

The *East Wind* now drew alongside the pier where the comprador and Koa Kang waited.

"Don't let Koa Kang see that you carry my gold as well as his," Crystal Lily warned.

Before Koa Kang could order his men onto the boat, Nicholai called down. "No one comes onboard. You can smell the gas in this boat... a careless spark from one of your men and it'll blow sky high. We'll hand the gold down to you."

Fifth Street was lifted onto a makeshift stretcher. He would be the first to reach the shore. "How are you feeling?" Nicholai asked him.

"Terrific..." He was fighting to stay conscious.

"Crystal Lily will get you to a safe doctor in Hong Kong as soon as she can." Nicholai touched his shoulder. "Engineer, thanks for everything that you made of my boat."

"It took you to have faith I could do it." Fifth Street put his hand in Nicholai's and gripped it. "It was a hell of a run..."

The Triad gold was lowered from the boat, the ingots weighed, numbered and carried to a waiting truck.

"I have paid off my father's debt to you," Crystal Lily told the lodgemaster of the 14K Triad as the last of his gold came ashore.

"All debts are canceled," Koa Kong said. "And... what happened to your enemies in Macau?"

"They are dead," she informed him.

Koa Kang was impressed. What she said had to be true, he realized, or they would never have let her leave Macau. He pressed his face close to hers. "It's a pity my Triad cannot accommodate women. You would have been worthy of a place. But I am master here and there is no room for the House of Sun. Don't stay in Hong Kong. Go back to Macau." The warning was clear, unmistakable.

"Everything is loaded, lord," Koa Kang's master of incense reported. Crystal Lily knew she would have to work fast to intercept the gold, otherwise within a few hours it would be hidden away in the New Territories among the villagers who owed allegiance to the Triad.

Koa Kang gave the signal to his heavily guarded bullion truck to pull out. It would have been inviting police attention to follow it. Instead Koa Kang and his master of incense climbed into a second car. They would make their separate way back to the city and pass innocently through any police roadblocks along the way...

"Another one who would prefer we not remain in Hong Kong," the comprador said as he came up behind Crystal Lily.

"He'll soon find I've left him no choice in the matter," Crystal Lily said, watching the Triad vehicles move out of sight. Now that her feet were on dry land she felt some of her confidence returning.

One of her lookouts further up the hill shouted a warning, followed by the beat of rotor blades. That helicopter came in low over the ridge of land and flew across the next bay. Slung below its belly was the royal marines' lethal-looking rigid raiders—fast, shallow-draught, light-attack craft. Through the gloom Crystal Lily and her comprador heard another helicopter pass to the north bringing in more marines from Mirs Bay.

"Hurry," she urged, "there's no time left..." In response to a guarded light signal, a second truck that had been hidden in the hills nearby rumbled down to the pier, followed by two Land Rovers.

Crystal Lily now ordered her Manchus who swarmed down from the truck to unload her gold. It was only a few minutes until dawn, when they would surely be spotted. Her Manchus formed a human chain to the *East Wind*, working feverishly to lift her three tons of gold from its hold into the truck.

Keng Po pasted transfers of police markings onto the sides of the Land Rovers. In the back were bundles of police uniforms. "Change into these," the comprador told the crew as the last of the gold was landed. "We must time our interception of the Triad's bullion truck before it can pass over Sharps Peak. After that there are too many roads it can follow, we could lose it—"

The engines of the *East Wind* suddenly broke into their deep rhythmic chant.

"Where's Nicholai?" Crystal Lily demanded.

"He's still on the boat—"

Which was now easing away from the jetty. Nicholai came on deck, leaned against the bridge rails, and she realized what he was going to do.

"Don't, please... remember our dream... The two of us... you *promised* me..." Yet even as she spoke she knew he was doing this for her.

"I was never part of any deal with the British," he called to her, "and the marines will be here in minutes. I can draw them after me... We both knew it had to be this way..."

She shook her head. "Where will you go?"

"Back out to sea."

"He'll never make it," Fifth Street told her. "That hull is still filled with flammable gas. He wasn't kidding when he said one spark..."

"He'll make it because I'm going with him," Udo growled, and thrust his uniform back into the comprador's arms. "We can buy you maybe twenty minutes' start."

"What about me?" Keng Po called out across the widening gap to Nicholai. "Haven't I been with you from the beginning? Do you think I haven't the guts to follow you now?"

"You've more courage than this needs, but you stay," Nicholai told him. "You've been chosen Crystal Lily's new comprador when Yu Shik Lieu is gone. She needs you now more than me..."

"It has been so arranged," Yu Shik Lieu said, adding his confirmation to Keng Po. "My lady has agreed. If you wish, the position will be yours."

To guide the fortunes of a Princely House with all the power and wealth that entailed... of course Keng Po wanted it. Still, to be separated from Nicholai...

To Crystal Lily Udo now said quietly, "Look after Fool Boy for me."

Crystal Lily nodded.

"Wait a minute," Fifth Street told Udo before his stretcher was lifted into the back of the Land Rover. "We figured out one final escape plan for a deal like this, but the Snake Boat Man's not going to use it. He's going to try to break his boat through the blockade, so you look out for him, understand?"

"I always do," Udo said, and leapt from the jetty, grabbed a hold on the *East Wind* and pulled himself through the railings onto its deck.

"I'll send a sailing sampan before nightfall to pick you up at Tai She Wan," Crystal Lily called to the boat. "It'll take you safely to the islands."

Keng Po ran the length of the pier keeping pace with the gunboat. "You heard that, you crazy bastards?" he shouted, not wanting to be parted from his oldest friends. "So don't get yourselves killed. All you have to do is lie low until we can make a deal with the governor for your safe return to Hong Kong. Trust me... trust my Lady Sun..."

Udo climbed to the shrapnel-pitted bridge. "All right, where the hell *are* we going?" he asked Nicholai.

"You, the *East Wind* and I are going where the British will never find us."

"I hope that doesn't mean to our ancestors," Udo muttered...

As Crystal Lily and her people climbed into their vehicles the *East Wind* swung away and crossed the bay. Before it could gain the channel three rigid raiders, each with a complement of eight royal marines, and with light machine guns mounted in the bows, rounded the neck of the bay. They caught sight of the *East Wind* moving slowly through the shallows, looking battle-scarred and crippled. The marines promptly took off after it, as Nicholai had expected they would.

The *East Wind* now entered deeper waters in the narrows that ran past Urn Island into Rocky Harbor. Nicholai opened the bridge throttles wide and the gunboat powered up to maximum speed, skimming on top of the water. But the rigid raiders with their huge outboards were faster than the *East Wind*, and they were gaining on her. The machine gun in the lead assault craft opened up, spraying the sea almost within range.

"By all our gods, don't let them hit us." Udo made an unabashed prayer. "One bullet in all this gas..."

"Don't worry," Nicholai tried to assure him, "wait until their shallow skimming craft hit our wake. They won't be wasting any time on fancy shooting then...What are you doing?"

Udo was struggling with something behind him.

"Making smoke," he said, flinging away the safety rings of the smoke cannisters he'd ignited, looking with satisfaction at the wall of smoke curling along the *East Wind*'s wake, blocking them from the view of the marines behind—

Except that blocking their exit to the sea was one of the minesweepers. Nicholai ignored its signals to stop. The sun was rising, spearing the sea ahead with shafts of yellow light. It was a moment for the two exhausted men to share, the last minutes of their long, deep friendship, in the glory of the dawn, in the white spray in the slipstream, in the relentless howl of the *East Wind*'s engines...

Nicholai saw the gun flashes from the minesweeper. He had passed this night in stages of despair and hope. Now, here with Udo, there was a kind of exhilaration...and satisfaction...Within the personal challenge he'd set for himself, he felt redeemed. What was left was his determination to reach the sea with his old boat. As he waited for the shells to fall he called out over the roar of the engines, "Udo, it's like the old days when we used to run down the path of the moon from Macau and no one could stop us—"

Shells burst in the path of the *East Wind*. The sea boiled and seethed, but Nicholai held his course.

"I remember...I remember," Udo called back to him, clinging to a piece of broken bridge rail. "Those were our great days..."

And he hit Nicholai from behind.

Nicholai collapsed. Udo caught him in his arms and carried him to the stern of the boat, where one of the large white cannisters, which normally house the vessel's life rafts, was kept. He pulled a tightly fitting oxygen mask over Nicholai's face, opened the lid of the cannister, lowered Nicholai inside, then closed it. Udo squeezed his great bulk into a similar liferaft cannister situated on the port side. Both cannisters were joined by a length of chain. Udo fastened down the lid of his, pulled a lever release from the inside, and both drums rolled off the stern into the churning wake of the *East Wind*. Hidden in the smoke and spray, the drums went down...down...

A salvo fired by the minesweeper straddled the *East Wind*, one of its shells bursting amid pockets of nitrogen gas trapped inside the hull. And the *East Wind* was incinerated in a white-hot explosion. Waves were flattened for a circumference of five hundred yards. Nothing remained of the boat but a fireball climbing lazily skyward, the blast that marked its end echoing for miles against the hills surrounding Rocky Harbor.

CRYSTAL LILY stopped her Land Rover on the high ground, climbed out and ran to look back over the length of Rocky Harbor at the black-and-orange fireball rising into the sky. "Nicholai, Nicholai..." Her voice echoed back from the cliffs, and she silently importuned the gods, "Don't let him die, please, don't let him..."

Only the comprador had the courage to approach her, to tug at her sleeve and remind her, "We must see this through, your whole life is at stake..." He put his frail arm around her shoulders, and then from the high cliffs overlooking Rocky Harbor spoke Nicholai's epitaph: "My lady, nothing you have done could have changed this. Do not grieve for the Snake Boat Man. He would count himself fortunate. He began life as a refugee with no name. He had a quality that brought him love. And he died living up to the legend he made."

But she would not accept that Nicholai was dead. Keng Po had told her about the escape cannisters. They were no guarantee, but they were, for her, the stuff of hope...which she clung to as she finally allowed herself to be led away from the awesome, terrible sight of the fireball rising from the place where Nicholai's *East Wind* had been, and was no more...

The news that the *East Wind* had been blown out of the water flashed to the operations room.

"Do you believe the gold was still on that boat?" the secretary for security demanded of Malloy.

Malloy shook his head. "No, I believe the Snake Boat Man had landed it."

"Have the helicopters and marines turn back and search the bays," the D.P.C. ordered. "Move in the police." He made a broad ring on his map. "I want roadblocks set up on every track that can carry a vehicle in this area." Privately he thought if they'd eluded his forces all night one could be reasonably certain Lady Sun was just as well organized in Hong Kong.

The secretary for security also understood the situation. It was time to cut his losses, try to limit the damage. He turned to Denning. "Does Lady Sun intend to contact you here if she makes a successful landing?"

Denning felt an oppressive weight lift from his shoulders. He was not defeated, not yet... "Yes," he answered, more excited than he would allow these men to see.

"Then tell her we will agree to her terms, *if* she can stop the gold from being used by the Triad."

THE CANNISTERS drifted below the surface of Rocky Harbor. Udo, breathing through a submariner's air recirculator, emerged from his, and pulling himself along the chain, swam to the second cannister. He unscrewed the lid and managed to pull Nicholai out, then grabbed him by the scruff of the neck and swam with him to the surface.

Udo spat out his mouthpiece and shook Nicholai. "Are you all right?"

"You ox, you nearly killed me," he sputtered, feeling the painful lump on his head. Then, treading water, he turned and looked back over the silent stretch of sea. He glanced up at the sky, where his boat had disappeared. "At forty-five knots between dawn and the morning star... it's a fine way to die..."

"First, I'm a bear, if you recall, not an ox. And you are a crazy romantic bastard," Udo growled, losing his temper at the memory that, without him, Nicholai would have stayed with his boat. "There's the Lady Sun out there, who loves you, and the way Hong Kong's lease with China could end, she's going to need you—"

"Udo," Nicholai said, "close your mouth before you drown and start swimming. A sampan should be waiting for us at Tai She Wan, and we've a way to get to it before nightfall..."

342

CHAPTER 33

THE TRUCK carrying the Triad's gold wound up a lonely track into Sharps Peak. It was an isolated area on the eastern tip of the sparsely populated New Territories. The Triad soldiers in the back of the truck had begun to relax, feeling almost safe here from the police.

The driver executed a routine change into bottom gear to round one of the hairpin bends—and as he did so a roadblock loomed in front of him. He slammed on the brake, and from the corner of his eye caught sight of a figure detaching itself from the side of the road.

Michael Ansty, resplendent in the uniform of a chief inspector in the Royal Hong Kong Police, swung onto the running board and leveled his submachine gun against the temple of the driver. "You're under arrest, me boys. Don't try it," he advised the two bodyguards seated alongside the driver who were reaching for their guns, "unless you're wanting me to deliver you to Hong Kong sad corpses all riddled full of holes. Good lads...all right, out with you now."

Crystal Lily's Manchus, also in police uniforms and led by Keng Po, fanned out in a semicircle from the roadblock, each man holding at the ready a submachine gun. The Triad soldiers in the back of the truck, surprised and outgunned, descended with their arms raised and were manacled to each other.

L'eung Heung came to attention as Ansty approached. "Sergeant, march these beauties into the bush at the side of the road and settle them down. It'll take a while for the transport to get here to take them to Hong Kong."

Keng Po climbed into the driver's seat of the truck. Ansty signaled him to move out, and as the truck accelerated away he jumped back onto the running board. Hidden in the dense scrub further down the road was Crystal Lily's Land Rover. "It's all gone smooth," Ansty reported to her. "The Triad soldiers are bedded down in the bush where no one will find them for a while."

"Take the gold to the address you have in Hong Kong," she told him. "Keng Po will show you how to get there by a back way." And to her comprador she said, "We must convince Koa Kang that this has all been the work of Billion Dollar Choy, his greedy treachery. When the gold is safely hidden in Choy's godown, I'll let Koa Kang discover where to find it..."

KOA KANG waited impatiently in Kowloon for news of his gold. When the truck failed to reach its destination as scheduled, he knew that he had been robbed in the heart of his own territory, and was shamed to near-madness by his loss.

In his shabby labor office in a building overlooking the harbor he ordered his master of incense to "summon every soldier in the Triad, send them digging into every corner of Hong Kong. I want that gold returned to me, no matter what cost."...

The Triad's soldiers fanned out through the squatter camps and re-settlement areas of the colony, breaking down doors, beating on heads.

At last an informer brought Koa Kang the news.

"Billion Dollar Choy, my almost-partner?" His voice was a murderous whisper. He shifted his massive, sweating bulk from the chair. "Sure...now that he has the Princely House nearly in his grasp he figures not to split the profits with our Triad. *Where is he?*"

* * *

IN THE operations room at MARPOL the phone rang. It was Crystal Lily, who asked to be put through to Denning. "I'm in Hong Kong," she said, reminding him of the bargain they'd struck in the cemetery in Macau.

"...The terms have been agreed to for you to take up residency in Hong Kong," he told her.

She felt a profound relief that Denning had kept his promise. She'd been right to trust him. As they talked he caught the note of weariness in her voice and realized what she must have been through during the last twenty-four hours. "And in return," she was saying, "I tell you to send your Superintendent Malloy to raid number one-seventeen Nathan Road. It's a godown owned by Billion Dollar Choy. Malloy will find the gold he's searching for there, and possibly, if he moves fast enough, the lodge-master of the 14K Triad. I suggest Malloy go well-armed."

Malloy, who had been listening to the conversation on an extension, promptly radioed through to his assistant inspector, Rem Choy, who was standing by with a squad of marksmen police. He gave Rem Choy the address. "Stake it out," he said. "I'm on my way."...

Malloy's car battled with the traffic all the way up Nathan Road. Rem Choy was waiting when he arrived. He pointed out a dilapidated two-story warehouse across the street that was due for demolition. "Choy went in there in a great hurry ten minutes ago," he said. "He must have been tipped off—"

"Anyone else?"

The radio attached to Rem Choy's belt gave out a muffled squawk. He fitted in the earpiece and reported the information relayed to him by one of his men. "Koa Kang and senior Triad people...entering through the back of the building."

"Give him five minutes to settle down, then we go."

Two minutes dragged by. And then, above the sullen roar of traffic, both men heard a series of sharp explosions. "Backfire?" Rem Choy said, but knew better.

"Gunfire...send your men in *now*." Malloy sprinted across the street, his men hacked through the flimsy front door to the godown with their axes, Malloy went in at a dead run, his policemen pouring through the opening after him. Back-up teams came through the fire doors at the sides of the building and the rear exit.

They found themselves in an empty warehouse. On its floor a tarpaulin thrown back revealed the hastily stacked gold bars. Billion Dollar Choy's dead body lay in spreading pool of blood alongside it. His executioner Koa Kang, taken by surprise at the sudden arrival of the police, still held the gun in his hand.

"You must be slipping," Malloy told him. "Doing your own dirty work now. Good, makes my job easier putting you away."

Koa Kang was hardly listening... too much time in absolute power had led him to commit this rash, arrogant act. And now he was surrounded by police, each a witness. Malloy reached out and relieved him of his gun. Koa Kang was too stunned to resist. "You can't have known"— he searched his mind for the author of his disaster—"I've been betrayed. But who would dare...?"

What especially confused him was all his gold right there on the floor of the warehouse. How could anyone voluntarily give it up...? He understood no one not cast in his own mold. Billion Dollar Choy would not abandon it. Only Crystal Lily... but, of course, he had always underestimated her...

MAE LING was still in the detention area of immigration control, her head resting wearily on her hands. But at last the fog was lifting and she began to hear aircraft departures being announced. Footsteps approached and she looked up at the senior immigration officer. She had stuck to her story about her husband, and, disbelieving still, saw her passport in his hands. "Please," she said, "they've called my flight to Singapore... may I leave...?"

The immigration officer had checked the passport thoroughly, and except for the missing visa had found it was in order. This woman... what a beauty... was obviously genuinely distressed. Someone in his staff had been lax but it was too late to find out who now... "I'm most sorry for the inconvenience you've been caused," he said, smiling at her. She watched, heart in mouth, as he opened her passport and stamped it with an entry and exit visa. "Go through that door," he said, pointing, "and on to gate seven. Your plane should be boarding now." Another big smile...

"Window seat four rows down on the left," the stewardess said, checking Mae Ling's boarding pass. The man seated next to her tried to make conversation but she ignored him, her eyes tightly closed until the plane left the ground. Only then did she look back on Hong Kong, the harbor and the skyscrapers revealed in the morning light. It was her last sight of China, but she did not say good-by.

346

Someday I will regroup my father's followers, she promised herself. I will train them in Singapore and even in the jungles of Malaysia. And when Ho Chen and I are ready we will return to Hong Kong stronger than ever before... She thought of Nicholai, and how she would make him forgive her. And of Crystal Lily... I've left a man who belongs to me, she thought as the colony disappeared below the wings of the aircraft, and a woman I intend to return to—and destroy.

EPILOGUE

NOT LONG after in Hong Kong, on the fourteenth night of the seventh moon, to mark the special occasion, the governor gave a formal dinner party.

Crystal Lily, looking cool and beautiful, took her place among the assembled taipans at the silver-laden table lit by the warm glow of candles in Government House. She had chosen to wear a full-length classically styled dress of simple black silk crepe; but she caused something of a sensation with her priceless ropes of pearls and sparkling diamond earrings. She scarcely looked like someone whose father had started out life as a beggar, and who herself had controlled a multimillion-dollar underworld syndicate.

She was seated next to the governor. On her right was Joss Denning.

"I've heard that you two"—he nodded toward Crystal Lily—"are bidding against each other for the Swan Center group of companies?" Sir Howard Caley said to Denning.

The taipan nodded cautiously. "So I've learned today." He'd not expected competition to come from her direction so quickly. As the governor broke off to concentrate on choosing from a serving dish offered him by a waiter, Denning dropped his voice so that no one but Crystal Lily could hear. "I think it's time to decide whether we're going to be partners or rivals," he said.

She smiled at him, with the knowledge that her three tons of gold was safe in Hong Kong and unaccounted for. Still, she owed him fair warning. "Allies perhaps, if an occasion arises in the future, but in business I am no one's partner."

Sir Howard Calcy, watching her tête-à-tête with Denning, had been enchanted by Crystal Lily from the beginning, and now he had to remind himself that this lovely young woman had ruthlessly outwitted, and disposed of, all her enemies. He saw a great future for her in Hong Kong.

And now she turned her attention to him. "Sir Howard, would you excuse me? As you know, this is the night we Chinese honor the Feast of the Hungry Ghosts."

"Of course," the governor told her. He knew it was a tradition at this time for Hong Kong families to pay homage to the departed spirits of their loved ones. Later he and his guests would repair to high ground to view the spectacle of fleets of tiny ships, each with a lighted candle glowing in its hold, set sail across the bays and inlets of the colony carrying gifts of food and money to the hungry ghosts.

Crystal Lily was the first guest to depart. Her comprador, Keng Po, and her ward, Fool Boy, were waiting in her limousine and accompanied her down to the water's edge.

Malloy, whose men still watched her, unofficially, sought her out there. "May I join you?" He had never stopped suspecting her of helping Mae Ling reach Singapore. "Or do you now move in such high society that I have to make an appointment?"

"How can I help you, Superintendent Malloy," she asked coolly.

"It's chief superintendent, and let me tell you, this charade doesn't impress me one bit," he said, watching her prepare a miniature sailing junk while Keng Po held up a flaming torch brand to light her work. "I don't believe the Snake Boat Man is dead. That *East Wind* of his was an engineering freak. The explosion that blew it to bits was all very convenient. But where are the bodies? I want you to know I'm not giving up. He's somewhere here, and I aim to find him if it takes till bloody hell freezes over..."

Crystal Lily knew where Nicholai and Udo were. Of course she couldn't visit them, but she often imagined them at work, heads shaved and in saffron robes, in her new comprador Keng Po's monastery on Lantau Island. From Keng Po she had learned of the rigid regime of discipline and self-denial imposed by the abbot. Udo was already grumbling mightily about the lack of wine, women and decent food, but she felt a little abstinence might do him good.

"Why tell me this?" she asked innocently.

"Because I believe you're only waiting for your influence with the governor and your power in the commercial world of Hong Kong to build up and then you're going to start to bargain for the Snake Boat Man's safe return. Maybe we couldn't pin a crime on you in Hong Kong territory, but the Snake Boat Man's a different story."

Crystal Lily shrugged. "They say that in time everything is possible."

She launched her miniature ghost ship and watched it follow Fool Boy's and Keng Po's into the dusk. Painted on the sail was the prayer she had written, and in the flickering light of the candle Malloy strained to make out the words—"*Hsun feng*...temper the winds," and below that, "Keep the one I love in safety."

"*Chief* Superintendent Malloy," Crystal Lily said quietly, "if you were Chinese and believed in the spirit world, then you might find the Snake Boat Man was closer than you think."